DO YOU think Floris' death was an accident?" I asked.

His foot must have trod hard on the gas pedal, for the truck made a little jump on the drive before he braked it.

"Of course it was an accident, Jenny. Don't go thinking anything else or this whole place may blow up like a volcano right in your face. And you wouldn't like that. Everyone's playing it safe, and you'd better too. We can't afford the publicity. Maybe nobody wants to know what might have happened. You would want it least of all."

We were in front of the hotel entrance, and I put my hand on the door handle.

"Jenny—" His tone was quiet, and I turned. "Don't go up there in the woods anymore, will you? Stay away. . . ."

Phyllis A. Whitney

The
STONE BULL

FAWCETT CREST • NEW YORK

THE STONE BULL

THIS BOOK CONTAINS THE COMPLETE TEXT OF THE ORIGINAL HARDCOVER EDITION.

Published by Fawcett Crest Books, CBS Educational and Professional Publishing, a division of CBS Inc., by arrangement with Doubleday and Company, Inc.

ISBN: 0-449-23638-2

Alternate Selection of the Literary Guild
Selection of the Reader's Digest Condensed Book Club
Selection of the G.K. Hall Large Print Book Club

Printed in the United States of America

12   11   10   9   8   7   6   5   4   3

Foreword

One of the questions most frequently asked of a writer is whether "real people" have been used in a story. In my case the answer is an immediate and unequivocal "no." My interest as a novelist lies in creating my own characters and the incidents that happen in a story. However, real places often furnish me with the inspiration that leads to an imaginary background and totally imaginary characters.

The marvelously beautiful and romantic Mohonk Mountain House in the Shawangunk Mountains on the edge of the Catskills provided an inspiration for the setting of *The Stone Bull*. None of the dire happenings in this story ever occurred at the real Mohonk, of course, which is a lovely and entirely safe place for any visitor.

I would like to thank the management of Mohonk Mountain House for its hospitality and assistance during my visit. In particular I want to thank Ruth Smiley, Rosalie and Dan Wilson, Mary Whitefield, and Jay Davis. My thanks as well to Diane Greenberg, who told me about those "whispering voices" on the lake, and to Frank Lyons, who kindly drove me all over the Mohonk acres in his truck. None of these people bears any resemblance to the imaginary characters in my story.

Phyllis A. Whitney

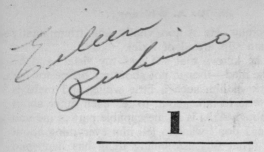

I

Tonight I am alone for almost the first time since my marriage. I sit here in our bedroom at the Mountain House, with all the lamps burning, and I am afraid. I know that soon Brendon will come upstairs and his very presence will dispel my foolish uneasiness. He will tell me that no one can mean me harm here at Laurel Mountain. But how can Brendon fully understand the sense of guilt that haunts me and is quite apart from this beautiful place, from the people who live here, or from those who come as guests to the hotel? Always my thoughts must return to Ariel.

Am I to blame for my sister's death? Perhaps I shall never be free of the question, the sense of blame. I try to accept the fault, face it, live with it, but even now when my life has changed so excitingly, so hopefully because of Brendon, I am never free for long of Ariel's shadow.

Someday I must talk to Brendon about her. But not yet. It's possible that I am still a little afraid of her—afraid of that far-reaching shadow, so that even to discuss her with him, to confess my feelings of guilt, would be to evoke her too clearly in his eyes—and I can't bear to do that. Not that Brendon would be attracted to the legend of a dead woman. He is too vitally and triumphantly alive. Yet I am still afraid of Ariel.

Of course he knows that she was my sister, and he knows how she died—though not about my blame for her death. I've known him such a little while, and there is still so much else to talk about, to tell each other about *us.* So even though Ariel is an inescapable part of me and always will be, I don't want to tell him everything about her. Not yet. That this astounding thing has happened to *me,* that I've been married to Brendon McClain for two months and we are on our honeymoon at his own fabulous Laurel Mountain—that is enough of a miracle for me to absorb for the moment. I must push everything else away. I must make the accusing thought of Ariel wait.

I met Brendon by such impossible chance that I can now believe in fate. A few steps in another direction by either of us, a few moments' difference in time—and we would never have come together. It happened in, of all places, the Opera lobby at Lincoln Center. Ariel's death was in all the papers, and the funeral would be the next day. Mother was, as always, managing bravely and capably, and I had run away for a little while, torn by the grief and self-blame I had to hide from her. I had still not confessed to her that last phone call of Ariel's.

The remarkable photograph that Martha Swope did of Ariel as Giselle was still hanging in the lobby, and it drew me across the city. Tonight she was to have danced *Europa,* which had been choreographed for her, and which she would never dance again. I had seen her do it with Maurice Kiov as Zeus, and it had been marvelous. I hadn't been able to cry as yet, and my eyes felt burning dry as I stood staring at her picture. All that love and hate, all the admiration and contempt that had been part of our relationship still boiled beneath the surface in me— the one who was left—and I could not cry.

Ariel! How fortunate it was that they had chosen the right name for her. She was only twenty-eight when she died—though that is getting on for a ballet dancer. I am two years younger, but we were look-alikes, with the same fine, straight black hair and huge brown eyes, the same delicate, chiseled features, though faintly blurred in me; the long, ballerina's neck, the look of fragility that we both wore so deceptively. I can think of nothing less fragile than a prima ballerina. We had the same long legs and slender feet, too, but it was all misplaced in me. I was earthbound Jenny and there was nothing airy about me. I was the one with two left feet. The startling resemblance between us was wholly outward. We couldn't have been more opposite in our skills and inner selves.

As children we started dancing lessons together out in Long Island where we lived, but I could never manage more than the wobbliest of arabesques, while from the first Ariel outdanced everyone in the class. It was Ariel who could float like thistledown, or soar like a gull. Even then her *grands jetés* were a miracle of grace and lightness, suspended in air, and she could execute those repeated *fouettés* that would someday give her the thirty-two for *Swan Lake*. Where I lost my balance and grew dizzy after two turns, Ariel could whirl the length of our practice room, with her head whipping around, never faltering uncertainly like the rest of us. Of course it was Ariel who went up *en pointe* as soon as she was permitted, Ariel who danced with a divine fire that would light the stages of the world and make her famous everywhere.

Strangely, in my mind, I used to feel that I was really like her. I could soar so beautifully in my imagination, while my feet thudded on the floor. Even my *barre* work was terrible, and I shrank from the pain that is forever part of a dancer's lot. True, the teacher praised me for a straight back and improving *port de bras,* but my long legs seemed to be made for climbing trees, my knees for hooking over branches, my feet for running in the woods. I was very good at that. Woods were always my element— not the make-believe of any stage. Or so I tried to comfort myself, and inside me I was grace itself.

Of course if you care about ballet, or perhaps even if you don't, you'll have heard of Ariel Vaughn, and if you are lucky you'll have seen her dance. The critics have raved about her mad Giselle, yet she could be that tender, lost girl in Tudor's *Pillar of Fire* as well—all passion and frustration and despair. And surely she was as lovely as any Odette-Odile there ever was in the classic perfection of *Swan Lake*.

So on that day after her death I had returned to stand before her picture, trying to make an impossible peace with both Ariel and myself, when a man turned from the box office window and noticed me standing near Ariel's likeness. I paid no attention until I realized that he was staring at me. I could feel his eyes and the old resentment rose with unreasonable anger as I stared back into that bright blue, curious gaze for the first time. I didn't need resentment anymore as protection, because Ariel was gone, yet my defenses went up automatically.

He must have been surprised to have a strange woman regard him so indignantly, but he came toward me down the lobby anyway, and stopped before Ariel's picture. Of course I knew why. We could have been twins, except for the way we wore our hair. In the photograph Ariel's was parted in the center and drawn smoothly back in the ballerina's twist, the smooth wings shining with highlights like black satin. I wore my hair long and free, except when I knew it was going to be in my way. When she was not dancing, which was seldom, Ariel had sometimes imitated me and let her own heavy hair hang down her back—and then there was hardly any way to tell us apart. That is, if we stood still, did not speak, did not move.

There was a certain arrogance in this man's look that I've since come to know, and that no longer aggravates me because he isn't arrogant toward me. But that afternoon it infuriated me. He looked so ominously dark there in the crystal lights of the lobby, with his thick brown hair and heavy eyebrows, contrasting with that electric blue of his eyes, and he was one of those assured men I couldn't stand. So I spoke to him rudely out of tense emotion.

"Yes, I know. We look alike. But Ariel Vaughn is dead and I'm left. I'm her sister." I almost added, "I'm nobody," but I managed to suppress that. My outburst was ridiculous, more childish than I liked to be, dredged up out of all those years of moving in Ariel's shadow. I saw his arrogance fade to pity—which was even worse. He might have spoken had I given him a chance, but I didn't.

"I suppose you'd hoped to see her dance tonight!" I cried, my voice splintering. "I suppose—"

This time he broke in. "No. I don't care for ballet. I never go. I was merely picking up tickets for my aunt."

Perhaps that was really the moment when I fell in love with him. I heard that deep vibrant voice denouncing the ballet world that worshiped at Ariel's shrine, and I fell—plunged!—into an emotion that was stronger than anything I'd ever felt before. Oh, of course it was only attraction then—a strong attraction, both physical and emotional, of the sort that can easily flash between a man and a woman. Love takes a little longer. That didn't develop for me until later that evening when we were, miraculously, having dinner together, and I realized for the first time that Ariel was gone and I was free to love. Perhaps it was that sudden razing of the walls I'd built about me that did it. Walls that I dared to look over for the first time since our high school days together.

The pattern started for us as sisters as early as that, and as we grew up it solidified. Not that Ariel ever meant what happened, but the boys who interested me took one look at her and were lost. Since she was older she usually met them first, and then they never so much as noticed I was alive. She always had that indefinable magic quality that men could never resist. It was all pointless, of course, as I could easily have told them if they'd asked. Ariel was given body and soul to her dancing, and while she loved adoration and thrived on it, indulging in light love affairs along the way, she was, as she often told me, not ready to be serious about love.

"Marriage can wait," she used to say. "A dancer's life is much too short, and I must have all of it while I can."

I could have told those boys, those men, that one pair of hands applauding would never be enough. Not with hundreds of palms clapping together in a darkened theater, not with those bouquets being handed up on the stage and all the world at her slender, high-arched feet.

But it was no use. After they met Ariel, I was only a friend they liked to talk to—about her.

So that was why, at twenty-six, I was ready for Brendon McClain's strength and arrogance and supreme confidence that he could have what he wanted. For the first time it was safe to fall deeply in love. That he was a man who had no interest in the ballet world made him doubly irresistible. Love at first sight? Of course it happens. I know. It has happened to me.

The mystery was that he should have been attracted to me as well. Perhaps not so swiftly or impetuously as I to him—yet he was attracted. Sometimes I tried to get him to tell me why, and his answer was one that always puzzled me.

"Because you're not an onion," he'd say. "Too many women today are like onions, with layers and layers to peel, only to find a hard little core all the layers were hiding."

"Layers of what?" I demanded.

His blue eyes tantalized me with the intensity of his look. "Layers of anything. You're not a child—you're a woman. Yet you're the unminted ore. You're genuine. No one has managed to shape and spoil you, or cover up what you are."

That wasn't true, of course. Until that moment in a theater lobby, my life with my sister had shaped and spoiled me, but now I was being born anew—as a self I was hardly acquainted with. Perhaps that was what he saw and why he was drawn to the very things that were unformed in me. The old appeal of Galatea. Just as I was drawn to his accomplished maturity, his advantage over me of ten years. In any case, I stopped questioning very soon. Instinctively, I knew that the wrong words might destroy emotion, that too much analysis wasn't good for something so fragile and delicate. I accepted and was content. Most gloriously content.

Of course when I learned about Laurel Mountain, which was his home, I was practically ecstatic, and Brendon was pleased with the things I had to bring to Laurel.

Years before I had determined that I must escape

from the apartment I shared with my mother and sister. Our father had died when I was twelve. So I'd gone in for the study of wildlife, flowers and plants and trees, and for the last two years I had been teaching an ecology course at a small college in northwestern New Jersey. I had lived close to the hills and within sight of the Delaware Water Gap. The beautiful countryside was still open and available and I could take my students on trips of exploration, working hard at the same time at my paintings of wild flowers. I'm no artist, but I can reproduce nature quite precisely and it's something I love to do.

Of course I told no one that Ariel was my sister. I knew all too well what would happen if I did, even at that distance from New York. If the relationship were known, there would be wondering whispers behind my back, a pointing out, and sometimes open staring: "She's Ariel Vaughn's sister"—as though some of the magic had rubbed off on me. To be talked about and stared at for my own accomplishments would be one thing, but it was ridiculous to single me out because of a mere relationship. I tried to be as different from her as I could, and I was lucky. No one noticed the resemblance. I kept my secret and I was almost content.

I even had men friends and tried tentatively to fall in love, though that part hadn't worked out. There continued to be an emptiness, a lacking in my life that no vocation could entirely fill.

Then I'd had that last frantic phone call from my sister. "Come to me, Jenny! Come right away. I'm desperate and if you don't come I'll kill myself!" There had been a lot more—a jumbled outpouring that I couldn't understand, or remember later. But it was all the old cry of "Wolf!" How many times I'd heard it over the years. A bad review, a missed step, one of the injuries that all dancers fear and are prone to—anything at all could upset her delicate balance. For years I had arranged with some difficulty to fly to her side whenever she called, sometimes at considerable cost to my own life. I had even lost a job or two on her account. So now I was calm and soothing and asked her what was the matter. A foot she had injured was acting up, she wailed. She was certain her dancing days were ended and what was she to do when it all stopped? She'd managed to kick her partner in the Black Swan *pas de deux* tonight at the charity benefit. She was losing her looks. No one loved her anymore. And on and on.

I told her quietly that I couldn't drop my classes at the moment, and I was sure Mother would look after her. "But I want *you!*" she cried. "I'll come," I told her. "I'll come for sure this weekend. Now be a good girl and put Mother on the phone." But Mother was away, and I gathered that was part of her pique. Mother had gone to visit our Aunt Lydia in Connecticut and wouldn't be home till tomorrow. Right when Ariel needed her most. "Take a sleeping pill," I'd said. "You'll be all right, darling."

So she had taken a whole bottle of sleeping pills and she hadn't been all right. When Mother found her in the morning it was too late. They'd rushed her to the hospital and the reporters were already swarming. I never told my mother about that phone call. I never told anyone. I gave up my job and moved back to New York to stay with Mother for a while.

For all those years Ariel had been Mother's sole concern, her career, really. She had played for Ariel's practicing, made her costumes in the beginning, sat in at her classes, gone with her later when she traveled. I think she hardly noticed that winter when my father died of pneumonia. I was the one who missed him. Mother had *her* work in Ariel. But now all that had come to a sudden, shocking end. She wasn't one to falter or show weakness while something remained to be done for Ariel, and she had coped as no one else could have with the details of that elaborate funeral. I had hated it all. The screaming headlines, the reporters who kept asking for more, the pressure put upon us by the curious. The police questions, the inquest. I had pitied my mother and wondered what would happen when it was over and she had nothing left to do.

On the day after my sister's death I met Brendon, and

my life took a new and exciting turn. Nevertheless, I stayed on with Mother through the summer, and Brendon stayed in New York. Mother met him and was politely indifferent, except for the concern that I might leave her. The inquest had brought out something surprising. Not that many sleeping pills had been consumed, after all. It was even possible that my sister hadn't meant to kill herself. Foolishly, she had also taken an amount of alcohol—and the combination had been fatal. Perhaps this knowledge should have relieved my feelings of guilt, but it didn't at all.

More than these revelations, however, seemed to be worrying Mother. Now and then I sensed that she wanted to tell me something, that it was possible she knew more about whatever had been tormenting Ariel than she had let anyone know. But even when I felt she was on the verge of talking to me, she always drew back, keeping whatever secrets Ariel might have burdened her with, in spite of my urging her to talk.

Finally, at Brendon's suggestion, I sent for Mother's sister, my Aunt Lydia. She was a masterful woman in her own right, and a recent widow. She came willingly to take hold, and in the end I had been able to marry Brendon with a clear conscience. The only person Mother really needed was Ariel, and Aunt Lydia could easily take my place.

There had been mild surprise over my marriage, but I don't think very much that was happening was real to my mother anymore. The real world, for her, had been Ariel Vaughn on a stage dancing. And that was over for good.

For me, the torment of self-blame went on. If only I had come when Ariel had called me. If only I'd paid heed, perhaps help might have been summoned for her in time. Perhaps there wouldn't have been that fatal combination. So I must live with this blame always. Yet, somehow, I must not let it spoil my marriage.

During that summer in New York, Brendon had time to tell me about Laurel Mountain and the Mountain House. He promised me flowers of every variety, forests of trees—some seven thousand acres of wooded land, untouched, unspoiled, where no cars were allowed, except on the access roads that brought guests to the Mountain House. All this high in the Catskills above the Hudson, up from the town of Kings Landing on the water. The structure of the hotel could well be something out of a European spa of the 1800s, he told me—a fabulous anachronism in all its outrageous grandeur. I was longing to see it.

We stayed in New York for the summer until we were certain my mother was settled. Brendon headed the management of Laurel Mountain House, which his family had owned for generations. His mother and her second husband, Loring Grant, to whom she'd been married for six years, were in charge, so Brendon could remain away and we could be together in our getting-acquainted period.

Now the lovely summer is done and we arrived here in the mountains, so that a new, wonderful life is beginning for me. Or that is what I hope for. Of course there must be a little strangeness at first, but I know that is to be expected. Not everyone is going to like me as quickly as Brendon did. So tonight I sit here alone in our rooms with all the lights burning and a strange chill in my bones. There is nothing to be done until Brendon comes upstairs, and I can only try to still this rising uneasiness by remembering all that has happened today.

We drove up from Kings Landing early this afternoon and I had my first glimpse of High Tower—that massive stone structure that dominates Hudson country for miles around and was built many years ago as a memorial to Brendon's grandfather, Geoffrey McClain, long since dead. It was Geoffrey's father before him who bought the lake and some of the acreage around it early in the last century, who built a small stone inn in that lovely spot. With the passing years and increasing wealth of the family, the holding has grown to its present seven thousand acres gathered in an area of mountains and gorges and precipitous cliffs. The original inn has developed addition by addition into an enormous hotel and Brendon has told me there are guests who have been coming here all their lives and count a year lost without a visit to Laurel Mountain House.

Every visitor had to be checked in at the entry to Laurel property, and Brendon braked his Saab before the little gatehouse with its peaked roof and sign picturing a handsome crouched panther. This, as I knew, was the logo of the Mountain House, and I saw it again in the insignia sewed to the guard's lapel as he came toward us to give Brendon a respectful salute. I was introduced as Brendon's wife and we were waved through.

"I'm not going to take you straight in," he said, as we followed the winding road with forest on either hand. "Do you feel like walking?"

I always feel like walking, as I always feel like climbing, surefooted enough outdoors, and I was in a mood to be amazed and delighted by whatever he wanted to show me. As I was so continually amazed and delighted with this man who was my husband.

When we'd driven a mile or two, with the hotel still not in sight, he pulled off the road in a suitable spot and we got out of the car, striking off along a path that climbed through the woods. I was already glorying in the clear mountain air and the sight of sunlight striking its beams through the heavy stands of trees. I counted beech and maple and oak all about us, as well as scattered stands of pine trees—the latter planted there long ago by early McClains and their descendants. Some of the maples burned at the top with fiery red because there had been a recent frost, and the air was bracing and cold for mid-September. We walked hand-in-hand and there was so much love between us that my heart brimmed and no words were needed. I mustn't question my luck, I mustn't ask why. I needed only to believe—and that I could do with my whole being. Brendon had already taught me how much he loved me.

"I grew up here," he said, as the narrow trail twisted and the way steepened. "I know and love every inch of the place. My father and old Keir Devin taught me. My father died eight years ago, and two years later Mother married Loring Grant. Keir is still boss of the whole out-doors and you'll meet him. His son—" He broke off and something hesitant came into his voice. "Never mind—you don't need to meet Magnus for a while."

We rounded a turn in the path and I forgot his words. We were out in the open beneath an arched blue sky, with the forest above and behind us. Immediately below, shining like a deep blue sapphire in its setting of sur-rounding green, lay the lake, an irregular oval, curving gently into the steep folds of the shore around it. Opposite us at one end spread the fairy-tale creation that was the Mountain House.

Its red roofs were towered and steepled and there were stone battlements as well. On one steeple a cock weather vane turned in the wind, and from another flew the flag of stars and stripes. The whole was a conglomeration of architecture that matched the whim of builders over the past hundred years and more, and it reminded me of some fanciful painting of Camelot. Hundreds of windows and balconies overlooked the lake, and little summerhouses blossomed here and there along shore and trails, their thatched or shingled roofs offering shelter, their wooden benches rest for weary walkers. A few small boats dotted the water at this afternoon hour and on the far side, where the hotel ended, there was a massive outcropping of rock.

Brendon, having satisfied himself with a quick glance at the view, was watching me, waiting. I looked up at him and saw the tenderness in his eyes and on that mouth that could be hard and arrogant. I saw as well the question.

"Yes!" I cried. "Oh, yes!"

He put an arm around me and held me close. "You've passed the test, darling. If you'd made one crack about its being monstrous and ugly, I'd have taken you straight back to New York and divorced you!"

He was laughing, but I knew he half meant it. He had grown up loving this place as a boy and a young man, and it was part of him. That it might be an architectural anachronism didn't matter. It was also splendid and beautiful as it floated there on the lake like something out of a dream.

Far below us, a few small figures moved about on the lawns before the hotel, and a few others could be seen on the mooring platform for the boats.

"I love to row," I said. "Do you think I can take a boat out on the lake?"

"Of course. I keep a boat of my own down on the lake and you can have it whenever you wish."

I nodded my thanks. The scene was utterly quiet. We had met no one on the trails, and the woods seemed empty.

"It's so peaceful," I said. "So quiet and—and safe."

"What do you mean by that?" Brendon's arm tightened around me.

I wasn't quite sure. I didn't know why the thought of danger should occur to me in the midst of these quiet woods.

"I don't know," I told him. "Perhaps there are fewer things to hurt one here."

"I'm not sure that's altogether true. Nature has its own threats."

"In a place like this?"

"Of course. We have our share of mishaps. Ask Keir."

"But hardly fatal ones, I should think."

His arm pressed me forward and I suddenly realized that just beyond the shielding shadbushes at our feet a rocky precipice dropped away.

"Don't be so trustful," he said, and drew me back. "If you tumbled off that, it would very likely be fatal. And out in the middle, the lake is practically bottomless."

The words sounded so ominous that I looked up at him quickly and caught the grim set of his mouth. When I shivered he turned me back toward the trail.

"Let's go down and drive in properly. My mother will be waiting for us. They've already called her from the gate and she'll be wondering where we are."

Because of that grim look I'd glimpsed in his face, I had to know more. "Have you had any deaths by accident on the place?"

"Only one that I recall, and we want people to forget about it, so don't go around asking questions."

Rebuffed, I walked beside him in silence. On the way down I stopped now and then to admire the various varieties of ferns that grew in the woods. I'd always loved to draw the detail of a fern frond, and I couldn't wait to come out with my sketching things.

As we neared the car, I began to think with interest of Brendon's family. At that moment I had no great concern about meeting Irene McClain Grant, his mother, or his stepfather, Loring Grant. Anyone related to Brendon I was prepared to like on sight, and I was eager to make their acquaintance and be liked in return.

Now that it is later, now that night has fallen and I sit here waiting, I am not so sure I shall be comfortable with his family. I have a strange sense that something more is wrong than I've glimpsed on the surface. As though something were stirring beneath the peace and serenity— something faintly sinister.

But I had none of that feeling as we drove on toward the hotel. At a place where wide lawns tumbled down the rolling hillside, and the shrubbery grew more domesticated, we met a truck coming toward us, marked with the insignia of the Mountain House—a panther crouched on a rock—that logo I'd already seen on the way in, and on notepaper and brochures. I had thought the drawing a good one, though I was puzzled as to why a panther had been chosen.

"There's Keir's truck," Brendon said, slowing the car, "and that's Keir Devin driving. I want you to meet him. He's been like a second father to me."

The truck stopped beside us, and we all got out onto the roadway. I liked Keir at once. I liked the strong clasp of his hand, the keen, studying look of gray eyes that told me of his fondness for Brendon and his interest in seeing him happy. I sensed that this man would not accept me with easy approval before he knew me. He would take my measure, and if it didn't add up to what he wanted for

Brendon, I knew he would reject me. But not without fair trial, and I thought I could meet his testing.

"I know about you," I said. "Brendon says you'll help me to know the woods and the trees and plants. Will you, please?"

He was in his mid-sixties, Brendon had said, and his hair was white, the skin of his face tanned and leathery from long outdoor exposure. Yet he seemed younger, with his vigor and youthful carriage. A plaid shirt with khaki pants made up his work clothes, and as he came toward us he'd removed his wide-brimmed felt hat. While he was as tall as Brendon, his shoulders were even wider, and I had an impression of wiry strength that could cope with the outdoors.

He held my hand for a moment, still studying me. "Of course," he said in answer to my request. "But there's a lot to learn."

Brendon smiled his affection for the older man. "Jenny knows a bit more than how to tell a dandelion from a daisy, Keir. You'll approve of her. She's been teaching ecology out in New Jersey, you know."

"Fine. I'll put you to work," Keir told me, and then looked at Brendon. "It's good you're back. You're badly needed."

"Something wrong?" Brendon picked up his words.

"Everything."

"Loring?"

"Right. You've been away too long and he's got the bit between his teeth. He's talking about clearing the woods for cottages up near Rainbow Point. He wants to cut down an entire stand of Norway pine."

"We'll stop that, don't worry," Brendon said. "We have all the cottages we want in the area near the hotel."

"Loring thinks ten aren't enough, and he's talking expansion. Magnus is pretty mad, since it would be treading on his territory. He's likely to brain the driver of the first bulldozer that comes in, and I'm not sure I won't help him."

"There won't be any bulldozers," Brendon said shortly and turned back to the car, guiding me by the elbow.

Keir Devin stood in the road looking after us—a bit quizzically, I thought, as though not altogether reassured.

"I like him," I said as we drove on. "I hope he'll like me."

"He will. But Laurel Mountain comes first with him, and you'll have to earn your spurs. I know you'll do that."

"Who is Magnus?" I asked.

"His son." Again his answer was short, almost curt. "Look—now you can see the Mountain House."

Around the next curve it appeared in all its impressive grandeur as we moved toward it. The full spread was still hidden by trees, but its towers pierced the blue sky proudly and I could see its iron balconies more clearly now. On our left the gardens had begun, and for the moment they took precedence for me over the hotel. Even in September the formal plantings were colorful with marigolds, cosmos, scarlet salvia, chrysanthemums of various varieties, while up against the rocky hillside grew great masses of climbing hydrangeas. Below, near one of the beds, a woman in jeans and an earth-stained shirt was on her knees working.

Brendon touched his hand to the horn and she looked up, then jumped to her feet and came running toward the car.

"Aunt Naomi," Brendon told me. "My father's younger sister. She's a dear, but a bit of an individualist."

We left the car again, so that he could sweep her small, sturdy person up in a great hug. As he set her down she turned toward me and I held out my hand.

She was a small woman, weathered like a little nut, her tanned skin obviously never protected from the sun. Escaping under the red bandanna she had tied over it, her gray hair was short and a bit shaggy, as though she might have chopped it off impatiently with her own scissors when it grew long enough to annoy her. She held a garden trowel in her right hand and she shifted it so that she could take mine, but her hand lay surprisingly limp in my clasp, and there was no welcome in the face she turned toward me.

"As you know, Naomi, this is Jenny," Brendon said. "I hope you'll love her as I do."

I thought it a strange thing for him to say and wondered if he used those words because he strongly suspected that Naomi McClain was not going to love me at all, and that in her case I would receive no welcome. Rather quickly I let her small limp hand go. She hadn't said a word, but simply stared at me with eyes like hard brown pebbles.

"Naomi," Brendon said with quiet emphasis, and I heard the faint edge to his voice.

She seemed to start, and her eyes moved away from my face. "Hello, Jenny," she said, as if by rote. "Welcome to Laurel Mountain."

I looked down at her small face, with its pointed fox's chin, and murmured something agreeable.

Brendon waved a hand. "Naomi is responsible for all the beautiful plantings in this garden area. You two will have your fondness for flowers in common."

"They are beautiful," I said, but she only shrugged and walked away, her shoulders drooping as if in dejection. My presence seemed to have depressed her in some way I couldn't understand.

I followed Brendon back to the car. "She's not going to accept me," I said as we drove on.

"Of course she will." He sounded assured. "She's like a squirrel or a chipmunk. It may take a little time until she trusts you."

But what I had read in Naomi McClain's eyes had not been the caution of some wild thing—it had been open antipathy.

I so wanted nothing to quench my enjoyment in this arrival at Laurel Mountain House, and once more I gave my attention to the great structure that rose ahead of us— four stories high, with a width equal to the length of more than a city block. The arrival door was not on the lake side, and as we took the half-moon curve to the steps, two or three young men in the gray-green uniform of the Mountain House, again with panther on lapel, came down to greet us and opened the trunk to take out our bags. At the top of the steps a woman waited in the deeply arched stone alcove of the entry, and I knew she was Brendon's mother. Whatever his Aunt Naomi might have thought of me, it was his mother who mattered, and I braced myself for this next encounter, trying not to feel shaken by the rejection of one member of my husband's family.

2

As I sit here tonight in this big bedroom at the top of the hotel, with five lamps and the overhead light banishing all shadow, I feel terribly alone. I know that soon Brendon will come upstairs and then all will be well. He will understand about that sheet of hotel stationery that I've placed on the desk, and there will be no more need for uneasiness, or fear of unknown malice.

At the time of our arrival, in spite of the encounter with Naomi, I felt none of this, had no premonition of uneasiness to come when Irene Grant smiled her warm greeting as we came up the hotel steps. Her smile included me as well as Brendon, and allayed any uncertainty I might have felt about meeting her.

Brendon didn't sweep his mother up in a hug as he had Naomi. She was a woman to be treated with greater dignity, and he put an arm about her and bent to kiss her cheek. Then he turned to draw me to the top step beside them, and when she'd kissed him back she held out both hands to me.

"My dear! I'm glad you've come. I've been waiting for you for years."

It was a lovely greeting and I felt tears reach my eyes as I gave her my hands. Once she must have been a beautiful woman, and she was still pretty in a somewhat faded way. Obviously she cared about her appearance, as Naomi did not. Her light beige skirt and cardigan were neat and the brass buckle of her leather belt shone polished at her waist. She was fairly tall, with soft brown hair puffed into a rounded coiffure, and gentle brown eyes that looked lovingly at the world. As she took my hands she pulled me to her and kissed my cheek lightly so that I caught the scent of her light, flowery fragrance.

"We're giving you the suite on the top floor of the stone wing," she told her son.

He nodded approval. "Jenny will like that tower room. Where is Loring?"

The tiniest shadow seemed to touch soft brown eyes. "He got caught on the telephone. Will you stop in the office before you go up?"

"Yes, of course, Mother. I want him to meet my wife." Brendon said nothing of Keir Devin's concern, but led the way past the check-in desk and into a rambling lobby.

The Mountain House, as Brendon had told me, stayed open the year-round, and besides the regular guests there were always special groups coming in to spend a few days or a week. This, however, was a slack week and he had chosen it on purpose for our arrival. There were only a few guests in evidence and those we passed seemed to look at us with friendly eyes, unlike the guarded visitors to New York hotels. I glimpsed one or two lounges and a sunny library on the lake side, but Brendon didn't pause to show me around. We followed the jog of the corridor past the doors of various offices, and at one of them Irene paused and beckoned us into a small anteroom.

In the larger room beyond, a man was putting down a phone. Rising from his desk, he came quickly to meet us, his hand outstretched to Brendon. He was attractive, handsome in his late fifties, with hair that grayed only a little at the temples. His eyes were shrewd, his chin forceful. I quickly realized that one couldn't be in the same room with Loring Grant without sensing the dynamic force that drove him. He shook hands with Brendon and then turned to me with a warmth that I somehow distrusted. There was a flicker of something cool in his expression at the first glimpse of me, to be shut off quickly as he took both my hands and welcomed me with a kiss on the cheek.

"You certainly surprised us this time," he said to Brendon. "Not even giving us time to get to the wedding. But I must say I approve. An interesting development—yes? I mean all this sudden falling in love for an old bachelor like you!"

I glanced uncertainly at Brendon and saw a hint of anger in his eyes. Not for me, but for Loring, who ceased his outburst as though a faucet had been cut off.

"Do you know who that phone call was from?" he asked Brendon. "It was the police chief down at Kings Landing. He's still ready to stir things up, though I thought the matter had been closed months ago. Maybe you can talk to him. In case you feel it's not good for the hotel."

"I'll try," Brendon said to his stepfather. "But not now. We've had a long drive and I think Jenny would like to see our rooms and get unpacked."

I had the feeling that my husband was again cutting Loring off, his manner a warning not to talk in front of me, and I felt slightly piqued. If I was going to live at Laurel Mountain, I wanted to know all about the place. Especially if there had been a police matter so recently.

Loring said nothing more, but the look he turned on Brendon was bright with something that might have been spite.

Irene came with us in the elevator, to make sure, she said, that all was right in our rooms. Though Mrs. Hendrickson was an excellent housekeeper and kept an eye on everything.

The elevator was roomy and modern, its shaft rising beside a broad, old-fashioned staircase. At the fourth floor we left the car to walk down a wide corridor that zigzagged from addition to addition of the hotel. The carpets were a bright and cheerful turkey red; there were numerous photographs and old lithographs, and maps hung along the walls. I had noticed this downstairs as well, glimpsing dress and hair styles from the past as we moved along.

"They're a record of our history," Brendon said, noting my glance. "Each new generation adds to them. Get Mother to tell you about them sometime."

Here and there, when we came upon a cul-de-sac in the elbow of a jog, comfortable chairs were drawn near a window, where one might rest and admire the view. There was no time for views now, however, and Brendon went ahead, key in hand.

"This stone section was an addition built nearly eighty years ago," Irene said as we went down two steps into a narrowing corridor. "Its granite came from our own quarry."

"The place is like a self-contained kingdom," I marveled. "It's as though I were coming to live in a castle."

Brendon's mother smiled at me as we walked together, dropping behind. "I used to pretend that it was a castle when my parents brought me here to visit as a child. Marrying Bruce McClain was like marrying the prince. Geoffrey McClain was the king and ruler, of course. And he really ruled. We still feel we must follow some of his edicts."

"So I have married the king's grandson," I said. "The heir apparent."

She slipped her arm through mine and her hand pressed gently. "I want you to be happy here. I want you to make Brendon happy." There seemed a sudden, odd intensity in her words.

As I sit here now in my room some hours later, I can remember the very tone of her voice and in my lonely disquietude I wonder. But I gave her intensity only passing attention at the time.

"There's nothing I want more than to make my husband happy," I assured her.

"I know, Jenny. I can see it in your face. You *must* be happy here. Oh, please be happy. He loves you very much. You should see the letters he's written about you."

There was no need to assure me of his love—who knew it best of all—and again there was passing wonder at her emphasis.

Ahead, Brendon had paused, turning his key in the lock, and his eyes were bright with affection for us both. He put out his hand to stop me, however, before I went through the door.

"Wait," he said. "Let Mother look around first."

It was like the moment up on the hillside when he had wanted me to have my first marvelous view. Irene seemed to understand. She walked into the room and I heard the sound of doors opening. Then she came back to us.

"Everything is fine. Your suitcases have been brought up, and tomorrow, Brendon, you can move in more of your own things from the house, if you like. I'll leave you now, my darlings." She kissed us each on the cheek and hurried back along the corridor.

"I already love her," I told Brendon over the lump in my throat. Perhaps I would find more of a real mother in my husband's than I had ever had when Ariel was alive— or now that she was dead.

"Come," Brendon said and held out his hand.

We walked together across the room and I hardly looked at it, because the double doors to the balcony were open, inviting us. Outside we stood at the iron rail, with Brendon's arm about me, and all the breath-catching beauty of the scene spread before us. Our rooms over-looked one end of the sapphire lake, and immediately below were wide lawns and a road, and trails leading off up the mountain. But it was the mountain itself that held me. Laurel Mountain, which gave its name to the area. At its rocky summit High Tower crowned the top of the cliff, from which stone dropped away in a sheer precipice to the forest below. Around the rest of the lake trees grew down the steep hillside to the water's edge —except where there was rock—folding sapphire into deep green jade. Many of them were evergreens, I noted. The air sparkled clear and pine-scented, and there was hardly a sound anywhere.

"It's so peaceful," I said, as I'd said before up on the mountain.

"Yes. And we want to keep it that way. My grand-father wanted it to remain untouched always, no matter what happened to the rest of the world. He used to say we had the gift of peace to give those who grew weary of fighting and came here to renew themselves."

"I like that," I said.

How safe and sure I could feel just then, with Bren-don's arm around me, knowing myself his wife. Some-where on the grounds below there was laughter and a boy and girl came swinging down one of the trails hand-in-hand, the silence pleasantly broken.

Now we could turn back to our rooms and I had time to explore. We had entered through a charming sitting room, more personally furnished than any hotel room. Of course this suite was special, as Brendon pointed out, and had always been used for guests of the family. It delighted me to find that a section of the room opened into the circle of a tower that protruded from the face of the hotel, with windows all around. Here a low walnut table was set with a bowl of yellow chrysanthemums, a dish of fruit and a silver knife. The small touch welcomed me—my comfort and pleasure had been considered.

The rest of the room was equally attractive. A charm-ing Queen Anne kneehole desk, with brass drawer pulls, stood beside gold draperies, a rose-patterned Chinese lamp lighting the polished surface with a rosy glow. The rug had a floral design, pleasantly faded with the dignity of age. A water-color painting of Naomi's gardens hung over the rose damask sofa, and I went to look at it more closely. I'd always envied the artist who could paint land-scapes. All I could do was re-create flowers and plants exactly from nature.

"It's a beautiful room," I said, turning back.

Again Brendon was pleased. "My grandmother fur-nished it originally, but my mother has added touches of her own."

A large bedroom opened off the sitting room, and it too had its balcony overlooking the lake, though the built-in tower did not reach into this room. Even the small, shining-clean bathroom had a view. Closets with sliding doors had never come with the room in the beginning, I knew, but added now to its comfort.

"I'm happy, happy, happy!" I cried and did a not-too-clumsy pirouette across the room. I could even *feel* graceful now.

Brendon pulled me into his arms and kissed me for quite a long and satisfactory time. But we needed to unpack and hang up our clothes, make sure I had something unwrinkled to wear tonight, so the love we longed to show each other had to be postponed.

"Do you dress for dinner?" I asked Brendon as I opened my suitcase.

"You'll see long skirts and some pants suits in the dining room. No real evening clothes. We're fairly informal and our guests do as they please, though we frown on jeans in the dining room at night. Dinner is early—six-thirty—and we'll eat at our own table. However, there's a house ritual that we enjoy before dinner. Naomi takes charge of that. We'd better go down around six o'clock and mingle."

"Why is Naomi so ready to dislike me?" I asked, shaking out a long black and turquoise skirt that would do for dinner.

"She doesn't know you yet. And she's very protective of Laurel Mountain House. And of me. Give her time."

He had said that before, but I wasn't completely convinced. Never mind—I would make a special effort to win Naomi over and reassure her that I meant no harm to either Brendon or this beautiful place. But there were still other things I wanted to know.

"What was that all about in Loring's office when he spoke of a police matter?"

Brendon was hanging a plaid sports jacket at his end of the big closet and he didn't turn around. "It's a bit unpleasant. Do we have to talk about it tonight?"

"Hadn't I better know? Before I blunder and say the wrong things because there's something I don't understand?"

He turned back to me almost fiercely. "There are a lot of things you aren't going to understand immediately, Jenny. And no one will expect you to. But if you must know about this, come here."

His hand on my arm was not altogether gentle and I looked at him in surprise as he led me back to the balcony and pointed across the lake.

"Look! Do you see that mass of tumbled boulders just across the water at this end? It's something we call the Wolf's Lair. You'll have to get used to our whimsical names for trails and special spots of interest. It's convenient to have everything named so that guests can wander about following their maps and keeping track of where they are. That's real forest out there, you know, and you can get lost. People do."

"What happened at the Lair?"

His tone hardened. "A woman died there last May. It's a rocky labyrinth of a place that hikers like to climb through, with a good-sized cave at the end. She was crushed by a falling boulder and we haven't let anyone in there since."

I shivered. "But why the police?"

"There had to be an inquest, though no one was at fault, and that's all there is to it. It was a tragic accident, but it's the only serious one I can remember, so our record is good."

"Loring sounded as though the police were still interested."

Brendon sighed and turned back to the room and his unpacking. "I don't know what that's all about. I'll talk to him later."

"Was she a guest—the woman who died?"

He paused before his open case, a sweater in his hands. "No—she lived here." He hesitated and then went on. "She was Floris Devin. Keir's daughter-in-law. Magnus' wife."

I'd never heard his voice sound so hard, so cold, and the tone frightened me more than a little.

"I'm sorry," I said. "You're angry with me. But I don't know what I've done."

He dropped the sweater and came to me at once, held me to him, so that my face was pressed into his neck and I couldn't see his eyes.

"I'm sorry, too, darling. I suppose we all blame ourselves for what happened that day. Someone should have known that boulder was ready to roll. Bringing all this up again is disturbing. It's going to upset Mother terribly. Sometime I'll tell you about it. But Jenny, let's postpone all that for a while. Just let it alone. I want you to learn to love this place. I want to—to be sure that you'll want to stay before we get into things that happened in the past and that mustn't be allowed to affect us now."

"But of course I'll want to stay!" I cried. "Why ever would I not?" What a strange thing for him to say.

He held me from him at arm's length, and looking into his eyes I seemed to find, for the first time, some uncertainty there, and that in itself was disturbing. Uncertainty about what? About me? Brendon had always seemed the most confident person I had ever known. Almost arrogantly confident, so I felt that he knew who he was with the utmost assurance and could deal with the world on his own terms. Now there seemed a wavering that troubled me.

"All right," I said. "Let it go for now. But not for too long, darling. If I'm to be a part of your life, I need to know everything—the bad as well as the good."

He smiled at me then and shook his head. "Not everything. No human being should ever tell another everything." But he seemed suddenly cheerful again as we finished our unpacking, and I sensed a relief in him because talk had been put off for now.

It was hard for me to recover my sense of joy. Through my bath and dressing, even while I sat before the flounced dressing table near a window brushing my hair, my thoughts were troubled. I had too great a sense of something unknown and threatening hanging over my happiness—something that Brendon had been able to put away from him for the moment, but that I could not. He at least knew what he was putting away. The unknown can be much more frightening. I told myself that I must hold firmly to the knowledge that we truly loved each other and that we would never let anything come between us and harm that love. As I watched him across the room, I knew it was foolish to think of anything coming between us.

Yet the thought of that unknown woman—Floris Devin, Magnus Devin's wife—who had died so tragically cast a shadow, lessening the pure joy that I wanted to feel.

In passing, I repeated the name of Magnus Devin to myself and wondered why it seemed vaguely familiar. But I couldn't remember where I might have heard it, and as I busied myself dressing I put the question from my mind.

For the evening I put on my long skirt with the drifting turquoise and black panels, and a draped blouse of matching blue crepe, its cowl neckline becoming. I hadn't bought clothes like this in years—not since I learned never to compete with Ariel. But Brendon had wanted me to have a "trousseau" and I had tried to oblige, though I still had a feeling that I played at dress-up when I put these things on. It was some assurance that my mirror told me I needn't worry. I could think of myself now and not of Ariel.

Brendon fastened the sapphires he had given me around my neck, and I wore the little sapphire earrings that had been a Christmas gift from Ariel several years ago. Not think about Ariel? That wasn't easy, when so often the thought of my sister was there to stab me, never quite releasing me from pain. That all her beauty and vitality and genius should end so soon . . . It was hard to think only of me.

As I tucked a strand of hair into the coil I had managed with the help of tortoise-shell combs, Brendon watched, and I met his eyes in the mirror, saw the warming of approval that nurtured me and gave me a confidence I had never had in my life before. I *must* let Ariel go.

"The nicest thing about you," he told me, "is that you really don't know how beautiful you are." He bent to kiss me behind the ear and I leaned against him, able for the moment to banish all haunting doubts.

In the corridor he pulled the door shut so that it locked automatically. "Here's an extra key for you," he said, and I tucked the bit of metal away in my black velvet bag.

"Are there guests in the rooms up here?" I asked.

"No. We don't use this section unless we're exceptionally crowded, so we have the place to ourselves. Through that archway down there is an alcove with stairs to the roof. I'll take you up there sometime. Once or twice a night someone patrols these empty sections, but in the main we'll be alone."

I liked that. It was almost as though we had our own house, instead of a suite in the castle. We followed the red carpet to where the hall widened, passing an occasional guest as we moved toward stairs and elevators. This time we went down to the second floor—the dining-room floor, Brendon had told me.

When we left the elevator the sound of a Gershwin tune played softly on a piano drifted toward us—"Love Is Here to Stay"—and now there was a murmur of voices, muted and never shrill, but present to remind me where we were. Small rooms opened off the corridor we followed, and I glimpsed Victorian furnishings—plush sofas with carved rosewood frames, whatnot shelves crowded with bibelots, round pedestal tables covered by velvet that dripped fringe. I paused in delight in one doorway where there were touches of chinoiserie in twin cabinets, but it was the row of windows along the west wall, looking out toward a dipping sun, that caught my eye. The lake side faced east, but here the great western spread of valley lay below us, running clear to scalloped mountaintops on the horizon. Mountains that stood gray-blue against a sky that had begun to gild.

"It's so beautiful it hurts," I whispered.

Brendon was beside me. "Yes. And it's never static. The sky is always changing and the mountains can look different in every new shading of light."

"Everything here seems so—so far away from the

world," I said. "Unearthly. No television. No radios or newspapers crying doom."

He laughed. "Oh, there are newspapers, and they still cry doom. We do have a shop on the lobby floor. But those who choose can escape from the world for a little while. It's not Eden, though—never think that. There's no Shangri-la anywhere. Only surcease, rest, a little forgetfulness—that's what we have to offer. And it's good for those who come here. That's why they return repeatedly. Just as I will always come back, no matter where I might wander."

There was no reason for his words to make me slightly uneasy again. I would never want to take my husband away from this beautiful place—would I? Surely I would always be content to be bound to it, as he was bound.

We continued down the corridor, looking into more little parlors, all furnished with lovely antiques, and offering intimate settings for guests to use, unlike any hotel I'd ever seen.

"Most of these things were collected in my grandmother's day," Brendon said. "Now this floor belongs to Naomi. She's become very knowledgeable, not only in charge of the gardens, but also as our Victorian expert as well."

In the jog of a corridor we came upon the piano player and he looked up to smile at Brendon. There was no music on the rack and he slipped effortlessly from Cole Porter to Berlin to Rodgers and Hart.

"No hard rock here," I whispered to Brendon and he nodded.

"We do have younger guests coming, but we feed them nostalgia and they seem to love it. Nostalgia inside, nature outside—the combination is irresistible. That's why I'm not about to let Loring spoil it."

Guests were gathering in some of the rooms, chatting, visiting with each other, comparing small adventures of the day. Many seemed well acquainted. Yet this was more a visiting ritual than the cocktail hour of New York, and no drinks-in-hand were to be seen.

"They're not drinking," I murmured in surprise.

"There is no bar," Brendon said. "But if you'd like a drink before dinner—"

I shook my head. "I prefer it this way."

Sometimes when Ariel wasn't dancing she had drunk too much, and since I was forever flinging myself in opposite directions from my sister, I drank very little.

An elderly, white-haired lady in long black lace saw us in the doorway and left a horsehair sofa to come toward Brendon with outstretched hands.

"My dear boy. How good to see you. I've been here all summer, and not a glimpse of you. But I understand." She turned a friendly look upon me. "I want to meet the new bride."

Brendon introduced me and she took my hand, her pale blue eyes a little speculative. "Well—you are a surprise. I knew your husband as a small boy running about these very hallways. I've been coming here all my life, you know. My parents brought me when I was hardly more than three, and then my husband and I often took our vacations at Laurel. Now that I'm alone—I still come. So I'm happy to see that the McClain dynasty will be carried on. There aren't enough children anymore. Not belonging to those who live here."

Brendon got me away from her a bit hurriedly and I wondered why, since she was only being kind. We went on, and now and then we were greeted, though nearly always by the middle-aged or older. The younger guests hadn't been coming long enough to know Brendon that well as yet.

"We'll find Naomi in the family parlor," Brendon said. "It's where guests come when they want to see the McClains. Another tradition. We're full of those."

"It's lovely to have traditions," I told him. "Who stands still long enough these days to do the same thing twice?"

The family parlor wore red velvet and no horsehair, and rich garnet draperies looped in gold were pulled back from the windows for a full view of the sky and faraway mountains. Irene sat with a certain gentle regality in a tapestried chair—the queen mother reigning. Yet there was no sense of make-believe to the scene. All this belonged to Laurel, and had always belonged. The outside world hadn't yet crushed in to destroy it. Or had it? Unbidden, I thought again of the woman named Floris who had died here last May, and in whose death the police were still apparently interested. "It's not Eden," Brendon had said.

But I forgot the small cloud quickly because Brendon was taking me about the room, introducing me to men and women who could still be gracious and unhurried here, no matter what happened to them in their distant homes.

Naomi was not immediately in evidence, but even as I looked about for her she flitted in, no longer grubby as when I had seen her in the gardens, the bandanna gone from her head, her gray hair fluffed and curly, but not wildly windblown. To my surprise she seemed to be in costume—in an India silk dress, snug of bodice, with a slight train and just the hint of a bustle. She must have seen me staring because she came toward us, flouncing a little.

"How do you like me, Brendon? Grannie's trunks are bottomless. I don't think I've worn this gown before."

Brendon smiled his affection. "The dress is fine, but you don't quite make the transition into Victorian lady. There's a difference in the walk when you run around in pants all day."

"I'll mince from now on," she promised and went off wriggling her train a little, and using a step that was more bounce than mince. She hadn't looked at me once. I might have been invisible as far as Naomi McClain was concerned. I watched her greeting guests, inviting admiration for her gown, still flouncing a little.

"I wonder what she would have done if they'd ever let her out in the world," Brendon said. "She's only fifty now —she was the baby of the family, and Grandfather had a curious notion about protecting her from the 'outside.' She's still lively—and I suppose she's happy enough here. There was a man once, but he died in the Second World War, and she's never found anyone since to care about as she does about Laurel. But I think if she had escaped when she was young she might have been successful at a job, even a career."

"Why can't you think of Laurel as her career?" I asked.

"It's too limiting. A small kingdom can also be a prison, unless you get out once in a while, as the rest of us do. But now she'll never leave, and perhaps it's her touch that keeps a lot of the old traditions working. The guests—the older ones—are devoted to her, and she's devoted to Laurel."

"Why does she think I've come here to hurt her favorite place?" I asked Brendon under cover of nearby laughter.

He was as evasive as before. "It's not that. Sometime I'll explain. Let it go now, Jenny. Smile. I want everyone to admire my beautiful wife."

There was no dinner gong. At the end of the corridor outside the parlor, big double doors opened silently, and there were already guests—mostly the young hungry ones—lined up to go in. We waited until the parlor had emptied and Irene came to take her son's arm. Her smile for me was as warmly friendly as Naomi's pretense that I didn't exist was chilling. Loring appeared just as we went through the door, and he seemed to be in a rush, as was usual for him.

As he spoke to Brendon, his words carried a ring of triumph. "I've got it sewed up, finally. A conference of oil company executives from all over the world is meeting here next spring. Not only our people, but perhaps a sheik or two as well. It's the biggest thing I've been able to land so far. They'll spend plenty."

I saw Irene turn her head quickly to look at Brendon. Naomi was striding ahead, forgetting to mince, and hadn't heard.

"We'll talk about it later," Brendon said coolly to his stepfather. "How definite are the arrangements?"

"Definite enough." Triumph was still bright in Loring's eyes.

The head waiter disposed of the group ahead and then turned to greet us, giving me a special bow as Brendon introduced me. Naomi bounced on ahead down the vast room, and we followed more slowly, so that I had a chance to look around.

I had been in Europe only once—when Ariel and Mother had insisted that I go along in order to see my sister dance in Paris, and this dining room was larger than any I had seen there. A strange mingling of the elegant and the rustic made it individual. Overhead, great dark beams rose to the peaked ceiling, and while the wood-paneled walls were dark, white tablecloths gave light to the room and there was an abundance of rosy lamps on the tables and bowls of autumn flowers everywhere. Crystal and silver shone from much buffing. Opposite the door a roaring fire sent flames leaping high in a giant fireplace. Again, however, it was the windows that gave the room its special, dramatic character. The end of the room we approached was built out upon the hillside in a great semicircle, with huge glass windows making a solid wall, dramatizing the splendor of sky and valley and mountains.

The family table was near one of these windows, and a smiling young waitress attended us. While Loring seated his wife, Brendon pulled out chairs for Naomi and me. I was determined to savor, to enjoy, every new experience I had at Laurel Mountain. Too soon everything would become familiar—perhaps commonplace. So now I sat looking out the windows, watching the gathering of color in the west as clouds were tinted to chrome yellow and chartreuse and deep rose.

Brendon had told me that it was Irene who kept the hotel cuisine to a level of excellence that was known around the country. While there was no elaborate choice at meals, the cooking was imaginative, sophisticated, delicious.

I enjoyed my smoked oysters, lentil soup, succulent duckling, and the salad of greens and tiny tomatoes grown in the hotel gardens. For dessert I let every mouthful of French cheese cake melt in my mouth. During the course of the meal there was desultory conversation, but it was not as pleasant as the food, as I became quickly aware.

Brendon's mood had darkened and I suspected that he was brooding over the *fait accompli* of Loring's plans. Irene was clearly worried about them both, torn between husband and son, while Naomi had ceased to bounce and ate gloomily as though what was set before her might be her last meal. I had been placed next to her at the round table, and once I tried to engage her in conversation by telling her how much I liked everything I had seen of Laurel Mountain.

I didn't get very far because she set down her fork with an air of impatience, as though I had interrupted important concentration, and looked at me briefly. Her glance was no more than that. A flicking of her eyes to my face and then away, but I saw again the evidence of antipathy and felt shocked and troubled. This was not the place to try to draw out the reason for her hostility, or attempt to diminish it, but I knew there would eventually have to be a meeting between Naomi McClain and me if we were both to live where we would see each other constantly. She said nothing in response to my remarks, but simply gave me that quick look and then turned to speak to Loring on her other side.

At that moment I happened to look at Irene and caught her eyes upon me, knew that she had seen, that she was aware. She tried to smile at me—in reassurance, I think—but her lips quivered before she tightened them, suppressing evidence of whatever she was feeling. There was no suppressing the look in her eyes, however, and I sensed that something had frightened her, or at least worried her extremely, and that it had to do with me. I was beginning to feel like Bluebeard's bride. What had happened in this place to make Brendon's bringing me here as a new wife something to cause concern in one woman and decided aversion in another?

At least I could rely on the fact that everything was perfect between Brendon and me, and I enjoyed my meal determinedly. When we were leaving the dining room I put a hand on my husband's arm.

"Will you walk with me outside? Perhaps there'll be an

early moon tonight, and I'd love to see Laurel by moonlight."

He covered my hand with his. "We'll do that, darling. But on another night. Loring and I have business to attend to that can't wait. It will probably take a while, so I may be late coming upstairs. I'm sorry, but I'm sure Mother will welcome your company for the evening."

I shook my head, thrusting back my disappointment. "I understand. But if I can't be with you this evening, I'm tired enough to want to be alone. I'll go up to our rooms and read for a while and then get to bed early. This has been a long day."

"Yes. Long for me too. But I've had my reward. You *are* going to feel about Laurel the way I do. And that's all I can ask."

Brendon and Loring went downstairs to the lobby floor for their conference. Naomi had disappeared, and I stood for a moment in the hall with Irene, thanking her for the lovely rooms and the welcome she had made me feel. She reached for my hand and held it gently.

"You *are* welcome here, my dear. I couldn't ask for anyone lovelier as my son's wife. Not just because you're so pretty, but because of all he has told me about you. Besides, I make up my own mind very quickly." Something flickered in her eyes as though she might have said something else, but she looked away. "I know everything is going to be all right. Just give Brendon time to stop being a bachelor."

Her choice of phrasing seemed to hint that she'd harbored a fear of its not being "all right."

"Of course I'll give him time," I said quickly. "We'll both need time to get used to marriage. What I've never understood is how I was lucky enough to find him. Lucky enough not to have had some other woman snap him up long before this."

She smiled and released my hand. "Oh, there have been girls. That's no secret, and you mustn't suppose otherwise. Not with a man like Brendon. But he never wanted to settle down with only one before. I'm glad it was you, my dear. Now—if you haven't any plans for the evening—would you like to come over to our house for a while? It's close by—the house my father built, so he could get away from the hotel some of the time. Naomi lives there with us, though she has her own little office on the main floor of the hotel as well."

"Thank you," I said. "I'd like to come another time."

"Of course. Run along and have a good rest. Laurel will be waiting for you tomorrow."

Her words had warmed me, and when we'd said good night, I walked toward the elevator with a lighter step. From the beginning I had told myself that I would not be curious about Brendon's past. He asked no questions about men I might have known, and I would never ask him questions about women. Our lives together had begun with *us*. And that was enough. What problems I might have to work out at Laurel Mountain would not be because of my husband.

The walk from the elevator toward what they called the Stone Section seemed endlessly long. The additions that had been built on to the hotel over the years had taken a curious zigzag pattern, so that each new section was set a little back from the old—perhaps to follow the line of the lake, about which nothing could be done. At least I was glad of cheerful red carpets and good lighting, until the corridor narrowed and the overhead lights grew dimmer. I hadn't been aware of emptiness up here before. With Brendon beside me I hadn't listened to the utter quiet, but I was aware of it now. A hangover from city living, undoubtedly. Though I hadn't been afraid out in the New Jersey countryside, and the Mountain House was even safer. It was just that I wasn't accustomed to a totally empty hotel corridor where no one else occupied the rooms on either side.

It was a relief to reach our door. I slipped my key into the lock, let myself through, and closed the door behind me, shot the extra bolt. Eerie, that feeling I'd had in the hallway. And very silly.

Across the room the balcony beckoned me and I went through the open doors and stepped outside. The entire face of the hotel on the lake side was made up of just such balconies—long verandas, really, all broken into separate enclosures by decorative wrought-iron railings of the sort one seldom sees today. On either hand the fourth-floor balconies stretched empty, though here and there a lighted room threw patches of yellow across the darkness. The night was completely dark now and I gave myself over to its enjoyment.

Stars bloomed across the deep blue sky, and far below, the reflecting lake lay quiet—like black glass in the shadows, twinkling with star points out in the middle. Lights of the hotel made paths across the water, and on the opposite shore where that labyrinth of rocks called the Wolf's Lair tumbled down the hillsides, I could see a small, thatched-roof summerhouse—a little gazebo—with a light standard near it. Other lights flickered through tree branches here and there about the grounds, while high on the rock of the mountain opposite, the High Tower light was brightest of all—sending its gleam across the Hudson Valley and beyond, the dark arm of the tower holding its beacon high.

A warm response to all that was beautiful and peaceful about Laurel Mountain rose in me. That this was to be my home from now on delighted me increasingly. Where others had to leave after a short visit, I could stay on and see it in every season and under every weather change. In that moment of intense feeling I was doubly grateful to Brendon, who had given me this and who would be forever a part of its perfection.

From the room behind me came a faint, unaccountable rustle. Perhaps Brendon had opened the door without my hearing him. But of course he couldn't have because it was bolted. I walked back into the room, wondering what could have made the sound. The answer was quickly evident.

Someone had slipped a sheet of hotel stationery beneath the door, and I glimpsed the proud and watchful panther of the logo again. A message from the desk, perhaps? I picked it up and carried it to the glow of the Chinese lamp, to find that a few words had been typed across its surface. Words enclosed in quotation marks:

"Let no guilty man escape."

That was all, and it sent a stabbing of alarm through me. Because *I* was guilty. Ariel had called me; I had not gone to her in time, and my sister was dead.

But this was ridiculous, and I shook myself angrily. No one else knew about that phone call. Not even my mother. It was my own guilty conscience causing the sort of stab I would probably experience for the rest of my life. If this sheet was not for me, however, then it must be intended for Brendon, and that was somehow far more frightening. I didn't like to think of such malice being directed toward my husband.

Quickly I unlocked the door and looked into the corridor. The long tunnel of the hallway was empty; the eerie stillness and sense of emptiness were still there. The alcove that housed the stairs to the roof was a shadowed cave. Once this section had been a main part of the hotel and had echoed to the voices and footsteps of guests. Now no one but Brendon and I and the hotel help would come here. Yet someone had come. Someone who had slipped this sheet of paper under the door, and it could hardly be considered a message from the desk.

Never mind. It would have to wait until Brendon came up to bed, I decided, and placed the sheet beside the lamp, wondering where the quotation had come from and what it could possibly mean. Brendon would know and explain it all away.

To comfort myself, I opened the box that contained my water colors and acrylic paints, and leafed through the sketchbook I'd brought with me. In New Jersey I had worked on my collection of wild-flower paintings, and it distracted me now to look through them. I smiled over my careful representation of the lowly skunk cabbage—*Symplocarpus foetidus.* I'd thought it a fascinating plant in the way it uncurled into bloom in the early spring, with great green leaves and the curious, purple-streaked hood that was its flower. The aroma one could ignore.

My drawings were exact in every detail, since I liked to be meticulous, and I sometimes felt they might almost

be picked from the page. That satisfied my striving to
make them as flawless as I possibly could.

The room was beginning to feel cold, and I put my
sketch things away and went to close the balcony doors
against a rising wind that rushed through the forest. Heat
had started to gurgle in the radiators, and I was glad to
close the doors, because entry from that direction would
be all too easy by way of connecting balconies. Probably
a foolish thought here in this peaceful place. Then I went
into the adjoining bedroom and lighted all the lamps. I
have been sitting here ever since, waiting and thinking.
Always listening, while my uneasiness grows.

But I knew this was getting me nowhere and eventually
I undressed and put on the bright fleece dressing gown
of Chinese red that Brendon had not yet seen me wear. A
full-length mirror on the bathroom door told me that I
looked dramatically beautiful—and quite unlike myself.
The robe had belonged to Ariel and Mother had insisted
that I take it with me. "I can't bear to give all her beautiful things away to strangers," she'd said. "Keep this at
least, Jenny, to remember her by."

I needed nothing more to remind me sorely of Ariel,
and the gown wasn't right for me. When I had a chance,
I would replace it. I bound my hair into a long braid
and let it hang over my shoulder in a dark rope against
the red fabric. Perhaps he would like me to be dramatic
once in a while, and dressing up made me feel more
courageous and less apprehensive about that sheet of
paper on the desk.

When I was ready I got into bed with a book to read.
But I was more weary than I knew and I fell sound
asleep quickly, with all the lights left burning around me.

3

This is another night and I walk the path on the far side of the lake and watch the stars flickering in the water. Against the dark sky the steepled roofs of the Mountain House make a still darker silhouette. What is it like up there among those fantastic towers? What a view it must command. But I have no heart for such exploration now.

No one knows I am out here, but I need to be alone so I can think. I'm not sure I will ever know what to make of this strange day I have somehow lived through, with its isolated and shocking occurrences that all seem to be building toward some inevitable climax that I am afraid to reach.

It began last night, really, with a knocking on the door that roused me from deep sleep, penetrating my vanishing dreams. I sprang up from the bed, startled, remembering the bolt that was keeping Brendon out.

"Coming!" I called and ran in bare feet across the carpet.

The bolt slid back with a clatter and I pulled open the door. I had never seen him look so tired and there was a lingering of anger in his face that I knew was the residue of his long session with Loring Grant. His eyes didn't light at the sight of me as they usually did, and when I tried to fling my arms about his neck he held me off.

"Don't ever wear red," he said. "It doesn't become you," and he strode past me into the room.

I was left to stare after him in astonishment and distress. "I—I'm sorry you don't like the gown. It belonged to my sister and Mother wanted me to have it."

"Take it off," he told me, "and go back to bed."

He had never spoken to me in that tone before, and I felt both shock and resentment. As I unzipped myself from the lounging robe and got into bed, he gathered up his night things and went off to the bathroom, leaving me to fume. But my pique didn't last for long because I was trying hard to be an understanding wife. Brendon had undoubtedly come from a difficult time with Loring and he was worried about things that had nothing to do with me. His annoyance had spilled over because I was there, and that was all it meant. I must be quiet and not add fuel to an already angry blaze. What had happened was simply a new fact that I had learned about my husband—that he didn't like red—and I would add this to my growing fund of knowledge. Adjustments were what marriage was all about, and it couldn't be easy for a man of thirty-six to suddenly get used to a new wife who knew so little about him.

By this time I'd begun to feel virtuous and self-approving of my calm and tolerant reasoning. The red fleece gown lay discarded on the carpet, and tomorrow I would give it to Irene to dispose of.

Brendon came back into the room, set the balcony doors ajar and went about turning off the lights I had set burning. I watched him over the top of the covers and saw that the strain had lessened a little in his face and in the muscular lines of his body above his pajama pants. I loved the way he looked—lean and strong, with never a hint of fat.

"There's an energy shortage, remember?" he said, moving toward another light.

I thought of the note and the reason for my wanting as much light for company as possible, but in the same breath I told myself that it could wait until morning. I didn't want to upset him any more now. So I watched and was silent.

With an air of deliberate avoidance, he stepped around the puddle of red the robe made upon the floor and went to turn out the Chinese lamp on the desk. There he saw the sheet of paper and picked it up, moving toward the bed.

"What's this?"

I had to answer. "I don't really know. Someone pushed it under the door after I came back to the room tonight. I thought you might understand what it means."

If he knew he wasn't going to tell me and I noted in dismay his violence as he ripped the paper across and across and let the pieces flutter toward the wastebasket. When he had turned out the last lights, he came to lie beside me on the bed, not touching me, but stiff and unrelaxed, as though he couldn't bear my nearness.

I was really frightened now. "What is it, Brendon? Tell me what's wrong."

The groan that seemed to be torn from him had a despairing ring, but at least he turned on his side and drew me close, held my own trembling close to him until I quieted against his warm body, reassured about nothing except that his arms were around me and that he loved me still. While he explained nothing, his love convinced me of what I needed to know.

I slept all night in his arms, and I think we both slept deeply out of weariness. It was I who awakened first and raised on an elbow to watch the still marvelous novelty of finding him asleep beside me. The lines of worry were swept away from forehead and mouth, and he looked rather young and boyish. A dark smudging of beard showed across the firm chin that I had come to love, and long lashes lay upon his cheeks, hiding the bright blue of his eyes. He wouldn't have liked it if I'd told him, but I thought he was a beautiful man.

Beyond our balcony windows the sun was shining and I got quietly out of bed, stretching widely. The scarlet pool of Ariel's robe still lay on the carpet and I scooped it into a bundle that I thrust far back on the floor at my end of the closet. If some association with red disturbed my husband, then I would take care that he not be annoyed by it again.

Nevertheless, this morning, I didn't feel like letting the matter go entirely. Last night something had turned him from me, however briefly, and unless I was to stumble again in the future, I needed to understand why this had happened. It would be too difficult to live with someone whose nerves might turn raw at any moment that I unknowingly irritated him. We couldn't live like that, and today I would find a time to ask him openly what had been the matter last night, and why he had torn up that note so savagely. Whatever happened to him from now on, I was a part of his life, and I had to understand.

When I had bathed and dressed in brown slacks and a rust-colored shirt, Brendon wakened and smiled at me sleepily. "You're up too early. What's the rush?"

"It's such a beautiful day that I couldn't go back to sleep. Laurel is waiting for us out there. Will you show me everything today?"

His look was loving and there was none of that brief rejection I'd glimpsed in him last night. "At least we can begin. The dining room opens at seven-thirty and I'll be ready."

I carried my jacket when I went downstairs, and took along my sketching things as well. We breakfasted alone at a table near the windows, since the others had their first meal of the day at their house. I watched cloud shadows chase themselves across the sunny valley, painting shapes of dark and light on distant mountain slopes.

As we ate he told me more about the McClain family and the long years of custom and tradition that had gone into the building of the Mountain House. The main stem of the family, the inheriting branch, as far as Laurel was concerned, were all here at the hotel. The entire property had been left in equal parts by Brendon's father, Bruce McClain, to Irene, his wife, Naomi, his sister, and to his son, Brendon.

"So we are the board that runs things," he explained.

"Then Loring comes into it only through Irene?" I asked.

Brendon dabbed dark honey on his toast. " 'Only' isn't the right word. He has come to have a very strong influence upon my mother in the six years of their marriage, and sometimes she sides with him against me. Naomi is devoted to Laurel, but she can blow with the wind, so it's a rather sticky situation. I set down my opposition very clearly last night to the things he wants to do. He's already set some of them in motion, and that makes for complications."

"But isn't it hard to keep going these days? Why don't you want that oil company conference coming in?"

"Tradition again, I suppose. We like to attract a different type of conference from the commercial hotels, and we've been doing very well with them. In a few weeks there will be the annual gathering of old carriages here. You'll be surprised at the horse-drawn rigs that will turn up. We have a number here in our own collection down at the Red Barn. That's a place you'll have to see. Much of it is a museum now. Then we're having a gathering of organic gardeners and natural-food people coming next month. We're interested in organic gardening ourselves. We go in for writers' and artists' conferences too. There's a group of mystery-story fans coming this winter. Maybe none of this is in a class with oil magnates, but these affairs pay our bills and serve our purpose, in that we're interested in conservation and health matters that concern pollution, and we like to encourage groups interested in any of the arts."

"It sounds wonderful," I said. "Worth doing."

"We think so. We've never wanted to go commercial and attract big business. We don't want to be exploiters or hucksters. In fact, we're content to be a modest business ourselves. Though I'm afraid that's not what Loring wants. To give him credit, he has a good deal of managerial ability and he used to work for the Hilton chain. But he's more ambitious for the Mountain House than I like to see. Part of our charm is not being commercial on a big scale."

"What about your aunt, whom I met in New York? Doesn't she have any vote in what happens?"

"She's not on the McClain side of the family and she has never taken any interest in what we're doing. When her husband died he left her well off, so she doesn't need any help."

When breakfast was over and we were leaving the dining room, we met Naomi, again dressed in jeans and bandanna, ready for working outdoors. She smiled at Brendon and once more ignored me. Sooner or later I would have to come to some sort of understanding with Naomi McClain, but Brendon didn't seem to notice, and when he'd helped me on with the jacket I'd brought downstairs, we went outdoors, my sketch kit under my arm.

In the cool, bracing air the morning sparkled with sunlight and the lake shone, its surface crinkling in the breeze that blew toward the hotel. Brendon led the way to a path that started up the mountain.

"We'll take the short way up," he said. "The longer road around is easier, but you've told me you like to climb."

Underfoot, the trail was a mingling of earth and fine black gravel, and the footing was springy with occasional patches of pine needles and dead leaves. Here in the woods, under the lee of the mountain, the sun had vanished and it was cool and shadowy. Leaves were turning bright to a greater extent, and we passed a golden locust, and several maples burning into flame.

It would take about half an hour to get to the top, Brendon said, and then I would be rewarded with a spectacular view.

As we climbed I set myself a private goal. When we reached the top and were resting there, I would talk to my husband about what happened last night. It would be harder to quarrel—if there was to be a quarrel—out here in these beautiful surroundings.

When we had followed the trail a little way up, he led me over a rocky side path to one of the small summerhouses above the lake. It was built with a thatched roof and open sides, and a rough floor made of split logs, and it seemed to grow out of the great boulder on which it perched. I stepped into the shelter gingerly and Brendon reassured me.

"Don't worry. These rest houses are anchored into the rock and we test them constantly to make sure floors and railings are safe."

As I sat down on a rough bench, I realized that the rock on which the little house was built was one of those great tumbled boulders that had poured down the mountainside during some upheaval in the prehistoric past. All was not entirely safe, however, since a woman had died among those very stones below our perch.

Looking down upon the broken pile, I caught movement far below and saw the tiny figure of a man climbing through the Lair. He was dwarfed to matchstick size by the great boulders all around him and I pointed him out to Brendon.

"I thought the Lair was closed."

"It is," he said, and leaned above the rail. "Hello!" he called. "You, down there!"

The man looked up and waved.

"You aren't supposed to be in there," Brendon shouted. "You'd better turn back toward the lake. Some of the rocks may be loose and there's a sign at the entrance telling you to keep out."

The man below us called back that he had climbed down from the rocks near where we were, and he would find his way out.

Brendon watched until he had disappeared behind a boulder. "He's probably safe enough, and perhaps Keir will consent to open the trail again before long. There isn't anything loose now. In fact, Keir says there wasn't anything loose there to start with. He's just being cautious."

I stared at him. "But then how—"

"We don't know," Brendon said shortly, and I knew he had shut me out again.

Across the lake the massive structure of the hotel spread along the rock bank of the far shore, and its red roofs and pointed towers were beautiful in bright sunlight. Now I could pick out the Stone Section—that tower where we had our rooms.

"I'll never tire of looking at it," I said, as we left the summerhouse and went on up the trail, climbing now above the huge boulders of the Lair that lined this part of the shore and dropped away on our right.

"I've never tired of it in all the years I've lived here," Brendon said and put his arm about me as we walked.

We met only one or two people on our way, as the morning was still early, and most of the hikers weren't up and about as yet.

When we stood at another lookout point above the Lair, I ventured a question. "Where was it that the rock fell?"

After a brief hesitation, Brendon pointed. I could see the depression in the earth where a great boulder had once rested, see the scars of its fall as it had struck rocks on either side before crashing into the wide crevice below. The pit of my stomach quivered and I could almost hear the shattering sound of that fall, almost hear the screams of a woman trapped.

"There's something wrong about it, isn't there?" I said. "Something you haven't told me?"

"Come along," he said curtly and pulled me back from the sheer drop of the precipice.

He didn't put his arm about me again, nor did we walk companionably hand-in-hand as we had done yesterday in the woods, and I felt the loss sadly. I was discovering that Brendon was more a man of moods here at Laurel Mountain than he had been in the city, and today was not so propitious as yesterday for intimacy. Something had happened to separate him from me, though I didn't know what it was. More than ever, I felt determined to find out, and when we reached the top I would summon my courage and open the subject in a way that he couldn't turn aside.

For now, as we climbed, I interested myself in the things I knew best, identifying trees along the way, enjoying the clusters of white snakeroot flowers that grew in great profusion beside the path. I didn't want to stop now, but another time I would come back and make a few drawings.

At one point Brendon stopped me and gestured up the hillside. "Do you see that door up there?"

Since it was partially overgrown with Virginia creeper, I hadn't noticed the metal door set into the hillside. "What is it?"

"There's an underground tunnel in there big enough for a man to walk through. It carries electric cables and water pipes up to the tower. I'll tell you more about it when we get to the top."

Now the way steepened in places, though the climb was never difficult. I filled my lungs with the glorious, pine-scented air and was hardly out of breath by the time we neared the top and stepped out upon a rocky plateau. Here the granite tower, built on a circular out-cropping of sheer rock, rose against the sky.

"We can climb to the top of the tower, if you like," Brendon said. "If you don't mind stairs."

We went through the arched door of the tower, with its memorial inscription overhead. Inside, the stone cavity echoed deafeningly as several boys came running down the stairs, shouting to rouse the tumultuous sounds of voices crashing against the stone. They grinned at us, unabashed, and rushed outside. I was grateful when the echoes quieted and we could climb the wide, open stairs in silence.

Out through the door at the top wind rushed upon us, whipping my long hair into a tangle, snatching my breath away. Brendon steadied me as I leaned against his arm. He bent his head to kiss me lightly, and my spirits rose because I knew he was glad to have me with him, showing me the places he loved.

On all sides around the tower spread the tremendous view. Toward the east the Hudson wound away beyond hills that hid Kings Landing on the river, and we could look out over the countryside beyond. To the south lay sun-swept valleys and more hills. As we turned to the south-west I saw two slanting mountain peaks that seemed to fling themselves into the air at a perilous angle, their stony crowns thrusting outward as if they were flying. Eons ago some mighty upheaval had launched these rocky crests into space, so they would stand alone like twin waves rising to break at their very peak—yet frozen for all eternity.

"It's so beautiful." I whispered the words I'd spoken before.

His arm tightened about me. "Yes. The earth and sky, the water and those dramatic mountains! It's only men who can be ugly."

The words sounded an unexpected bitterness and I pressed my hand upon his arm. "At least you furnish a counterbalance here at Laurel. That's worth accomplishing, isn't it?"

He turned from me, withdrawing his arm. "Sometimes I think it's all been spoiled, contaminated. Sometimes I'm afraid it will never be the same again."

"Because of—of that woman's death?"

"That's part of it."

"Please tell me," I said. "Don't shut me out, Brendon. I don't want to live here wondering about some mysterious happening that is being kept from me and that seems to turn you away from me."

He had moved on along the stone parapet and stood looking out toward the lake and the Mountain House, not answering. I went to lean against his arm.

"Please tell me."

He put a light finger to my lips. "Hush, darling. Not now. Don't spoil what we have. What's past has to be forgotten."

I couldn't forget what I didn't know, but I had been silenced, and I could only stand beside him looking down at the jewel of blue lake and that red-roofed fantasy at the far end, dropped into a sea of green forest that rolled away on every hand. In the distant valleys I could glimpse twisting roads, with small houses sprinkled here and there like white sugar, but no towns to be seen. The quiet and the loneliness were complete.

Again he pointed. "Do you see where the rock cliff

across this end of the lake ends in a sheer precipice? That's another walk you must take, Jenny. To Panther Rock, where you'll have a magnificent view of High Tower."

Once more the panther. I wondered why the Laurel emblem made me faintly uneasy and inwardly I rebelled against the curb that had been imposed upon my questions. I knew my thoughts would never be still until I knew the answers. I could sympathize all too well with Bluebeard's wives—though I hoped I wouldn't meet such a fate if I persisted in asking for answers. Brendon was no Bluebeard, and for now I could only go along with what he wanted.

"Were there really panthers here?" I asked.

"There used to be. In the West they're called mountain lions, but here people called them panthers. They're long gone from the area now, of course, because men have driven them out, just as most of the snakes have been driven away."

"I'm glad of that," I said, but now I wasn't thinking of snakes. Or panthers either. All my questions had to do with men—and one woman.

"Don't be sad, Jenny." His words were unexpectedly pleading. "I remember how sad you looked that day when I saw you standing in the Opera lobby before your sister's picture. I remember thinking that I wanted to see you smile. You've smiled a lot since then. Smile for me now."

So I smiled a little tremulously, and he kissed me again.

"Bear with me, Jenny. I'll tell you about everything when the right time comes. Right now—" He let the words drift off into the silence and I knew that I dared ask him nothing more.

When he knew he'd stopped me his tone grew lighter. "Even the most sensible men can have aberrations," he went on. "My father built this tower years ago to honor Geoffrey McClain, my grandfather, who did so much for Laurel Mountain. It was Grandfather Geoffrey who looked ahead and started our conservation program. But when the tower was being constructed, my father had a room hollowed out of the rock underneath. There's still a door into it where the stairs begin, but we keep it locked. That tunnel I showed you opens into it."

"What was the room for?"

"It was going to be a sort of grand ballroom and meeting room. But it proved to be too far for guests to come without transportation, and the project was given up before it was finished. Bruce's Folly, they call that room."

It was strange to think of a huge, closed-off room still existing beneath High Tower.

"Isn't the room used for anything now?"

He looked away from me, and for a moment seemed to hesitate. "No, it's not used. Not exactly."

"I'd like to see it sometime."

His gaze returned to my face. "I really don't think you'd enjoy what's down there, Jenny. Forget about that room."

Once more his sudden evasiveness puzzled me, but I asked no more questions.

As we leaned on the parapet, the clopping of horses' hoofs reached us, and I looked down to see that a horse-drawn carriage, with cross seats holding several passengers, had pulled up below the tower. I watched as the passengers got down and walked about, exclaiming over the view.

"So there is transportation?"

"For sight-seeing purposes. Those who don't want to climb can take buggy rides all over the grounds. We keep a stable of horses, though not as many as in the past. That's our hotel stage—right out of the century's turn."

"There's a wide enough road?"

"Of course—the slower way we didn't take. Our own trucks have to get about, in order to take care of the place and patrol it, though they are the only motorized vehicles allowed. The roads have to accommodate Keir and his rangers."

I had moved on around the stone enclosure to where I could look out over thick woods of oak and maple that grew up the northern slope. At one place another rocky outcropping rose above the trees, and down the slope from it a clearing was visible, with a peaked rooftop showing among the trees.

"Is there a house down there?" I asked. "I didn't know anyone lived up here on the mountain."

"It's only a cabin," Brendon said. "That's Rainbow Point over there, where Loring wants to build cottages. There's a level space of land on this side of the cliff."

"How would anyone get to them?"

"There's a road to the cabin, and it's Loring's idea to allow cars on it. Of course we'll permit none of this to happen."

His voice had hardened, and glancing at him I thought Loring had better watch out with his bold plans. I didn't think my husband would be an easy man to deal with if he were roused.

"Are you ready to go down?" he asked.

I had another question to ask. "Whose cabin is that? Does someone live there?"

"It's Magnus Devin's log cabin. He lives there with his father."

"Magnus Devin? I wonder why that name sounds familiar when I hear it?"

"Probably because it is," Brendon said with that odd note that came into his voice whenever he spoke of Keir's son. "He's very successful. Out in the world his work as a sculptor is well known. Some of it is in museums around the country."

"Of course! Magnus Devin! I've seen some of his outdoor work in New York. It's on a rather large scale, isn't it? But why does he stay up here?"

"Like the rest of us, I suppose he likes it. He's also something of a recluse. We try to keep guests away from him. The road to the cabin is private. That's another reason why Loring can't build over there. Keir wants to keep it out-of-bounds to visitors."

My eyes must have lighted with interest because Brendon shook his head at me firmly.

"Jenny! Don't turn adventurous. Magnus doesn't welcome visitors."

"That must have been lonely for his wife. She was the woman who died?"

"Come along, let's go down. I do have work back at the hotel. I'll fix you up with a map so you can do some exploring on your own."

We went down the stairs, meeting the more venturesome of the carriage passengers on their way up. Before we could return to our path, however, a truck rumbled up the main road and I saw that Keir was at the wheel. He braked beside us.

"Good morning, Mrs. McClain," he said, and then turned to Brendon. "You're wanted down below. They sent me up to get you."

Brendon grimaced. "Okay, I'll go back with you. Do you want to come with us, Jenny?"

"Thanks—no. I have my sketching things, and now that I'm here, I want to enjoy it for a while. I can find my way down by myself."

Brendon climbed into the seat beside Keir, who was busy on the intercom to the hotel. I watched as they drove down the road, circling gently around the crown of the mountain. A few visitors stood about, and I smiled at them as I walked across the area below the tower. I was discovering that those who met on the trails were automatically friends, with all of Laurel in common. The views were almost as stunning from here as from the top, though I couldn't see the far countryside to the same extent.

When I'd had my fill of gazing, I wandered a little way down the road. Overhead the sun was higher now, and though there was still a wind, the morning had warmed and I took off my jacket and spread it on a rock, so I could sit down.

Now I had time to make a few rough sketches of flowers that grew near the woods. Wild flowers always appealed to me more than their tame garden cousins. Naomi could have her formal flower beds—I would take these beauties that straggled like gypsies along the roads and through the woods.

I drew a quick sketch of yarrow with its ferny leaves

and flowers like tiny daisies that would bloom till November. There was plumy goldenrod too, and my favorite of all—Queen Anne's lace. I took the time to make a very exact painting of the last before I put away my colors and went on.

I could move at my leisure, savoring as I went. Since it would give me a different scene, I chose the carriage road down, and followed its winding, gentle descent.

Wind rustled through the trees, rattling leaves that had begun to dry, and here and there dead ones drifted down. I saw tall striped maples in the woods, green with visible stripes on the bark—a tree I hadn't seen before, and I left the road and walked through underbrush to have a closer look. Poison ivy, already crimson, climbed a nearby stump, brilliant against the greens and browns. In these surroundings I could feel peaceful and happy again. This was my element, and once more I knew I wanted to stay here forever.

The things I didn't understand about Brendon would be cleared up eventually. He had promised me that. I mustn't worry. I mustn't turn into a brooding female who never smiled. True, it was more in character for me to fly at problems and push for a solution. I liked everything to be set neatly in order as quickly as possible, and I must restrain this urge. For the moment I could only hope that we would both adapt compatibly when we came to know each other better.

For now, at least, I would be patient. Brendon was still as unknown a quantity to me in many respects as I was to him. So for now I would postpone all puzzling and think only about trees. Think safely about trees.

The forests at Laurel had a healthy, diversified look and I knew they had been carefully planted in the past. Sometime I must talk to Keir Devin about them and learn their history. Many of the chestnut oaks had been killed off in the last fifty years, I knew, and they had been replaced by hemlock, by gray and white birch and stands of pine. I paused before a grove of white birch, admiring the beauty of these northern trees. When I reached out to touch the papery bark, my hand came away powdered with white. How beautiful such trees were—more stalwart than the smaller gray birch that sprang up weedlike everywhere in neglected fields or burned-out areas.

Down the hill a little farther, I came upon a clump of gray birches, their heads all bent gracefully in one direction. Ice storms would cause that bending, and the trees often never fully recovered their upward stance.

As I walked on, back on the road again, I noted with approval that the woods were full of dead and fallen trees. Ecologically, this was the way it should be. In Europe there were forests where you could walk for miles with no interfering underbrush, but that was because the people of the countryside had been poor for generations, and wood was sought after to build fires, cook food, give warmth. Here there had been some obvious cutting where roads might be endangered, or a fallen tree might injure a live one, and undoubtedly wood was taken out to burn for fireplaces, but most of the dead trees were left to crumble into the organic matter that would enrich the forest floor and keep new growth coming. On fallen logs bright-colored fungi were already at work, helping along the necessary decay. Mingling with the pine scent, the scent of growing things, there was an earthy smell that was natural to a healthy forest.

I was moving happily along my way, comforted by the scene around me, when I came to an uphill path marked *Private* and I stopped before the sign.

Now as I walk in the night darkness beside the lake, I am forced to consider my actions of this morning. Were they wise? Unwise? Have I done any real damage?

Across water that is more silver than black, the hotel windows shine, and there are outdoor light standards as well. But there is no light here, except from the stars. I want to be alone to think my own thoughts, undistracted, undisturbed. Strangely, I am not afraid out here— because no one knows where I am. In our rooms I would be available, by phone and by door. Even by the balcony doors. Here water laps at the lake's edge and I find that

I can take a few careful steps and enter another gazebo—
one of the many little summerhouses built above the water.
I sit on a bench in the comforting darkness and listen to
the night.

There are voices drifting across the lake from the
hotel—sometimes laughter, or a woman's high tones.
Sometimes the rumble of a masculine voice. Music reaches
me nostalgically. The pianist is playing "A Foggy Day . . .
in London Town." Nothing to do with me now, but a
tune Ariel used to like. Because she professed to love
London. She had danced there as a guest of the Royal
Ballet. I had never seen her dance in London, never seen
her dance Aurora in *The Sleeping Beauty,* but I could
close my eyes and see her dancing now. She'd had a ra-
diance on the stage, and a passion, a vitality that made
other dancers about her fade by comparison. It was hard
to believe that all her delicacy and grace and beauty were
gone—gone forever.

I can weep now. I can put my face in my hands and
cry for my sister here in this spot by the water, where
beauty is all around me—but never her beauty again.

The voices reach close to me now in the darkness.
They are very near, whispering and eerie. Yet I know they
are not human voices, and they are not whispering about
me. Where lake waters lap into caverns beneath the rocks
the hollow sounds they make are like a deep whispering.

I must go back soon. I must be in our room before
Brendon comes up to bed. I haven't told him yet what
I did this morning. Or what happened during the rest of
the day, and I am not yet certain how much I will say
to him. If he must have his secrets, perhaps I will also
have mine. And now I hold one almost too terrible to
bear.

The word on the sign stopped me for a moment.
Private meant to exclude me, as Brendon had indicated.
It meant to exclude anyone who came this way and had
no business following a path up through the woods. I
knew where the path must lead. I had come down the
road until I was undoubtedly opposite Rainbow Point,

opposite that cabin whose roof I had glimpsed among the trees, and I had only to step around the sign and start up through the woods to come upon it.

There was no one about to see and I took the first step, and then another. It was not a well-worn path and weeds grew thick across it in places, but it must be a shortcut from cabin to road, if someone chose to take it. There was probably another way, a better way, since Brendon had said that Keir could drive his truck to the cabin, but this path was good enough for me.

I had no plan, no intention. Only curiosity and a faint, nagging worry drove me. Brendon did not like Magnus Devin. And it was Magnus' wife, Floris, who had died here last May in a curious accident, killed by a falling rock that should never have fallen. All I really wanted at the moment was to look at the cabin. If the man came out and spoke to me, I would make his acquaintance. It was as simple as that. All to be played by ear, with no intention of harm on my part, or of any real intrusion.

So I climbed the path through the woods that grew close on either side, with maple and oak branches interlocking over my head. It was cool again in these shadows where the sun hadn't penetrated and I slipped on my jacket as I walked, following twists and turns, climbing little rises, till the path leveled off. And at last I reached the clearing.

This was not the one I had glimpsed from the tower, as there was no house to be seen. I came upon it unexpectedly and it had nothing to do with nature. Human hands had cleared this space, yet it seemed to belong to the forest like some hidden, magic circle of green. All about it dark hemlocks crowded in, hiding and protecting its secret. The circle of the arena was free of all growth except that rough carpet of grass that covered it.

"Arena" was the proper word—because in the very center of the ring, his head lowered for the charge, hoofs spurning the ground, stood a great stone bull. Entranced, I moved into open sunlight—the old feeling that I used to have as a child engulfing me. That strange, unreal feeling that I could dance as beautifully as Ariel. Here, surely, was Europa's bull, and inside me I was all grace and flowing movement that would conquer stumbling feet and elbows that never rounded. The stone bull had been waiting for me all my life in this enchanted wood and I dropped my sketching kit to the grass, raised my arms and ran toward him.

If he had been alive he could have gored me with those wicked horns as I came on in my rush. But the lowered head with its heavy mass of neck muscle did not move, and the snorting nostrils made no sound, the galloping hoofs never left the earth.

He had been carved—hewn—from granite and I could see the marks of the tools that had been left on the stone. There had been no effort to smooth and make him realistic in every detail. He was more like the spirit of a bull charging across a ring with a suggestion of enormous energy and anger, so that all his tremendous force drove him with one intent—the killing of his enemy, the man. I wished that Ariel could have seen him. Ariel, who had danced her make-believe ballet of maiden and mythological bull to Maurice Kiov's Zeus.

I walked around the great stone animal—he was more than life-size—admiring the power and skill that had wrought him. In New York he would have brought crowds to view and applaud his magnificence, yet here he stood at the end of a mountain path marked *Private* and there was no one to see. Except for myself, who came as a trespasser. Ariel would have danced before him, worshiping at his pagan altar, but I could not. I could only manage that one dash of delight that I had made in his direction.

Circling him, I saw that on his far side, close to the lowered head, a large stone had been placed. Surely a stepping stone, since it invited my foot, and when I stood upon it, I found that I could raise my other foot to his head, balancing between the horns, until I had pulled myself up over the rough hump at his neck, where muscles swelled. In a moment I stood in triumph on his broad back, and the flat rubber soles I'd worn for walking clung firmly to the stone surface so that I had no problem of slipping.

I was once more enchanted, moving out of instinct, unself-consciously, as though the bull was male and I female, and yet it was I who had conquered him.

Above me the sky was cerulean, with a single billow of white cloud, and all around the magic circle green hemlock arms reached out in protecting secrecy. From this high place, I could glimpse the rocky top of Rainbow Point above the trees. I could have danced on that broad back—almost. Amused by my own fantasy, I raised my arms, rounding them in ballet's fifth position. My long black hair fell back from my lifted head, and I felt beautiful—invincible.

The voice that shouted at me in an angry bellow might have come from the bull himself, and it shocked me completely.

"Get off!" he roared. "Get down off there!"

A dreamer must never be awakened so rudely. My sense of grace, of mastery over my balance, vanished and I wobbled on the stone, felt myself plunging. I would have struck the ground like a weighted stone if great arms hadn't caught me. There was nothing gentle about their clasp. I was simply engulfed in hard bands of muscle and flesh, and set rocking upon my feet with a jar that clattered my teeth.

For an instant everything blurred before my eyes and I stumbled on solid ground. This time he made no effort to steady me, and I braced my own feet apart and looked up at him. He stood well over six feet tall, with a massive chest barely restrained by a denim shirt, arms like the stout branches of an oak tree and great thighs encased in denim jeans. His hair was red and it curled long at the back of his neck, while an expanse of curly red beard covered the lower half of his face. Set deep in that massive head, his eyes reflected the green of the forest behind him, and they seemed to spark angrily as he stared at me.

With an effort I recovered a semblance of equilibrium —both physical and emotional. "I—I'm sorry. I know I'm trespassing. I'm Mrs. Brendon Mc—"

"I know who you are," he said roughly. "And you've no business here."

There was no possible way in which I could explain that I had only been living out a fantasy, yet I had to try.

"I have—I had—a sister who was a dancer. I was—I suppose I was pretending I was Ariel Vaughn. He's so marvelous—your bull. He put a spell on me."

Strangely, unexpectedly, his look softened—almost as though he understood what could not be understood. But he said nothing, merely waiting for me to go.

I picked up my sketch box and started away from him across the expanse of green, only to stumble again. Somehow, with the force he had used in setting me on my feet, I had twisted an ankle, and I found myself limping ignominiously as I moved away.

"You're hurt," he said curtly.

I bit my lip against pain and showed him my back, trying to move with dignity. He came after me at once.

"Don't be a fool. You can't go down that long road with a hurt foot. Now that you're here, you might as well come inside and have a cup of coffee. I've got some fresh on the stove."

I tried not to wince as his meaty hand took my arm, turned me about as though I'd been a kitten in his grasp and marched me toward an opening in the trees, opposite the one from which I'd entered. Though "marched" isn't exactly the word. After a few stumbling steps, he picked me up like a sack of meal under one arm and carried me through to the other clearing. I knew there was no use squirming against this further humiliation and I let my hair hang over my face to hide my rising fury. Not until I felt him mounting steps did I push the hair aside to see that I was being carried into a cabin of rough-hewn logs.

The cave man was bringing home his captive, I thought indignantly—except that he didn't want me here in the first place. Inside the big rustic room he dumped me without ceremony on a couch and went to the stove to pour coffee. I set my sketch box on my knees and looked around. The big room, though rough, was not without grace. At one end was a huge fireplace, with a cooking pot suspended over it in the old way. On the floor were worn Indian rugs, and an Indian blanket had been spread against a wall. The stove at which Magnus Devin stood was wood-burning and the graniteware coffee pot that rested on it was immense.

With an effort I wriggled my foot. The ankle felt sore, but I didn't think it was serious, and I could make it down the mountain all right. I didn't mean to stay an instant more than I had to with this bear of a man, but just for now I would sit still until I could recover my strength and wits. Then I would gladly leave him to his stone bull and never come near this place again.

4

"Have you ever tried honey in your coffee?" Magnus asked over his shoulder.

I blinked, thrust off balance again. "It sounds horrible."

"It's not, and it's better for you than sugar."

I watched in dismay as he dipped a dollop of honey from a jar and stirred it into my coffee.

"No cream," he said. "Dad hasn't brought up the milk from the farm yet, and we don't have refrigeration here—just the springhouse out in back."

He brought me the mug with remarkable care in those huge hands, and I held it, letting it warm my fingers. It was cool here in the cabin and the fire in the open hearth had died to red coals.

"Drink it," he said.

With a feeling of repugnance I brought the cup to my lips and sipped. There was a faintly different taste, but sweet was apparently sweet, and it was strengthening and not unpleasant.

"It's even better in tea," he informed me, and I looked up to see that the red beard had parted to show a smile as gentle as a child's—and in this man astonishing.

"You like my bull?" he asked.

On this friendlier level I tried to respond. "He's splendid. Magnificent. As good as anything I've seen of yours in New York. But isn't he wasted out here in the woods where no one can see him?"

"I can see him," Magnus Devin said. "And you'd be surprised at how many adventurers from the hotel pay no attention to signs and wander up this hill."

"Do you treat them all so furiously?"

The smile faded and I could see the straight line of his mouth between red fur.

"Most trespassers don't climb on his back."

"But how could I hurt him? There's even a stepping stone near his head. Why were you so angry?"

He let that go and leaned forward to touch the box on my knees, recognizing its import. "You're an artist?"

"Not really. Just for my own amusement."

"Let me see."

I had no desire to show this man my amateurish work, but he waited for no permission, simply taking the box from my knees and opening it. When he found my sketchbook he spread it on a table and looked at the paintings and sketches one by one, while I sipped my coffee nervously—like a novice at an audition.

"It's obvious you like wild flowers," he said after a time. "What are you going to do with these?"

I wouldn't tell him my vague plan for a book and be laughed at. "I'm not sure. They're just for fun, really. I hope I can add to them here at Laurel Mountain."

He packed the sketches back into my box and set it on the sofa beside me. "Very nice," he said, as though he spoke to a child.

The words were polite and so unlike him that I felt slightly wounded. He didn't approve of my work, and clearly didn't feel it was worth commenting on.

From outside came the sound of a truck and he strode to the door and looked out. "There's Dad now. He'll be able to take you down." As Keir Devin came toward the steps, Magnus called out, "We have a visitor," and a moment later his father entered the cabin.

Big as Keir was, he was dwarfed beside his son. As he came in and saw me, he removed his broad-brimmed hat, his white hair like a light in the shadowed cabin. I wondered if it had ever been red, or if Magnus' mother had had red hair.

There seemed to be shock involved in Keir's finding me here, for he stopped to stare, and then came toward me slowly. "Mrs. McClain?" he said, as though he doubted my identity, even though we'd already met.

"Of course it's Mrs. McClain," Magnus said impatiently. "She likes signs that say *'Private.'* She thinks they mean 'Come in.' Maybe we'll have to take that one down and put up something else. Like, 'Beware the bull.' "

I was feeling more and more like a chastised child and my resentment was rising. When I'd finished the coffee I stood up with all the dignity I could muster and spoke to Keir.

"Will you drive me down, please? I seem to have given my ankle a twist. It's nothing serious, but I'd rather not walk."

"Sure," he said. "Of course." Then he turned to stare across the room at his son and the two exchanged a long, strange look, in which something close to antagonism bristled, and perhaps a warning. I was beginning to suspect that Magnus got along with very few people.

"Thank you," I said to my host, sounding stiff and unfriendly—which was all right with me.

He grinned at me through his thick red beard, as though he knew quite well that my dignity was assumed and entirely false. I turned my back and walked toward the door, managing not to limp as badly as I'd done at first.

"Hold on to my arm," Keir said, and we walked together to the truck, where, with his help, I hauled myself into the high front seat and looked back at Magnus, standing in the doorway, his deep-set green eyes sardonic, neither liking nor disliking me—but still distrustful.

At least I needn't see him again, and I would take care not to invade his privacy. My only regret was that I hadn't had another chance to look at that tremendous stone bull, and I thought again of how Ariel would have loved him.

"Your son isn't very friendly," I said as the truck turned down the winding road.

"He likes the woods to himself. He likes solitude. And he has his work."

"Wasn't his wife lonely, shut away like that?"

There was a faint hesitation before Keir answered, and beside me his profile seemed as chiseled as though it had been something his son had carved from stone.

"Floris managed," he said.

"What was she like?"

Keir turned his head and looked at me carefully. "You ask a lot of questions, Mrs. McClain."

"I know. I'm sorry. You see, it's just that I want to learn everything I can about Laurel Mountain. And of course the people *are* Laurel."

We went slowly in the truck, in low gear down the grade.

"Magnus hasn't been the same since Floris died," Keir said. "You know about the accident, don't you?"

"Yes, Brendon told me. It must have been tragic for your son."

"He was glad," Keir said calmly. "Relieved. She was the sort you'd call neurotic nowadays. Plain, and energetic enough. Hard-working. But twisted inside. Mixed up. She made Magnus' life hell the last few years. He married her too young, when he didn't know any better. Magnus once worked for her father—that's how he met her."

"What business was her father in?"

"Tombstones," he said shortly.

I don't know why the skin should prickle at the back of my neck. Someone had to carve tombstones, and it seemed somehow appropriate for Magnus Devin.

"How old are you?" the man beside me asked.

"Twenty-six. Why?"

"You seem younger. You and Brendon haven't known each other long, have you?"

Brendon had warned me that I would have to earn my spurs with Keir Devin.

"If you want to know," I said, "I love him very much,

and I think I always shall. It was such a lucky chance that brought us together, and I'll always be grateful."

He gave his attention to his driving and I couldn't tell whether my answer had satisfied him. Something he had said earlier still puzzled me and I asked another question.

"Forgive me, but what did you mean when you said that Magnus has changed since his wife's death? How could that be if, as you say, he was relieved?"

"He's not one to accept his own relief. He can torture himself."

That gave me something in common with Magnus, I thought wryly. But I wanted the man beside me to be my friend because he was devoted to Brendon, and there wasn't much time left, since we were nearing the driveway to the hotel.

"Thank you for talking to me, Keir. May I call you that? And I'd like to have you call me Jenny."

His hand left the wheel and patted my arm. "Just step softly for a while, Jenny. Raw wounds have to heal over. Given time, they grow a new skin."

But what raw wounds had affected Brendon? I wondered. If Floris had been plain and neurotic and unpleasant, I couldn't believe that her death could have meant all that much to Brendon.

"Do you think Floris' death was an accident?" I asked.

His foot must have trod hard on the gas pedal, for the truck made a little jump on the drive before he braked it.

"Of course it was an accident, Mrs. McClain. Jenny. Don't go thinking anything else or this whole place may blow up like a volcano right in your face. And you wouldn't like that. Everyone's playing it safe, and you'd better too. We can't afford the publicity. Maybe nobody *wants* to know what might have happened. You should want it least of all."

He could be as intense as his son, and I could only nod uncomfortably, having no idea what he meant.

We were in front of the hotel entrance and I put my hand on the door handle.

"Mrs. McClain—" His tone was quiet, and I turned. "Don't go up there in the woods anymore, will you? Stay away from Magnus."

I didn't understand, but this was not the moment to probe for more answers. I offered my thanks again for the lift back to the hotel and got out of the truck. Keir didn't look after me when I turned to wave, and I knew I had been clumsy again, totally without finesse. I was a klutz—just the way I'd been as a child. Nearly falling off that bull because someone shouted at me. Annoying Magnus, annoying Keir. And Brendon? Was he annoyed with me too? Why did I have to go around being a thorn, when I wanted only to be a lovely rose? Brendon had said I had no layers to peel down. But I had, and I'd never really got down through them myself.

My foot still hurt a little when I walked, but by favoring it I could manage fine, and it was the least of my problems.

Brendon wasn't about when I wandered through the lobby, and his office was empty, so I set myself to an exploration of the ground floor of the hotel. A few guests were about, in all stages of dress, though probably wearing a little more than they must have in summer. I smiled vaguely at those who smiled at me, realizing that some of them knew who I was.

The small library room was empty and offered a place where I could sit and rest my foot while I pulled out books and turned pages in a desultory fashion. The chair I chose was near a reference shelf and I bent to read the titles of several volumes. One of them gave me an idea and I pulled out the fat tome of Bartlett's *Familiar Quotations*. When I looked up "guilt" I found nothing pertinent, but the word "guilty" came right beneath and I quickly found the complete quotation I was looking for.

"Let no guilty man escape, if it can be avoided."

U. S. Grant had said that when endorsing a letter that had to do with the Whiskey Ring—whatever that was. Hardly a quotation that spoke volumes to either Brendon or me. Yet the mere extracted words had in themselves been made to sound appropriate. I had reacted to them, and so had Brendon. Someone who had easy access to this volume had typed those words, knowing that it wouldn't matter what they were taken from.

Another quotation came unbidden to my mind. *"The guilty flee where no man pursueth."* Except that the note thrust beneath our door meant that someone was pursuing. Not me, but Brendon.

I know now who pursues. I know now what the words meant and for whom they were intended, but I can find no reassurance in this knowledge. I have left the dark shelter of the summerhouse across the lake and come upstairs, to sit here in our rooms, with all the lights burning again, while I wait once more for Brendon. He went down to Kings Landing this afternoon on some errand, and I am frantic with waiting, yet afraid to have him come. It is Brendon I need to confront. He *must* tell me the truth now. And I am afraid.

I had found Brendon at the hotel earlier this morning, but I'd hesitated to tell him about seeing the stone bull. Before he left on his errand he took me out to the place on the edge of the lake, not far from the hotel, where he kept his own boat. He couldn't come with me, but when I'd climbed in and set the oars in place, he pushed it off the bank and stood watching for a few moments while I got used to the rather heavy wooden boat. The hotel boats were made of a fiberglass combination and were lighter, but I wanted to be trusted with Brendon's dinghy.

"Of course you can swim?" he called to me.

I nodded and smiled, and he went off toward the hotel. I wasn't going to tell him that I couldn't swim very well and have this pleasure denied me. I didn't expect to do anything reckless that would tumble me into the water.

I found sheer physical joy in pulling hard on the oars, sending the boat out upon the shining placid lake. I rowed toward the far end where the forest came down the bank below High Tower, and few hotel guests ventured.

Yet despite my pleasure in the physical exertion and in
being in this heavenly, quiet spot, I felt lonely for Brendon. I realized that management of the hotel's affairs
must now occupy much of his attention. Increasingly, I
was coming to recognize how very much Laurel Mountain
meant to him, and how much it would demand of him.
In New York we had been together every moment, but
of course it couldn't be the same here. Like every bride,
I must learn to accept my husband's absorption in his
work. Later perhaps he would tell me more about what
he was doing and allow me to share his interests. There
hadn't been time for that as yet.

Without warning, as I sat with my oars idle, drifting on
the water, windy clouds appeared above enclosing tree-
tops and it began to rain. I turned back, rowing strongly.
At least it was fortunate that I had the wind behind me
and I returned to my mooring faster than I'd gone out.

This afternoon, because of the rain, I was further
thrown back upon the hotel's resources. First there was
lunch to get through.

We all met at the table again—all except Brendon,
who was still in town. Because of finding that quotation
in Bartlett's, it was difficult to sit with them and talk
quietly, guarding my tongue, careful to let no suspicious
word or glance fall toward any of them—yet all the while
wondering which one bore such malice toward either
Brendon or me.

The lunchtime meal was a popular institution at Laurel
Mountain House, as Irene told me. A sumptuous buffet
was always provided, set out on long tables near the
entry door, the food attractively arranged for color contrast and appetizing effect, with great assortments of
salads, raw vegetables, cheeses and dishes of crackers and
breads, nuts and fruit. There were hot entrées for those
who wanted them, but I heaped my plate with a cold
sampling and carried it to our table.

Irene and Loring were already there, and Naomi joined
us a little while after I sat down. The same hint of a
flowery scent floated about Irene, and her manner at the
luncheon table was calm and gentle. Except for the hint

of a deepening line between her brows, I would have thought her unworried. She wanted to know about my morning, and I told about climbing to High Tower with Brendon and of my delight over the view.

"And then?" Naomi leaned toward me, her bright dark eyes intent. "What did you do *then?*"

So she knew, I thought. Already Keir must have told her about my visit to the clearing in the woods.

"I explored," I said. "I found a stone bull in a grassy glen."

Irene gasped softly, and I knew Loring was staring at me with a look that probed, but I kept my attention fixed on Naomi. She had taken off her bandanna, leaving her gray hair wind-tossed, and she hadn't bothered to smooth it. She wore jeans and a green sweater that folded up in a turtleneck, almost engulfing her small, pointed chin. Before my insistent look, she dropped her gaze, avoiding my eyes.

"So you found Magnus' stone bull?" Loring said. "Didn't you see the sign marked *Private?*"

"I saw it. But I live here, don't I? Surely it isn't meant to shut out the McClains?"

Loring grinned rather nastily. "Magnus wouldn't mind shutting us out. In fact, he once ordered me off the place. It could be that he'll now have to move down from Rainbow Point. What happened this morning when you went there?"

I skipped a little of what had happened. "He invited me up to the cabin for coffee."

Naomi made a sputtering sound, but Irene smiled.

"How very nice of him," she said. "Magnus can be quite kind when he pleases. I'm glad you've made friends."

"I don't think we've exactly made friends—" I began, and then saw that Naomi seemed to be choking on a bit of celery, her cheeks bright red and her eyes stormy.

When she caught her breath, she pushed back from the table. "I can't stand it! It's going to happen all over again! It's horrible, horrible!"

"Calm down," Loring said and put a hand on her arm. She shook it off and stood up. "I don't have to listen

to any of this!" she cried and almost ran the length of
the dining room in her anxiety to get away.

I stared after her in astonishment and then turned to
Irene. "What happened? What have I said to upset her?"

"She's easily upset," Loring said. "Pay no attention.
She'll go back to her garden and quiet down. Flowers
always soothe her. The next time you see her she'll be
fine."

"But what's wrong? I need to know what's wrong, so
I can be more careful next time. There's something no
one is telling me."

Irene bent toward me, her look concerned. "We apologize for her, Jenny. It's not your fault. It has nothing to
do with you. She's been like that ever since—well—you
see, Floris was her friend and—" She let the sentence fall
into silence with a slight, helpless shrug, and I saw the line
between her eyes had deepened.

"You mean Floris *used* to be her friend," Loring said.
"Irene, don't you think it would be better—"

She stopped him almost frantically. "No, dear. Please!
We want everything to be happy here for Jenny. I'll talk
to Naomi. She mustn't be allowed to behave like this."

I had meant to return to the buffet tables for a second
helping, but my appetite was gone. It was Brendon I
needed to see. He must be the one to explain. No longer
would I let him put me off.

"When is Brendon coming home?" I asked.

"He may have gone on up to Albany from Kings
Landing," Loring said. "But he should be home this evening. Business came up that had to be taken care of. He
hasn't exactly been on the ball around here lately."

"Now, dear," Irene said, always the peacemaker.

"I'm sorry," I told Loring. "I suppose I'm to blame.
But perhaps getting married is important too."

"Of course." Irene's tone was gentle, affectionate. "And
Loring has managed beautifully on his own. Everything
has run perfectly."

Her husband gave her a look that made her subside
apologetically, and I began to dislike him actively. He
was attractive, dynamic, clever—and I didn't in the least

like the way he treated Irene, who was so obviously gentle and eager to avoid friction. I thought of Brendon's words again—"It's not Eden." I was beginning to discover the truth of that statement on all sides.

I finished what I could manage of my lunch while looking out the great picture windows toward the mountains. About us in the huge dining room guests were laughing, chattering, and though this was not a busy week and there were many empty tables, the line at the buffet was continuous. Loring talked to Irene about hotel problems, and I only half listened. I needed something to do besides exploring the grounds, and this idleness made me restive. It gave me too much time to brood and worry.

"Can you find me something useful to do?" I asked, breaking in on their talk. "I'm used to having a job, and now my days are going to seem empty unless I find something to do here. I won't even have a house to take care of—no duties at all. And I can't live without something to do."

Irene nodded sympathetically. "Brendon said you painted."

"Just little sketches of wild flowers. I've thought of collecting them for a book, and I can work from life around here."

"Lovely. That will keep you busy."

"She can't paint all the time," Loring said, surprising me by understanding. "I know a job for you, Jenny. The hotel library is in a thoroughly muddled state. What about setting it in order, working out some sort of filing system? The desk gets complaints every year because guests can't find anything."

I jumped at the opportunity. "I'm sure I can manage that. I used to fill in at the college library once in a while when I was teaching. This morning I looked into the library room and it's an attractive, sunny place. I'll be happy to work there."

"We don't buy as many books as we should," Irene said. "Mostly guests have been generous in giving them to us over the years. There are a lot of old books in there that date back to early in the century and before."

"Lovely! They should all be catalogued. I'll begin this afternoon, if that's all right with you."

Irene looked pleased with her husband for his suggestion, and pleased with me, and when I left the dining room I went directly to the library and took a survey of what needed to be done. There appeared to be no card file, no records of the books available, and I decided that a simple system could be made to work. When I'd looked into one of the offices and equipped myself with a pad and pen and a box of filing cards, I returned and went to work.

Not until rain slashed against the window panes did I realize that the storm had increased and it was raining harder than ever. A door at one end of the library opened onto a broad veranda overlooking the lake, and I set my work aside for a breather and went out to walk across wide bare boards. This must be an older section, and the veranda was like those I'd seen in photos of turn-of-the-century hotels.

All along the broad railing chairs had been set—empty now because of the change in weather. The veranda was well sheltered beneath its overhanging roof, however, and though it was cold I walked to a rail and stood looking out over gray water that danced in the rain.

The view was as beautiful as when the sun was shining. Far above the lake, High Tower stood on its rocky summit with mists wreathing its head. On the opposite shore from the hotel, those enormous boulders of the Wolf's Lair shone wet in rivulets of rain, and the sight of them drew me with a certain fascination. What had she felt that day—Magnus' wife—a woman who had been labeled by her father-in-law as unpleasant and neurotic? Had she heard the rock in its tumbling fall? Why hadn't she run in time to escape?

I shook myself and returned to my work in the library. Floris Devin had begun to haunt me, and I was increasingly aware that whatever unhappy mystery lingered here had to do with her life and her death. Already I had the feeling that I would see Magnus again, despite his father's warning, because perhaps he, of them all, might be the source of things I wanted to know. He had the brawn of a blacksmith, and perhaps his work with stone required a similar strength. And yet he had smiled at me once as gently as a child, and though he had been rough, he had not been unkind about my twisted foot. If Brendon would not tell me—Magnus might.

Loring was another possibility. In fact, he was already on the verge of revealing whatever secrets were being kept from me, and only his wife's hushing had stopped him from talking. But I didn't want to hear anything from Loring Grant. Whatever the truth might be, I didn't want to have it filtered through his cold and merciless personality. His main love seemed to be the hotel he had married into, and he would twist everything to serve that mistress. I felt a little sorry for Irene, whom I already liked, for giving her affection to a man like that.

I began working on my knees at the far end of the library, pulling out one book at a time from a bottom shelf to enter title, author, publisher and the date of publication on a filing card. It was evident that a vague sort of alphabetical system had once prevailed, and that an attempt had been made to arrange the books by authors. But everything had become so thoroughly mixed over the years that all the books would have to come off the shelves to be put back in the right order. First, however, I would list each book as it came.

When a guest walked into the room I didn't look up until she approached and stood beside me.

"Oh, good!" she said. "Ever since I've been coming here, I've wished someone would put these shelves in order. By now I've read most of the books, but I can't ever be sure because there's no system."

I pushed the hair from my face and smiled up at the plump, pretty little woman with slightly blue hair who stood looking down at me. I didn't in the least expect the sudden consternation I saw in her eyes. She stepped back from me with a cry and clapped a hand to her mouth.

"But—but you can't be! She—I read that she—was dead!"

So it had happened again, even in this remote place, and I could feel my smile freeze.

"No, I'm not my sister Ariel Vaughn," I told her. "And it is true that she died a few months ago."

The little woman dropped into a chair and took a handkerchief from her bag to blot her face. "What a shock you gave me! You look exactly like her. You could be twins."

I fought the familiar knot inside me and suppressed an impulse to run. "I suppose you've seen her dance?"

"No—my husband doesn't care for ballet, so I've never gone. But I've seen her a dozen times or more right here in this room. I've even talked to her, though she wasn't always friendly. I suppose one can't blame her. She came here to rest, to run away from the strains and pressures of her life. She told me that once. So of course she wanted to be left alone."

I had dropped my head again, so that the dark curtain of hair shielded my face from her eyes. The feeling at the pit of my stomach was as though someone had thrust a fist into it, and I couldn't speak. I couldn't move.

"She was so beautiful," the woman went on, almost wistfully. "Like you are. Only she used to go around in dark glasses, and she wore old clothes when she came here—denim jeans and a man's shirt. A sort of disguise, I suppose. And now her sister has come to Laurel too. Are you working for the hotel, dear?"

I managed to thrust the book I held onto a shelf, gathered up my cards and pen and put them away neatly, where I could find them again. My fingers felt like thumbs.

"I suppose I am working for the hotel," I said. "I'm Mrs. Brendon McClain."

I got up from my knees and walked past her without looking into her face again. Not for anything would I let myself see whatever might be mirrored there. The elevator was waiting and empty, and I took it to the fourth floor, where I got out and walked uncertainly along the corridor. I moved automatically, knowing only that I must get away by myself and be completely alone. Only then would

I dare to examine the information that had been given me so unexpectedly.

At no time had Ariel ever told me that she had come to a place called Laurel Mountain. True, she sometimes ran away when her nerves grew tense and she couldn't bear the strain anymore. When there was a free week or two, sometimes she would disappear, but she made a habit of going off alone, and not even Mother always knew where she went. It was the one thing Ariel had been completely secretive about.

Now I had to face the fact that she had come here. But that was something I couldn't bear. This place was *mine*. I didn't want her to ever have been here. This was, for me, the one safe haven that my sister had never invaded.

My thoughts were taking me along a dangerous road, and I was fearful of what I might find at the end.

At the door of our rooms I stopped to take out my key, but in the act of slipping it into a lock a sound reached me and I paused, listening. Far off, somewhere in another section of the hotel, someone was playing a piano. But the pianist who worked for the hotel played only in the evening, and he couldn't be heard up here anyway.

I left the door and walked down the corridor, away from our rooms into a portion of the hotel that I had not yet explored. My ankle was not bothering me now and I could walk almost normally. I followed the narrowing hall around a jog into a still older section and passed the alcove of stairs to the roof. Now the music reached me more clearly. Someone in a room on this floor was playing.

The music was light and gay—melodic—and as I recognized it I felt again a prickling of the skin at the back of my neck. That was the dance of the little swans—from *Swan Lake*. Ariel had used it sometimes to practice to, and it would always speak to me of her.

The music drew me now, hypnotically. I went on along the hall toward an open door at the far end, from which the music was emerging in an unbroken flow of sound.

5

The entrance to the apparently large room at the end was through double doors, and as I approached I could see that it had once been some sort of meeting room that had served this older part of the hotel. It was empty now, with only a folding chair or two set against the wall, and the piano out of sight around to the left of the door.

My steps slowed as the music changed. That was the *pas de deux* now—where Odette–Odile danced with the prince. Once I had seen Ariel dance to that very music with Nureyev, and not even his vibrant and dramatic personality had overshadowed her own passion. What an Odile she had made—stronger in the evil role than when she danced the innocent Odette.

Resolutely, I walked through the open doors and stood looking toward an upright piano set at a right angle to the wall. Naomi McClain sat on the bench, playing, her expression rapt, her fingers light on the keys, and as she played tears rolled down her face. Again there was that sense of a fist punching into the pit of my stomach.

Perhaps I would have retreated, but from the corner of her eye she saw me and the music stopped with a crash as she turned her head and looked at me directly.

"You knew her, didn't you?" I said. "You knew my sister Ariel?"

One brown hand made an angry gesture of brushing away tears and she stared at me with fury in her eyes.

"Why did you come here? Why couldn't you have stayed away and let her memory be? We don't want you here. None of us wants you here!"

"You know that isn't true," I said as quietly as I could manage. "Though I've been aware of your hostility ever since I came. I'm sorry you feel that way. Believe me, I didn't know that Ariel had ever been in this place."

"You look like her. You're the image of her—but you're not Ariel. You're nothing like her! You can never touch what she was in your whole life."

I recognized suffering when I saw it, and I could only be gentle with her in spite of the pain and fright that waited for me.

"I know," I said. "I'm different. I've never wanted to be like her. I suppose you've seen her dance?"

"Of course I've seen her dance! Once on a stage in New York when she sent me a ticket and invited me to come. The ballet she danced in was Antony Tudor's *Lilac Garden*. She was Caroline, and Maurice Kiov was the Lover. But mostly I've seen her dance here. Here in this very room. Look around you!"

She gestured and I followed the movement with my eyes. On one side of the room a large mirror had been hung against the wall—a dancer's mirror, and across from it was a ballet *barre* attached to the opposite wall. Here at Laurel Mountain House a practice room had been arranged—for my sister Ariel.

"She had to practice, of course, even when she rested," Naomi rushed on. "So we had this room fixed for her, and I used to play when she danced. It's the only use I've ever really found for playing a piano. I knew all her music by heart. She could say, 'Play this, or play that,' and I knew every solo number she danced. And practically all of *Swan Lake*."

"You must have been a wonderful friend. She must have needed you."

"Of course she needed me! I was the one she came to with her secrets. I was the one she trusted. Not even her

mother could ever have done for her all I did. That last
time she was here she cried in my arms—before she went
back to New York."

"When was she last here?" I asked carefully.

"In May. Because she loved the mountain then. That's
when the laurel and dogwood and rhododendrons are all
in bloom. And the azaleas are on fire. I only saw her once
more after that. Though I went to her funeral. You were
there. I saw you and hated you—because you were alive
and she wasn't. She was everything and you are nothing—
but you are alive. Look there, behind the piano!"

The hatred in her words slashed across nerves that had
gone raw with shock and pain, but I had to obey and I
walked around the piano where it was set out from the
wall. A folding chair stood close beside it and on the
seat was something that made my breath catch in my
throat.

A pair of pink satin toe shoes rested there, the toes
slightly soiled, the ribbons my mother's loving fingers had
sewed to them spilling from the shoes. Ballet slippers that
had belonged to my sister. At any performance she would
use several pairs, and she might bring six or eight to the
theater, so that she could wear what felt best for each
dance. I could remember how she used to bang fresh toe
shoes on the floor to soften them up a bit before she broke
them in. Yes—those were slippers that would have fitted
her long, slender, dancer's feet.

Naomi had stood up from the piano to watch me, to
savor my agony.

"You were to blame," she said. "She phoned you because she needed you, and you didn't come. *I* know. Because she phoned me too and told me so. I said I'd get
there as soon as I could. But it was already too late, and
there was nothing I could do. You could have saved her
if you'd told her you'd come at once!"

I couldn't bear to hear any more. I didn't want to know
any more. If I stayed she might tell me other things—
things I didn't want to hear. I ran out of that all-too-
empty room and down the hall, leaving a dreadful silence
behind me. I could imagine Naomi sitting there, staring

blankly at keys that would never again play for the dancing of Ariel Vaughn. Now I knew who had thrust that note beneath my door—and why. "*Let no guilty man escape.*" There seemed a threat in the words, and she might very well know that punishment would come from within me.

My fingers were shaking so that I could hardly open the door to our room. When it was closed behind me and the bolt shot—as though I could shut out the terrors that beset me—I went to the balcony and stood outside, watching rain slant in gusts across the gray lake. No one moved out there now and the trees were a wet, dark green. I could hear the sound of their dripping and I thought of the stone bull up in the woods, standing there alone with rain glancing off his back as all his muscles gathered in the force of his charge. I thought of Magnus shouting at me to get off his back, and I knew why he had reacted like that.

Once Ariel had danced in that very clearing. I knew her so well. Knew what would charm and entrance her. She would have leapt gracefully to the back of the stone bull and stood there in all her triumphant beauty. Magnus had hated to see me there, clumsy and unlike her. I had heard fury in his voice when he'd roared at me. Because I wasn't Ariel and I had no right to be where she could not be.

And there was Brendon. But I was afraid to think of him. I slammed a door in my mind and went into the bedroom to fling myself on the bed. Emotional exhaustion struck me and gave me release. I fell sound asleep and slept the afternoon away—because I couldn't bear to be awake.

It was nearly dinnertime when I sat up suddenly to look about the darkening room. Brendon had not yet come home. For that, at least, I was glad. Because I still didn't know what I would say to him. He would have known Ariel when she stayed here. Yet he had not told me this. He had looked at me in the Opera lobby and assured me that he didn't care for ballet. A lie? How well had he known her?

If only I could go back to the time before that silly woman had walked into the library and recognized my face. It was better not to know. Not to know anything. Could I go on and pretend that I was still ignorant of the fact that they all had known my sister? But Naomi would tell them now. She would enjoy telling them.

Dinnertime went by and Irene phoned my room. I told her I had a headache and wouldn't be down—just to let me sleep. Of course she didn't. In a half hour she was upstairs, bringing one of the boys from the dining room to carry a tray. When he had set it down on a table near the bed, Irene closed the door after him and drew up a chair.

"Something has upset you, hasn't it? Has Naomi done something, said something?"

So Naomi hadn't told her yet. I shook my head. "I'll be all right. I just need to be quiet."

"You've been up here all afternoon, haven't you?"

"I was tired. I slept."

She sat looking at me a little sadly. "You mustn't let the things Naomi said at lunch today disturb you. She has a vivid imagination and she has never quite recovered from Floris' death."

Floris—Magnus' wife—and Ariel up there in the woods. Ariel, who had always taken what she wanted, and never minded if it belonged to someone else.

"What was Floris like?" I asked, a little surprised to note that my voice sounded natural.

"Difficult. I can't say I was fond of her. None of us were. She hated Laurel—it was only a prison to her and the last few months before she died she tried in every way she could think of to get Magnus to leave. Of course he wouldn't. He believes that he can only work in a place like this, and it's probably true. His art would die if he had to live in a city. It would destroy him."

It was better to think about Floris than about Ariel—and me.

"Do you think someone was to blame for her death?" I asked.

Irene's gentle calm fell away and she answered almost

shrilly, astonishing me with the swift change, "Of course not! You mustn't think things like that. It was only an accident—that stone falling. You mustn't question it."

I remembered Keir saying that everything might blow up in my face like a volcano if I persisted in questioning. But I couldn't stop now.

"I'm beginning to question more and more. Because everyone shies away from the idea as though it burned them. No one will tell me the truth."

With an effort she seemed to collect herself and her tone was lower when she spoke again. "There are some things it is better not to think about, Jenny dear. Not to question."

"Is that why the police are interested in opening up the case again?"

This time she remained unshaken. "I don't really think they are, dear. Loring told me that somebody phoned in an anonymous call. Some crank, undoubtedly. The police called Loring about it, but they aren't going to pay any attention. Everything was decided quite clearly at the inquest. So don't *you* go imagining things. Come now, Jenny—I've brought you some hot broth and a serving of delicious broiled fish. I'm going to stay right here until you eat something."

To please her, since she was being kind, I got out of bed and sat in a chair. At least the soup was warming and the fish was delicately broiled with herbs. I even ate half an apple and a wedge of Brie to finish my meal, and had to admit that it made me feel better.

"I'll put the tray outside the door so you won't be disturbed," Irene said. "Then I'll let you rest. Brendon phoned a little while ago and he expects to be home tonight. He wanted me to tell you."

I nodded, unable to feel any joy. More than anything else at the moment, I dreaded seeing Brendon. Before she left, however, I thought of something and went to the closet where I had thrown Ariel's dressing gown into the corner and forgotten it. I drew it out and shook it to release some of the wrinkles.

"Can you give this to someone?" I asked. "It was my

sister's, but Brendon doesn't like me in red, so I want to be rid of it before he returns."

The worry line between her eyes had deepened and I thought she looked a little frightened as she took the gown from me and promised that she would find someone to give it to. Then she dropped a light kiss on my cheek and went quickly away.

I couldn't bear to wait for Brendon in that room. The rain had stopped and I put on my coat, went down to the lobby by way of the back stairs, slipped out a side door. For a long while I sat in the summerhouse across the lake, watching the hotel lights, listening to the whispering voices of the water until I finally returned to my room.

Once inside, I didn't bother to bolt the door. Now I knew where enmity lay, but I didn't think Naomi would come to see me tonight, or write any more notes.

My heavy afternoon sleep made me wide awake now, but I couldn't settle down with a book. Instead, I sat at the Queen Anne desk and wrote Mother and Aunt Lydia a long letter, filling it with an account of the beauties and delights of Laurel Mountain, with nothing about a stone bull that stood alone in the woods, or about Ariel ever being here. When the letter was done, I went outside to sit in a balcony chair and watch the night.

I am still here. The air smells fresh-washed and fragrant with pine, and the lake is star-speckled and very still, with only its natural currents running. From here I can hear no sound of whispering voices along the shore, though occasionally there are other voices.

Couples walk hand-in-hand in the lighted area at this end of the lake—old people as well as young. Older couples who have grown closer than ever with the passing years. As I walk about the hotel I see them and I can sense the affection between them, and I am aware of emotions once young, now grown stronger with the bond of long years together. I feel sad and a little afraid when I see them. Afraid because it may never be like that for Brendon and me. Now, in my youth, when love is young and hot with longing, and never fully appeased, I crave for an assurance that there will be for us a later, quieter time for deeper love than we can know now. Because then we will truly know each other. Sitting here with the calm and peace of the mountain night beyond my balcony, I realize how little I know him, and how little he knows me. Will it be possible for our love to last through that learning-to-know? Or even possible for it to last through tonight?

I am very cold, yet I sit here waiting. Is his car coming up the valley on the far side of the mountain even now? Can he see the light from High Tower beckoning him home? Home to me? But why *me*—if Ariel came here in the past? Or is that really the answer? Because I look so much like my sister? Because he can hold me and pretend that it is Ariel he holds in his arms?

I cross my own arms in front of my body, shivering, holding myself as perhaps he will never hold me again, once I have flung down my challenge. I dread to hear the sound of his key in the door. I've left it open so that he can come in at any time. My teeth are chattering. I must go inside to my warm bed. Our bed. Or will he sleep elsewhere tonight?

I heard him in the hall before he reached our rooms. He was running—running all the way down the empty corridor, his feet thudding on the red carpet. Then he opened the door and came into our sitting room, tossing aside jacket and briefcase, hurrying into the next room—calling out to me as he came.

I had no chance to speak or greet him before he was sitting on the edge of the bed, gathering me exuberantly into his arms, his blue eyes alight, his lips eager.

"I've missed you!" he said against my hair. "I hated to go away all day and be nowhere near you. Darling, how nice you smell. I love that woodsy scent you wear. Do you know how often I think of you in the midst of my work? It keeps me sane to have you here waiting for me. How empty I was before you came."

Empty because she had gone away from him? There

was no way to tell him what I knew without cutting down his joy and delight in being with me again. I had to cling to him and return his kisses—I had to believe. And when at length he lay beside me sleeping, my eyes felt dry and burning in the dark, and all my thoughts were tumbled and confused. How could I possibly destroy with my own words all that we had between us? Wasn't it better to be a coward and to believe what I wanted to believe, and not what all my experience of my sister had long ago taught me to know? So I fell asleep at last with my cheek resting in the hollow of his shoulder, and my churning thoughts quieted at last.

When I awoke in the morning he was already up and dressed, and he smiled at me in the mirror as he combed his hair. I awakened groggily, with something heavy and menacing dragging at my thoughts, though I couldn't remember what threatened me in those first drugged moments of coming to life. When Brendon came with all his confidence and vitality to kiss me awake, I had no heart for unpleasant discussion. I could only play what was happening by ear. Sooner or later it would all come into the open, and in the meantime I would be a coward and pretend that our love was for always.

That way it was possible to go calmly down to breakfast with him and be glad that we could eat alone every morning. It was possible to postpone my next meeting with Naomi, even to avoid Irene and Loring until later in the day. I didn't tell him about meeting Magnus in the woods—I didn't tell him anything. Duplicity had to be my way of life from moment to moment, and I listened instead to his account of his trip to Albany, to his talk of hotel business. I even found that I could be absorbed by all that interested him, and I could contribute remarks that were not unintelligent. But when I tried to remember later what had been said, I found that very little had penetrated my protective fog.

Only when breakfast was over and I was left on my own again did my thoughts begin to take form, and once more I began to plan. It wasn't in my nature to drift for long. My work in the library could wait. I knew what I must do with my morning, knew what plan I must follow. It was Magnus I must talk to. Magnus had known her—I was sure of that. Perhaps he had loved her. There had been pain in that roar he had hurled at me when he'd told me to get down from the bull's back.

So now he must talk to me. I would force him to talk to me—as no one else but Naomi had been willing to do since I'd come here. I couldn't discuss any of this with Brendon yet, but Magnus was another matter, and I must be armed before I faced Brendon.

It was at least two hours ago that I planned to seek Magnus up in the woods. I wasn't able to, however, because just as I came down the hotel steps I saw Keir's truck go by, and Magnus was sitting beside his father in the front seat. The truck disappeared in the direction of the main road and for the moment I had to give up my plan.

Now I wander about in this huge, mysterious barn—a gloomy place of cobwebs and preserved history, feeling more alarmed than ever, and afraid to go back to the real world, where all my shock and my terror of whatever is to come must show in my face. It is safer to stay here for a while and try to marshal my thoughts into some sort of order, to find out what it is I really feel and believe. The sunny peace of Laurel, the safety of woods and lake have been destroyed for me—destroyed forever. All because my sister came here a few months ago and because of the terrible thing that is being whispered about her.

As I poke about, exploring idly, I come upon a dilapidated two-seater buggy, and the shadowy seat invites me. I put my foot upon the square step and pull myself up past the carriage lantern into a dusty cave. There is a smell of ancient, cracking leather and neat's-foot oil. Rising dust makes me sneeze, but overhead the rib-braced top offers shelter and I can feel hidden here.

The buggy is hitched to nothing, the shafts and moldering reins go nowhere. I fancy that this room of old carriages, opening off a harness room, still carries the smell of sweat from the horses that once drew them. I could disappear forever if I chose, I think whimsically. Who would miss me, since I'm not Ariel?

I have already wandered through the museum parts of the Red Barn, but it is also a fabulous place of underground rooms and passages, of echoing tunnels from one section to another, and now that I have found this retreat I sit here and try to order my thoughts, try to decide what I must do. Is there any saving action that can be taken—or must I simply run away? Perhaps say good-bye to no one, never see any of them again.

"Oh, Ariel!" I whisper her name aloud and echoing whispers rush back upon me. But there is another name in my mind and one blocks the other, so that even my pain is confused and its source uncertain.

How innocently I began my adventure in this place. When I found that I must postpone my meeting with Magnus, I wandered down through the grounds, past formal gardens where I glimpsed Naomi working again. When I saw her, I turned aside and took a branching path that led me to the great quadrangle of the Red Barn. A doorway into the wing marked *Museum* invited me, and I discovered that there was a great deal to see. Few guests moved among the exhibits just then, and the curator was talking to one of them. I went on from room to room idly, until I found a closed door with a sign that read *Employees Only.* Since I was not a guest, I opened it upon stairs that I descended to the underground level.

Here, I gathered, everything that was old and no longer in use was brought to be stored. It seemed as though nothing had ever been thrown away. In the harness room every imaginable type of harness hardware hung upon the walls. There were hames and bridles, bits and chains, all on wall hooks, and festooned with cobwebs. From the harness room a tunnel-like passageway opened, and when I followed it I found stairs that led me back to the ground floor, ending in a long room of many stalls. These open boxes went up one side of the room and down the other— and I counted to a hundred and twenty. What a stable Laurel had once had! There was still a faint odor of horses lingering, of leather and of dust over everything.

Light came in through high small windows above each stall, but the stables were now elsewhere, and this was a room left over from the past.

My steps echoed as I walked bare boards and as I wandered I fancied an echo to my steps. Once I stopped and listened, but all was quiet about me, eerily still in this place where restless hoofs had once stomped, where there had been whinnying and the chomping of oats. I walked again, and again footsteps walked with me. Yet when I whirled about, no one was in sight. When I called out to know who was there, no answer came to me.

The feeling of being watched and followed was unpleasant and I returned to the stairs and fled underground again, since I knew no other way back to the main part of the barn and the public museum. However, there seemed to be more than one tunnel, and when I'd run the length of enclosed space, I came out in a dark room where discarded objects stood about. I could identify an old anvil and broken farm machinery—the whole room a dead end of disuse. Now the footsteps began again, sounding openly and coming closer, following my path through the tunnel. There were no windows here, only traces of daylight that filtered in from the tunnel, and I struck some iron object, and was reminded of the ankle I had hurt yesterday. It hadn't bothered me till I'd bumped it.

For a moment I stood still in that dark and dusty place, rubbing my ankle and listening. My follower was making no effort now to conceal the sound of steps echoing hollowly on wood, and when I turned I could see him silhouetted against the door through which I'd come. Suddenly a light clicked on overhead as the man at the entrance to the tunnel reached for a switch. I stood blinking in the glare from a naked bulb that swung above me, and saw Loring Grant regarding me curiously.

"Are you lost?" he asked, a faintly derisive note in his voice.

"I suppose I am," I said. "Why were you following me?"

"Did I frighten you? I'm sorry. I saw you heading into

the old part of the barn, and while I didn't want to spoil your exploration, some of these rooms are no longer safe, and I thought I'd follow and make sure you didn't get hurt."

My voice had a tendency to quiver in reaction, and I steadied it by an effort. "What could hurt me down here? And why didn't you answer when I called?"

He answered my first question, but not the second. "Broken floors. Things that fall. We'd have sent someone along with you if we'd known you were coming here."

"I didn't know it myself."

"If you've seen enough, perhaps I can show you a pleasanter area upstairs. Then we might talk a bit, Jenny."

I wasn't sure what he wanted to talk about, or whether I wanted to listen. I had the uncomfortable feeling that he had wanted me to feel uneasy, perhaps a little frightened. However, I brushed away clinging cobwebs and followed him back through tunnels and rooms and up stairs until we reached a large display space on the second floor.

Here light flooded in through windows at both ends, and I saw that various exhibits were ranged down each side of the long room, with a wide passage left between. This must be the room over the stables below. From the ceiling hung a huge American flag, and Loring came to stand beside me as I looked up at it.

"There are forty-five stars," he told me. "That flag was in use here at Laurel in 1896, when Utah came in, until 1907, when Oklahoma became the forty-sixth state."

But we weren't here merely to look at exhibits, and he led the way past an old Model-T Ford and a two-horse treadmill to where a bench near a window allowed us to sit in a band of sunlight. I felt a continued unease in this man's company, and in spite of his explanation of why he followed me, I distrusted his motives. He wasn't the first person at Laurel I would have chosen to talk to, but I suspected that whether I liked it or not, something was now going to be brought into the open. It had been Loring who had wanted to talk to me earlier, and Irene had stopped him.

"Irene tells me that you were very much disturbed about something last night," he began.

"I don't think I want to discuss it," I said.

"Naomi has talked to you, hasn't she?"

I turned my head and looked into eyes that had a flat sheen, as though they were made of metal, and I was aware once more of a barely suppressed vitality in this man. There was no use pretending any longer that I didn't know the truth.

"She told me that my sister Ariel used to come here."

"Yes. There's been no way to muzzle Naomi. Brendon warned us all that you weren't to be told, though I was convinced that it could not be kept from you indefinitely."

"Why didn't he tell me from the first that you all knew my sister?"

"I'm afraid you'll have to take that up with Brendon. That's not what I want to talk with you about, however. Irene has told me that last night you were asking about Floris Devin—about her death."

I was silent. Floris didn't matter to me now. Not when Brendon's full duplicity was coming into the open. Sooner or later I mut know and face why he had kept this monstrous secret from me, and the thought left no room for concern about Floris.

"You had better know," Loring went on, "that your sister caused the death of Magnus' wife."

His words shocked me back from my preoccupation with Brendon, and I stared at him. "What do you mean?"

"Oh—not that it was deliberate. At least, we hope it wasn't. Ariel was standing on that big boulder above the Lair—the one that fell. Somehow she dislodged it and sent it crashing down—and Floris was killed. Irene didn't want you to know, but I feel there has been enough concealment. Sooner or later someone would tell you, so it's better to hear it impartially from me. Ariel left for New York the next day. We thought it best to send her home. None of us wanted an exploding story in the press—least of all, Ariel."

"Don't the police know?"

"Not a word, as far as she was concerned. Since it was

an accident, there seemed no point in involving Ariel, and we simply sent her away. There was no need to tell the police and make all the headlines. We all agreed on that."

All this was in May, I thought—early May, when Floris had died. And Ariel had taken those pills the last week in May. Yet she had told Mother nothing. Told me nothing. Or had she tried to tell me? There had been a jumbled outpouring that I hadn't understood and couldn't remember afterward.

"Of course there have been whispers of suspicion," Loring said quietly.

"What do you mean?"

"Ariel was involved with Magnus, you know. During her last visit here she stayed with Magnus and Floris in their cabin. Floris was making threats against her, but Ariel only laughed at her."

I could imagine that laughter—gay, sparkling, without any sensitivity for those she might hurt. Yet whatever she had been, my sister was no murderer.

"She would never have sent that rock tumbling on purpose," I said.

"That's what we all told ourselves."

"Told?"

"Can we help having doubts? There's proof that someone prepared that boulder so it would fall. It needed only a little rocking to send it tumbling into the chasm."

"What proof?"

He smiled at me most gently, but his eyes had a cold gleam. "Since it is evidence that was—shall we say—held back from the police, it's better not to go into it now. Brendon will deal with these new inquiries—whatever they are, and it will be best if you know as little as possible."

"I don't think there's anything to know, as far as Ariel is concerned," I told him with conviction. "But if there are whispers, as you say, then they ought to be stopped."

"Just how would you do that?"

"I'm not sure. I'll have to think about it."

He reached out and took my hand in his. "Don't, Jenny. Don't think about it at all."

His hand was cool, the flesh dry, and I drew my own away. "Thank you for telling me," I said stiffly and stood up. "Of course I'll want to think a lot about what you've told me. I'll want to know a great deal more. If there is any suspicion that Ariel Vaughn was deliberately behind that woman's death, then it will have to be disproved."

He repeated his earlier question, "How will you manage that?"

"I don't know. But I will. I owe that to my sister."

"Why are you so sure of her innocence?"

I stared at him for a moment, not speaking. Then I walked away from him down the long room, seeing nothing of the exhibits on either side. He didn't follow. I had the frightening feeling that I wanted to hide, that I must get away alone, where no one would find me. Some place where I could face my own thoughts and no one could watch me.

When I was sure Loring hadn't followed me, I fled back to the barn's labyrinths. Watchful now of broken floors and falling dangers, I groped my way to this creaking, leathery haven of an old buggy. Here I can sit undisturbed and try to find order in chaos.

Undisturbed except for my own tormenting thoughts. Magnus in love with Ariel? I could believe that. I knew very well the attraction she exerted toward men. In this case, with Floris standing between Ariel and a man she wanted, as she so obviously must have done, my sister would have had no scruples—none whatever! And yet— murder? No, not Ariel. I must somehow still my own terror at the thought.

After a time I left that dark, musty room and found my way back to the outdoors and sunlight. With the sun on my face, I felt a little more courageous. And then, though still deeply concerned, I began to feel a new, unexpected relief. Because now, explanations for Brendon's actions were coming to mind, and I could find ways to excuse him for his silence.

Of course he hadn't wanted me to know that Ariel was having an affair with Magnus. He'd said he didn't care for ballet, so perhaps he had never liked Ariel him-

self and hadn't wanted to tell me that the day I'd met him
in the lobby. Probably he meant to tell me everything
eventually, but he had known even then that the fact of
her being here wasn't important to *us*. He had been right.
It wasn't.

I could be glad now that I hadn't exploded last night,
hadn't hurled foolish accusations at him. Everything was
going to be all right between Brendon and me. But I had
spoken the truth in what I'd said to Loring about Ariel. I
owed her something. I owed my own guilty conscience
something, and I would not rest until such whispering
about my sister was silenced. For the first time I wondered
who it was that whispered. That was a question I should
have asked Loring.

When I followed a walk in the direction of the hotel,
I saw that Naomi was no longer working in the nearby
gardens, so I turned onto a cross path that allowed me to
wander among the great beds of autumn flowers, red and
gold and orange, and spiced with barberry and rosehips
and bittersweet. A wide spread of lawn ran up the hill to
where climbing pink hydrangeas made a wall of bloom,
the blossoms only slightly tarnished by nipping frost.
There was another gazebo there, and I climbed up to it
across the grass and sat on a bench where I could look out
toward towers that from here seemed clustered together
and more than ever like a glimpse of Camelot.

Had Ariel been troubled by guilt because of the rock
she'd unwittingly dislodged so that it had crashed down to
kill her lover's wife? Was this why she had taken those
pills? It didn't seem characteristic. Self-guilt was not a
common indulgence with my sister. More than ever now,
I knew that I would have to see Magnus. Whether he liked
it or not, I would have to talk to him about my sister
Ariel.

As I sat on the bench in this high vantage point, I saw
Keir's truck following the road that wound below me, and
again Magnus was with him. The truck turned uphill,
away from the hotel on the road to High Tower, and I
knew they were going back to the cabin. By the time I

walked up there, perhaps Keir would have left, dropping Magnus off, and his son would be alone.

For the second time that day, I braced myself for a confrontation with Magnus, but was glad now that I had waited. I could go to this meeting with him knowing far more than I had known earlier this morning. And I could go with a lighter heart as well. It was not, after all, Brendon who had loved my sister, and the knowledge gave a lift to my steps as I started up the mountain.

6

My climb was not clear to High Tower this time, as I was following the more moderate rise of the carriage road, watching for the branch that would lead through the woods to the cabin.

There was no urgency in me, now that I was on my way. Once I left the road, climbing past a clump of goldenrod to reach a shadowed spot where grape ferns grew, their leafy fronds turning bronze as the season changed. Earlier the spore cases would have been yellow-green. What treasure these woods would hold for me when I had time to go plant hunting. If only Brendon would come with me. It appeared that I was to see much less of him than I'd expected.

This road bypassed the clearing where the bull stood frozen in his eternal charge, and when I came to the path that would have led to him, I walked on, refusing to be deterred. My fierce stone friend must wait for another visit, however much I wanted to see him again.

Long before I reached the cabin, I heard the ringing sound of mallet on steel, telling me that Magnus must be working this morning. When I had last been here, my attention had focused upon Magnus himself and his treatment of me, and I hadn't studied the house particularly. Now, when I came into the cleared space around it, I saw how well the split logs of the walls and the wood shingling of the roof suited their surroundings. This was a forest cabin—it belonged here. No curling smoke rose from the fieldstone chimney, and as I neared the source, the ringing sounds of a mallet grew louder, coming from beyond the cabin. I walked around its far end and stood looking at the scene before me.

This morning Magnus wore no shirt in the warm sun, and his chest with its fuzz of red hair, his brown arm raised to lift a wooden mallet, seemed massive—like the mountain rock itself. His open-air workshop was littered with stones of all shapes and sizes—some of them chips he had hammered or drilled away. On a sturdy table stood a huge stone face that reminded me of pictures I'd seen of Easter Island carvings, except that this bore the individual stamp of Magnus Devin's own imagination. The stone he was working on, however, was not a sculpture. It was obviously the shape and size of a headstone, and I remembered that carving tombstones had once been Magnus' work. Beyond him stood a protected shelter that held his tools and some of the machinery he used for moving huge blocks.

He didn't hear my approach because of the noise he was making with mallet on steel chisel, and I picked my way among the bits and pieces of chipped rock and came to stand in front of him, where he could hardly fail to see me. Yet for a few moments longer he paid me no attention, but worked on, shaping the rough slab of granite. When his last stroke satisfied him, he dropped mallet and chisel to a workbench, removed the goggles that protected his eyes and straightened to stare at me. His red hair and red beard seemed afire in the morning sun, and the deep green of his eyes challenged me in some way that made me uncomfortable.

"Good morning," I said.

He nodded without greeting. "I've been expecting you. You had to come back, didn't you?"

"Why would you think that?" I countered.

"Because when you knew the truth, you would have to come. Because you're her sister. There's been a loss of innocence since yesterday, hasn't there? The innocence of ignorance."

There seemed a brutality in his words that shocked me, though I knew instinctively that this was not a man who would step prettily away from dangerous topics. Yet if I rushed at him with questions, he might very well shut me out and return to his deafening work. So I stood before him, waiting in silence.

"Who told you?" he demanded.

"First a guest at the hotel. Then Naomi told me more. I found her in a room at the hotel playing Ariel's music and crying."

"That miserable little creature!" His scorn toward Naomi seemed as enormous as everything else about him, but unjustified.

"Ariel charmed her," I said. "And anyone Ariel charmed had to love her. It's always been that way."

"Except for you." Eyes as deeply green as the pines behind him continued to challenge me.

"I loved her," I said. "I loved her and hated her, and I didn't always know which was which. You loved her too, didn't you?"

"And sometimes I hated her," he said simply.

I bent to examine the headstone more closely. No lettering had been engraved upon it as yet.

"Do you do much of this sort of work now?" I asked.

"Only when it's needed here at Laurel."

I understood. This was a stone for Floris' grave.

"Someone has told me that you used to work for your wife's father."

"I did for a time. Every sculptor ought to work in a stonemason's yard for experience. We need to know something about the qualities of different stones before we try, as sculptors say, to open up the stone."

I moved toward the crude shelter that had been built to protect his machinery and tools, and to store some of his work. A few smaller stone beasts crowded the area in various stages of completion, but the thing that drew me stood on a rude bench in a corner of the shed. Glaring out from the shadows was a curiously mad face carved in some reddish stone. The teeth were bared, the eyes stared wildly and a nubby horn grew from the forehead. It was difficult to say whether the thing was man or beast, and the sight of it—evidence of a demented imagination—disturbed me. It was a face out of nightmare.

Behind me, Magnus started toward the cabin, picking up a lumberjack's shirt and pulling it on as he moved. "We can't stand talking out here, and it's possible that we do have something to say to each other. So come inside."

I cast a last uneasy glance at that personification of evil in stone, and followed him obediently, having no wish to be picked up again like a sack of potatoes and carried indoors.

The big room was still gloomy, its overhanging roof shutting out direct sunlight, though the Indian rugs glowed in soft warmth on floor and walls. At the far end the huge grate was black with burned-out logs and the iron pot hung empty.

"Coffee?" he said. "I've got some top milk this morning."

I shuddered faintly at the thought of that dollop of honey, and said, "Black, please," just in time. He poured from the graniteware pot as delicately as a lady with a china tea set, and I took the mug he proffered and moved about the room, seeing more than I had on my previous visit. Today I could feel less at a loss, more on top of what was happening. At least Loring had given me that. There was no point in moving cautiously now, however, since there were things I wanted to say to this man, wanted to know, and I had better get on with it. I might frighten him off by being direct, but at the same time I felt that directness was a part of his own character.

"I've been talking to Loring," I said, stopping before a shelf where handsome pieces of small sculpture had been placed. Apparently Magnus didn't always work larger than life. "He says there are whispers about my sister. He told me she was standing on that rock before it fell."

I avoided looking at him, but I had a sense of waiting silence behind me—a wary, almost animal silence, like that of a wild thing startled. When I turned slowly, I saw that he had spilled the coffee he was pouring for himself, but he paid no attention to a brown puddle on the table—his whole focus of attention on me, waiting for whatever came next.

"Ariel would never have killed anyone," I said. "She would take what she wanted and never worry about consequences, but she wouldn't kill because she never wanted anything that much. I think it must take great passion, great fury, to kill someone."

Outdoors Magnus' voice could rise to a shout that seemed to come in a roar from his chest, but now he spoke softly, almost gently.

"She had passion. She could be angry."

"Only on a stage," I told him. "That was all she lived for—her dancing. She wanted adulation, onstage and off—and she commanded it easily."

"You do hate her, don't you?"

"Not anymore. There were times in the past when I did. But not hating her doesn't mean that I can't see her clearly, or that I can't love her as well. What did Loring mean when he used the word 'whispering'?"

"Hadn't you better ask him?"

"But you would know, and you must see that I must confront whoever believes such things about my sister."

"I'm not exactly on a close relationship with those who run the hotel. I don't know anything about it."

"The police appear to be interested again. They've received an anonymous call. I can't stand by and see the case reopened."

Finally Magnus moved, picking up a cloth to wipe the spilled coffee, pouring himself another cup. When he'd drunk a swallow that must have scalded, he set the mug down and came toward me across the room.

"I wonder if you knew her at all? She might even have married me, if Floris hadn't stood in the way."

"Never! She wanted her dancing first. Always."

"Not during those last weeks. Not while she stayed here under this roof."

"Why didn't she stay at the hotel?"

"Maybe you'd better ask Brendon that."

But Brendon didn't come into this, and I pushed his words quickly aside.

"I've got to find a way to disprove whatever is being said."

"I've forgiven Ariel. Why can't you?"

Strange words. I didn't know what they meant, and it didn't matter.

"I'll find a way," I promised.

"Then I wish you luck. However, isn't that a dangerous undertaking?"

"What do you mean?"

"If you think that rock was deliberately prepared to roll, and if Ariel didn't set it up to fall—then who did? If you disprove one thing, then mustn't you prove another?"

Somehow I had been so bent on my concern for clearing Ariel from suspicion that I hadn't come to the point of wondering who might have acted against Floris if my sister hadn't. This was a thought too uncomfortable to consider—that a murderer might still be here at Laurel Mountain, believing himself safe.

My attention focused on a wall shelf before me as I sought distraction, and I began to study the lovely sculpture in marble, nearly life-size, of a young boy's head. What a far cry from that horrid redstone head I'd seen in Magnus' outdoor shelter.

"Did you do this?" I asked. "It's exquisite."

"My son. He died a few years ago—when he was five."

I sensed a father's grief in the simple statement. "I'm sorry," I said, and then sighed. "How inadequate that word always sounds. People have been saying they're sorry to me ever since Ariel died, until I've begun to hate sympathy. Death is so—unmendable. It leaves so much shattering behind."

He said nothing and I moved on to look at another object on the shelf. This was something that had been cast in bronze, but I couldn't make out from the oddly twisted shape exactly what it was until I picked the heavy thing up in my hands. It had once been a dancing figure, perhaps ten inches high—a girl in tutu and toe shoes, posed in a ballet attitude with one arm curved above her head. There its beauty ended. Something had been used to smash the delicate head and face into an unrecognizable scarred surface. I turned to Magnus in horror and held up the figure.

"What happened to this?"

"Floris destroyed it," he said. His tone was without emotion, his own passion controlled, yet I knew by his eyes that something barely hidden seethed beneath the quiet surface.

After a moment he went on. "Ariel never hated anyone. She created beauty and love. Floris could hate. Hatred was her best creation. And she was destructive as well. If it had been Ariel who had died beneath that rock, no one would have looked far for evidence of murder."

"But it was the other way around!" I cried. "And what you say is true. My sister never hated anyone."

"If you are going to live in this place," Magnus said, "you had better let the whole thing alone. You can't help Ariel now."

"Oh yes I can!" I heard my own vehemence and it surprised me as I hurried on. "If the police come back into it, if they point to what happened as murder and Ariel is blamed, it will all spill into the papers. It will ruin everything she was, everything she did, and it would break my mother's heart."

"Tell me about her death," he said. "I only knew of it through the papers. Did she really kill herself?"

I set the smashed figure down and went to sit in a chair near the cold hearth. "I don't think she meant to. I think she only wanted to worry us because she was unhappy. She phoned me to come to her, and I didn't. Perhaps if anyone is to blame, I am. She didn't take enough pills to matter, but the combination with alcohol killed her. I could have been there and I wasn't." I could hear my own voice rising. "Even Naomi would have gone to her if she could. *I* could have and I didn't. So that's why I have to clear her name now, if something untrue is really being said about her. I owe this much to my sister."

He was staring at me strangely down the room, and

when he spoke his words took me by surprise. "Will you pose for me, Jenny Vaughn?"

I could only gape at him in astonishment. Particularly since he had called me by my maiden name.

"I might model you in clay—though it's not my favorite medium. Just your head. Then I could cast it in bronze again and repair that figure. It's the only thing I ever did of her."

How strange an immediate emotional reaction can be when it wells up out of old unconscious pain, without restraint, without calculation—suddenly there, revealing you to yourself. It happened now—old bitter rage against Ariel springing into being again. Because once more it was *she* who mattered. I was nothing. I was only a reflection of something so beautiful, so beyond me, so out of reach, except in a surface resemblance that I couldn't help.

He saw my reaction at once. "Don't be angry, Jenny. Why should you be?"

And of course I was not angry the moment reason thrust back that sudden rush of devastating emotion. But in that instant of self-revelation, I understood what it might mean to destroy. Only it had been Floris who was destroyed—not Ariel, who might have asked for her own destruction over and over again.

"Of course I'll pose for you," I said.

He smiled at me—that dazzling white smile that parted the red beard, and his look was gentle, understanding.

"Thank you."

I finished my coffee and stood up. "Is there anything at all you can tell me that might help? Was there anyone besides Ariel who might have hated your wife, been angry with her?"

"I hated her," he said. "And I suppose she hated me. It should have been ended between us long ago."

"I don't think you're a murderer either," I told him.

"I could be."

There was something deadly in his voice, and I remembered that extraordinarily evil face I had seen out in his workshed. From what inner rage or anger had that head been created?

"I'd better go back now," I told him. "Do you mind if I visit your stone bull again on the way down?"

"Of course not." Once more he was smiling. "I'm over my first shock at seeing you there. Come along and I'll go with you."

He went ahead down the path through the woods from one clearing to the other. The bull waited for us in all his magnificence, and I could sense again the gathering of power in great muscles as he prepared to charge.

"How did you do him?" I said. "Did you have a live model?"

"There used to be a bull down at the hotel farm. I guess I made him angry a few times, just so I could get him to charge, while I went over the fence. I made sketches—dozens of sketches. And I studied photographs, of course."

I walked over to place my hand on stone that had warmed in the sun, and I could almost feel the pulsing of all that power and force beneath the hump of muscle in his neck. It was just below that muscle that a sword would find the vulnerable place and thrust through to the heart.

"He's not a farm bull," I said. "He's right out of a bull-ring in Spain."

"That's what I intended. That's why he stands in a ring—if only of grass. I've seen bullfights in Madrid, and I wanted to show my bull triumphant."

I hadn't known how close Magnus had come to me, and I had no inkling of what was about to happen until I was picked up suddenly in massive hands, raised in the air and set asprawl on that great stone back. Gasping, I struggled for my balance and drew up one knee, letting my other leg hang down the great beast's side while I clung to his hump of neck.

Magnus stood back and looked at me while I fought for my balance—emotional as well as physical.

"I'd like to make a smaller figure of the bull—with you on his back. Just the way she used to pose there," Magnus said. "Oh, not in slacks, of course. Maybe you could find some sort of flowing dress—"

I didn't bother to get down by way of stepping stones—I simply hurled myself off that stone back and landed on my hands and knees on the grass. I had never felt so furious.

"I will *not* pose for you!" I cried. "I'm not my sister—so you can stop imagining that I am."

His roar of derisive laughter split the silence of the woods. "No—you're not your sister in the least. She never made an ungraceful movement in her life."

I stood up, brushing grass from my hands and knees, and tried to walk with some dignity toward the path I'd taken up from the road yesterday. Behind me I heard no further laughter, and he said nothing as I went. When I reached the trees I couldn't resist looking back. He stood beside the stone bull, one hand resting on its flank. He had already forgotten me, as he would never forget *her*.

I ran down the path, and when I came out on the road I followed it until I saw another trail leading off from it, dropping toward the lake. There were always signs nailed to trees, and every path, every trail had a name. This one took me steeply down over rough ground until I came out on the way I'd taken yesterday with Brendon—the path that ran above the Lair. Once more great boulders tumbled below me, as though some giant hand had arrested them in full motion. Now I could pick out the place where the falling rock had killed Floris.

For me there seemed a morbid fascination about this spot, and I stood staring down upon it for a long while. Then, inescapably drawn, I left the path and went across to the space of bare indented earth from which the boulder had fallen. Standing there, I could look straight down into the chasm where a woman had died. Rock walls were sheer, and the pit at the bottom wide enough for the chunk of stone now plugging the way that had once led through it. She would have been hemmed in, perhaps unable to escape quickly, even when she heard the rock coming.

The hand that grasped my shoulder so startled me that, if I hadn't been jerked back from the edge, I might have fallen. As it was, I stumbled over rough rock and had to right myself with a wrench. It was not Magnus this time, but his father. Keir Devin stood beside me, his tanned hand on my shoulder.

"You shouldn't go so close to the edge," he warned. "You gave me a scare. A scare in more ways than one."

"And you gave me a scare," I told him indignantly. "I nearly jumped out of my skin."

He paid no attention to that, his gray eyes, not unlike his son's in their lively expression, regarding me strangely. "You look so much like her that you made me think I was seeing things. She used to sit right there for an hour at a time, just looking out at the lake and the Mountain House, or watching people go through the Lair down below."

They all remembered her so vividly, I thought, and I found myself remembering too—out loud.

"Yes, I can recall times when she was like that. Times when she could be absolutely still. But it wasn't in character for her. Her work was all movement, after all, and it never ceased. No matter how all-out she'd danced at a performance at night, there was always a class to take early the next morning. She was never let off. So sometimes she tried to let everything go and she'd be very still, trying to renew herself. Sometimes she'd run away, and not even our mother knew where she'd gone. She never told us that she came here."

He joined me in reminiscence. "I picked her up in my truck one day when she'd twisted her foot on a rock—just as you did. I found her sitting in one of those gazebos down there, crying. I told her she'd better call her home if the hurt was bad. But she wouldn't. She didn't want anyone to know where she was, and I don't think she was crying about a hurt foot."

"No, she wouldn't be. I've known her to dance with broken bones in her feet—ballet dancers do sometimes. They always live with pain. It all looks so graceful and light, but there's a lot of physical suffering. It's part of their lives and they don't cry about it."

He shook his head. "It's not natural—what they do.

Anyway, it would have been better if she'd never come here."

I could only agree. But there was something I wanted to know and I asked a direct question.

"Who told you I knew she was here?"

"I saw Loring a little while ago. He asked me to keep an eye out for you because you were pretty upset about learning that your sister had come to Laurel. But it's okay, you know. You're nothing like her."

From him, it seemed a compliment, and I tried to smile.

"Your son wants me to pose for him, the way Ariel did," I told him. "Do you think I should?"

"No." The word was curt. "Stay away from Magnus."

"You've said that before. Do you mean for my sake or his?"

"Maybe for both. You might as well know I never liked your sister. I didn't like what she did—breaking up everything between Floris and Magnus."

"Perhaps it was already broken," I said.

He shook his head. "They got along all right until she came. They were used to each other. Your sister damaged everything she touched. But I don't think you're like that, Jenny."

There was a gentler note in his voice, a kindness in the gray eyes.

"Sometimes I don't know what I'm like," I admitted. I had recovered from the shock of his hand on my shoulder, and I remembered that I wanted to make friends with this man who had always been close to Brendon. "Don't forget," I went on, "that you promised to take me around the grounds sometime. Brendon thinks no one could do it better. Will you have any free time this afternoon?"

He considered this soberly, perhaps a little doubtfully. In spite of his avowal that I was different, he wasn't quite sure of me yet. Then he smiled—a smile that seemed almost shy in his weathered face—and ran a hand through his white shock of hair.

"Sure, Jenny. I'll be free late this afternoon. Suppose I pick you up in my truck around four o'clock."

"Fine," I said. "I'll wait for you on the arrival side of the hotel."

He touched his hand to his temple in a salute that suggested an acceptance of me as Brendon's wife, and went back to the road and his truck.

For a little while longer I stood looking at the place where Ariel had liked to come, and where she had been the day that rock had fallen. It must have been her dancer's agility that kept her from rolling with it. She must have felt the movement beneath her feet and leaped to safety. Once more I looked down the precipice and saw that a man had just begun working at the bottom with a sledge hammer, breaking up the rock that blocked the passage. Before long the Lair would be opened to guests again, and perhaps I would walk through it, and look up from the crevice to this perch so far above.

Out on the lake little boats dotted the water. I glanced at my watch and saw there would be time before lunch to go out again in Brendon's boat. Rowing was physical and tranquilizing, and the calm blue lake drew me. I hurried around to the secluded place on the shore where the dinghy was beached, and in a few moments I was out on the water, pulling hard on the oars, enjoying the use of my own muscles. I felt a proper superiority to those guests who chose the little paddle boats for their excursions. I preferred real rowing.

Somehow the thoughts that troubled me fell away, and I felt soothed and calmed by this physical effort. I must have rowed for nearly an hour before I turned back to shore and docked my boat. As soon as I started toward the hotel, however, questions swept back.

By now, I supposed, everyone would be aware that I had been told about Ariel. I was sure to see Brendon in the dining room, if not before, and I wasn't certain how I could face him in public, knowing that he had held back from me the fact that Ariel had come here. Even if it had been Magnus with whom she was involved, Brendon had headed the conspiracy of silence and enlisted the others. He had told them not to tell me that Ariel had been there. So there was a breach of understanding be-

tween us that must be bridged. I must try to be generous.
I must give him time to tell me why he had felt such
silence necessary.

I ran down the path that led from Panther Rock while
a crimson sunset stained the sky and distant mountains.
I was late for dinner, so I had to hurry, though I thought
it might be better if I was very late and could eat alone.

Because all is not yet well between Brendon and me—
because none of it is in the open yet. The conspiracy of
silence goes on, and the fact that others think it necessary
frightens me. As if they are holding back from some explosive situation that alarms them. And as if Brendon is
avoiding me.

Lunch, earlier, was an uncomfortable affair. We filled
our plates at the buffet and carried them to our table.
Loring was there, and Irene, who watched me anxiously,
so I knew *she* knew I had been told. Naomi didn't look
at me at all, or speak to anyone except in monosyllables.
Brendon came in last. He dropped a kiss on my cheek,
pressed my shoulder in signal of his love—and obviously
knew nothing about what had been revealed to me. I
tried to take heart from the very fact that he could be
so openly loving toward me. If there was anything really
disturbing to conceal, there would surely have been in-
dications and far less openness in his manner.

Nevertheless, it was a nervous meal for everyone except
Brendon and Loring. I sensed wry amusement in Loring,
though he betrayed nothing. Irene seemed so jittery that
Brendon commented on her state, and she blushed miserably. Naomi surfaced only for baleful glances in my direction, but there was tension in her every move. I suspect
that Irene had commanded her silence, or it might have
been she who would have brought everything into the
open.

When I could get away from the dining room, I
escaped to our bedroom upstairs, locked the door and
lay on the bed. Lately it seemed that I could always fall
asleep, as though something in me sought the safety and
escape of the unconscious state. Now I rested until it was

time to get up and meet Keir. At least no one had sought me out, and I was allowed privacy when I wanted it.

When I'd brushed my hair, letting it hang free and long down my back, I went downstairs. Again I had the feeling that I must play this by ear. Keir, too, might be a source of information for me, but he was a man I must be careful not to offend, or he would shut up like a clam.

He was waiting for me in the truck with the panther emblem on the door, and I climbed into the high seat beside him. As we set off up a road that led away from the lake, I found him more friendly than before, a little easier with me. Perhaps he was coming to accept me, just a little.

I'd brought my sketching things along again, only regretful that it wasn't spring, when many more flowers would be blooming. Still, the early fall varieties had their own interest, and white snakeroot grew plentifully on either side of the road.

We followed a trail that led up the cliff on the opposite side of the lake from High Tower, and Keir said Panther Rock was our goal. When we neared the top, he parked the truck by the roadside and we both got out.

"I'd like you to meet a frind of mine," he said, and we climbed a steep hillside, where masses of Queen Anne's lace grew in profusion. Quietly he put a hand on my arm. "Look—over there," he said softly.

The doe and her two fawns were beautiful, their movements leisurely and unalarmed as they fed off shoots and the tender branches of fallen trees. Once the mother looked around at us calmly, but did not take flight, apparently accustomed to the sight of Keir. Without hurry they moved on, until a branch fell in the nearby woods, startling them, and they took off in a flash, showing us their white tails.

"How beautiful they are," I said. "I'm glad I saw them."

He nodded approval of my response, and we moved on until he stopped me again and started to make a curious gobbling sound. In a moment a wild turkey emerged from a thicket and came toward us, his wattles aquiver.

Keir took a packet of corn from his pocket, poured some into his palm and knelt to hold out his hand.

"I brought you something special today," he said. "Help yourself."

With delicate good manners the bird pecked at the kernels and listened courteously to the flow of words addressed to him. I kept very still and he paid no attention to me. When the corn was gone, Keir introduced us.

"This is my friend Hilly-Billy. I think he has a wife back in the woods, but she's timid and I haven't met her yet."

When Keir had taken leave of his friend, we started up through the trees again, following a rough path.

"The road curves around below this rise," he told me. "But when we get to the top you can see everything at once—as you can't from the road."

In a short distance the trees thinned as we came onto a rocky outcropping from which the land dropped away on all sides. At the top of the rise a great stone figure waited for us, and I knew this was Magnus' work again. Almost a part of its natural setting, the granite panther crouched, one paw outstretched, the head alert and watchful, the long tail almost whipping into life. One knew at once that it scented danger and was waiting to pounce. Here was Laurel Mountain's logo in person!

"He's perfect for this place," I said.

The man beside me shrugged. "Maybe. I like the idea of real ones better. They used to come here long ago, you know."

I walked around the stone beast, sensing once more the flow of power Magnus was able to uncover in inanimate rock, as though sinew and muscle lay beneath the surface stone. Yet here again there seemed a sense of threat— power to be unleashed—that I had already seen in his bull. At least there was natural beauty here, unlike that dreadful head I had glimpsed in his workshed.

"It's the view I brought you here to see." Keir sounded impatient with my interest in a stone panther, and I went to stand beside him.

As the full sweep of valley and mountains came into

view, I caught my breath. Across a valley to my right the two winged mountains that I had seen before seemed to thrust themselves into space, while around to my left a tree-filled chasm dropped away in talus to the foot of Laurel Mountain. We were very close to the great mound of stone that held High Tower, and across the chasm the tower itself rose dramatically into the sky above us. Beyond winged mountains on one hand and the tower on the other, the land dropped away into a fertile, apple-growing valley that spread out for miles.

When I'd looked my fill at the tremendous view, I glanced at the white-haired man beside me, his attention caught and held by a scene he knew well. I sensed that he belonged to this place as much as the deer or the turkey or the mountain itself. He must have grown up here, as Magnus' panther had not.

After a moment he remembered me, and when he turned his head to smile I felt a warm rush of satisfaction because he was beginning to accept me, to like me—as perhaps he had never liked or accepted my sister.

"Have you always lived here at Laurel?" I asked.

"Most of my life. I was born down there in the valley in a farmhouse you can see from here. But I came to work and lived at Laurel Mountain when I was a kid. Geoffrey McClain took a fancy to me, and I did most of my growing up here."

"Geoffrey was Brendon's grandfather?"

"Right. I worked for the old man, and Bruce and I grew up together. Brendon's father. I guess you might say I helped to raise Brendon. I can remember this place when the trains came to Kings Landing on the river, and guests drove up the mountain in carriages. Some of those carriages are still preserved down in the Red Barn."

"I know. I sat in one of them this morning."

He went on, his eyes on the tower. "There have been too many changes. Not all for the good. Geoffrey McClain meant to have all these thousands of acres preserved in their wild state, and that's what we've tried to do. Brendon will hold it the way it should be. We can count on him."

"What about Irene? Does she listen to Loring?"

"Irene's changed," he said. "She's gone too much under Loring's thumb. Now maybe you can weigh things in the other direction. Influence her. If she likes you. Does she?"

The question was point-blank and I faltered. "I—I hope she does. She has welcomed me warmly, and she's been more than kind."

"She's a kind woman. She was kind to your sister too—even when she didn't deserve it. But she can be pushed too far. I've seen her get angry once or twice."

I wanted to ask point-blank questions myself, but somehow I didn't dare. Keir was a little like his own wild friends, and too direct an approach might frighten him off. It was better to encourage him to talk in his own way.

"The mountain and the tower are dramatic from this view," I said. "All that rock—as though it had been carved into that round shape, bare and empty right down to the base, with trees still green and thick below the talus. Some of them are beginning to turn. The color will be breath-taking in a little while."

"It's always beautiful around here. In autumn, of course, and in the spring when the mountain laurel blooms around the lake and the shadbushes turn white. And wait till you see the rhododendrons! But it's beautiful in summer green too, and again when there's snow everywhere. I hate ice storms because of the damage they do, but there's hardly anything more beautiful than the woods after an ice storm. You'll come to know all this, Jenny." He paused, his eyes upon me, keen and searching, and his words startled me. "I'm glad your sister never came back. I'm glad you've come in her stead."

I held out my hand gravely. "Thank you. I've wanted you to approve of me. But I didn't come in her stead—I came on my own, for myself."

He nodded agreement as he took my hand in his big one. "Stay and fight," he said strangely. "There's plenty worth fighting for here. But don't go near Magnus. Don't ever go near Magnus again."

"Fight? What do you mean? And what is the matter with Magnus?"

"He fell in love with that woman—that ballet dancer. He isn't over her yet. He could get the notion that she's come back to him in you. So let him stay up there with his rock carving. That's something I've never understood. Me—I like to let the rocks stay as they are—the way nature carved them."

"But his stone bull is marvelous, and so is this panther. You have to admit that."

"Pagan—that bull," he said. "Bull worship's not for me. Or for you, either. Magnus can be dangerous. Brendon doesn't like him. As Brendon's wife, you'd better remember that."

His words disturbed and puzzled me, but I knew I must ask him no more questions. He was silent for a time, looking out across the farming land of the valley, where puffs of cloud shadow made patterns of light and shade. I tried to speak to him of his own world.

"This is good healthy forest at Laurel," I said. "The growth is diversified enough so it should resist pests."

"Right. And we keep it that way without spraying. A healthy tree is more apt to be resistant." He broke off suddenly, his attention on the rocky cliff that dropped away at our feet. "Look, Jenny—down there!"

I saw the great soaring bird in the canyon below us, and as we watched it dropped like a dive bomber after some small prey, snatching it in midair with incredible speed and disappearing onto a rocky ledge out of sight below us.

"That was a falcon!" I cried. "A peregrine falcon! But it's not possible. They're practically extinct here in the East."

"They were," he said, pleased with my recognition. "That's a young one. It's been close to twenty years since we've seen them here. Chemicals and DDT got to them through their food. The strain that used to populate the East is completely gone—because men killed them off. But they're still found in the Arctic and a few other places. A man at the State University in New Paltz has learned how to breed them in captivity, and Cornell's ornithology lab has started raising young birds. They brought us three young ones this summer and installed them in a nest box down there on the cliff. Students stood guard over them till they were old enough to fly and hunt their own food. They'll be migrating south for the winter soon."

The bird was out on the air again, following the currents with wide-spread wings, rising above us now in unbelievable grace.

"I'm glad I saw that," I said. "Thank you for the deer and the turkey and the falcon."

He nodded, pleased, and we followed the path to where it dipped down in a steep drop to the road.

"It's time for me to go back," he said. "You can stay, if you like. You'll be all right if you just follow the road down there. It circles Panther Rock, and then goes back to the hotel."

I watched him striding off toward his truck, and then I climbed down to the road and crossed to another of the little gazebos perched on a rock. When I'd sat down on the bench, I took out my sketching things.

For some time I worked almost contentedly, duplicating on paper the details of tiny snakeroot flowers. The sort of work I did had to be meticulous—each little flower drawn in detail and with great precision. I was more botanist than artist and it was the art created in nature that interested me. If my drawings and paintings were beautiful, it was because my reproduction of nature was exact and had to be beautiful in turn. Perhaps someday they might be used in a classroom. The flowers themselves weren't always available, but in this way I could provide their counterpart for those who wished to study them.

As I worked, I put from my mind Magnus' lack of comment on my sketches. I had wanted him to approve, yet his silence had told me that he didn't, and I wasn't sure why. Most people liked my little paintings. But Magnus was an artist, and praise from him would have pleased me. No matter—I'd never pretended to be more than I was.

I worked in deep concentration until I realized that a
rosy glow lay over the land and distant mountains, tinting
my paper. The sun was dipping toward the western
Catskills and I would have to hurry back to the hotel. For
a little while, as I worked with my sketching, I'd experienced the surcease from concern that such activity
always gave me. As the wild flowers themselves were
serene, so I became serene when I was reproducing them
in my sketchbook. But as soon as I put my equipment
away in my carrying box, all that was disturbing swept
back to engulf me.

What had Keir meant when he'd said "Stay and fight"?
Of course I would stay. But whom was I to fight? The
words meant nothing. The moment I ceased to distract
myself, worry took over and grew stronger.

Ariel had spoiled everything. There was no way in
which I could put the thought of her entirely from me.
Wherever I walked, her light feet had been there before
mine. Whatever beauty I looked upon, her eyes had already seen. Had she come to this very spot with Brendon,
perhaps? Had he found time for her when she'd stayed
here?

But I mustn't think of that. It couldn't be. Magnus was
the man who had attracted her, and I could see very well,
knowing her, how that could have happened. Magnus
was like his own stone bull—all male power and aggressiveness. The very traits Ariel would respond to. She was
always Europa, waiting to be violated by Zeus in the guise
of a bull.

Yet Brendon had known her, and he had not told me.
And now it was growing late.

That was why I was running down the trail, hurrying
away from Panther Rock and its tremendous views, hurrying as well from my own pursuing thoughts, my own
fear of something unknown and terrifying that I couldn't
escape and must rush toward as though carried by a
wind, like the falcon.

In me there was a yearning and an urgency to be with

Brendon. I knew I must reach him *now* and beseech him to answer all my questions. I could put this off no longer. Just to be with him, to be close to him, would reassure me. I could bear no more postponement.

7

But "now" was not possible because he was gone again. More business had taken him elsewhere. Always away from me. This time it was some new contract for repairing an old wing of the hotel. I understood only vaguely what Irene told me. I knew only that I had seen my husband all too little since I'd come to Mountain House. At mealtimes, perhaps, and at night when he returned to my arms, and words were hushed between us. Just twice had he walked with me on the mountain. Because it was too painful for him to remember walking with her? Too painful to be always avoiding my questions?

Listlessly I put on a dress of celery green with a drifting skirt, and a gold necklace that dressed it up for evening. It was a dress Brendon liked.

But he didn't come to our rooms, and he did not appear at the gathering before dinner. In fact, he didn't come to the table at all. Irene seemed troubled and evasive, Naomi had turned sorrowful—but her sorrow had nothing to do with me. I knew for whom she grieved. Loring, to give him credit, tried to cheer us all, tried to instigate conversational gambits, but he had little co-operation, and I still had the sense of his being an amused spectator.

After dinner I got away from them as quickly as I could, yet the thought of sitting again in my room, waiting endlessly for my husband, didn't appeal to me. It might be better tonight if he could return to an empty room, in which, for once, I shouldn't be waiting for him. But where could I go?

I walked beside the lake for a time, but the air had turned cold and the sky overcast, so there was no moon or stars. The water lay like black glass, reflecting only the dark sky, and at one end the multiple lights of the hotel. Currents lapped in deep caverns along the shore and the whispering voices seemed more ominous than ever. Had they whispered to Ariel? I wondered. Had they warned her of coming disaster, as they seemed to warn me? Or would she have heard them? And hearing, would she have laughed?

I could almost hear her laughter echoing over the lake, as once it must have done. Surprisingly husky, her laughter had been, a little like her speaking voice, which never matched the light airiness of dancing feet.

When I left the lake, I walked around the near end of the hotel, and went on past dark tennis courts until I came to steps that led uphill. I was wandering idly, so when I saw lights above, I climbed the steps, merely killing time. In the clearing beyond the steps a house shone white in shadowy artificial light, and there were more steps that mounted to a broad, old-fashioned veranda. One end of it had been screened, and rattan furniture still lingered there for summer lounging. A nameplate gleamed beside the door, and in the overhead light on the veranda I could read it: *McClain*.

So this was where Irene and Loring and Naomi lived. Where Brendon had lived as well, until I came and we'd been given our own private suite in the hotel. My first impulse was to turn quickly away, to avoid any further contact with a family that held so many secrets against me.

And yet . . . ? I remembered Irene's increasingly nervous manner tonight, her obvious concern lest I open up some subject she feared to broach. Perhaps because she didn't trust herself, if that should happen? So why—since Brendon was avoiding me—should I not talk to his mother?

With new resolution I went up the steps and put my finger to the bell. No one came to the door, but I could hear someone inside playing a piano. That would be Naomi again, probably. Yes—Stravinsky. The music from *Firebird*. How she was haunted by Ariel!

In an unwanted flash of memory, I could see my sister's face with its special *Firebird* make-up, the eyebrows winging upward and bright feathers crowning her hair. No—I wanted none of Stravinsky tonight, and I was beginning to think Naomi a little deranged. Yet I must still try to see Irene, and I pressed the bell again.

This time the music stopped, and I heard running feet in the hall. The door was pulled open and Naomi stood looking out at me, her eyes alight with something a little frightening in its avidity. Her tiny person was enveloped in the fleece lounging robe of Chinese red that had once belonged to Ariel, and which I had given to Irene.

"Come in," she said, and flung the door wide.

"No—no—" I tried not to falter. "I wanted to see Irene. If she isn't home—"

"No one is home but me. Come in."

There was something compelling about her tone of voice that I had no will to resist. I stepped over the sill past her and into a wide, gracious hall that bisected the house. She flitted ahead of me, holding up the trailing folds of the robe, lest she trip over them, and stopped to open a door at the rear of the hall.

"In here," she said. "Where we can talk. No one will interrupt us here. No one comes here unless I invite them."

Still wanting to run away, yet unable to, I stepped into the small, warm sitting room. Wood burned brightly on a hearth graced by a white marble mantelpiece above, and Naomi gestured me to the chintz-covered sofa drawn before it. To my relief, she did not sit beside me, but took a small rocking chair placed to the right of the fire.

Without looking too closely, I had an impression of red all about the room. Redbuds in the wallpaper, wine red draperies at the windows, a red and gold lacquer box on the coffee table, the red bindings of books, a deep-piled, red figured rug before the fire. And Naomi in red fleece.

Inevitably, my eyes were drawn to stark black and white above the mantel—the photograph I had been immediately aware of, and was trying not to see. In spite of myself I shivered. How well I knew that picture. The crossed feet *en pointe,* the despairing gesture of the hands, the intensity of longing in every line of her body in that full, old-fashioned dress, eyes closed, the stamp of agony in the face.

Naomi rocked in her chair, squeaking a little, unaware of the sound as she watched me.

"She was the best Hagar since Nora Kaye," she said softly. "In Kaye's time no one else dared dance *Pillar of Fire*. Not until Ariel Vaughn did it."

"I thought you only saw her dance once on the stage?"

"That's true. But there are books—all those books with their descriptions and photographs. She's in them, as you know." She waved her hand toward a low shelf and I knew by sight the titles on some of the book spines—well-known standards on ballet. I could almost pity her for this single-minded worship, this vicarious living she must have done through Ariel. Perhaps I could even understand a little.

"Did you ever dance yourself?" I asked.

"Of course. I used to long to be a dancer. I even took lessons as a child. But my parents wouldn't let me go on. My father forbade it. So I only danced in my head. I knew all the steps, but I could only dance them in my imagination."

I could understand that too. I had done it myself—moving so beautifully, so gracefully in my mind, as I never could in life.

Naomi rocked again. "It was all make-believe until that first time Ariel came here to rest, and I got to know her, became her friend. I gave her this room because she wanted a place of her own. I let her fix it up to suit herself." Something insidious and sly seemed to come into

Naomi's voice. "Now it can be your room—just as it was your sister's. You're welcome to come here any time, Jenny, just as she used to do. You'll always find her here."

She paused as though waiting for some utterance of gratitude from me, but I said nothing and she went on.

"So much of my life stopped being make-believe when Ariel came. It was all real then. As real as this robe that Irene was going to throw away because it had belonged to her. How often I've seen Ariel wear this very robe. Do you remember how she loved red? That's why there is so much red in this room. I let her do what she wanted with it. Of course she used to wear this red fleece for Brendon because he bought it for her. No wonder you wanted to be rid of it. It must have been a terrible shock to see you in it. How sickening that must have been for him!"

It was difficult to get my breath and the heat from the fire seemed to stifle me. Above the mantel the closed eyes of the photograph were the closed eyes of death. But I was not sure who had died—was it Ariel, or was it I?

Naomi left her rocker and came to sit close to me on the sofa—too close, so that I edged away.

"You didn't know, did you? He never told you. What a liar he has always been! I'm not so angry with you now, because I know what he is doing to you. He never loved anyone but her. I used to give them this room sometimes when they wanted to be alone, and there was nowhere else to go. So many things here are hers, because she wanted them here to please him. Sometimes she would tell me what it was like afterward. The sofa was too small for them, of course. But they would lie on that very rug before the fire and make love. It must have been beautiful, beautiful—because everything she did was beautiful."

I wanted to run out of the room. I wanted to fly from the sound of her tormenting voice, yet I couldn't move.

"Oh, she was careful not to make a scandal, of course. This is a big house and there's a back door. So no one knew when they were here. No one but me. Or if anyone guessed, they didn't dare say anything. Not to Brendon. Sometimes I kept watch. He wanted to marry her, but she couldn't make up her mind. Sometimes she'd say 'Yes,' and sometimes 'No.' And then she went away and died, and it was too late."

Silence lay heavy upon the room, except for the crackle of wood in the fireplace. There were words I must speak, denials I must make—but no words would come. Shock has a numbing effect and while there was a sickness at the pit of my stomach and my hands were trembling, I could find no words.

"How he has fooled himself!" Naomi ran on. "As soon as he saw you, he tried to make it all come to life again. He tried to bring *her* to life again—through you." A whipping of scorn in her words told me what a poor try she thought that had been.

This time I managed to speak. "But it was Magnus she loved—Magnus she was involved with—"

"Later." Naomi smiled as brightly as though she gave me some lovely gift of knowledge. "Because of course she couldn't stay with one man forever. Magnus is a primitive, and so was Ariel in some ways, for all her sophistication. She grew tired of Brendon's importunities —how could she marry anyone, when she belonged to the world? So the last time she came here she stayed with Magnus in his cabin."

"With Floris there?" I managed.

"Oh, Ariel was a guest, of course. Floris was too stupid to see what was coming. And when it happened, it was too late. Magnus can be pretty overwhelming. She told me about him, too. She called him her Zeus."

Somehow I pushed myself up from the sofa and walked to the door. Naomi went back to her squeaking rocker, still murmuring to herself.

At the door I turned and stared at her. "At least *you* have never mixed me up with Ariel," I said.

Her head came up, firelight touching frizzled gray, and there was venom in her eyes. "Of course not! Though you were a shock to me at first sight. Even though Brendon had warned us, you were a shock because you look so much like her. He wrote Irene that no one was to tell you about Ariel until he got around to it. Now you can go back to where you came from and stop trying to take her place. Why don't you just go away tomorrow? He's already discovered his mistake. Don't stay until he hates you."

I put a hand on the doorjamb to steady myself. "I am not going away. For all I know you may be making up everything you've told me."

She flew out of the rocker and stood with her back to the fire, staring at me across the room. I didn't know what her look meant, and I didn't stay to find out, but ran down the hall and out the front door. In the lighted area outside I gulped great drafts of cold air in an effort to clear away the numbness, the fog that seemed to engulf me.

I don't believe her, I told myself as I walked toward the huge, lighted bulk of the hotel. *She's not to be trusted and I don't believe anything she's said.*

But I did believe. Conviction lay heavy as a stone upon my spirit. Inside the Mountain House I flitted through the corridors and up the stairs, not waiting for an elevator, where I might see someone, have to speak, have to say "Good evening." My feet made no sound on the red carpet as I fled down the fourth-floor hall and put my key in the lock. A haven. I wanted a haven. Time alone, so I could fight off my confusion and fright, make some sort of sense out of the things Naomi had said, most of which were undoubtedly lies.

But they weren't lies. I know that now as I lie in bed alone, with Brendon gone and my marriage shattered. Where am I to turn? What am I to do? What can I do but think?

The moment I opened the door, I knew he was back. His jacket lay over a chair, and from the bathroom came the sounds of his showering. Panic struck me and I backed into the hall, closing the door softly. Because how could I stay when I was so little ready to face him? I couldn't bear to see him now.

There seemed no place to go in this vast building, yet

my feet led me without will and I found myself following the narrow corridor into the old section, where once Ariel Vaughn had come to do her practicing.

Along this section of hall there were no lights, and the line of doors was closed upon empty rooms. No one would find me here. I wouldn't have to face Brendon when he came out of his bath. My hand followed the wall, guiding me past closed doors until I found myself in the empty room at the end. Here the blackness lessened because there were windows over the lake and the night outside was not as black as this room.

Carefully I felt my way. Piano keys gave a faint plink under my fingers before I found the wall and followed it back to the door until I touched a light switch. Clustered lights in the ceiling came on. She had danced here—Ariel. And she had betrayed me once again.

No—that wasn't true. I had to be honest. Brendon and Magnus had both been hers first. I was only trailing along in the path of a shooting star as I'd always done. I had no right to Brendon. I had no right to judge Ariel—but only Brendon. The betrayal was his.

Behind the piano soiled pink toe shoes were all that remained of the beauty that had danced in this room. Moving with a strange compulsion, I threw off the coat I'd put on over my green dress and sat down on the piano bench. Very carefully I put on her shoes, wrapping the pink ribbons back and forth around foot and ankle, tight and firm. Our feet had been identical in size since we'd grown up. Then I walked flatfooted to the *barre* where she had exercised and took hold of it with one hand, raising myself on the blocked satin toes. Lamb's wool that she had packed into the shoes cushioned my toes, and I already knew how it felt to be *en pointe*. I'd had all those ballet classes when I was young, and I'd tried on her shoes more than once when we were both grown and she was famous. As though they might carry magic in them like the Red Shoes of the movie ballet.

Not that I understood what I was doing in that blind moment. I attempted a few *petits battements*, remembering the Swan Queen's beating of foot against ankle in the second act. I did all the positions of the feet, forcing myself to pain, since my feet and legs were in no way trained to such placement. I went up and out in a simple *échappé*, not quite so awkward as might be expected, though it hurt a lot. Then I tried vainly to travel out across the floor in little *bourrée* steps, *sur les pointes,* the pain exquisite, till I dropped back on the floor.

Across the room a sudden glimpse of the mirror made me freeze with my arms overhead—freeze in shock. For *she* was there, dancing in the glass. I moved and Ariel moved, watching me gravely. The skirt of my green dress floated to half-calf, and tonight my hair was pinned into a low knot at the back—like hers.

"Are you trying to *be* your sister?" Brendon's voice asked from the doorway.

I whirled about, caught in terrible disarray. He stood in the doorway watching me, dressed in his navy robe and slippers, and I saw the shocked expression on his face.

"I've seen Naomi," I said. "I know."

"Take off those shoes and come back to the room," he ordered me coldly. "It's time we talked."

I went to the bench and bent over, untying the ribbons, hidding my face from him. Time? It was long past time. The time he should have told me was when we first met in that Opera lobby in New York.

When I'd slipped into my own shoes again, and raised my head, the doorway was empty. He had gone.

With slow fingers that hardly knew what they were doing, I pulled the tortoise-shell pins from my hair and let it flow down my back, as though it might remove me further from my sister to let it hang loose. I left her shoes on the floor, pink ribbons trailing out of them, and walked with feet as heavy as lead down the dark hallway toward light at the end.

He had left the door of our sitting room open, and I walked in and closed it softly behind me. Brendon stood in the tower section of enclosed windows, with his back to me, looking up toward the light on the mountain. The door made a slight sound as it closed, but he did not turn, and a fierce anger that grew out of pain began to rise in me. Was *I* to be treated as though all the fault were mine, as though *I* had lied and deceived and cheated?

"You lied to me from the first, didn't you?" I challenged and heard my voice uttering words as cold as his. "You told me you didn't care for ballet."

He spoke over his shoulder. "I didn't lie. I've never cared for ballet. Only twice did I ever see her dance. I knew her here on the mountain, not in her ballet world."

"But you loved her. You've never gotten over loving her! You came to me in the lobby that day because I looked like her and you've been trying ever since to put me in her place, to bring *her* back to life."

This time my words pierced whatever defense he had raised against me and he turned sharply. "Yes. You reminded me of her. She was dead and it's true I came to you in pain."

"No wonder everything went so fast!" I cried. "From that first moment it was Ariel you loved. And you just went on loving her! You held me and you loved *her*. I can't tell you how contemptible I think you are."

His eyes had turned dark blue with fury. "I'll move into another room tonight. Tomorrow I'll have the limousine take you back to New York, if you want to go."

"No! You needn't bother. I'm staying."

He stared at me in angry silence.

"I mean to stay until I find out the truth about who was to blame for Floris Devin's death. I'm not going to leave my sister's name with any stain of suspicion on it. I know what she was like, but she was never a murderer."

"Then you're wasting your time." He went into the bedroom and I followed as he began to pick up his clothes, his shaving things, his shoes.

"You're wasting your time," he repeated, "if you think you're going to exonerate her. She went to Magnus, didn't she? And she wanted Floris' death."

"Are you the one who has been saying these things about her? How could you when you loved her?" My fury was rising out of control. "How despicable! There aren't any words— Please go as quickly as you can."

He went even more quickly than I asked, and when the door had closed firmly behind him, I turned as limp as an empty sack and dropped to the floor because there was no strength left in my legs. Perhaps deep inside me there had been a tiny, forlorn hope that he would deny his love for Ariel, that he would tell me that he'd loved me just for myself. I knew better now—and I hated him fiercely, hoping the fire of my hatred would burn out my love.

For a long time I sat on the floor beside the bed with my head on my arm. My eyes were dry again, burned out with anger, and my throat was choked with tears that could not be released. I don't know how much time passed, but after a while I got up and went through the doors onto the balcony. The wind was cold on my face and I drank in the chill to let it freeze away the heat of the anger that burned in me. Down on paths near the lake couples moved together—so close together—as I had once moved with my love. But now there was only emptiness and pain and loss. Something worse than loss through death. Because what I had lost I had never really had. It wasn't me he had loved, but always Ariel.

So why must I stay here and torture myself when she had destroyed my life, however unwittingly? Yet I knew it was because it had been unwitting on Ariel's part. I'd never known Brendon until she was dead. Perhaps too I must punish myself for my sister's death. If I had gone to her, she would have lived, and none of this would have happened. I wouldn't be standing now on this balcony. I wouldn't have lain in Brendon's arms for all these weeks. I would never have known what it felt like to be loved as he had loved me. In a sense, she had given me something I had never known before, and would never know again.

What if I should do what she had done? What if I should just go down there to that cold, waiting water and give myself to it? If I did, *I* would make no phone calls hoping for rescue. I would seek oblivion gladly. Anything to turn off the pain.

But there was another voice inside me that made me listen:

Stop it! You've been a fool, but you needn't go on being one. Ariel had all the courage in the world when it came to her work, her dancing. But she had none at all when it came to living. If she didn't immediately get what she wanted, she went to pieces. You're not like that. If adversity makes anyone strong, it has made you strong. You're not Ariel, and you'll live. You're not the first woman who has been betrayed. Others have suffered before you, and most of them lived and found something happier, something better. There are other men. You'll meet one in time. There are men who are good and honest. In the meantime, stay long enough to find out what you can about Floris' death. Pay your debt to Ariel.

The inner voice had its way. I turned out the sitting-room lights, since there was no longer anything to fear in the dark. Then I went into the bedroom, flung off my clothes, turned off more lights and got into bed as quickly as I could, shivering a little, until my body warmed the bed.

There would always be cold beds from now on.

That too I thrust away as I lay there thinking. Always the cure for anything is to plan. Plan some sort of action. Anything that will give the next day purpose. It doesn't even need to be meaningful purpose, but just something that will keep the body moving, the mind more or less occupied. I knew now what I would do.

I would climb the mountain again and visit Magnus. At least he hadn't deceived me. He had been open and honest, even when it was unflattering. So I would say to him, "If you want me to sit on the back of your stone bull and pose for you, I will." And perhaps he would talk to me—tell me things I could use to help me understand more about Ariel.

With that settled, I fell eventually into troubled drowsing. Not until it was nearly morning did I fall deeply asleep, as though I'd been drugged, so that it was ten o'clock before I awakened. The dining room would long be closed, but I knew there was a small coffee shop as an annex to the lobby store. When I was ready in slacks and a sweater, my handbag slung over my shoulder, I went downstairs and sat at a tiny table where I drank my coffee and munched on a doughnut.

I'd seen nothing of the family since I had come downstairs, and I avoided the corridor where the offices were, letting myself out on the lake side, hurrying toward the paths that led uphill, so that trees could quickly hide me from the hotel. I had no idea what Brendon would decide to do. Certainly our estrangement could not be hidden for long from his mother and Loring and Naomi.

Every direction my thoughts took carried me into pain, but there was no help for that. Perhaps I would eventually break down and cry desperately for a while, but I was still staving that time off. My mother had always been annoyed when I cried. Only Ariel's tears were justified. What could *I* have to cry about?

This morning I chose the steeper, shorter way up the mountain. I needn't go to the top, since there were side paths along the way that led to the cabin in the woods. Determinedly, my eyes registered and identified as I walked, so that my gaze wouldn't turn inward. Once more I had brought my sketch kit along, though I didn't stop now to use it.

In the spring there would be lady's slippers here, and arbutus blooming. Butterflies and bees would be busy. Now woodbine climbed over a broken stone wall, and with the chill nights the trees were turning yellow and red and rusty brown. From among the stones a chipmunk rose on his hind legs to study me with bright, beady eyes, before vanishing more quickly than my sight could follow.

When I found a path leading upward at a right angle to my trail, I followed it until I came to a quiet glen, where maple trees hung their scarlet banners all around. I could still find solace in such a place. With its offering of peace and growing beauty, I could drug my mind with forgetfulness.

Then I climbed again, through pitch pine and white pine, upward to the wider road that led to High Tower. Here I had to retrace my steps in order to find the cutoff to the Glen of the Bull, as I had begun to call it in my mind.

Again I found satisfaction in what was happening in these forests. Though some of the chestnut oaks were dying, their places were being taken by white and gray birch, and soft and striped maple, plus hemlocks and other evergreens. I came upon a beautiful larch tree, with a few of its rosettes of needles left, the others already shed.

Distraction, I thought. Anything for distraction. Because the one thing I must not do was to think about Brendon. It was my sister I must think about now, and only about her. I had an everlasting debt to Ariel, and I could at least pay it in some small part. My feelings toward Brendon—an unhappy mixture of love and anger and pain—must not be allowed to distract me from the one purpose that now kept me here.

This time I seemed to come upon the bull even more suddenly than before. Perhaps because of my effort not to see the woods for the trees. He stood in the center of his grassy ring, seeming to paw the earth in all his impatient power—all his male aggressiveness—as though he might toss me onto his horns, toss me onto his back and go galloping away with me, as Ariel's bull did in her ballet. How she must have delighted in this place, delighted in Magnus, who had created so primitive a creature. What had Keir said, sounding scornful?—"bull worship"? Well, why not in this primeval setting?

This morning the woods did not ring with the sound of mallet on steel, and when I left the bull and found my way to the cabin, I saw blue smoke rising from the chimney, and caught the fragrant scent of burning wood. The door stood open and there was no knocker. I mounted the steps and called out.

"Is anyone home?"

Magnus came to greet me, wearing a green lumberjack shirt open at the throat to show a tuft of red hair, his corduroy pants worn and faded, wrinkled from recent washing. His smile showed all those dazzling white teeth again, making me a little uncomfortable with its welcome —as everything about him made me uncomfortable. That bull in the woods was, I suspected, a projection of himself, and I had never quite liked such overpowering evidence of male vitality. Brendon was male enough—but there was a tempering in him. Only I must not think of Brendon.

"Good morning," I said.

As usual, he didn't return my greeting. "So you've forgiven me?"

I shook my head, staying where I was. "No. And I shan't. I don't like that sort of treatment. But I've decided to overlook it, providing it never happens again. I'd like to offer myself as a model."

His smile vanished, but he stepped back from the doorway. "Come in then and tell me why."

There was a certain hesitance in me about entering his house again, though I had no fear of him today. In his way, I sensed that he could be a kind man, though sometimes imperious, so I thrust back my own hesitation and walked past him through the doorway. A fire of great logs burned on the hearth, the flames crackling and leaping, sending showers of sparks up the stone chimney. The fire drew me and I set down my sketch box and went to it to warm my hands. Memory tricked me again, as it probably would for a long while, and I thought of Naomi's little sitting room, and the red figured hearth rug before her fire. Had Ariel lain on this rug too, making love to this bull of a man? And how could she, after Brendon?

"You're worried," he said. "Sit down and warm yourself. Some days I light a fire just for company. Do you want coffee?"

I shook my head. Yes, he would need company in this empty cabin. He had lost two women, almost at the same time.

"All right," he said. "Sit and think awhile, and then tell me why you've come. I've left our dishes since last night, and I'm just washing up."

I made no female offer to help him, and I knew he didn't expect it. It was likely that he was not a role-playing man, and I wondered unexpectedly if I might really be able to talk to him. Then I dismissed the thought. There was no one—no one anywhere to whom I could talk openly and honestly. Certainly not to anyone who had loved Ariel.

Behind me I heard the splashing and rinsing and gurgling of water, and all the while I sat in a stupor watching the fire, grateful for its hypnotic spell. It was best to watch the flames and think about nothing. Empty myself.

Eventually he finished, and when he'd left stacked dishes on the drainboard to dry themselves, he came to join me at the hearth before leaping flames. He didn't bother with one of the crude wooden chairs, but sat on the Indian-patterned hearthrug and crossed his legs with their laced boots that came above the ankles.

"Silences must always come to an end," he said. "Have you decided what to tell me, and how much?"

How green his eyes were, I thought, when I turned my head to meet his look. Green, with firelight in them, and how red his hair, with firelight striking into its natural blaze.

"I've come to bribe you," I said. "If you will tell me about my sister, I will pose for you."

He gave me a long look that seemed to see deeply into me. "I'll tell you anything I can. Though shouldn't you go to Brendon first? I can tell by your face that you know they were in love. You've changed since yesterday. Yesterday you were still happy, even though you'd discovered that she was here. Today you've met with despair."

"Not despair," I denied. "Never despair as long as there is something I can do."

"About the rift between you and Brendon?"

"No. That can't be mended. It's not your affair and I don't want to talk about it. I want to talk about Ariel. Naomi says she came to you."

He nodded, waiting, and his look seemed open, unguarded.

"You were in love with her too. You knew her well."

I made statements and his silence denied nothing.

"Would you have left your wife for her?"

"What Floris and I had when we were young was over a long time ago. She knew that. She knew there had been other women."

"But not one who came and lived in your house. How could she endure that?"

"She didn't mean to. That was the whole problem. Floris couldn't recognize that Ariel was quicksilver—that no man could ever grasp and hold her. Floris had only to wait her out. But she wouldn't do that. She was going to blow everything sky-high."

"What do you mean? What was there to blow?"

"I'm not sure." He got up to poke a log in the fire and then sat down again. "She had some scheme in mind, but I don't know what it was. It doesn't matter. She had to be stopped—and she was."

I'd been staring at the fire, and now I turned my head quickly to see a calm assurance in his face—an acceptance of simple fact that shocked me a little. He was indeed a primitive—like that stone bull in the woods. Yet surely not evil? Quickly I put from my mind the memory of that redstone face with the glaring eyes and grimacing mouth.

"Someone murdered your wife," I said.

His smile was grim and there was no flashing of teeth. "No one knows that for sure. It could have been an accident. A stroke of fate."

"From some punishing god?"

"Perhaps."

"It could have been an accident," I said. "And I'd gladly accept that if Loring hadn't said that accusations were being whispered against Ariel."

Again, Magnus waited.

"Don't you know that her presence on that rock was concealed from the police? Don't you know—"

"Of course I know." His tone was suddenly harsh. "I threw all my weight into persuading the family to leave Ariel out of it. For once, they listened to me. I didn't want to see her dragged through an investigation. She wasn't strong enough to stand up to anything like that."

"Ariel was the strongest human being I've ever known."

"In her work as a dancer, yes. Physically. And strong of will. But when it came to trouble—no."

So he understood this about her too.

Pain rushed through me. Pain because of Brendon—which I must deny. Pain because of Ariel—which I could give voice to.

"It was my fault she died," I said dully. "I've told you that. She phoned me to come to her. But she'd done that so many times before. She had cost me jobs because I dropped everything and ran to her. So this time I wouldn't. And she took those pills and died."

There was a long silence and I didn't dare to meet his eyes. I didn't want him to condemn me. When he spoke it was strangely, with words that chilled my blood.

"So now you know what murder feels like, Jenny McClain."

I tried to swallow and choked. He went calmly to the sink and ran water into a glass, brought it to me, stood above me while I drank.

"That's a horrible thing to say!" I cried, when I'd managed to empty the glass.

"It's no worse than what you've been saying to yourself, is it? And perhaps better to say it aloud."

"But it's—brutal—when it comes from someone else."

"I meant it to be brutal," he said.

He continued to stand above me in all his massive size and strength, and for the first time a tiny quiver of fear went through me. I didn't know enough about this man. I didn't know what motivated him.

"Why?" I said. "Why should you want to hurt me any more than I'm hurting myself?"

"It might be necessary. But you haven't come to the real point yet. The real point of this—bribe—you're offering me. If you're breaking off with Brendon, why are you staying on? Why all this trumped-up interest in Floris?"

"I'm trying to tell you! If the police come into it again and Ariel's name is smeared in the papers—oh, I won't have it! I've got to spare my mother that, and spare the love that people everywhere feel for my sister."

"You want the legend kept unsullied? Is that it?"

"Of course. I won't stand by and let something ugly happen. I'm going to find out who was behind it. I'm going to expose whoever is really guilty."

He answered me quietly. "But it was Ariel who stood on that boulder. If there was any guilt, it was hers, and that's what you may be exposing. That's why I've said things you've termed brutal. Because I wanted you to feel some sympathy and understanding for your sister."

"But she *wasn't* a murderer!"

He looked at me with that green, calm gaze that accepted what I couldn't possibly accept.

"No!" I cried. "It's not possible. She might do something like that in sudden anger, not meaning the outcome. But Loring says that the boulder was fixed so that it would roll easily. He says he has proof that it was made ready to roll. So that Ariel—or anyone else—coming unwittingly onto it would cause it to fall. Though how it was arranged that Floris would be below, I don't know."

Magnus walked about the room, suddenly angry. "I thought you were imagining things yesterday. How do you mean that stone was 'fixed'? I don't believe it."

"Would you rather believe it was Ariel?"

He came back to face me. "I do believe it was Ariel. She was furious with Floris. They had a blowup. If Floris had killed Ariel, I wouldn't have been surprised. As it happens, it was the other way around. Floris could have been lured to the place in some way, and Ariel could have waited for her above."

"No!" I was vehement. "How can you say that if you ever loved her?"

"I loved her as she really was."

"I won't listen to this. I thought you might help me. But the things you've said are unspeakable. I don't believe them, and I won't listen."

"Because you have a guilty conscience, Jenny McClain? It's not so much that you'd like to clear your sister as it is that you want to be able to live with yourself. Isn't that it?"

I would listen to nothing more and I ran to the door

and pulled it open. He was after me in a moment and his great hand on my arm made me helpless to move.

"Oh, no—you're forgetting something. There was a bargain—remember? If I would talk about your sister, you would pose for me. So now you're going to start posing. You're going to stay and start posing for me right now."

I had the feeling that he would keep me here if he chose, no matter what I might say or do, so I gave up and went limp in his hands.

8

I have found the burial ground. It is hidden away in the woods on a road with a chain across it, not open to visitors. I would never have discovered it if Magnus hadn't sent me here.

The day has warmed and this is a quiet, enchanted place. I walk among the old stones and read the names aloud, liking the company of my voice. The first McClains who came to Laurel Mountain, who gave it its name, are buried here, but Geoffrey McClain, who came later, has the largest stone. His son Bruce must have seen to that, just as he saw to it that the tower on the mountain was a memorial to his father.

There are other names on the family tree that I have yet to learn. Or perhaps will never learn now, since this will be my home no longer. Brendon will someday sleep here, but I will not be by his side in death, any more than I can be in life. But I try not to think of Brendon as I walk on around the small enclosure.

It is a mountain cemetery and the fence around it is made of stones gathered from the hillside. Small animals can come and go here as they please, finding it a friendly place to sun themselves. There was a woodchuck here when I came through the gate, sitting up on fat haunches, his jaw munching rapidly on a handful of greens. He gave me a look of that curious disdain an interloper deserves, and waddled off when I appeared. There is still a chipmunk flirting with me from behind a granite headstone, not particularly afraid, but not completely trusting either.

Not all of the stones bear the name of McClain and I am sure that those long associated with Laurel Mountain may also have been brought here to rest, where the mountain slopes gently toward the east, and sunrise must touch the stones with gold every morning. Except for the exposed side, with its distant view, hemlocks grow all around, dripping green fronds in a solid enclosure beyond the stone fence. In one shady corner ferns grow undisturbed. My mind gives me the name automatically. *Osmunda cinnamomea*—cinnamon fern.

It is easy to identify the one grave that waits for its stone. That stone that Magnus Devin is preparing so painstakingly in his backyard studio. He showed me his further work today. He has been abrading and polishing its face, making it ready for the carving to be engraved on its surface. I asked him what words he would put there, and he told me curtly that he would carve her name and the dates of her birth and death. Nothing else. No "beloved wife of . . ." Of course not.

I sit beside the pile of earth that has not yet fully settled as the other graves have done. Grass is growing sparsely up its sides, but no one has brought flowers here lately, and it has a neglected air that makes me feel a strange pity for a woman so unloved.

The sun warms me and I sit here almost somnolent, thinking back over words that were spoken in Magnus' cabin, and of that strange time when I had gone with him to the Glen of the Bull to keep my promise and pose.

When we reached the glen, the huge stone figure seemed to be waiting for us, pawing the earth in perpetual fury, and I was caught up once more in admiration.

"He's tremendous," I said. "Did you carve him from a rock you found here on the mountain?"

"Of course not." Magnus dismissed my ignorance. "I had a fresh block of granite brought here from the quarry.

Weathered stone develops a skin that's hard to work. I liked the experience—getting into the stone to discover him."

"Has he a name?"

"Only the obvious one Ariel gave him. Zeus. Inappropriate, of course."

"Why inappropriate?"

"Because he's a sacrificial bull. Whether by one of the old religions, or in the ring, he would be sacrificed. Last May Ariel wove a chain of daisies for his neck in the old way. But she was the one who died."

His voice held no emotion, yet I knew how much he suppressed.

"Why do you stay here?" I asked. "Couldn't you find a place with fewer unhappy memories?"

"I have such a place waiting for me," he admitted, setting out his tools. "I've a few acres over in Pennsylvania. I'll go there someday. It's my own land—not leased like this."

"Then what holds you here?"

"My father, mainly. He couldn't live anywhere else, and I need to stay around and look out for him."

I couldn't imagine anyone who needed looking after less than Keir Devin.

"I'm all he has left," Magnus went on, "however much he disapproves of me at times. But he can't be uprooted. So I'll wait awhile."

I liked him for that, but I couldn't put my warming toward him into words.

"What do you want me to do?" I asked, approaching the bull.

"I'll sketch you first on his back," he told me. "I'll make drawings from several angles, and then you can leave if you like. I'll have to decide about what material I'll use. Perhaps marble—if I can find the right piece. I do have some, and the block itself will determine the size."

All I needed to do just then was to climb onto the bull's back and let him pose me there. This time he made no rude gesture of picking me up, but stood back politely, albeit with a green gleam in his eyes that I didn't altogether like, watching as I stepped from stone to head, between the horns, and stood again upon that broad back.

"Tell me about Ariel's costume," he said. "You're all wrong, of course, in pants. What did she wear for *Europa?*"

"Not a tutu," I told him. "Flowing layers that clung and parted when she moved. Shades of green, from dark to very light, and falling to her knees. Semi-Grecian, I suppose. The lady was daughter to the king of Phoenicia."

"She should have worn purple," Magnus said gruffly. "Royal purple to honor the bull. To honor royal Zeus."

"Purple was for Romans. And I don't think Europa cared much about honoring him when he was carrying her off by force. He swam across the sea to Crete, didn't he, while she clung to his back?"

"All maidens should be carried off by force the first time," Magnus said, walking around the bull while I stood awkwardly on the creature's back.

I refused to be outraged by his words, since I was beginning to understand that outrage was Magnus' stock in trade, and I meant to say nothing to encourage him.

"I think you'll need to lie down up there," he said after walking around us twice. "Let's see how graceful you can be."

I lowered myself to lie on one side, with my arm reaching toward the lowered head with its wicked horns.

"No," Magnus said. "Don't sprawl."

His mind's eye was giving him Ariel, I knew, and there was no way in which Ariel could make an awkward move. Vainly I tried to improve my position, feeling ridiculous and rebellious again, and wondering why I had ever let myself in for this. What I had wanted from him in return hadn't been forthcoming, so perhaps we were neither of us getting the best of the bargain.

When he'd set his sketch block and pencil down on a rock, he came over and rearranged me on the bull's back, his hands surprisingly light when he wasn't manhandling me, his touch firm but not rough as he pushed one leg out along the back with the toe pointed, the other knee bent and drawn beneath me, my arms flung toward the horns in a gesture of entreaty.

"Forget about Jenny McClain," he said. "Forget about Ariel. You are a woman being carried away against her will and full of fear and grief. You're entreating him to let you go. You're putting your whole soul into that entreaty."

Fear and grief were something I knew about, and without bidding I thought of Brendon.

"That's good," Magnus cried. "Don't move. Whatever you're thinking—keep thinking it."

He snatched up his block of paper and sketched rapidly, tore it off and sketched again. I remembered now that I'd left my own sketch box at Magnus' cabin. I must pick it up later. The discomfort of hard stone grew into an agony, physical as well as mental. When I felt that I couldn't bear it a moment longer, he dropped his sketch block and came over to the bull.

"Come down," he said, and held out his arms.

When I dropped into them, he held me carefully, almost tenderly for a moment, and then set me gently on my feet, with none of the jar that I'd experienced yesterday.

"Would you like to see?" he asked, and picked up the sheets of drawing paper he had scattered about the grass.

How skillfully and swiftly he had worked. I gazed and was both disturbed and astonished. It was Ariel's face that looked back at me from white paper—her eyes wide with fear, the agony of suffering stamped upon her mouth. I had seen Ariel look like that on a stage, where she was a superb actress, as all great prima ballerinas are. When it came to the rough drawings of the body lying upon the back of the bull, there was less grace, but here too a sense of suffering. The body was mine, and he had drawn me without concealing garments, as though he knew my very flesh and bone structure.

I shook my head. "I'm sorry. I can't ever be as graceful as Ariel was."

He took the sheets from my hand and studied them again. "It's doesn't matter. Maybe Europa wasn't all that graceful either. Perhaps it's better this way. Classical ballet movements don't always convey heights of emotion. Martha Graham could do it better. You've given me what I want. You were thinking of Brendon, weren't you?"

"I was thinking of how hard and cold that stone felt under my body," I told him sharply. "Am I free to go now?"

"For now, yes. But you'll come back? You'll promise me that?"

There was entreaty in the words, and I stared at him in surprise. My impression had been of a man who was likely to take without asking—not one who would ever beg. Yet for an instant there was unguarded sorrow in his face, and he *was* begging me.

"Of course I'll come back," I said. "Even though it's not really me you want as a model."

"Ah, but there you're wrong!" he cried. "Yesterday I looked at you and saw only Ariel. Now Jenny is getting in the way. And perhaps this will be a better, more original work because of that. Run along now, and don't get lost in the woods."

But I didn't run along. Instead, I stood staring at him in surprise, because I was grateful for his unexpected gift. The gift of myself. He had looked at me and seen me—not Ariel.

"Thank you," I said.

He didn't understand what I meant, but his smile was wide again in that great red beard, and something in his eyes seemed oddly triumphant. When I turned away and started across the clearing he came with me to where the path began.

"There's something you ought to see down there on the hill," he said, pointing. "When you reach the road keep going that way until you come to a path that's blocked off with a chain. Go over the chain and follow that road through the woods. You're a McClain and there's something there you should see."

I wasn't sure how long I would be a McClain, but I nodded and started down the trail, feeling oddly confused and far from reassured. He was a strange man, and it was never possible to know what he was thinking, or to guess what intent he might be hiding. As I walked along, I had the uncomfortable conviction that he had conquered me in some way, and that he had fully intended that conquest. When I posed for him in the future, I would be a little more on guard.

How different it had been with Brendon. With my husband I had never been on guard at all. I had believed in something wholly false from the first moment that I'd seen him. How cleverly Brendon had made me believe that he didn't know Ariel. How cunning he had been to dismiss ballet as something he didn't care for.

No—I mustn't think. I mustn't remember. Numbly I walked on, following Magnus' directions until I came to the handsome grillwork of an iron gate set between stone walls, and looked past it into the burying ground that had served the McClains and those close to them for so many years. Was this the place Magnus meant me to see?

I went through the gate, only then remembering once more the sketch box I'd left at the cabin. It didn't seem to matter now. I could always pick it up later. I had no desire to sketch wild flowers and plants in my present state of mind. What had always been an escape for me seemed so no longer.

Sitting there on the rough grass beside Floris' grave, I had my back to the gate, and I didn't see or hear Irene when she entered. Nor did she see me, half hidden as I was by the monument that marked Geoffrey McClain's grave. I wasn't aware of her until I heard the sound of a sob nearby and turned, startled, to see who was there.

As always, her dress was neat. This morning she wore a brown wool skirt and ribbed sweater, with gold chains about her neck. Her brown hair was combed carefully into its puff over her forehead and her brown brogues were well polished. Her coloring matched the touches of autumn in the woods, but her face, in its faded beauty, was splotched with tears as she stood crying openly beside Bruce McClain's grave.

This was something I shouldn't witness, but I didn't

know what to do. If I kept still, she might see me later and be all the more embarrassed. There was nothing for it but to stand up and greet her.

"I'm sorry," I said as I got to my feet to leave. "I don't want to intrude."

She was as startled as I, and as taken aback, but when I moved past her toward the gate, she touched my arm.

"No, don't go, Jenny. Stay with me a little while. I haven't seen as much of you as I'd like. My duties at the hotel—all of the menu planning, you know—have kept me busy. But I do want to know my son's wife a great deal better."

A hand worked swiftly to brush away tears, and she managed a tremulous smile.

"I'd have liked that too," I said. "But it's not going to be possible. You see, I know everything now. I know about Ariel and why Brendon married me. I know I must go away soon."

Her eyes fell, not meeting mine, and the uncertain smile was wiped away. "Oh, no, Jenny! He meant to tell you, but I know he was afraid. He wanted you to be happy here first, so that you could forgive him."

"There's nothing to forgive. He loved my sister and he tried—understandably—to put me in her place. Someone who is suffering will do almost anything to make the pain stop. *I* know that. Only I can't go on living with a man who is pretending I'm my sister."

She offered no denials, made no defense of her son, but her hand tightened on my arm and she drew me toward a place where the stone wall warmed in bright sunshine.

"Let's sit here and talk a little, my dear. You mustn't run away because you've been hurt. Give him time, so he can learn to love you for yourself."

"I won't do that. I can't do it anyway. Now that it's all out in the open, he's furious with me for breaking the spell. We can never see each other as we did before, when it was all make-believe."

"Oh, dear," she said unhappily, and began to cry again. I put my arm about her shoulders and felt their shaking. She was my only friend here, and we might have grown into an affection for each other, so I felt a sadness as I tried to comfort her.

Perhaps because dependency was part of her nature, she leaned against me, as though she could take some comfort from the touch of my arm.

"It's so awful," she murmured. "I don't know what to do. I'm being torn in all directions. Oh, I wish Bruce were alive. He was always strong and wise, and he always told me the right things to do."

"Perhaps it's time to figure out for *us* what must be done. Perhaps that's the only way we can be honest with ourselves."

"But I can't figure it out—I can't! Help me, Jenny, help me!"

Her appeal was disturbing, and too demanding for what I was able to give. "I'd like to, but I don't know what you want of me. I'm an outsider, and—"

Irene moved back so she could look into my face. "You're not outside. You've seemed like a daughter to me from the first time I saw you. Yet I never felt like that about your sister. I thought she was a destructive force—dangerous in ways she couldn't help. Perhaps really dedicated artists aren't entirely human. I knew she was going to hurt Brendon. And she has—so badly that he may never get over it. Please offer him a little healing."

"No," I said quietly. "I'm sorry, but I can't. I want too much for myself, and I've spent too much of my life trying to be satisfied with what Ariel didn't want. There isn't any way for Brendon and me to come together again. Last night we were furious with each other. He walked out on me and I haven't seen him since. I wish I never had to see him again."

"That's anger!" There was pained protest in Irene's words. "And anger cools. You'll surely make up again."

I could only shake my head. "I'm not wildly angry anymore, though I still feel that he cheated me, lied to me. I suppose resentment will die out eventually. But the cold, plain common sense that follows is worse. I feel less like taking him back this morning than I did last night. But if there's any way I can help you in the little time left to me here at Laurel, tell me what I can do."

"I suppose there's nothing, really. Just your friendship."

"Can't you go to Brendon about whatever troubles you?"

She turned her head to look at me, almost in fright. "Oh, no! He's part of it. He's fighting Loring. And sometimes Loring punishes me for that. Brendon never wanted me to marry him, but I was lonely and when Loring came along——" She broke off and dabbed at her tears with a handkerchief.

I could see how it might have happened. Loring would have come on the scene with all that dynamic charm and vitality, and he would have swept her off her feet, as Brendon had swept me off mine. We had both been damaged by forceful men.

"Now Loring wants to run the hotel," she went on. "He wants me to side against my son. He wants Brendon out. All my husband's plans are the exact opposite of my son's."

"And what do you want?"

"Only to be loved, to be taken care of. To have a son I can count on, lean on."

"I mean what do you want for the hotel?"

She hesitated and her gaze wandered toward the grave she had come to visit. "I suppose I want what Bruce wanted. If only he hadn't died! I'm not strong enough to stand up to Loring, and I can't bear to make him angry with me."

"I think you're stronger than you believe," I said. "I think if you were cornered you would fight. Women do, you know. I am going to."

"I'm glad," she said. "Brendon's worth fighting for."

"That's not what I meant," I said impatiently. "I mean to fight for my sister's good name. Loring told me that accusations have been made against her, that rumors about my sister, blaming her for Floris' death, are going around."

Irene's gaze avoided mine. "I haven't heard anything of the sort."

"Haven't you? Irene, *who* has been spreading this gossip that Loring talks about?"

For a moment she said nothing. Then one hand moved in a gesture of helpless entreaty. "Please, Jenny. No one pays any attention to that sort of thing."

I put a hand on her arm as she sat beside me on the wall, forcing her to look at me. "Who was it that started this rumor?"

"I—I don't know—" she began, and my hand tightened in its grasp. For a moment longer she tried to resist, and then gave in with a frightened air. "It's only Loring who has been saying these things."

"Loring!" I let her go. "But why? Why should this matter to him?"

"Jenny, I don't know. That's why I feel so frightened. He's planning something, but I don't know what it is."

"Then I'll have to find out. I'll have to find out what really happened to Floris. My sister's role in this is only coincidental. But I want to know who intended Floris' death. That's the only way I can stop what's being said."

Irene's fright had turned to terror, and she slipped down from the wall to stand facing me. "Please, please, Jenny, let it alone. No one is going to blame Ariel seriously. Don't stir everything up!"

"What do you really know, Irene?"

"I know nothing—nothing!"

I had upset her badly, and she didn't linger to talk to me further. Before I could stop her, she ran away between the graves toward the gate. In a moment she was through it and had disappeared into the woods.

I sat still on the sunny wall, wondering what her outburst and frightened departure meant. What was it Irene might tell, if only she would? The quiet cemetery around me seemed utterly lonely and deserted, now that she had gone. I tried to open my senses to its peace, aware of two chipmunks who came skittering along the wall not far away. There were still birds left to chirp in the trees—they hadn't all gone south—and there were even newcomers who would spend the winter. A small gray and white snowbird lighted on Floris' grave and began to peck about in new grass.

But there was no peace for me in this quiet place. Loneliness was an aching all through me. This was what the rest of my life was going to be like. I could never again afford to sit quietly anywhere and be completely still. Only if I moved, if I acted, could I turn my thinking outward and feel myself a part of living again. For the immediate moment I would leave this place and put my feet on some active path. Whatever might offer, I would do.

When I left the burial ground, I found my way down to the trail by which Brendon had first brought me up the mountain. As I followed it, I came upon the huge boulders of the Lair piled between trail and lake. Purpose moved my feet, and I hurried down to where another path led around the lake, below those great stones. Watching the rocks above me carefully, I walked along the water's edge, choosing a path I had sometimes taken at night, until I came to the entrance to the Lair. Keir's lettered sign was still in evidence, warning that the path was closed, but Brendon had said there was no danger now. In fact, there had probably never been any danger of a rock falling accidentally. Only that one boulder had fallen, because someone had loosened it to fall. So now I would have a look at the spot where it had crashed down and where Floris had died.

The way in was hardly more than a crevice, with high walls on either side, and a narrow earthen path to follow. The sun vanished from overhead as great rocks closed above me, leaving only an occasional glimpse of sky. Almost at once there was climbing to do, of a simple sort, and I was glad of the corrugated soles on my shoes. When the rocks opened up a bit, I saw a small maple growing sideways above me out of a patch of earth, and around a turn I had a glimpse of three gray birch trunks, their heads invisible.

Already the lake seemed far behind me, the Mountain House lost, and there were no voice sounds in this labyrinth. I kept on along the tortuous way, coming occasionally upon red arrows painted on the rock to point my direction. In one place crude log steps had been built to bridge a difficult crack in the rocks. Once I came out into full sunlight, where I could look up toward a little gazebo perched on the rocks far above, and I had an uncomfortable sense of all that mass of stone poised above me, ready to fall, as part of it had fallen on Floris. Some of those boulders were far larger than the block from which Magnus had carved his bull.

But that was only imagination, of course. If the mass of rock wasn't firmly set and wedged, no one would ever have been allowed to climb through the Lair. I clambered around a sharp protrusion—and came to an abrupt stop. Because this was the place.

The workman I had seen here earlier was gone, having cut a way past the fallen boulder, so that it was now possible to go on. I had no wish to pass it, however. The very thought of it forced me to imagine more than I wanted to, and I felt a little sick. The rock that had fallen was very large, but there had been room for it to fit into this opening exactly. Floris must not have been crushed beneath it or they couldn't have removed her body without removing the fallen rock. So she must have been caught between the wall and the great boulder. There were no stains upon either rock, perhaps only because someone had abraded them away—the rock looked scratched and newly wounded.

I closed my eyes and leaned back against hard stone, with the fallen boulder hardly the width of my body away. Yes, she could have been trapped here in this one open place. Speed and agility would have been required to move in either direction—and it might all have happened too fast. She might have been too startled to save herself.

Craning my neck, I looked up toward the place from which the boulder had dropped, but the sun was in my eyes, blinding me. As I blinked, a spattering of tiny pebbles struck my raised face. I ducked hurriedly in alarm, though I knew no big rock could fall upon me. I was well protected by the very stone that already filled the passageway. Perhaps some climber above had dislodged a few pebbles.

I brushed the dirt from my face and felt the sting where tiny stones had scratched my skin. The second fall of rocks came hurtling about my head with considerable force, and these were larger stones, so there was a great echoing of sound in my crevice. Quickly I backed away, found the narrow place through which I'd entered the section and took shelter there. All was quiet again, and I could hear only the quickened beating of my heart.

From where I crouched looking upward, I thought for an instant that a tiny figure stood black against the sun. Then it was gone, and I was not sure what I had seen. There were no more showers of rock, and those that had fallen hadn't hurt me, though I'd endured a few thumps about my head and shoulders. Nevertheless, I was thoroughly frightened because now I knew a hand had cast those rocks. Someone had stood up there watching my progress below. Someone who knew I was here. Perhaps there had been no intention to injure, for the stones had been too small for serious damage. Yet I knew that I was being warned. Someone who didn't want me to investigate Floris' death had cast those stones.

On legs that trembled now, I found my way back along the path I'd come, and I didn't breathe easily again until I was on the road beside the lake and heard the clomping of horses' hoofs as a carriage full of hotel guests rolled by.

How am I ever to stay alone in these remote rooms after what happened today? Last night, after Brendon and I had quarreled, I went to bed without the extra bolt on the door. My sleeplessness had nothing to do with any fear of danger for myself. Now everything is different. I burn all the lights again, and the doors are bolted—even the one to the balcony. I am glad of the phone within reach of my hand on the bed table. Yet if anyone got in, the phone would never save me in time. So I sit huddled beneath extra blankets and listen to every sound. Heat in the radiators startles me, and the old building creaks.

My worry is not only because of that shower of pebbles that fell on me in the Lair this morning, though that is part of it, and I look with doubt at everyone I meet, wondering whose malicious hand cast those stones. Somehow I must find out, because I am certain now that hand is the one that caused Floris' death, however it was managed. I have told only one person what happened to me in the Lair.

But other disturbing events have occurred today. One piece of information is especially revealing. I know now that Floris went into the Lair that day because she was *sent*. But I still don't know by whom. And Loring, so far, isn't talking. My attempts to question him have only brought sardonic looks and no enlightenment.

The worst thing that happened today was that dreadful fight down on the veranda. Short as it was, the hotel is still buzzing over it, and Brendon is furious.

It happened after lunch. I had sat reading inconspicuously in one of the little parlors near the dining-room door, and when I was sure the family had all finished eating, I went in and dined alone. As yet, I had told no one what had happened to me in the Lair, because I wasn't sure which of them it was safe to trust.

It had been a relief to eat alone in the emptying dining room. At resort hotels there are few late diners, as everyone on holiday seems permanently hungry, and meals are an event of the day, to be met promptly. When I had managed a salad and a bit of cheese, I went back to my library work for a while. Then when my eyes tired, I wandered onto the broad veranda built out over a portion of the lake, and fed the tame trout below that came to take my bread crumbs.

I felt completely aimless, without any immediate goal. It wasn't that I lacked an important purpose, but I had no idea what next specific step I could take to learn more about what had happened to Floris. Worst of all, whenever I tried to think of what I must do, I thought instead of Brendon.

How was I to live without thinking of him every moment of every day? I couldn't brush my hair without remembering the way he'd watched me in the mirror—as he must have watched Ariel. I couldn't look out at the beauty of lake and mountain, or up at High Tower, without feeling for the first time in my life that beauty, witnessed alone, is without meaning or satisfaction. I knew this wasn't true, but reason had nothing to do with the way I felt. I could reason endlessly that time would cure, that pain of loss would lessen. But in the meantime how was I to live? This morning in the burial place, Irene had said that she just wanted someone to hold her and love her and take care of her. With all of my being this was what I wanted too—from Brendon.

The fish feeding had become automatic and the trout and I were growing bored with each other, so I went to sit in a rocker by the veranda rail. At least there was something hypnotic about rocking gently back and forth and staring at a plane of water. My turbulent mind seemed to empty itself at last and think of nothing. Perhaps that is the best possible state for inviting new thoughts, new ideas, and one such idea was just beginning to offer itself when Loring came out on the veranda and saw me sitting there.

"Hello," he said. "What are you doing under a roof on a fine afternoon like this?"

His cheeriness struck a wrong note with me. "I'm not a guest, Loring. I'm not looking for entertainment."

I had seen him about the hotel greeting guests, charming a variety of ladies, and the smile he gave me now was a duplicate of those other smiles and I couldn't feel impressed.

He sobered at the solemn look I gave him. "Do you mind if I sit down, Jenny? I know how you must be feeling, but I think it's all for the best."

"What is for the best?"

"Let's not play games. I told Irene it would never work when we first knew Brendon had married you. Then when he brought you here and we could see how different you were from your sister, I knew it would be only a matter of time before everything blew up. It's happened even sooner than I expected, though. He was a fool not to tell you the truth right away."

Brendon was not a fool, and I didn't like to hear him so labeled. There was nothing I wanted to say to Loring Grant on this subject, however, and I rocked in my chair and stared at the lake.

"You're wise to leave," he went on, undisturbed by my lack of interest. "To end it before it's really begun. You'll recover all the sooner. Brendon's tried to fool himself, and he fooled you until now. I haven't any sympathy for him, but I do have for you. I thought this whole deception pretty rotten from the first, and I'll be glad to see you out of it. You don't deserve what has happened, Jenny."

His words were so kind, and yet somehow so false, and I continued to stare at the lake, wondering why he wanted me away from Laurel.

"When are you leaving?" he asked.

"When I find out about Floris," I said.

He seemed taken aback, but only for a moment. "Oh, that. How can you hope to follow so cold a trail? Besides, there's only one possible ending to such a search, and it's one you, of all people, should want to avoid. Of course Irene and Brendon want to avoid it too."

"Because you'd like everyone to think Ariel murdered Floris?"

"How very blunt you are." The smile I detested was in place. "But I suppose it could be true."

"And the publicity, if it all comes out, would be bad for Laurel Mountain House. Is that it? You're threatening Brendon with that?"

"Naturally it would be bad to have an unpleasant scandal in the papers. I think Brendon must move very carefully now."

Perhaps I was beginning to understand a little. "Carefully in a direction you want? You're using this as leverage?"

The smile was still there, and I found its smugness

intolerable. "What if the police come back into this, Jenny?"

"Why should they be interested again at this late date?"

"The idea has possibilities."

So I was on the right track. "You've been making it up, haven't you? All that about the police coming in again. What are you trying to do, Loring?"

"Nothing you need trouble your pretty little head about."

My hands clasped the rocker arms so hard the wood cut into my palms. He was maddening, and it was all I could do not to hurl angry, emotional words at him. With an effort I managed to speak quietly.

"It all ties in with what you know about Floris' death, doesn't it?"

"What a girl you are for leaping to conclusions." His voice and manner suddenly hardened. "None of this is your business, Jenny. The one wise move left to you is to go away from Laurel Mountain and never come back. There's nothing for you here."

I left my chair and leaned against the rail. "Oh, yes there is! There's the matter of the lies you've been telling about my sister. You're the one who has been *whispering*, as you call it. The only one!"

He answered me blandly. "Whispers do have a habit of spreading, don't they?"

Just looking into his bland, handsome face made me ill, and in another moment I would have left him and gone back to my library work. But I wasn't to touch it again that day.

It was at that moment that Magnus Devin chose to stride across the veranda boards, coming up behind Loring. His huge grasp plucked him away from me and, with no noticeable effort, tossed him the width of the veranda, as a charging bull might toss its prey. In that sudden instant I felt a deep, primitive sense of satisfaction—because that was exactly what I would have liked to do to Loring myself, and I was ready to cheer for Magnus. Only later did I begin to feel frightened.

9

Loring struck the back wall of the veranda with considerable force, but managed to stay on his feet. Rage seized him as he recovered and hurled himself toward Magnus. Loring was dwarfed in size beside the other man, but had the advantage of being a thoroughly dirty fighter.

I don't know which of them might have fared worse, given time, but there were outcries from within the hotel, and a moment later Brendon rushed out to grab Loring and hold Magnus off.

"You're both crazy!" he told them. "Now what's this all about?"

Magnus shook himself like a great red bull whose one intent had been to kill, and Loring went limp in Brendon's hands.

It was Magnus who spoke first, angrily. "He sent surveyors up to Rainbow Point today. He's trying to carry through his scheme to build cottages up there. You might as well know I'll kill the next man that sets foot on that land."

Loring wrenched himself from Brendon's grasp, pulling his clothes straight and wiping a smear of blood from his chin where Magnus' great hand had struck him.

"I'm going straight to the police," he said. "Magnus has been a squatter in that cabin long enough!"

"No police," Brendon told him, and though he spoke more quietly than either man, there was a whip of authority in his voice. "And there'll be no more of this sort of thing. Magnus has a lease, as you very well know, and he can stay as long as he likes."

"And for as long as I stay," Magnus broke in, "I mean to see that land preserved as God intended."

"It will be," Brendon promised him. "Come along, Loring. We need to talk." For an instant before he moved away, Brendon's eyes flickered over me as though I'd been a stranger, and then he was gone through a door to the lobby, and Loring, smiling all too brightly, but keeping out of Magnus' reach, had gone with him.

Peering faces vanished from the veranda windows, and only Magnus and I were left.

"You did what I felt like doing," I said.

The front of his shirt was torn, but otherwise he seemed undamaged, and he grinned at me. "Too bad I couldn't finish the job." He strode past me down the veranda steps, walking toward the mountain.

All my tension had subsided, as though it had been released when Magnus attacked Loring, and now I could stop trembling with fury. Deliberately, I walked the length of the long veranda several times, thinking now of the plan I'd begun to make when Loring had found me.

Irene was the key. The trick was to find the way to use her in the lock that had been fastened against me. She knew something about the day Floris had died, and there had to be a means of coaxing her to talk. The only way I could manage that was to keep trying and I might as well begin now.

I went inside and wandered down the office corridor. Brendon's door was closed and I could hear the sound of voices beyond, no longer raised in anger. Two offices down, a door stood open and I looked in to see Naomi at her desk. This was where she did the planning of her gardens and arranged her nature walks for guests, making herself generally useful. As I paused in the doorway, she looked up with bright, hostile eyes.

"Do you know where Irene is?" I asked.

Naomi left her desk and came to look into the corridor past me. "What was all the commotion?"

"A fight," I said. "Magnus and Loring. Brendon stopped it."

She licked her lips nervously. "Why? Why did they fight?"

"It was something about Loring's intention to build cottages up at Rainbow Point. I take it Magnus won't have that."

"It wouldn't be on his land."

"But too close to his cabin. You can't approve of what Loring wants?"

"I'm not sure. He thinks it might help the hotel. And that's a good level spot with a beautiful view." She didn't sound convinced of her own words, but seemed to be testing my own reaction.

A pang went through me at the very thought of bulldozers spoiling Laurel Mountain's beautiful face, but I thrust it back. What happened here now was no longer my affair.

"Tell me where I can find Irene."

"Why?" Naomi said.

"If you were so fond of Ariel, I should think you'd want to know more about Floris' death, so there'd be no hint of blame on my sister."

For an instant she looked taken aback, and then she shook her head vehemently. "I don't want to know anything. It's better not to know. It's too late anyway, with Ariel gone."

"Her legend won't die for a long while. I don't want to see it tarnished. And it will be if Loring has his way."

She stared at me, biting her lips, suppressing some emotion I didn't understand.

"Floris was an evil woman," she said at last. "No one mourned her death. But what does it matter now? Irene's at the house, if you want to see her. She wasn't feeling well after lunch and went to lie down."

I left Naomi studying an arrangement of bright autumn leaves she'd placed under glass on her desk. This time I knew my way, and I was glad of an opportunity to catch Irene apart from the others.

Approaching in daylight, I could see that the house was sturdily built, plain and old-fashioned. The McClains had bothered with no outside furbelows, except for touches of carpenter's gothic in gingerbread around the veranda and at the eaves. Sitting gray and solid on its hillside, it made a contrast to the Victorian elegance of the hotel. A gray shingled roof slanted over the veranda, with dormer windows above. Its setting was the autumn woods crowding in behind, and a tall stand of Norway pine.

I walked up wide, recently painted steps and rang the bell. One of the uniformed chambermaids from the hotel opened the door, a vacuum cleaner buzzing behind her. She shut it off and looked at me inquiringly.

"I'd like to see Mrs. Grant," I told her.

She stepped back and let me in. "I think she's up in her room resting. I don't know if—"

Irene's voice interrupted from the head of the stairs. "Who is it, Helen? Oh, hello, Jenny. You wanted to see me?"

"If I may."

The stairs were dusky, the upper hall unlighted, and I couldn't see her well. After a moment's hesitation she flicked a light switch and beckoned me up.

"All right, dear. Come up to my bedroom, please."

I was glad not to go near Naomi's sitting room at the back of the house, and I climbed green carpeted stairs, my hand on a shining mahogany rail. If a male McClain had built the house plain and sturdy on the outside, the McClain women had seen that it was graciously furnished inside. I glimpsed a polished hall table and brass candlesticks, a bowl of asters. Hung beside the stairs were the portraits of two men, and I could guess who they were.

"Is one of these Geoffrey McClain?" I asked.

Irene nodded. "Yes, the lower one is old Geoffrey. I can still remember him like that—all shaggy eyebrows, with a beak of a nose that dominated his face. Yet he used to smile a lot too—rather fiercely, as that portrait doesn't show. In fact, he had a ribald sense of humor that often embarrassed his wife."

I climbed a few more steps and looked at the second picture. "And this one?"

"Bruce, of course. My husband." Her tone softened as her eyes rested on the face in the portrait.

I could see a resemblance to Brendon in the strongly carved features, the firm mouth and strong-willed chin, the eyes that sometimes saw more than you wanted them to.

Irene turned away hastily, as though she might again be moved to tears, and went ahead of me toward a bedroom at the front of the house.

As I stepped over the high doorsill, I saw that the furniture was a glowing Chippendale tiger maple, and the carpet on the floor a colorful English Wilton. The big bed had been canopied in honey yellow, and a Chinese tea service was set upon a low round table. Chairs were drawn beside the fireplace, and on a maple dresser rested a golden bowl of chrysanthemums.

"It's a lovely room," I said.

"Bruce's mother furnished it. I haven't changed much. Do sit down, Jenny. You wanted to talk to me?"

I hadn't seen her since she had fled from me in the cemetery that morning, and I thought she looked even more tired and worn—as though she might be sleeping badly. I sat down facing her.

"Have you always lived around here?" I asked.

"Yes. I was born down in the valley. I grew up in Mountain House territory. Keir Devin and I are distant cousins, and I grew up knowing Bruce. Bruce and Keir and I all went to school together. But this isn't what you want to talk with me about."

"No. I'm sorry if I upset you this morning. Naomi said you weren't feeling well."

"I'm all right. I just couldn't stand being cheerful to guests for the rest of the day. You did upset me, Jenny. I hope you're not going to keep on this course you've chosen."

"Why do you want me to give it up?"

She rubbed a forefinger between her eyes as though to erase the frown lines that seemed to be deepening.

"I suppose I'm afraid that you may stir up some scandal that could hurt the Mountain House. Bruce never liked publicity. He always said word-of-mouth was our best advertising, and it always seemed to work in the past. We've upheld our traditions and we've never lacked for guests. Though sometimes lately—but Loring *is* trying to mend that."

"Did you see Floris just before she died?" I asked directly.

Brown lashes lay on her cheeks as she closed her eyes, not meeting my look.

"You must tell me," I said.

When she opened her eyes and stared at me despairingly, it was as though she couldn't struggle against me any longer. "Yes, I saw her. I met her on the other side of the lake, a little way up the hill. She was in a hurry, and she told me that someone was caught in the Lair—a woman who had sprained her ankle and needed help. Floris had some nursing experience, and she used to help us out on occasion until a doctor came. She said she would go into the Lair and have a look, and she asked me to see Loring and tell him. I—I didn't find him right away."

I sensed that she was holding something back, but I knew it would do no good to prod her.

"And then?" I asked.

"Before I found him, that boulder fell and—and Floris was killed."

"What about the woman with the sprained ankle?"

Irene took up a poker and bent toward the fire. Wood chunks fell in the grate under her determined thrusts. "I don't know. If there was a woman there, she never identified herself, and we never found out who she was. No one else was hurt when the rock fell."

"So perhaps there wasn't anyone there at all? Perhaps it was a trap for Floris?"

Irene dropped the poker and sat down, her face in her hands. I bent toward her.

"Tell me," I urged.

She shook her head. "Please, please let me alone! Don't stir this up again, Jenny. Please don't make trouble. Everything was quiet before you came."

"No, it wasn't," I said. "And it's Loring who has been stirring things up."

"Yes, I know." She took down her hands, her eyes wide open. "And he mustn't—oh, he mustn't! How can he be so—so foolish? How can he run such a risk?"

"Risk?" I challenged, but she only shook her head as if in confusion and I went on. "I think he's trying to use what happened to force Brendon to do as he wishes with the hotel and Laurel Mountain. If Brendon doesn't agree, Loring will threaten publicity and the police."

For just an instant I thought she looked relieved, as though I'd said something she hadn't expected. Then she began to shake her head again.

"He mustn't do this. He mustn't!"

She left her chair and roamed nervously about the room. She couldn't flee from me now as she'd done from the cemetery. Before the bowl of flowers, she paused to pluck out a dead blossom or two.

"Who told Floris there was someone hurt in the Lair?" I asked.

"I don't know. Truly, I don't know." She came back to toss dead blooms into the fire. "Floris didn't say, and I didn't ask her. It was all too urgent just then. Later it was too late to find out."

"Whoever told her that lie planned her death," I said. "And I don't think it was Ariel."

She answered me frantically. "You don't know that! You can't know it. It's better if it was Ariel, isn't it? Then that would be the end of it. No one who is living would be hurt."

I couldn't suppress my indignation. "Do you mean

you'd spare whoever killed Floris at the expense of Ariel's good name?"

Her eyes dropped and she was silent, flushing. I pressed her a little harder. "When did you see Loring again that day? If you couldn't find him in his office at first, where was he?"

"I—I'm not sure. What does it matter? When the boulder fell it made a terrible roar and the ground shook. So a number of us ran out to the Lair, and he was there, along with the others. That's all I know."

"Do you know that Magnus and Loring had a fight a little while ago?" I asked.

This time I had really startled her and she dropped into a chair. "Oh, Jenny, how awful! Was it bad? Did anyone get hurt? Perhaps I'd better go to Loring—"

"No—he wasn't hurt, and neither was Magnus. It was Magnus who started it. Brendon stopped them. He's having a talk with Loring now. Apparently surveyors were sent up to the land near Magnus' cabin and Magnus was furious."

"Such things never happened when Bruce was alive," Irene mourned.

I knew I would get nothing more from her at the moment and I stood up. "Thank you for talking to me. May I come back again for your help?"

"There's nothing I can do," she said gloomily. "I can't even stop you from a foolish course. Just be careful, Jenny."

I bent toward her. "You do believe someone killed Floris, don't you?"

"Only Ariel!" she cried. "And you'll be hurt if you find that out—won't you, Jenny?"

But I knew that this was not her real fear. For a moment I considered telling her about those pebbles flung at me in the Lair, but I knew she would only be further alarmed and still unwilling to help. So I touched her lightly on the shoulder and went out of the room to find my way down the stairs. The vacuum cleaner was humming in the living room, and I let myself out the front door.

The day was still beautiful, and couples were playing on the tennis courts as I went by. The ping of the balls against rackets had a pleasant sound. I found myself walking aimlessly, not knowing where to turn next. There was a deep and constant soreness in me and I knew its source very well. Brendon. No matter how much I found to do, no matter how much I tried to concern myself with Ariel and Floris' death, the heavy aching at the pit of me was because of Brendon. In a sense, this was like suffering death, and I must learn to live with it. Yet it was all the worse because he was not dead, and no matter how angry I felt toward him, or how hurt I was, love couldn't be dismissed by an act of will. The aching and the longing persisted.

I heard Keir's truck before I saw it come around a curve on the hillside, and I stepped into a clump of snakeroot to let him go by on the narrow road. Instead, he pulled to a stop beside me, reached across and opened the door on the passenger side.

"Get in," he told me curtly.

His tanned, weathered face was not one to show what he was thinking, but I sensed an anger with me behind his words, and I felt even more depressed. I had begun to think of Magnus' father as a possible friend at Laurel Mountain, and there had seemed the beginning of trust between us when he had taken me to Panther Rock. Now that feeling was gone.

I pulled myself into the high seat by the handhold and he put the truck into gear so that we moved slowly along the road past the hotel.

"I'm going to New Paltz," he said. "Do you want to come along?"

I had no feeling that this was an invitation given out of kindness, as might have been the case earlier, but I knew I must accept. I wanted to know what was troubling him. It wasn't hard to guess, but I wanted to hear it from Keir himself.

In silence we drove along the road that led to Laurel's gatehouse. There he checked us past the guard and headed for the main road. Another frost had touched the mountain last night, and more maple trees were ablaze, making splashes of startling color against more modest tans and yellows.

"You'd better tell me what happened," I said after a time. "I know you're angry with me."

"What kind of woman are you, to break up with Brendon like that?" he asked.

"I suppose I'm a human kind of woman. He married me because he was in love with Ariel and he wanted her back."

"Ariel was no good. I told him that from the first. I thought you might turn out to be different."

"Maybe that's the trouble. I'm too different. It was all make-believe. Now that I know that, there's no use going on."

"You're no better than she was," he said harshly. "Running up there to see Magnus."

"At least Magnus doesn't mix me up with Ariel," I said. "And if he wants me to pose for him, I'll do it."

"Brendon deserves better. If you're like her, you should go away."

I turned my head and stared at his granite profile that told me nothing. "Everyone seems to want me to go away. This morning, when I was exploring the Lair, someone tossed a handful of pebbles down on me. I wasn't hurt, but it frightened me. Who would do a thing like that?"

"I don't want to know," he said, and braked the truck to a crawl.

A deer and her fawn were crossing the road in great leaps ahead of us. When the two had vanished into the forest, he stepped on the gas again.

"Do *you* think Floris died because a rock accidentally crushed her?" I asked.

"Your sister was standing on it."

"Only by chance," I said.

"You have to believe what you want to believe, I suppose."

Everywhere I turned I met with this stone wall of dis-

belief when I tried to claim that Ariel would never have
deliberately harmed anyone.

Again we were silent, and there seemed no way to
reach this man who sat beside me, any more than I could
reach the others. They had all been against Ariel. Except for Naomi and Brendon. And perhaps Magnus.

We were nearing the town when I asked another question. "Were Magnus and Floris ever happy in their marriage?"

"I suppose they did as well as most people. Until that
dancer came along."

"But there were always other women. Magnus told me
so himself."

"Sure. But he never went overboard with the others,
and Floris didn't care. This time she cared a lot and she
went a little crazy."

We were in town now, though I hadn't been paying
much attention, and Keir braked again and drew over to
the side of the road.

"I'll leave you here," he said. "This is the old part of
town. Plenty to see. Suppose I pick you up right here in
about an hour?"

Disconcerted, I found that I had been dumped un-
ceremoniously by the side of the road, and I watched the
truck rumble off. Keir hadn't liked that straight-out question I had asked, and while he hadn't admitted it, I suspected that he had no doubts about Floris' death. But why
had he asked me into the truck? What had he wanted of
me?

Since there was nothing else to do, I began to walk
about, discovering that I was on Huguenot Street in the
original town, and that all about me were houses that
had been built nearly three hundred years ago. There was
every type of architecture, from early Flemish stone to a
handsome brick that belonged to a later, Federal period.
One of the houses was open as a museum and I wandered
past roped-off rooms, mingled with a small party that had
come by bus, invisible in my anonymity. Here no one
would suddenly cry out that I looked like Ariel Vaughn.

Yet even while my eyes studied and admired, my mind

struggled to plan. Keir was a puzzle to which I had never found the key. I wasn't even sure how he felt about his son, though he had been quick enough to warn me away from him. That he was devoted to Brendon, I didn't doubt, and now that I had fallen out with Brendon, the friendship that had seemed to be beginning between Keir and me had been lost. He trusted me now no more than he had my sister.

I was beginning to think they were all banded together to protect one of their own number, and I wasn't likely to stir any one of them into a betrayal of who that was.

When I returned to the place where Keir had left me, I sat on a stone step until the truck came into sight. When I was in the front seat again and we were heading across the Wallkill River toward Laurel Mountain, I tried once more to engage Keir in conversation.

"I suppose you know your son tried to give Loring Grant a beating this afternoon?"

Oddly enough, he hadn't heard, and he gave me a quick, startled look. "What do you mean? What happened?"

"Magnus was angry because Loring sent surveyors up to Rainbow Point near your place. I suppose he came down to the hotel to settle things with Loring in his own bullish way. It took Brendon to break them up. Nobody got hurt, but I'd say there's a lot of bad blood being stirred up."

"There are better ways to handle this," Keir said. "Magnus has always let his temper fly too fast. I'll talk to him. Brendon won't allow Loring to put his schemes through."

"Isn't the hotel run by a board?" I asked. "Brendon and Naomi and Irene have to vote, don't they? And isn't there a danger that Irene will listen to her husband's advice, and Naomi may go along with her?"

"There could be." His face darkened. "Irene could be too scared to do anything else."

"Of Loring?"

"Relax. Nothing's been spoiled yet. If you were going

to stick around, Brendon might have trained you to serve on the board."

"But I'm not going to," I said quickly. "I'll only be here a little while longer. Only until I find out what happened to Floris."

He gave me another sidelong look. "What if I try to help you on that?"

"Would you?" I said eagerly. "Would you really?"

"Maybe. I'll think about it." His tone had softened toward me just a little.

The curving, climbing road wound up to the entrance to Laurel Mountain House, and Keir slowed to speak to the guard before he drove on through to drop me at the hotel.

I sit here now with my doors bolted and remember all the unpleasantness of the day, glad to have it passed, so that it is one day I need never live through again.

I sit here and once more I am afraid. These rooms are too lonely, the corridors too deserted in this old wing. I know I have only to ring Irene and ask that my room be changed and she will put me in a more populated section where there will be guests coming and going, and I needn't fear the emptiness. Yet I make no move. I sit here, waiting.

Perhaps because it was here that Brendon and I were happy together, and I somehow fool myself that he will come back to me here. That he will tell me that it is me he loves, and all will be as it was before. I know this is nonsense and that the shadow of Ariel that has fallen between us can never be erased. Yet I sit here and wait. For what? A knock on the door? For the telephone to ring?

When it rings just as I think of it, I am startled out of my chair and sent running to answer. I pick up the receiver and speak into it in a voice that has gone more tremulous than I like. But it is only Magnus on the wire, and hope expires in me like the emptying of air from a balloon.

"I'll be ready for you tomorrow," he says. "I'm going

to do this in marble and I've spent the day on opening up the stone, with my sketches to guide me. So will you come?"

"I'll be there," I tell him, and my voice sounds firmer as I speak.

"What's the matter?" Magnus asks.

He is too perceptive, too alert.

"Nothing. I'm fine."

"You thought it was Brendon, didn't you? But you'll have to get over that. And don't come in pants—wear a dress."

"What time do you want me tomorrow?" I ask coolly, hoping that my tone will reprove him.

"You can come around ten o'clock, if you like. Dream well. And think about Zeus tonight—waiting for you on the mountain."

He is gone, the phone is dead, and I sit for a time with the receiver in my hands until it begins to make reproachful clicks, asking me to hang it up.

Before I get into bed, I go out on the balcony and stare up at High Tower with its beacon light. Somewhere on the mountain, hidden in the forest, the stone bull stands. The half moon that shines on my balcony and makes a shimmering path across the lake shines as well upon his grassy circle with the dark hemlocks crowding around. I think of Magnus' words—that Zeus waits for me. But it is Magnus who waits. I know that, and somehow I am more fearful than ever.

What is it Magnus wants of me? Why must I go to him? What do *I* want of Magnus?

For some reason the thought of that ugly stone head I had seen in Magnus' workshed returns to me. What sort of man could imagine so horrid a creation? I hope I will not see that face in my dreams tonight.

10

When I reached the cabin the next morning, I found it empty, with a note tacked on the door: *Zeus awaits you.* I couldn't feel all that whimsical this morning, and the words didn't please me. My temper had frayed badly overnight, so that I seemed to be angry with everyone. Especially with Brendon, who had taken my life and then thrown it away. As quickly as possible I wanted to escape from Laurel Mountain and never see its forests, or lake, or any of its people again.

So I bristled a little as I marched through the woods to the clearing, where both Magnus and his great stone beast waited for me. The bull looked as furiously ready for attack as ever, but Magnus' mood was the opposite of mine, and he greeted me with that flashing smile that could overpower me—if I allowed it to, and I braced myself against it. This morning he wore goggles again, to protect against flying chips, but he took them off when I appeared.

"Right on time," he said. "Unlike your sister."

My bristling showed. "Ariel was never late for a performance or a rehearsal in her life."

"I only knew her here on the mountain," he said mildly.

Those had been Brendon's words too, and for the first

time I wondered if there had been another Ariel—one I had never known.

Indian summer had descended gently upon the mountains and in the warm morning I could shed my jacket. I had put on my dress of celery green, with the drifting skirt, since it was the closest I could come to something Grecian, and Magnus approved me with a nod as I stood before him.

"Good. That will do nicely. Though I'll make a few changes. Such as a bare shoulder. And we'll have to find you a crown of flowers eventually."

He had brought a sturdy wooden stand out to the woods, and the block of marble stood upon it. Some of the extraneous stone had already been drilled away, so that a rough form was emerging.

"If you'd like to climb up there, we can get started," he said, being polite with me this morning, and rather formal, as though he sensed my nervous, angry mood, and wanted to do nothing to aggravate it further.

As I approached the bull I saw that an incongruous red plaid blanket had been spread across its back—so I wouldn't have to suffer cold stone today. I ignored the hand he offered and climbed up between the horns to seat myself on the blanket.

"Do you want me the way I was yesterday?" I asked, equally formal. There was no reason to take out my seething anger on Magnus.

He held up one of yesterday's sketches. "This is the pose I like best—if you can copy it."

I arranged myself as well as I could and he moved a foot this way, a hand that. When I had stretched out, he made chalk marks on the stone beyond the blanket, so that I could come back to the exact place after a rest. From where I lay in what I hoped was a maiden's graceful desperation, I could watch as he worked with his tools. His eyes were hidden by the protective goggles and I found that I missed seeing their green brilliance. With his eyes concealed, I could tell less than ever what he was thinking.

"We don't have to be quiet," he said after a silence

broken only by mallet on steel point. "I can concentrate and talk at the same time. I can even listen."

"There's nothing I want to talk about," I said.

"Oh? Dad tells me you're continuing your wild-goose chase to exonerate your sister."

"Your father didn't call it that. He said he'd try to help me."

"He has a tender heart under that gruff façade, and he's begun to feel sorry for you. But we both think that the sooner you face up to what passion Ariel was capable of, the better it will be."

"I thought you loved her?"

"When I'm attracted, it's with my eyes open. Unlike Brendon. I knew very well what I was doing when it came to Ariel, and I knew it couldn't last."

There was no kindness in me this morning. "That must have been pretty hard on Floris."

"Floris and I understood each other, as I've said before."

"Until Ariel spoiled that understanding?"

"You're feeling vitriolic, aren't you?"

"I don't find the world especially pleasant this morning. And I shouldn't think you would either."

"On a day like this?" he marveled, waving his mallet at the great arch of blue overhead, at the hemlocks, less grimly dark in bright sunlight.

"It must have been even more beautiful at the time when Floris died," I said. "And Ariel. May—spring. Tragically beautiful. Floris because someone took her life, Ariel because she took her own."

"And you don't see the connection? You don't see cause and effect?"

I pushed myself up on the blanket to answer sharply, but his voice cut like a whiplash. "Don't go squirming around! If all your thoughts make you angry today, you'd better keep them to yourself."

For a while I was still, struggling with emotions I couldn't manage. Perhaps didn't want to manage. No longer was I willing to be weak and hurt and tearful.

"It's a good thing I'm not ready to work on your face

today," Magnus said after a quarter of an hour had passed. "Yesterday you caught the right feeling. I was going to take a few snapshots today, but obviously I'd better stick to general outlines."

I bit my lips and was silent. I ached all over. Even with the blanket under me, the stone was hard and I felt the strain of trying to hold a pose. Inside, I was desperately wounded, yet resenting my own grief, angry with myself as well as with everyone else. Because of Brendon.

"Take a rest," Magnus said. "Before you go numb and fall off."

I sat up, stretching my arms overhead, wriggling my shoulders, drawing deep breaths of pine-scented air, because I realized I'd been breathing shallowly for too long.

"Get down and walk about," Magnus directed.

I slid from the bull's back, pulling the blanket with me. I felt colder now, and I wrapped it close as I walked around the ring of grass. When I came opposite Magnus I paused to look at the block of veined marble on the stand before him. The rough shape of the bull was becoming evident in the stone, with what might be the form of a maiden stretched along its back.

"Do you ever model in clay?" I asked.

"Only when I mean to cast in bronze. Clay isn't my favorite medium. You have to build it up and it lacks resistance. Perhaps I like to fight the stone. With marble or granite, you know everything is right there inside, and you have only to set it free. For me there's more excitement in that. I don't even like to use a maquette—a scaled model—to work from. For me it's difficult to hold the creative feeling when I must copy from a model. An idea can get tired when I struggle with it too long."

His talk about his own work relaxed me a little and I picked up yesterday's sketches to study them.

"You draw so well—have you never wanted to paint?"

"Not really. Painting at its best is an interpretation, an extension. But when you sculpt, you deal with something closer to reality—your own reality in stone. To the sculptor dimension is everything. What you create is there in the round—with its own lights and shadows that change as the world changes. You can walk around what you've done and see every angle. It has a life of its own."

As he spoke he illustrated, moving around the block, touching the point to it here and there.

"Marble is a satisfying stone to use. It's softer than granite, and the work goes faster. I've done almost all I need to do with drill and point, since I worked for hours yesterday. I'll use a claw tool to draw the figure in the stone, and then I can make my final statement with various chisels. That's the most meticulous part."

"And if you cut away too much stone?"

"That's the challenge. And the skill. With clay you can build up or tear down. What I do in marble is pretty final. But tell me about you, Jenny. Those sketches and paintings you showed me—what do you mean to do with them? What are you working toward?"

I hesitated to tell him because I knew he hadn't approved of what he'd seen in my sketchbook.

"I don't think you're just a dilettante," he said.

That forced an answer from me. "No—I don't want to be. I've thought in terms of a book eventually—when I've collected enough paintings. Perhaps something that could be used in a classroom to give the details of plants and wild flowers—exactly as I find them. This is my subject, you know—botany, nature. It's what I've been teaching in school."

He seemed to think about that for a moment, while more chips flew. "I remember now. Ariel told me she had a sister who was a teacher. Yes—I suppose that sort of book would be suitable."

I felt unaccountably put down, damned once more by faint praise.

"I forgot my sketching things and left them at your cabin," I said stiffly. "I'll pick them up today."

"Must you? I'd like to keep them a little longer, so I can have another look."

I didn't want him to have another look, and I said nothing for a moment, staring at the shimmering block of marble, feeling thoroughly angry with him again.

"Will it be Ariel, or will it be me?" I asked abruptly.

He took off his goggles and regarded me with his disconcerting green gaze. "It won't be either," he said and picked up his gritstone to sharpen a tool. "It will be Europa. Whatever you are would get in my way, just as Ariel's confusion got in the way when she posed for me."

"Confusion?"

"Yes. Didn't you sense that? Your sister was a woman torn in two. She wanted to love, and she was afraid of love. She had to dance, but she feared the future when the dancing came to an end."

"I know."

He went on as though I hadn't spoken. "She wanted marriage, a home, children—ordinary things."

My laughter sounded harsh. "Ariel? Never!"

"Then you know very little about her, it seems."

"I grew up with her!" I cried. "I knew everything about her!"

"Did you indeed? When you knew nothing about her coming here—knew nothing about her relationship with Brendon, and with me?"

"I don't need to know details. She always had light affairs. She needed something new and exciting—to feed her art. 'I need to restore my toes, Jenny,' she used to say. But the new always became old and she got bored and dropped it the moment her dancing called her back."

He put on his goggles, picked up his mallet and made a ringing period to our talk. "If you're limber enough now, can we get to work?"

Feeling more disturbed than ever, I spread the blanket over the bull's back, stepped up between the horns and arranged myself according to the chalk marks on the stone.

He worked in concentration, the blow of steel against stone carrying a rhythm in the striking that I knew would save his energy.

I let my head rest on an outstretched arm and found myself dozing a little in warm sunshine.

But he couldn't stay silent forever. Like many a man

who keeps to himself, Magnus liked to talk on those occasions when he left his solitude.

"I only saw her dance once," he mused. "Not in New York. Not on a stage. She danced for me here in this ring. No costume—just a leotard she wore for practice. And she improvised, made up her steps on half toe as she went along. I can still remember her leaps—though what she was doing wasn't ballet. She said she had to have a smooth floor for intricate ballet steps. But she danced *Europa*—flirting with the bull, being enticed at last onto his back, so he could carry her away. It was marvelous acting."

I could see her here in this glade. *Europa* had been more like modern dance in the Graham style than a classic ballet, yet Ariel had done it beautifully to Maurice Kiov's bull. And with very few props to help her. She had always liked an empty stage and hated clutter. Kiov wore only a cap of horns and black tights, his muscular torso bare. At the very end, they had stood like figures on an amphora while the curtain came down to wild applause.

"Tell me what she was like on a stage," Magnus said.

This was something I could talk about easily, and I closed my eyes, seeing her again beyond the footlights, filling a stage with her luminous presence.

"She was nothing but raw nerves when she stood in the wings," I told him. "Yet onstage her technique could hardly be surpassed. She had much more than an ability to conquer the mechanics of dancing, however. She was a romantic ballerina, I suppose, and she could make your breath catch with those wind-swept movements. Yet she had something else—perhaps a vulnerability that was terribly appealing. Just the way she held her head, or bent her neck, could break your heart. She could make a fairy-tale role come true, so that you believed in her lovely Swan Queen. But she could make you believe again when Odile took Odette's place and Ariel danced with that cold, wicked brilliance that was hers in the other role. There was no one like her—no one!"

I opened my eyes and saw that Magnus' goggles were

off, his hands quiet. He was watching me with an unexpected sympathy.

"You loved her, after all, didn't you?" he said.

"Only on the stage!" I cried. "Only there!"

"Yet I think Ariel wanted to escape the stage. She wanted sometimes to escape from her own prison of dancing. She told me what a dancer's life could be like. She felt ignorant of so much because she never had time to learn anything but ballet. Life was a mystery to her, and she could be lost and frightened when it touched her. She told me once that dancing was a twenty-four-hour thing. Something a ballerina couldn't put aside when she left the stage or the rehearsal studio. But there were times when she wanted to escape from it. That's why she came here and tried to pretend she was a real woman in a real world."

I had never heard him speak so gently, or with such tenderness. Nevertheless, I tried to discredit his words.

"You're wrong! The real world for her was always her dancing. Nothing else mattered. Oh, she had depressions sometimes. But they came because she could never feel that her best was good enough. She always wanted to reach new pinnacles, though there were hardly any left for her to top. I don't think she fully understood how good she was. She had to hear more and more applause to make her believe that anything she did was worth doing. She had to be built up all the time."

For once, he agreed with me. "Yes, I know that was true. She used to come here to Laurel to try to find out who she was. But at the end she was afraid to know. Floris' death shook her badly."

I snatched at a straw. "Of course it would. Because she was innocent of any intent."

"I don't think she was sure of that. I had only a little time alone with her before she was sent back to New York, and she told me she didn't know whether or not she was guilty."

"Exactly!" I pounced again. "If she'd had anything deliberate to do with what happened, she could hardly have doubted."

"Maybe," he said, and returned his full attention to the work beneath his hands, cutting off our talk.

I drowsed again, trying to empty my mind, trying to thrust away the quandary of what I must do—if there *was* anything I could do. Perhaps I was half asleep when Magnus spoke again.

"Oh-oh. I think we may need to take a coffee break."

I looked at him, puzzled, saw the direction of his gaze and turned my head. At the place where the path opened upon the ring of grass, Brendon stood watching us. How well I knew the language of his body, knew by the very carriage of his head and shoulders how furious he was. I didn't move, and both Magnus and I waited for whatever explosion might be coming.

There was none. Brendon was good at holding himself in check when he chose, and he came across the grass and stood beside the stone bull, regarding me coldly.

"When will you be through here?" he asked.

His presence was as disturbing as always, but the anger that drove me today revived at the sight of him, and I returned his cold look.

"That's up to Magnus," I said.

"We can stop for a while, if you like," Magnus told him obligingly.

Brendon reached out a hand to me. "Get down, please. I'd like to talk to you."

I ignored his offered hand, slid down from the bull's back, blanket and all, and stood before Brendon, waiting. Whatever he wanted, I didn't mean to help.

"Let's go up this way," my husband said, mockingly polite. "I don't believe you've seen Rainbow Point?"

I wrapped the blanket about my shoulders again and looked around at Magnus. "I'll be back," I told him, and followed Brendon up a rocky path that led toward the Point.

He strode ahead of me without speaking until we came out shortly upon a plateau that overlooked the eastern side of the mountain. In the distance, between hills, I could glimpse the Hudson, shining in the sun. It was easy to see why Loring had the idea of building cottages here. There was a great, flat indentation on the mountainside that would hold as many as he cared to build. Above the space of level land, overgrown with brush, a prominence of rock raised its head. Brendon climbed ahead of me and in moments we stood together in that high place where the Hudson Valley lay spread out in the distance and the Catskills rolled away behind us.

The beauty of the view left me sick at heart. Only a little while ago Brendon's arm would have been about me, and we'd have shared what lay before us. Now there was no sharing. We were separate and far apart.

When he spoke there was no change in his chill manner, and I had never before seen his eyes turn to blue ice. "Sit down, Jenny. We won't be overheard here."

He waited until I had chosen a step in the rocky outcropping that served as a bench, and when I was seated, he took the other end of it.

"You might as well understand," he said, "that as long as you remain at Laurel Mountain, you are my wife. You carry my name, and I expect certain rules of conduct from you. I don't want you posing for Magnus Devin, and you will not visit him here on the mountain again."

I couldn't have felt more outraged. "I'll use your name only as long as it takes me to drop it legally. I am not your wife any longer, and I shan't take autocratic orders from you. If you wish me to move out of the hotel, I'll do so. Perhaps Magnus will give me a room."

Nothing I could have said would have infuriated him more, and I knew I was astonishing him too. He had known me as a pliable young wife, wholly in love, and willing to comply with all her husband's wishes. There had been no conflict, because what Brendon wanted, I wanted. Now it was different, and even though a weak trembling had started inside me, I knew I had to face him down and refuse to be dominated.

"Don't be absurd. Keir won't stand for that," Brendon said. "It's his cabin too."

Obviously, I had no intention of staying with Keir and

Magnus. I was merely trying to goad and infuriate Brendon—all because I was shattered and desperate, and had stopped caring about my life.

"Then that's up to Keir," I told Brendon. "Not you."

He looked out over the mountain toward the distant river. "Keir will do as I ask."

"Why? What difference does it make to you what I do now?"

"I have some concern for the name of McClain. And I don't want to see history repeat itself."

"Because Ariel threw you over and turned to Magnus?" I challenged.

"You know very little about anything," he told me more quietly. "I want you to leave Laurel Mountain before you start something you can't stop. If you haven't already started it."

"I don't know what you're talking about."

"I think you do. I've been told that yesterday rocks were thrown down on you while you were climbing through the Lair—where you had no business to be in the first place. Deliberately thrown."

"Who told you?" I demanded.

"Keir, of course. He thought I should know. I don't want you hurt, Jenny. Tomorrow I'll have a limousine drive you to New York."

There was bitterness in me as I answered. "And then everything will be as quiet on the surface as it was before? And whoever caused Floris Devin's death will continue to be safe? Is that what you intend?"

He turned his head to look at me, and though his expression was grave, the chill was gone and there seemed a real concern in his eyes. "If you will go away—far enough away so you'll be quite safe, I'll see what I can do here."

"What do you mean?"

"I'll try to find the answers to the questions that are troubling you. I'm in a better position to do that than you are."

"Except that you don't believe there's anything to find out."

"I've changed my mind about that. Perhaps there is. Perhaps we both owe something to Ariel."

Now the thrust of pain was savage and once more caught me unprepared. For a brief moment I had imagined that his concern was for me—but once more I must share it with Ariel. I stood up on the rock beside him.

"I'll think about it," I said. "But now I'm going back to pose for Magnus."

I'd angered him again, but this time he must have known that he was helpless to order me. Without a backward glance, he strode off along the mountain's spine, leaving me alone.

By making an effort I managed to erase all feeling from my expression as I went down the steep path to rejoin Magnus. He was gone from the little glen, however, and only the stone bull awaited me in his endless charge. The table with the marble block upon it was still there, but a plastic covering had been placed over the work, and Magnus' tools were gathered into a box. Work had obviously been discontinued for the time being. My jacket lay on the grass where I had dropped it, and I traded the plaid blanket for it, slipping my arms into the sleeves, buttoning it high because I was so cold in the brilliant sunlight.

Now I was undecided. Should I follow Magnus to his cabin and find out when he would next need me? I didn't think he would accept Brendon's indignation over using me as his model. Undoubtedly, he would want me to come back. Yet somehow I couldn't face Magnus now—not in my present hurt and unsettled state.

When I turned down the mountain, I chose a different road that I hadn't followed before and walked through deep woods until I came out above the bright carpeting of Naomi's gardens. I could see her there, kneeling beside a crescent flower bed planted in yellow chrysanthemums. Perhaps I could talk to her again. There was still a great deal that she hadn't told me, and she of them all had been most in Ariel's confidence.

I bothered with no path, but went straight down over steep green lawns that winter's fingers hadn't yet turned to brown. She heard me coming and looked up to watch my descent. Once more a bright red bandanna tied back her shock of gray hair, and she wore a sweater and jeans. Her stare did not waver as she watched me come down the hill and pick my way through the narrow walks of the gardens. There seemed something almost avid about her look as she gazed up at me when I was close at hand.

"How are you doing?" she asked. "What astonishing things have you ferreted out this morning?"

"I've been posing for Magnus," I told her. "He wants to do a small figure of the stone bull—with Europa on his back."

"Ariel's bull!" she countered. "It's not you who should be posing."

I tried to be gentle with her. "I know that. But it seems a small thing to do for him."

She dropped her weeding tool and sat back on her heels. "There is one thing I'd like to know. When all those stories about her death spilled into the papers, how did you manage to keep it quiet about the baby?"

The power of words deserted me and I stood staring down at her blankly.

"You didn't know?" she marveled, pleased with my shock. "You really didn't know?"

"I don't know what you're talking about."

"Ariel's baby. And Brendon's. That's what I'm talking about. She was carrying his child when she left Laurel that last time."

I tried to smile a dismissal of her words, but my lips felt stiff. "That's isn't possible. There was no baby. After she died there was an autopsy because of the circumstances. A pregnancy would have been discovered."

Naomi dusted earth from her fingers and stood up to face me, shorter than I, but strong and wiry. I could feel her strength when she grasped my wrists in thin brown fingers.

"Don't try to tell me lies. A baby was on the way. Ariel confided in me. She didn't tell Brendon because he would have tried all the harder to make her come back to him. She had a dreadful sick spell after Floris was killed, and she thought she might lose the baby. But she didn't. I took care of her until they shipped her off to the city so the police wouldn't question her."

"She must have been lying to you," I said. "There was no baby."

Anger lighted Naomi's dark eyes and for just an instant I thought she might strike me, and I stepped back. But she let fall the hand she had raised.

"Ariel would never have lied to *me*. Your mother knew. I was with Ariel when she phoned her from here. So why don't you check with your mother?"

I swung away from Naomi and walked toward the hotel, angry at being told such lies. On the way someone spoke to me, but I scarcely heard, and by the time I reached the steps I was running. Straight up to my room I hurried, and put through a call to New York. Aunt Lydia's voice answered and I asked for my mother.

In a moment she was on the phone. "Darling, how nice to hear from you! Are you still a happy bride?"

I couldn't answer that. Only a surprise attack might give me a truthful answer.

"I want to know something about Ariel," I told her. "Was she pregnant before she died?"

There was a long silence at the other end of the wire, and I could hear my mother's quickened breathing.

"How did you find out?" she said at last.

So it was true. I leaned back in my chair, feeling sick. "What happened? Why didn't the papers . . . ?"

"We had it—taken care of."

"Why wasn't I told?"

"Ariel didn't want you to know. She didn't want anyone to know. We had to move with great care so it wouldn't be discovered."

"Didn't she want the baby?"

"Of course not." My mother sounded surprised. "She didn't want anything to interfere with her dancing."

"There are ballet dancers who have children."

"Not Ariel. She knew she would make a terrible mother, just as she would have made a terrible wife. There was no room for anything but dancing in her life. That was why she was so great. She never divided herself. . . . Jenny, are you there? Jenny, are you all right?"

"I'm all right," I said. "Perhaps I'll be coming home soon."

She sounded more puzzled than alarmed. "For a visit, you mean?"

"Yes—for a visit."

I said good-bye and hung up. Afterward, I sat on in my chair for a long while, trying to cope with the facts I had just learned.

Brendon's baby—yet she had never told him. And I don't think she could have told Magnus either, or he wouldn't have touched her. Magnus, I thought, would have had a certain sensitivity in a case like that. Even he, who paid little attention to sexual morals, would have balked at a woman who was carrying another man's child. At least I knew him that well—I thought.

Brendon's baby. His flesh and bone and life cells—and she had sacrificed them so easily. Or had it been easily? Since I had come here I had been learning things about my sister that surprised me. Magnus seemed to think that she hadn't been as single-minded about her dancing as had once been the case. He had seen her as a woman torn between her make-believe life on the stage and a real life she didn't know how to handle.

Yet she had gone ahead to destroy that beginning life, with my mother's willing and never-questioning connivance. Mother would have managed everything capably, of course, including keeping the whole thing secret. In New York only Mother had known. And apparently only Naomi McClain here. Until now, Naomi too had kept Ariel's secret.

This I would never forgive my sister. The fact that she had taken my husband from me was not her fault. He had belonged to her first. But to have carried Brendon's child—and then ended its life—this I could never forgive.

A sudden thought startled me. Had she perhaps not forgiven herself? Was this why she had died? She knew well enough the danger of combining barbiturates and alcohol. So had we overlooked a possible intent there? Had she had qualms of self-guilt, so that a few weeks later she had decided that she could not face her life after all?

If this was so, would we ever know?

And how could I bear the truth, whatever it was? Brendon's lost baby, his lost love. And I—hopelessly caught and turning in my own chains. Floris dead, Magnus alone, and always Ariel spinning her intricate pirouettes at the center of our lives. Even now, when her feet had been stilled for these months, they seemed to dance on, binding us all to her with cobweb strands that had the strength of steel.

What was I to do? How was I to live? My search for Floris' killer was real enough, yet it was only a marking of time. Something to keep me from thinking, from facing my life as it must be lived from now on. As it must be lived away from Laurel Mountain and all it stood for. Away from Brendon.

The knock on my door startled me. I wanted to see no one. Not even the hotel help, so I sat very still in my chair, waiting for whoever it was to go away.

But I hadn't bolted the door. A key was slipped into the lock and it was turning. The door was pushing slowly, secretively open.

11

An attack has been made on my life. This time it was
not a matter of a few warning pebbles flung at me down
in the Lair. This attempt was managed with deadly intent, and I believe it was done out of fear, because I am
too close on the heels of discovery and it has become
necessary to stop me.

Yet for the moment I feel safe, since by a miracle it
failed. Here in a strange bed, huddled beneath heavy
blankets, with a fire burning in the grate nearby, and
Irene dozing in a big armchair an arm's length away, I
can feel warm again, and sheltered. If I keep my eyes
closed, if I refuse to think, refuse to remember, perhaps
I can hold everything off and avoid the terrors of returning reality.

I cannot do this, of course. I lie here and long for
Brendon to come and sit before me, to hold my hand and
promise me protection. But all he is willing to promise
is an escorted journey back to New York. Am I to accept this and never see him again?

I know now that it was idiotic of me to quarrel with
Brendon out of my first misery and shock. It might have
been better to have remained silent, to have pretended
that I didn't know, so he could continue with his make-
believe loving. Until—perhaps?—he came at last to love

me. Only me, and not Ariel. But I had thrown everything in his face, flown at him in a rage and destroyed the fragile thing we had between us. It has been destroyed, and I don't know whether it can ever grow again for him. Because now he can no longer pretend.

My knowledge of the baby makes everything that much more difficult. How would he feel if he should learn about that? Would he come to hate Ariel for what she did, and thus give me a chance? Or would he reproach himself all the more for the bitterness of her death?

I can solve nothing. I can only turn in endless circles. Nor can I quiet my mind. Perhaps all I can do for the moment is to go back over what has happened and try to make sense out of the senseless.

It began this morning with the turning of that key in the lock of my door, forcing me to rouse myself and call, "Who is it?"

The door paused in its opening and there was a moment's silence before it began to pull stealthily shut. I flew out of my chair and snatched it open to confront the man who stood there.

"Loring!" I said. "What do you want?"

He smiled at me blandly. "I'm sorry. I thought you were out of your room, or I wouldn't have opened the door. I didn't want to bother you while you're resting."

I wasn't afraid of him. I refused to be afraid of him. Too much was at stake. I decided to attack.

"Why did you come up to my room, hoping I would be out? What are you looking for?"

"Is there something I should be looking for, Jenny? Whatever do you mean?"

"Never mind," I said. "I'm tired of games. Just tell me why you came here."

He considered me for a moment, his look still mild, concealing his thoughts. Then he seemed to come to a decision and strode past me into the room, leaving the door open behind him.

"All right, I'll tell you. I agree that there's been enough of these silly games. This was Irene's little plot. She wanted me to come to your room when you were out and simply move all your things down to the house. Then you'd have no excuse to stay here alone."

"That's outrageous!" I cried.

"I agree. But she can be all of that sometimes underneath her helpless dependency. When she really gets an idea between her teeth, she'll go to any ends to accomplish what she wants."

I found myself remembering that I had once told Irene that I thought she was quite capable of action when it was necessary. But moving me out of this room was hardly necessary. Unless she knew something I didn't.

"I choose to stay here," I said.

"I don't blame you for wanting to stay under the circumstances. It won't be altogether pleasant at the house. But I think you might as well do what Irene wants. She thinks she has your protection in mind. Although that's nonsense, of course."

I changed my course. "What if she's right? What if I do need protection?"

When Loring chose he could put anyone down with a smile that was not quite so open as a sneer, but which suggested that one had little intelligence and must be treated with condescending pity. He gave me that smile now.

"You're quite safe anywhere at Laurel, I'm sure, Jenny. The only two people who could have been dangerous are dead. Floris and Ariel."

I could feel a flush of resentment rising in my face. "You're the one who told me you had proof that the boulder that fell was prepared ahead of time so it would roll easily. So there must have been someone else. A third person. *If* you have any such proof."

"Would you like to see it?" he asked.

The offer took me by surprise, since he appeared to have been guarding this secret so carefully. I managed to nod and he went back to the door and closed it, then returned to me.

"Do sit down. We might as well be comfortable."

I felt increasingly uneasy because I couldn't trust him,

yet I was not exactly afraid. If Loring Grant meant me any harm, it was not likely that he would hurt me here in the hotel.

When I'd chosen the straight chair at the desk, he took an envelope from an inner pocket and removed from it several photographic prints that he laid on the desk before me.

"These are small, of course. I have enlargements in my safe downstairs. But I think you can see what's there easily enough."

Snapshots in black and white had been taken of the spot from which the boulder had fallen. Other rocks nearby and below identified the locality, and I remembered the stunted pine tree growing from a narrow ledge there on the left. Each picture had been taken from a slightly different angle. In one there seemed to be evidence of tool marks on the remaining rocks, as though something had been dug away from their surface. In another snapshot some sort of rod protruded from the earth.

Loring took a pen from his pocket and pointed. "Do you know what this is?"

I didn't know, and Loring was happy to explain.

"It's a crowbar. You can see that it must have been wedged beneath the rock at an angle and could have been used for leverage beneath the boulder that fell. Once some of the supporting rocks on the other side had been dug away, it would have taken no great strength to tip the big rock on its course. Almost anyone could have done it. Or anyone who put weight on it from above could have enhanced the pressure of the crowbar and sent the rock rolling."

I went through the snapshots carefully. "How did you happen to get these?"

"When Brendon went inside to phone for a doctor and the police, I went up there to have a look. When I saw what was there, I thought it might be a good idea to photograph the area. So that's what I did."

"But why didn't the police make something of this?"

"Because"—Loring regarded me with a certain malicious triumph—"as soon as I'd made my shots, I pried out the crowbar, and effaced the marks on the other side with dirt and small pebbles. The police never saw anything wrong."

"Didn't Brendon and the others know?"

"Certainly not. I couldn't chance all that stiff-necked integrity of Brendon's. The last thing Laurel Mountain needs at this time is ugly publicity that could lead to a suspicion of murder. It was bad enough to have a death on the place. Of course it could have been left to look as though Ariel had caused what happened, but everyone was bent on getting her away, and I went along because it meant that much less publicity."

"Do you know who the crowbar could have belonged to?"

"It could have been picked up anywhere around the place."

"Why wouldn't whoever used it take it away after the rock fell?"

"That's a bit of a mystery. Maybe your sister scared off whoever was working on that crowbar as a lever. Or maybe it would have been removed later, if I hadn't got there first."

I handed the pictures back to him. "And you've known about this all along. Known that Ariel had nothing to do with what happened. It would have taken a man's strength to tip that rock."

"Not necessarily. None of the women around here sit about in rocking chairs. And you forget that it *was* Ariel whose weight tipped the balance. Maybe it was she who coaxed Floris into the Lair. Because Floris stood between Magnus and your sister. Because she meant to cause all the trouble she possibly could—to the extent of a whopping scandal."

"Why do you think that about Floris?"

"Because she told me so. Because she came to my office earlier on the day she died. She was issuing ultimatums right and left to anyone who would listen. I told her exactly where she could get off."

"And nobody else has seen these pictures?"

"Only Ariel," he said.

I stared at him.

"I developed and printed them myself right away. So I showed them to her before she left."

"What did she say?"

"Nothing. She took off as though she'd seen a ghost. And maybe she had. Either I scared her badly because of what I knew, or else she guessed who must have made those marks—and didn't want to talk."

"Who do *you* think made them?"

"Ah—that would be telling, wouldn't it?"

His tone was sickeningly arch, and I'd begun to feel a little ill, as I often did with Loring. "If you didn't want anyone to know about this, why have you saved the pictures?"

"They may be useful one of these days. Who knows? Don't look so upset, Jenny. Nothing can really hurt your sister now." He put the envelope of snapshots away in his pocket and turned from the desk where I was sitting. "Now then—let's get you moved out of this room."

"No!" I said. "Perhaps I'm the one who should go to the police."

His unpleasant smile was back. "I don't think you will. In any case, we can't leave you here. Irene is right. Shall I pack your things, or will you?" As he spoke he picked up the phone and dialed the lobby. "Send a boy up to Mrs. McClain's rooms right away," he told the answering voice.

Abruptly I gave in because I had the horrid feeling that he might go ahead and move me anyway if I did not. Beneath Loring's suave and sophisticated exterior lurked something rough that I didn't like and didn't want to arouse. Irrelevantly, I wondered if Brendon could ever win against him. Brendon would fight clean. Or would he? Wasn't Loring's opinion of his integrity overrated? Brendon hadn't been honest with me.

Loring pulled my suitcases from the closet and I began to pack them in haste, while he helped by emptying drawers and carrying things from the closet to lay on the bed. By the time the boy came up from the lobby, I was nearly ready. A few things had been left on hangers to carry as they were, and we made a small parade down the hall to the elevator. In the lobby we chose the exit away from the lake and carried everything out to Loring's car. Several of the staff members lived in houses away from the hotel, and there were cottages nearby to which guests were allowed to bring their cars. When we'd dumped everything in the trunk and back seat, I got in beside Loring.

He looked at me for a moment before he turned the ignition key. "We might as well try to be friends," he said. "There will be enough people for you to fight with, without including me."

I shrugged. "It doesn't make any difference, does it? I don't expect to be here long."

"Too bad you and Brendon couldn't hit it off. But your marriage had to be doomed from the first. We all knew that. Nothing ever hit him as hard as Ariel did. Oh, well." He started the car.

I bit my lips hard and was silent. If there was anyone I had ever detested more in my life than Loring Grant, I couldn't think who it might be.

At the house Irene came running out to the porch and put an arm about me in greeting. I walked away from her without responding. My touchiness wasn't something I enjoyed, but I couldn't seem to help it.

Loring carried my suitcases upstairs as she showed me to my room, and he left us there.

The bedroom that had been prepared for me was done in soft greens, with yellow touches at the windows, enhancing the sunlight. The bed looked inviting, and all I wanted to do was put my things away and rest.

Irene made an effort to collect herself, though strain showed in her eyes. "It's past our usual lunchtime, Jenny. Why don't you leave everything until after we've eaten? Then I'll help you settle in. It really is a good idea to have you here."

"I don't care for high-handed tactics," I said.

She came to me at once, ready to plead. "Jenny, I knew this might upset you. But you wouldn't listen, and I had to get you away from that empty wing. You couldn't stay there alone with Brendon gone. I've talked to him about it and he agreed."

"Is Brendon staying here?"

"No, dear. You needn't worry about embarrassing meetings. He has taken a room by himself in another part of the hotel."

"Then please go and have your lunch. Since I'm here, I'll make the best of it."

I tried to smile at her, since there was no use punishing Irene for all I was feeling. She put her arms around me and held me for a moment.

"Be patient with us, Jenny. We all want to help you."

"Not all," I said.

She drew back from me. "There's a kitchen downstairs, so when you've rested you can fix yourself something to eat, if you like."

I nodded, but I still couldn't be warmly responsive, and she dabbed at her eyes and went away.

When I had worked doggedly at unpacking, hanging up, putting away, I kicked off my shoes and lay down on the green and yellow counterpane. The room was pleasant enough. Less formal than our rooms at the hotel, with odds and ends of old, rather good furniture, and a thick carpet the color of goldenrod that felt soft under my feet. There was an adjacent bath, and I was grateful for that. From where I lay I could see only quiet woods beyond the windows—a stand of tall Norway pine, a little grove of birch trees. Unexpectedly, I missed the view of the lake and the tower on the mountain. No more could I lie in bed and watch its beacon at night. At least the quiet was blessed, with only occasional reassuring shouts from the tennis courts to break it. I was not so far from human company here, and perhaps that was better—wiser—after all. Yet I knew that Brendon would not come to me here. Brendon . . . Brendon . . . I must try to think about the things Loring had told me—yet whenever I was still, it was the thought of Brendon that surged back.

Was there anything I could do, now that my anger was dying and I felt less and less like stirring the blaze anew?

Was there any possibility that I could still fight for my
love and win him back to me?

I didn't know. There seemed no quiet haven for me
anywhere. My body yearned for some sort of releasing
action, and at last I put on my shoes again and went
down the wide stairs to the front of the house. There I
stood hesitating. Everyone would be over in the dining
room having lunch, and for a moment the house was mine.
Naomi's little sitting room at the rear of the hall seemed
to draw me, but I resisted the temptation to go back
there. There was nothing except pain for me in the room
where Brendon and Ariel used to meet, and I never
wanted to set foot in it again. Yet even as I told myself
that, the pull seemed to increase. Before I left Laurel
Mountain, I knew I would have to visit Naomi's sitting
room once more. Perhaps I wanted to hug pain to me,
hold it close so as to make myself understand how real
it was.

I let myself out the front door and moved down the
steps, walking around the house to the rear. Since I'd been
outdoors, the sun had disappeared and the sky had darkened, with gray clouds sweeping in as they could do so
quickly in the mountains. A path nearby led upward
through the stand of Norway pines, and I followed it
idly, until it ended in the open above the lake. Now I
knew where I was. Just below me was the place where
Brendon kept his boat. I'd been out rowing in it only yesterday, and the thought of the quiet, empty lake appealed
to me.

I scrambled down through brush to the open place
where the boat was pulled up on the bank, its oars resting
along the seats. I realized the moment I stepped into it
that it was not the boat I had gone rowing in before. It
looked older and more shabby, but that didn't matter and
I didn't question the substitution. A boat was a boat.
True, there was a little water in the bottom, but there was
also a tin can for bailing, so I didn't worry.

In a moment I had cast off the rope, pushed down from
the shore onto the water and seated myself. When the
oar pins were in their sockets, I turned the boat around,

rowing toward the center of the lake. Only then did I notice that the day had grown considerably colder. No matter, my jacket was warm and my brown slacks were wool.

The entire lake was mine for the moment, and I set out for the far end. Even the Mountain House vanished as I rounded the curve that put this end of the lake out of sight of the hotel. Rowing was harder for me than it had been the other times, because this boat seemed more sluggish and heavy, and also because a cool wind had begun to blow, and I was heading into it. Nevertheless, I put effort into my strokes and held my own, gaining gradually as I headed toward the wild end of the lake. There was something satisfying, something releasing in the physical effort I had to make. While I was fighting water and wind, there was no time for pain and indecision.

Once I stopped to bail out some of the water that sloshed beneath the boards in the bottom of the boat. But if there was leakage, it didn't seem serious, and soon I went back to pulling on the oars.

My strokes were steady and strong at first, but my arms weren't used to such effort. After a time, when I paused to rest, I turned my head so I could look up at High Tower directly above me, its great drum of rock rising beyond trees that crowded to the water's edge. Mists had moved in to wreathe the tower, hiding its top in drifting white, and as I looked up a spate of rain lashed my face. So I wasn't to have any moments of quiet after all. The wind was sharper now, with a bite to it, and rain cut slantingly across the water. I pulled my collar high and began to row hard toward the wilder shore, which by now was nearest to me. Rain beat across my back and I rounded my shoulders against it and peered ahead to find a good landing place. In gray storm light I couldn't make out the shoreline clearly.

My feet felt cold and wet in the rain and I looked down to see water lapping over my shoes—much deeper than before. Once more I began to bail, only to realize that the level was rising so fast that bailing would do no good. Even as I stared in dismay, water gushed in, not from the rain, but through old seams that had opened in the bottom of the boat. Where Brendon's boat was completely seaworthy, this one was not. In moments I would be foundering. Yet there was no way to stop the water that rose icy cold over my feet, creeping up to soak my legs.

Desperately, I tried to row toward shore, but the waterlogged boat scarcely moved as I drew on the oars. I was sitting in water now, and the wet cold numbed and shocked me. How soon would I be immersed in the water, forced to swim? I had never been a good swimmer, and I wouldn't last long in this icy, spring-fed lake. I tried to shout for help, but rain was coming down harder, and the trees all around rushed with sound. These shores were deserted in the storm, and no one could see me here, around the bend of the lake. No one could hear my feeble cries above the noise of rain and wind that overrode everything else.

Inexorably, the water rose to the gunwales and I sat in its wet cold, shivering, my teeth chattering, knowing that if I was not to succumb to the numbing chill, I must go overboard and swim for shore. Yet I had no confidence in my ability to cover what seemed a hopeless distance. At least the wooden boat wouldn't sink altogether, and if I clung to it in the water and continued to call for help, perhaps someone would hear.

Cold was an intense pain all through my body, and the rain was wind-driven with a greater force than ever, so that my shoulders and body were as wet as my thighs and legs.

How long I sat there with water washing over me, the gunwales level with the lake, soaked and freezing, my hair running cold rivulets down my face and neck, I don't know. It seemed forever, and my calls for help grew hoarse and always weaker.

When a voice reached me, shouting across the lake above the storm sounds, I looked in its direction, scarcely believing that rescue could be at hand. The sight of Magnus standing on the shore bellowing like a bull was the most wonderful thing that could happen.

"Hold on, Jenny!" he roared. "I've got a boat. Just hang on!"

I let go the oars and clung to my foundering shell, conscious of nothing except Magnus rowing strongly toward me across the water. Even the pain was lessening as I grew too numb to feel.

As he came alongside, he reached out to grasp my coat collar with one big hand, and hauled me without ceremony onto the boards of his own boat. Quickly he wrapped me in his jacket and began to row for shore. I lay there like a gasping fish, aware that he was scolding me about something, but unable to focus my wits on anything except the fact that I was alive. Perhaps sometime I would even be warm again, though I could hardly believe just then in so happy a state.

Yet I *am* warm. So beautifully, drowsily warm that not even my thoughts can frighten me. Not for a little while.

Magnus brought me back in his father's truck, since it was quicker than trying to row. At the hotel Brendon came out to take me from Magnus' arms. I was aware of his face, bleak and white as he drove me in his car to the house and carried me up the stairs. I was aware of unjustified and languorous contentment as long as he held me.

After that, it all grows hazy. I think he helped Irene to undress me, get me into a warm robe, and helped to heap blankets over me. I was packed with hot-water bottles, fed a hot toddy and scalding soup and given aspirin. And after a time my shivering stopped.

I remember Brendon bending over me when I was quiet and warm again. "How did it happen, Jenny?"

It was an effort to talk. "The boat. I went on the lake. It wasn't storming then. But it was a different boat and it began to leak. It sank under me when I was out in the middle. I might have drowned if it hadn't been for Magnus."

It was such luck that Magnus had been there, I thought. Such luck. I must thank him. His hadn't been

one of the faces that had come to look down at me in this
bed. Loring had come and I had closed my eyes at the
sight of him. Naomi had come, curious, and perhaps
pleased over my disaster. Irene had wept and fluttered until Brendon spoke to her more sharply than I'd ever
heard him. After that she controlled her emotions and
grew quiet. Even Keir came, somewhat later, to inform
Brendon. He had towed the foundered boat back to land
and reported that it should never have been left where
anyone would use it. The boards were rotted, and it hadn't
taken much pressure of water to cause disintegration. But
who had moved Brendon's boat to a nearby spot behind
a clump of bushes where I hadn't seen it, and put the old
boat into its place, no one knew or admitted.

Keir left a few bright maple leaves on the table by my
bed, and I remember looking up into his grave, penetrating eyes and asking where Magnus was.

"He's back at the cabin, Jenny," he told me. "Brendon doesn't want him here."

Brendon, standing on the other side of my bed, said
nothing.

After that I drowsed off, while Irene sat with her
needlepoint, and the fire hissed over sap in the logs and
crackled soothingly. I felt safe and utterly protected.

The feeling hasn't lasted, of course. For the moment I
am protected from everything except my own thoughts.
These I've had to face. The old boat must have been
deliberately substituted by someone who knew its condi-
tion, knew the chilling cold of the lake at this time of
year. Someone who wants to injure me—or worse. Someone is terribly afraid. Afraid enough to kill? I must know
who it is so I can expose a murderer. So I can live.

There is so much I must do, though everything is still
a little foggy. Also there is something I ought to question, some oddity in all this that should be recognized
and thought about. I fall asleep trying to remember what
it is.

12

I stayed in bed for all the next day, lazily enjoying my invalidism and postponing the things I knew I must do, and couldn't think about. A girl came over from the hotel to help Irene and they spelled each other in my room, so that I was never left alone. The following morning Naomi came to sit with me, her hands with their slightly grubby gardener's nails for once idle, except for the book she held. From where I lay I could see by the jacket that it was a volume on ballet. I didn't try to talk to her for a time, or she to me. I didn't like having her there and I had no confidence that she meant me well.

Our silence must have lasted for nearly an hour, and then Naomi broke it and started to talk softly, half to herself.

"Ariel always hated to talk about death. Do you remember that? She said there was a superstition about it in the theater, and she wouldn't talk about Floris' dying. I went to see Ariel in New York after she left here that last time. Not to see her dance. She wasn't dancing that night, and she took me out to a lovely restaurant for lunch. I wanted to ask her about Floris, but she wouldn't discuss what had happened at all."

"Of course she wouldn't," I said. "She must have felt horribly guilty."

"Yes. That is why I tried to get her to talk. I wanted to make her realize that she ought never to feel any guilt at all. Floris shouldn't have stood in her way if Ariel wanted Magnus."

"Magnus happened to be Floris' husband," I said dryly.

"As if that mattered! Silly rules weren't made for someone like Ariel."

"I'm sure she would have agreed with you."

Naomi ran on, not hearing the derision in my words. "She was capable of passion and deep emotion. She couldn't have been a great ballerina if she hadn't been capable of large emotions."

It was no use talking to Naomi. I had sometimes thought my sister's emotions paltry indeed. But then, it could be that I had never understood her. I only wished Naomi would stop talking, but she went on again.

"Once she quoted Danilova to me, Jenny. Danilova said, 'Love is never permanent, but art is permanent.' Ariel was always true to her art. But she had to have those grand passions in order to put them into her dancing. She used to say that in dancing you had to go beyond technique to other, undefinable qualities. All the great dancers do. Fonteyn and all the rest. She could always manage that. There are plenty of dancers who can do the steps perfectly but never touch the peaks. They're good mechanically. But unless you have the spirit—"

Her fingers drummed on the spine of her book, and I felt a certain pity for her. She was sharp, abrasive, and she detested me—yet once more I was sorry for her. It was tragic that she had never had the chance to live her own life in a larger world outside of Laurel Mountain. Vicariously, she had made the ballet world hers—but only in make-believe through Ariel. Since she wanted reminiscence, I tried to give her my own.

"I remember that Ariel never liked to rehearse," I said. "She used to drive her partners crazy sometimes because rehearsing a role seemed drudgery to her. She could practice endlessly alone, or in class, but she always wanted to come to a role fresh, as though it were for the first time, so that she could discover nuances she'd never sensed before. When she did rehearse—as of course she was forced to—she often danced badly. She didn't come to life until there was an audience out there waiting breathlessly —and she never disappointed them. Even when she wasn't pleased with her performance, she gave the audience what it wanted. She made them *feel*."

"Was she really dancing badly at the end?" Naomi asked.

"I don't know. I didn't see her then. Mother said she thought she was."

"Did you phone your mother? About the baby?"

"Yes. There was an abortion."

"I thought as much." Naomi nodded vigorously. "Though she wouldn't talk about it when I saw her. It would have been necessary, of course."

I found that I was still weak. Weak enough for tears to reach my cheeks. Brendon's child—who would never have a chance at life.

"She might have danced better for being a mother," I said. "Even emotion on a stage has to come from something real inside."

Naomi's head flew up, and she looked at me with spite in her eyes. "How could you know? A younger sister who grew up in the shadow of so much greatness!"

Her words lacerated. I'd believed for a little while that I had come a long way from letting Ariel's shadow affect me. But I knew now how little had changed. Brendon had taught me that.

"Just go away," I told Naomi. "I've had enough of lying in bed. I'm going to get up and start my life again."

Such as it was, I thought. But anything would be better than lying here listening to Naomi's spite. I could pity her, but I could never like her.

"All right." She stood up and came close to my bed. "I'm sure you don't need nursing anymore." Her smile was bright with familiar malice. "I'm glad you've moved here to the house, Jenny. It will be much better for you here. And of course you are always welcome to visit my sitting room—where Ariel used to come."

She went off, leaving the door ajar behind her, and I

was glad to see her go. A welcome from Naomi didn't please me. It was likely to mean that she had something else in mind that would torment me.

Now, however, I must decide what to do next. For that brief, lovely time with Brendon I had escaped Ariel, and I must escape her again. All last traces of anger with him seemed to have died out with my icy baptism in the lake. It was as though facing my own death had washed away petty and superficial emotions. Now I could put away my jealous hurt and face my own truth. I still wanted to be Brendon's wife. I wanted to win him away from Ariel and back to me. The real me—not someone he could pretend was Ariel. Now that anger and bitterness were gone, I was ready at last to fight for my life and my love.

The covers flung back, I stood up, my bare feet finding warmth and comfort in the thick carpet of goldenrod yellow. But even as my feet sought my own slippers, they touched something that made me draw back in shocked repugnance. There on the floor, placed neatly beside my woolly blue slippers, rested a pair of pink toe shoes, their satin ribbons tucked into the blocked toes.

Naomi, of course. Naomi, who was determined that I should never forget Ariel, never forget that Ariel, not I, belonged here. But after my momentary shock, I found I could pick the slippers up without being torn by emotion and set them on a table. My feelings toward my sister were as ambivalent as ever, but I would not let Naomi try to build a shrine to her—not with any help from me.

My long rest had done me good and I felt vigorous and alive, with weakness past, so that I was ready for some sort of purposeful action. I could not let them send me back to New York, as they all wanted to do. If I took that course, Brendon would be lost to me forever. I would try to be careful, I would take no foolish chances, and for the moment I felt fairly safe. Someone had substituted an old leaky boat for a sound one, but whoever had done so vicious a thing would need to move carefully now. Any attempt made upon my life must be managed with an effort to conceal the murderous cause. Now I must beware mainly of accidents. I didn't think anyone was going to leap at me from behind a tree and leave me bleeding on one of Laurel's trails. If Magnus hadn't rescued me, if I had drowned in the lake, the reason might never have been discovered, so whoever stalked me was also being careful.

In any case, attack on me was pointless. No matter how much I would like to expose whoever had killed Floris and tried to arrange my death, I hadn't a clue to work on. Not unless I knew something I didn't realize I knew. There had been flickers of some illusive thought ever since Magnus had fished me out of the lake and brought me home, but nothing I could grasp and recognize. Just some curious thing that I felt ought to be questioned.

No matter. If it was important it would eventually emerge.

When I had dressed I went downstairs and out into a gray morning. The rain had stopped and hotel guests were on the trails again, but it wasn't as warm and pleasant as it had been. I wore a coat, since my jacket was being cleaned, so I was comfortable as I set out a bit aimlessly toward the hotel. I wanted to find a purpose, a direction, but nothing specific presented itself.

At least my feet seemed to know where I was going better than my mind, and I followed them into the hotel and along first-floor corridors to Brendon's office. The door was open and he was there at his desk working on papers spread before him. In that moment I would have given anything to go to him in the old, loving way.

"Good morning," I said.

He looked up, and for an instant his eyes lighted—before the spark went out of them and he regarded me coolly. I knew with a pang what had happened—knew that reaction all too well. For an instant Ariel had stood there in his doorway, unexpectedly, and he had responded to *her*.

"How are you feeling?" he asked.

"Fine. The rest has helped. No aftereffects."

"That's good," he said. "How soon can you be ready to leave for New York?"

I braced myself. "I'm not going to New York. Not for

a while, anyway. I'd rather stay here. I like Laurel Mountain."

"Sit down," he said, and drew another chair toward his desk. "Will you please listen to me with that very good mind of yours, Jenny? Someone substituted that old boat so it would get you into the middle of the lake and then sink. You, not me. Because I haven't been using a boat lately, and you have. Besides, if it had happened to me, I'd have been able to swim for shore. What occurred was intended for you. So you can't stay here."

"But why—why was it intended for me?"

"Because you've been talking wildly about exposing whoever was behind Floris' death."

"So you accept that now?" I challenged. "So you're willing to concede that it wasn't Ariel who set the whole thing up? But are you willing to go to the police?"

He ignored my last question. "Loring has just shown me those pictures he took. Ariel would never have set up such a trap."

"So what are you going to do about it?"

"I'll handle it in my own way. Quietly. We aren't ready for the police yet."

Impatience with him surged up in me again. "All because you want to avoid scandal! Because that's all any of you ever cares about!"

Even as I spoke, I regretted my words, but I couldn't apologize and retract them because he gave me no chance.

"I'm quite aware of your low regard for me," he said, "but nevertheless, I'd like to see you stay alive."

He had flushed and I suspected that he would have liked to shake me. We were fighting again—my love and I, and everything was going wrong. I kept still for a moment and breathed deeply, so that when I spoke my voice was under control and I could make a quieter effort.

"Brendon," I said, "I'm still your wife. I don't want to go away. I've been hurt and angry, and I've said words I didn't mean. Because of all sorts of things in the past that you don't even know about. But can't we back up a little and start over—give each other a new chance?"

He looked wary, watchful—anything but loving. "How do you propose we manage that?"

"With a little understanding and generosity it might work. You might try to understand how I felt when I found out the truth. And I want very much to understand how it was with you when you walked into that lobby, mourning Ariel—and saw me. I can accept that a little better now. But·just the same, I find it hard to believe that you hadn't begun to love me a little—just me. Perhaps I'm only presuming. Perhaps I've destroyed an illusion that you wanted to hold on to. But shouldn't I at least stay and try to find out?"

He pushed back his chair with a gesture of impatience. "I don't think you understand as much as you believe you do, and I'm not ready for all this magnanimity. If you want to stay here for a while, I can't send you away. But I suggest that you don't go wandering around alone. Get someone to go with you. And now, if you'll excuse me, I have an appointment."

Without another look in my direction he went out of the room and left me sitting there, every bit as flushed and angry as he. So much for my effort to mend our marriage! Yet I felt sick as well as angry, and as always with him—defenseless. There was nothing further to be done now about Brendon McClain. So where was I to turn?

I went to the wide door on the lake side and watched for a time as guests came in from walking, or went out, and as carriages started up the trails. Then I saw Keir in his truck, with Magnus beside him, turning up the mountain. In the truck bed rested the headstone I had seen Magnus working on behind his cabin. Floris' stone. So they must be heading for the cemetery.

A special group of guests had come to the Mountain House for the weekend, and there were more people than usual abroad on this Saturday, so I didn't have to worry about being alone. When I reached the road that climbed toward the McClains' burying ground, I found walkers ahead of me, and I slowed my pace to keep them in sight. Only when I reached the cemetery trail did I strike up through the woods by myself. The truck was well ahead of me, but I would soon be with Magnus and Keir. Besides, no one knew I was up and around as yet—except Naomi and Brendon.

By the time I reached the iron gate, the two men had the stone out of the truck and were setting it up in the hole that had been dug to receive it at the head of Floris' grave. They were working silently with spades, absorbed in what they were doing, and I stood back a while, waiting to be noticed.

When Magnus spoke, however, I knew I had to listen. "Who do you think substituted that boat?" he asked his father.

The older man paused in spading earth around the bottom of the stone. "I think I know. But I don't want to talk about it yet."

"You've got to," Magnus said. "If you know anything, you've got to say so."

"Say so to which one of them?"

"To start with, to me."

Keir shook his head gravely. "Least of all to you. I don't want you rushing off to do murder yourself. When you get mad you act like a bull. Just let things simmer down for a while. Jenny will go away, and that will be the end of it. I don't think Brendon will let her talk to the police now. He's afraid to."

"As you are?" Magnus asked. "Because you're both protecting the same person?"

Keir ignored that. "The sooner the girl's gone, the better. You know that as well as I do."

I dared not hear more. I had to make my presence known, and I walked toward them as though I'd just come through the gate.

"Good morning," I said. "I saw your truck heading up this way, so I thought I would come along. I wanted to thank you, Magnus, for saving my life."

They both turned and stared at me as though I were some sort of apparition that had stepped out of the woods. Then Magnus' look softened and his wide smile split the red beard.

"You're looking fine, Jenny. How do you feel?"

"I'm not sure. How does one feel after—after nearly drowning?"

Both men were silent, still staring, and I walked around the stone with its handsome engraving of Floris' name.

"I'm luckier than she was," I said.

Magnus tossed his spade aside and came toward me. "When will you pose for me again? Or are you leaving right away?"

"Now is as good a time as any, if you're going back to the cabin. I'm not leaving at once."

Keir made a snorting sound, though I wasn't sure which he disapproved most—my staying here or my posing for his son. The words I'd just heard from these two men—about protecting someone—were disturbing, but I didn't know how to follow them up, short of asking a question that wouldn't be answered.

Magnus ignored his father's disapproval. "Fine, Jenny. I'll take you up on that. Will you drop us off at the cabin, Dad?"

The headstone stood with dignity in its place, though the grave remained without flowers for this woman who seemed not to have been very much loved, and was now so little missed. At least, when I followed Keir toward the truck, Magnus stayed behind for a moment, his head bent, perhaps beset with older memories of long before the time when Ariel came to Laurel Mountain.

Keir got into the truck and motioned me into the seat beside him. He stared off through the windshield as he spoke to me.

"You're the sort to go hell-bent for trouble. First Brendon—who never should have married you because he'd never got over *her*. And now you're sticking your neck out with Magnus. But he's a lot bigger trouble than Brendon. Too much trouble for you to handle."

"I'm only posing for Magnus," I protested.

"That's what you think," he said.

Before I could find a strong enough answer, Magnus climbed into the seat beside me, and we drove in silence to the cabin. When Magnus got out, waiting to help me down, I put a hand on Keir's arm.

"Please don't worry. I'm not like Ariel."

"Maybe I'm thinking of Brendon too," he said. "He wouldn't want you up here."

"There's nothing wrong about my being here. I have to belong to myself. I'm proud and pleased that Magnus Devin wants to use me as a model."

"Because you look like *her*," Keir said.

Magnus reached out one big hand and plucked me out of the front seat of the truck. "No!" he told his father. "Because Jenny looks like Jenny. Because she is Jenny. There's not going to be anything of Ariel in what I'm doing now."

Keir remained unimpressed. "She's still Brendon's wife. Just remember that." He put the truck into gear, backed around and drove off with an air of repudiating both of us.

Magnus looked after him ruefully. "He's a great guy, but sometimes he's seemed more like Brendon's father than mine. I suppose having a sculptor for a son has been hard for him to take. It's not what he regards as a 'real' job. My sort of success will never impress him."

I followed Magnus into the cabin and watched while he picked up a few things he wanted to take to the glen. "What was your mother like?" I asked.

"She was exactly right for him. She loved the outdoors and she could work hard at physical things right along with him. He's been lonely without her."

He handed me the plaid blanket, gathered up his box of tools and as we started through the woods he spoke of his mother.

"She was his first love," he said. "And maybe first love is something you never quite get over."

As Brendon was mine. I wondered who had been Magnus' first love. Had it been Floris? A young Floris, different from the sour, hateful woman she had grown into? It was depressing to think of how much people could change—of how even in this short time Brendon and I were changing.

"I wonder if Irene is happy with Loring," I mused as we reached the glen where the bull waited for us.

"Why wouldn't she be? She married him of her own choice, and she has what she needs—someone to tell her what to do, think for her. That's what she wants, isn't it? Isn't that what she clings to?"

"I'm not sure. I came on her in the cemetery yesterday and she was crying beside Bruce's grave."

Magnus sighed. "I'm very fond of Irene. After my mother died, she took her place to some extent. She encouraged me in what I wanted to do when no one else cared. I'm sorry if her life isn't a happy one."

"Anyone who could choose Loring—" I began, but Magnus broke in on my words.

"We'd better get started. You're not dressed for this today, but I'll work on the general form. You'd better keep your coat on. It's getting cold." He had turned from the subject of Irene with an abruptness that made me wonder why I had been cut off so suddenly.

I let the matter go and spread my blanket, climbed upon the bull's back, patting him between the horns as I did so, because he was my friend now and willing to endure my weight as I stretched myself along his back. Magnus uncovered the marble and I saw that the work had advanced still more since I'd last posed for him. The bull was emerging from the stone, and I had a feeling that was almost excitement at sight of the head, and the horns just becoming defined. I could understand a little of what Magnus meant about the feeling of discovery as the marble opened its secrets to him. Yet the figure he was uncovering was not the bull on whose back I lay.

"He's going to be different, isn't he—your new bull?" I asked. "His head is up in a challenging sort of way, and I don't think he's charging."

Magnus' goggles were in place again and once more there was the rhythmic sound of steel against stone. "Yes, of course. As I've told you, I don't like to copy. This will be a different concept. You know, I did a lot of reading before I started work on that first bull. There are more legends about bulls than I'd dreamed, and in more countries. I suppose they were always a symbol of male aggressiveness. In India the bull is a god of thunder and storm. But in most countries he was cosseted and then sacrificed. Before they used the knife, the Egyptians called down upon him all the evils that might befall the people and their land. He went to his death saturated in human wickedness, carrying the curses of the gods."

"Poor bull," I said, and patted the stone beneath my hand.

Magnus laughed. "At least the bull that's coming out of this piece of marble is different. His is only the disguise worn by a god enamored of a maiden. Interesting that the bull was the disguise Zeus chose for his escapade."

I was glad to see Magnus relaxing a little, seeming to be less watchful of me than he sometimes was, less wary. Now I could take him off guard with a question.

"You do have some ideas, don't you, about who might have substituted an old boat for Brendon's good one?"

He raised his head to look at me sharply, his eyes concealed by glass. "If I had, do you think I'd tell you?"

"Which one of them are *you* protecting?"

"Mainly myself," he said. "I'm very good at that. I hope you'll go away soon because I'd like to see you stay out of trouble. I've come to like you a lot better than I ever did Ariel. For a while I loved her. But I never really liked her."

"I don't see how the two can be separated. I couldn't love anyone I didn't like."

He wasn't smiling now and his mouth, what I could see of it, seemed grim and straight. "If you want to talk, stick to the innocuous."

"I can't do that," I said. "It's hardly innocuous that someone wanted my death enough to try to drown me."

For a moment the blows of his mallet rang through the glen, but his beard hid the expression of his mouth, as the goggles hid his eyes.

"I should think you'd be interested in staying alive," he said after a moment.

"I do have a certain interest in that very thing."

"Then why are you here in the woods alone with me?"

It was my turn to smile my brightest. "I trust you more than almost anyone I know. Perhaps as much or more than I would trust Brendon."

"You'd better explain that."

What I said surprised me as I thought out loud. "I think I trust you not to hurt me. I don't mean physically. Perhaps you're rougher than you know. But you can be gentle in other ways. Lately Brendon only wants to hurt me. I suppose that's because I can't stop loving him, and that makes me vulnerable." I couldn't think why I was saying these things—I only knew that I wanted to talk to someone—and Magnus was there.

He reacted gruffly. "Spare me the confidences, please. I'm not interested in your love life. In other words—shut up and let me work."

I wriggled a little on my hard bed, pushing lumps out of the blanket and pulling my coat around me. Somehow I was still smiling. It was strange, but Magnus' harsh words never lacerated the way Brendon's did. I could be comfortable with Magnus. He wanted nothing of me, nor I of him.

So, feeling comfortable, I yawned widely, rested my head on my outstretched arm and went to sleep.

So often these days I seem to find myself resting before wood fires, entranced and hypnotized by leaping flames of yellow and red and sometimes blue. This fire burns in the grate of Naomi's sitting room, where I wanted never to come again, and I sit on her sofa staring at flaming logs, trying to lick my many wounds. For once I have turned off the lamps and am willing to sit alone in the firelight trying to find answers to questions that are as elusive as ever, but which have grown in number.

From above the white marble mantel the portrait of Ariel as Hagar in *Pillar of Fire* watches me. Even though her eyes are closed—or nearly so—I fancy a faint gleam beneath the lids, as though she peers slyly out at me, wondering what I mean to do next. How strange that if it hadn't been for Ariel's actions I would not be here now.

I would never have known Brendon or Magnus, or any
of them. I would never have seen Laurel Mountain or
have nearly drowned in its icy waters. When I think this,
everything begins to have a dreamlike quality, as though
nothing can be real. Surely Ariel Vaughn is somewhere
tonight dancing on a stage, and I am busy teaching at
some school, believing in my work, accepting my accustomed way of life. Nothing has really happened. It can't
have happened. Then I hear the echo of words spoken
only a little while ago in this room—and I know it is all
too real. Everything is real and frightening, and I am lost.

How long I lay asleep on the back of Magnus' stone
bull, soothed by the rhythmic blows of his mallet, forget-
ful of the world around me, I don't know. Once or twice
I opened my eyes drowsily and glimpsed Magnus working
in deep concentration on the figures taking shape beneath
mallet and chisel. I could see the form of the maiden
now as she emerged from the marble. Magnus seemed
unaware of the times when I watched him, though now,
strangely, I had a feeling that something had changed in
him, and there was a growing distrust toward me. I
couldn't understand why, but it was nothing I wanted to
ponder since I knew it would trouble me, so I fell asleep
again.

The sound of a horse's hoofs awakened me. I lay for
a little while longer with my eyes closed, aware of where
I was but wondering why one of the carriages would have
come up this private road. Then the sound stopped and
there was an intense silence in the glen. When I opened
my eyes I saw Irene sitting astride a beautiful brown
mare, only a little way off, watching me and watching
Magnus.

She looked slim and surprisingly sturdy in her checked
riding jacket and fawn jodhpurs, a billed hunting cap
on her brown hair, and short brown boots on her feet.
Her elegance was a little startling here in the woods,
where everyone dressed as casually as possible.

"Hello, Irene," Magnus said at last, and I had the
feeling that he did not welcome her coming here.

"So this is where you're working?" she said. With a quick, lithe movement she flung a leg backward and dismounted, holding the mare firmly by the bridle.

I felt unexpectedly self-conscious in my sprawl on the bull's back, and managed to pull myself to a sitting position, stretching cramped arms and legs. She came toward me, drawing her mount after her. The mare, however, seemed skittish at the sight of the bull, and Irene had to pause to calm her with pats and soothing sounds. When this wasn't entirely successful, she took her back to the edge of the clearing, looped the reins around a sapling and then returned to me, her expression mildly reproachful.

"We didn't expect you to run away, Jenny. Naomi came over to the hotel to tell me that you were getting up and wouldn't listen to sensible advice."

She reminded me of Mother, who often treated me as though I were a child and slightly half-witted.

"I'm not sick," I said. "There were things I wanted to do."

Magnus sighed gustily, and when he spoke his voice grated. If he was fond of Irene, he was not showing it now. "Somebody has tried to drown your daughter-in-law, Irene. Perhaps she would like to know who and why."

"But that's exactly why we don't want her roaming about the mountain alone. Brendon would like to have her return to New York as soon as possible."

"I told him that I was staying," I said. "I don't think I'm in any danger here with Magnus."

"Nevertheless, I've come to take you back to the hotel." I sensed a firm intent beneath her gentleness that surprised me. Most of the time I liked Irene and I didn't want to fight her.

"All right," I said. "Do you mind, Magnus?"

He moved his shoulders in a shrug. "What can I say? It's too bad, since I'm just beginning to get the form of Europa on the bull's back. But perhaps I can work without you for a while. I've a pretty good mind's eye."

Using the stepping stone, I got down more decorously than usual and walked over to Irene. She slipped an af-

fectionate hand through the crook of my arm and nodded
to Magnus—perhaps a tiny bit triumphant.

"Come along then, Jenny. I'll take the reins and Mildred will follow us nicely."

I stared at the handsome mare, cropping grass at the
glen's edge. *"Mildred?"*

Her laughter had a pleasant ring to it, and I realized
that I had never heard her laugh before.

"Loring named her. He said she had a Mildred look in
her eyes and no other name would do."

Magnus looked up from his work on the maiden's head.
"The mare's name is Gazebo, in honor of Laurel Mountain, where she was born. Perhaps it's not appropriate
either, but I like it better."

I felt a reluctance to leave him so abruptly. I owed him
a very great debt—my life. But he had returned to his
work, as though he had already dismissed me. When
we started down the trail, I looked back and saw him
staring after us. No smile parted that great beard, and
I had the feeling that he would not be surprised if I
never returned to pose for him again. I didn't want him
to think that, and I stepped away from Irene and the
mare to wave to him urgently.

"I'll be back, Magnus. I promise I'll be back."

He shook his head at me. "Stay out of the woods when
you're alone. Phone me if you want to pose and I'll
come after you."

I nodded at him and fell into step beside Irene as she
led the mare down the path. She looked a little sad again.

"We all wish you wouldn't come up here," she said.
"When he was a boy I was very fond of Magnus and I
thought he had great promise. But he has turned into a
barbarian. He has disappointed Keir all his life, and lately
he's been miserable to Brendon. I find it hard to forgive
him that."

"Oh, I don't know," I said, feeling contrary. "Magnus
and his father seem to have a basically good relationship.
Keir must have done a fine job in replacing Magnus'
mother, and I imagine you helped too."

"That was all a long time ago. It doesn't matter now. I

suppose the real thing that disturbs us all is that Ariel did exactly what you are doing. She came to Magnus and posed for him, let him fall in love with her. And then Floris died. You can't blame us for feeling uncomfortable —even fearful—when you follow in your sister's steps."

"I'm hardly following in her steps," I said tartly. "That's the last thing I'd be willing to do."

She patted my arm as we walked along, soothing my indignation. The mare snuffled after us, nudging Irene gently with her nose once in a while. I hadn't thought about riding horses here, though I knew there were stables. Riding wasn't something I'd done a great deal of, but I could manage, and perhaps it would be a good way to get around—on the back of one of the quieter horses. I said as much to Irene and she nodded absently.

"Of course. One of the men down at the stable will fix you up. And I can lend you riding things, if you like."

"My own slacks will do fine," I said, and glanced at the woman walking beside me, taller than I, and still slender and younger-looking than I knew her age to be. I would have liked to be closer to Brendon's mother than I was.

We got back to the hotel for the lunch hour, and this time I couldn't very well hide away and wait for the others to eat without me. There was nothing for it but to face Brendon again, even though pain returned at the very thought, and I went into the dining room reluctantly.

13

It was as difficult a meal as I feared. Irene promptly told where she had found me, and Brendon's silence was hard to endure. He seemed no longer interested in what I did. Since I had opposed him and gone my own way, he had withdrawn himself even more, and it was as though he had told me to do as I pleased and that he no longer cared what happened to me. Only I couldn't believe that was true. I had the feeling that he cared more than he wanted to admit, and I longed to find a way to reach him.

Loring talked about the hotel, but no one joined in or paid much attention until he suddenly startled us.

"I understand that Jenny is considering going to the police," he said.

We all stared at him then, but it was Naomi's vehemence that broke the silence.

"No! She can't do that! We can't allow Laurel Mountain to be dragged down in a murk of scandal. I suppose that's what Jenny would like to manage, but you'll stop it, won't you, Brendon?"

"It's difficult to stop Jenny from anything she chooses to do," Brendon said. "How do you suggest we go about this, Naomi? Or perhaps Jenny has something to offer in her own defense."

Now the four of them looked at me, waiting, while

I stared at my plate and tried to find words to make them understand. Perhaps to make *me* understand, as well.

"I can't bear it that you're all trying to use Ariel as a scapegoat for someone else's crime. Something dangerous is happening and the police should be the ones to solve it. No matter what the cost is to Laurel."

Brendon looked at me directly, coldly. "I have said I would handle this, Jenny. You'll have to be satisfied with that."

I started to tell him that I could no longer wait for him to take some vague action, but an interruption stopped me. The headwaiter had come to our table and stood at my elbow.

"Mrs. McClain, word has just come from the desk that there is someone waiting to see you."

I looked up in surprise. "Who is it?"

"He didn't give his name, Mrs. McClain, but he's from New York. He asks you please to finish your lunch and then allow him to speak with you."

I pushed my dessert aside. "I'm finished now. If you'll excuse me—" I rose from the table, both puzzled and anxious. What had happened in New York that someone had been sent here to find me?

One of the clerks at the desk pointed the visitor out to me, where he sat alone in a shadowed corner. This section of the lobby was empty at the moment and as I crossed it the man saw me coming and rose to his feet with a familiar expression of shock.

"You look so much like her," he said. "Forgive me. If I didn't know—"

He had turned toward the light and I recognized him at once, though I had never met him. This was Maurice Kiov, whose present fame Ariel had helped to make by choosing him as a favorite partner. In person he was as impressive as upon the stage—a little overpowering in his virility that further exploded the myth that all male ballet dancers were homosexuals. Dancing with Ariel, he had made her seem all the more fragile and feminine.

I gave him my hand. "I know who you are, Mr. Kiov. I've seen you dance with my sister."

He was young—in his early twenties—and his eyes had a dark life of their own beneath heavily marked brows. His nose was beautifully Greek, his full lips sensitive. Black hair grew long at the back and very thick, drawn into points before his ears. His clothes were casual—a white turtleneck under a sport jacket, and well-cut gray trousers.

He had danced with Ariel the night she had died. A benefit performance. They'd done the Bluebird *pas de deux* from *The Sleeping Beauty,* one of the most renowned duets in classical ballet. I hadn't attended that night—I'd been off in New Jersey—but I had seen Kiov dance with her other times, and I knew how marvelous he was, how supercharged on a stage. He was a *danseur noble* who deserved the name, and he had twice the stamina of an athlete, to make everything look so easy.

"I apologize," he said, taking my offered hand. "I didn't want to send in my name—to spread it around that I am here."

"I understand. The library is empty—we can talk there, and you can tell me why you've come."

He watched me uneasily, moving with a dancer's grace at my side, and I knew he couldn't help but see Ariel in me.

"I'm not like her at all," I assured him when we'd found a place near a window.

He nodded that beautiful head—like the head from a Donatello frieze. "I know. No one could be. Along with many others, I was in love with her. Though only as a dancer, I think. I could never approach her as a woman— not until that last night."

"How did you find me?"

"I went to your mother. But I couldn't talk to her. I—" He made a helpless gesture that I understood well enough. When it came to Ariel, Mother could be difficult indeed to talk to.

"So she gave you my name and told you where I was?"

"Yes. I hope you don't mind. There's so little to say, really, and yet the matter has been troubling me all these months since Ariel died. I've been out of the country, you know. I couldn't even attend her funeral because I was in Australia before I learned what had happened that night after I'd danced with her for the last time. The next morning I was on my way out of the country, so I didn't know. And then there was nothing I could put into a letter."

He was becoming agitated, feeling deeply some guilt of his own, and suffering her loss all over again.

"I'm glad you've come," I said. "Please tell me."

"My tour has lasted until this week. As soon as I reached New York, I went to see your mother."

"I understand." He looked so miserable that I reached out and touched his hand gently. "It's all right, you know. Whatever it is, you're not to blame."

"No, I suppose not. But again and again I've wondered if there might have been something I could have done or said that night—something that might have helped. After the performance, when the theater was empty, I found her in her street clothes standing on the empty stage. When I went out where the spotlights had moved earlier, she clung to me and cried a little. She believed that she had danced badly—though that wasn't possible for Ariel Vaughn. She was sad and lost and without her usual confidence, so that she turned to me as though I were a younger brother."

His dark eyes clouded and his voice broke on the last word.

"I suppose I never loved her as I would a woman. More as an enchantment—something to worship from afar, even though I knew her weight and the feeling of her body in my arms. The first time I was allowed to dance with her, it seemed like a miracle. It was hard to believe that she was flesh and blood."

"What did she tell you that night?"

It was clearly difficult for him to bring himself to talk about it, though it was for that purpose he had come here.

"I took her a few blocks from the theater to a little coffee shop, and we sat in a booth and drank coffee and she talked to me. About this place, mainly—Laurel Mountain. There was a woman who died here under tragic circumstances—a woman named Florence?"

"Floris," I said. "Yes."

"Ariel stood on a rock that fell and killed this woman. She told me that. I think she was not to blame, but what happened had haunted her. She told me she had stood on this boulder and talked to the woman who was in the crevice below. The stone had moved a little beneath her, but she had paid no attention at first. The woman called to her that a man from the hotel had told her someone was hurt in this rocky place, and this woman—Floris— had come here to help this person. But there was no one there. So she wanted Ariel to go back to the hotel and check with this man."

"Did she mention the man's name?"

"I believe it was—Grant?"

"That's possible. Then what happened?"

"Ariel tried to move to the edge of the rock, so as to see the woman below and talk to her better, but the rock began to teeter, and she had to leap free. She began to cry when she told me—because what happened was so horrible. Perhaps if she hadn't moved to the edge of the rock, it wouldn't have rolled. But her weight started it and there was nothing she could do. She told me she would never cease to hear the last scream of the woman who was trapped down there. This—Floris—was someone she didn't like, but she suffered a great deal over her death."

The sigh I expelled was a long one. "Thank you for coming to tell me, Maurice Kiov. There have been some who have hinted that my sister meant to harm Floris Devin, though I've never believed this. Now you've given me the proof to the contrary that I need. I don't think there'll be any necessity, but if events should require it, would you be willing to tell all this to the police?"

"Of course. I would do anything possible to help you. But there is a little more. Something else she told me that night." ·

I waited and he moved a hand across his face as though to control his own emotion.

"After the rock fell, she stood frozen for a few moments, hearing the roar and crash, and the echo of that scream. Then she became aware that someone was watching her from below the rock. She often had moments of almost superawareness, and because of this feeling, she looked down—and she saw a face. It disappeared at once, and she heard someone run off through the brush out of sight. Then she rushed back to the hotel to tell everyone what had happened."

"Did she tell you who it was she saw near the rock?"

He must have caught the anxiety in my voice because he shook his head regretfully. "I have a feeling that she knew this person's identity, but she wouldn't tell me. Whoever it was must have been aware of her recognition before running away. I believe that it was someone important to her. She told me she was sure that the rock had been undermined so it would fall. She had been shown some snapshots."

"She was protecting someone, you think?"

"That's possible. I don't know. She blamed herself for what happened, though she had no real guilt. She spoke to me too of old age and the short life of a dancer. Ariel couldn't bear the thought of becoming ugly and old, of giving her life to teaching others, or of marrying and living in the shadow of her husband. The spotlight was her life. Sometimes I too feel that way, but I believe I am tougher, less vulnerable. If I must, I can do other things besides dance, and I will do them successfully. The discipline of any talent can be used in other ways."

I smiled at him. "I think you will be successful, whatever you try. And I can't tell you how grateful I am to you for coming here to tell me these things."

He rose and made me the courtly bow that was completely natural to him. I'd seen him bow like that on a stage.

"I thank *you*, Mrs. McClain. My mind is relieved now. I can sleep again without seeing her face demanding something of me."

"How did you come here?" I asked.

"By car. I will be driving back to New York."

"Would you wait just a few moments longer? Would you be willing to tell these things to my husband?"

There was a moment's hesitation, and I wondered what Ariel had told him about Brendon. Then he nodded agreement and I hurried back toward the dining room. Brendon was coming down the stairs from the second floor and I told him hurriedly about my visitor and asked if he would come and listen to what Maurice Kiov had to say. He agreed at once and we returned to the library, where the dancer waited for us.

Kiov was a shade less friendly with Brendon than he had been with me, and I had to believe that Ariel had said something about Brendon that had stayed in his memory. Nevertheless, he gave the same account again, and Brendon listened soberly, questioning now and then, though he got nothing more from the story than I had gotten. The dancer had told us both everything he knew.

We escorted him to the door and saw him to his car. Once more, the sky looked black and threatening and I hoped he would escape a storm on his drive home.

"What do you make of his story?" I asked Brendon as we turned back to the lobby together.

"That you were right to believe in her, and I was wrong to doubt her. If Loring sent Floris into the Lair, he has some accounting to do himself. Do you want to come with me to talk to him?"

I said I did and we went together to Loring's office. He was alone when we walked in and Brendon stood beside his desk. Perhaps we looked a bit like executioners, because Loring looked up at us with a startled expression.

"Sit down," he said. "Sit down and tell me the news. I can see by your faces that it's bad."

"No," I said. "It's very good. It's good enough to convince both of us that whoever caused Floris' death, it wasn't Ariel."

He raised his eyebrows mockingly and waited for us to sit down. Then he said, "Well, go on."

Brendon told him, almost word for word, pausing when he came to the mention of Loring's name.

"So you were the mysterious party who sent Floris into the Lair that day to rescue a mythical injured woman?" Brendon said.

A flush had come into Loring's face, but he was more angry than disconcerted. "So what if I was?"

"You might have explained this sooner," Brendon pointed out.

"And get myself caught up in possible ramifications? No thank you. It wasn't essential anyway. Since I wasn't the one to originate the myth."

We stared at him and Brendon said, "Then who was?"

"Someone phoned me that morning and said there was a woman in there with a broken ankle and we'd better get her out. I phoned Floris to get down there fast, since, as you know, she used to do most of our nursing-care jobs. And in the meantime I went out to see if I could locate Keir or one of the rangers to go in and get the woman out."

"Who phoned you?" Brendon asked.

"I don't know. The voice sounded hoarse, like someone with a bad cold, and I couldn't tell if it was a man or a woman. The identity didn't seem to matter just then, when the important thing was to get the woman rescued. By that time, of course, the rock had fallen on Floris. What else did Ariel tell this dancer?"

Before Brendon could continue, Naomi burst into the office, her pointed little face bright with excitement.

"Do you know who was just here in this hotel?" she cried. "I saw him out there getting into a car. I saw him with my own eyes. It was Maurice Kiov. Here at Laurel Mountain!"

"Are we supposed to be thrilled?" Loring asked.

"If you knew anything about ballet, you would be. Next to Nureyev and Baryshnikov, he's the greatest male dancer in the world. Ariel used to tell me how magnificent he is! I would have given anything to meet him. Why was he here?"

We all looked at each other, and Brendon got up to give Naomi his chair. "You might as well hear this too," he said and began the story all over again. This time there were no interruptions and he was able to get to the last part about a face Ariel thought she had seen and would not identify.

Naomi listened in frozen silence, as though Ariel herself might have been speaking.

"Who was it?" Brendon asked Loring. "Do you know?"

"Of course not. I haven't the faintest."

I glanced at Naomi, and her look slid away from mine, though she said nothing. "Who do *you* think it was?" I asked her.

Her bright look flitted about the room, never touching our faces, never meeting our eyes. "Why, it *must* have been Loring," she said. "You were out there looking around, weren't you? So who else would it be?"

"I can think of several people," he told her. "So it might be a good idea not to make accusations until you're sure."

I broke into this interchange impatiently. "In any case, the important thing to come out of this is the fact that Ariel never meant the rock to fall. When you call in the police you'll have to make all this clear to them."

"I'm not sure there's all that much to make clear," Loring said. "In talking to Kiov, of course Ariel would have put the best possible light on whatever happened. But there's still no proof she wasn't guilty."

"I think there is," Brendon said quietly.

"You never could see any harm in your ballet dancer!" Loring spoke scornfully. "But as things stand now, it's this man—woman?—who was there among the rocks who matters. If he isn't mythical too."

Brendon made a movement that suggested suppressed violence, and I leaned forward in my chair. "Loring, why are you so anxious to believe there was some sort of guilt on Ariel's part? *Who* are you protecting?"

His look seemed almost triumphant. "All of us, of course. We can't afford to have this look bad for anyone connected with the hotel."

I sensed the rising anger he was trying to control. Clearly nothing was to be done now. The arguments were left suspended, and in some strange way it was as though we all mutually agreed to postpone the real battle, and I said nothing more about going to the police.

When Brendon left, Naomi went off with an oddly secretive air, as though she might know more than she was telling. I glanced back at Loring as I followed them and caught the look of pleased malice in his eyes. How he disliked us all.

I wandered alone back to the house and found it empty, except for the usual maid with her buzzing vacuum cleaner. I smiled at the girl as I went upstairs and shut myself in my room, to sit staring at the yellow carpet.

What was to be done now? I found myself thinking of the young man I had just talked to—Maurice Kiov. At least he had not been one of her lovers—he had only worshiped at the shrine. How easy it had always been for her. A smile, a gesture, an enchanting look, and they came to her. Until she threw them away—as she had thrown Brendon—leaving her discards to figure out how they could live without her. How convenient I had been for Brendon!

"Stop it!" I cried the words aloud as I paced around the room. This was self-indulgence and I didn't need it. What I did need was to cut through all my own self-pity and self-delusions to what might remain that was real between Brendon and me. But how was I to do that when he had so clearly put me out of his life? Or was I out of his life because of my own words, my own behavior? Where did the truth lie, and how was I to find it?

There was one place that remained where I could go. The place I had told myself I never wanted to set foot in again, even though I was aware of its insidious pull. Perhaps this was the time, when the house was empty, and Naomi was busy over at the hotel. She wouldn't be needing her sitting room now.

It was a little like pressing the pain of a toothache. Why should that forbidden room, the room that held only hurt for me, draw me with so strong a demand? What could I do there but founder into images I didn't want to invoke, into memories that were not mine?

I went into the hall and listened at the top of the stairs. The cleaning was going on at the front of the house, and when I was sure I wouldn't be seen, I stole down and followed the lower hall to the rear. The china doorknob was cold under my hand as I turned it and let myself into the room.

It was empty, as I had known it would be, and I closed the door softly behind me. In the gray murk of the coming storm that would send hotel guests scurrying inside in dismay over lost hours, the room was dim and colorless. But someone had readied logs on the hearth and I knelt and set matches to kindling. In moments, flame licked upward, and the room began to glow red in the firelight—red with all the touches Ariel had made. I moved about, looking at everything as I had not done before, but never once glancing toward the picture of Hagar over the mantel.

I had no sense of invading Naomi's privacy, because she herself had already invited me—with malice—to use the room, and she would be pleased to find me here. She would recognize at once the journey I was trying to make back to my sister, and she would be glad if it gave me pain.

On a small rosewood table in a corner rested a brass incense burner with a small temple dog on its top, and I recognized it as a gift I'd made Ariel one Christmas when she was going in for a Japanese period. I felt no hurt because she had given away my gift. Nothing could be more natural to her than to give away anything she might have enjoyed briefly and tired of. Like a man. Were she here, I didn't think she would even begrudge me Brendon.

A pellet of incense rested in the burner and I lighted it and sniffed sandalwood. What was I doing here? What game was I playing? A not too distant rumbling made the window panes rattle. Thunder? I went to a window and looked out at the darkening pine trees behind the house.

The room felt chill and I was glad of the rising fire warmth behind me.

On I went in my idle searching—without real purpose, yet with my senses open to any impression they might receive. So easily could I visualize her in this room. But I saw her always alone. I wouldn't open the door of my mind to Brendon. I wouldn't allow the pictures Naomi had put in my thoughts to surface. I wouldn't look at the red patterned rug that lay before the fireplace. No—I hadn't come here to torture myself, but to try to understand something, though I wasn't sure what it was I must learn to accept and understand.

Not until I had wound my way around the room, examining bric-a-brac, looking at pictures, did I come at last to the mantelpiece and the photograph above it. Only then did I see Ariel's toe shoes resting there on the white marble surface below her portrait. I might have known that Naomi would retrieve them. Just as she had the red fleece robe.

Idly I picked up one slipper and thrust my fingers into the blocking to feel the lamb's wool that had briefly cushioned Ariel's magical toes. The life of such slippers was so short. They could be finished in a single dance, and new ones must be broken in constantly. What dance, I wondered, had her feet brought to life while she was wearing these particular shoes? I turned the slipper over in my hands and saw that down the length of the narrow, barely soiled sole ran a scrawl of writing made by a felt-tipped pen in green ink: *"For Naomi—to remember Giselle. Ariel Vaughn."*

I had forgotten that she sometimes gave her slippers away to favorite admirers, autographed on the sole. What a marvelous Giselle she had been—up there with the classic bests who danced the role. With the slipper still in my hands I turned my back on picture and hearthrug and sought a carved Victorian chair in a far corner of the room. It had no arms, its back a faded oval of crimson velvet. Had Ariel ever sat in this chair? Probably not. I had never known her to seek the outskirts of any room, but always the center. The center of any stage.

14

Now that he has gone, I am sitting here still, the tears drying on my cheeks. I am alone and desolate, and there is nowhere to turn. Yet what could I have done to escape this encounter?

I hadn't dared to move when he walked in, though all I wanted was to be out of this room before he discovered me. To have him find me watching him would be dreadful. Yet I could only sit quietly in my corner, waiting for whatever must happen, helpless to stop time or events.

If he noticed the scent of incense he must have attributed it to Naomi's use. A glance apparently reassured him that the room was empty, and he did not see me in my shadowy corner. He went to stand before the fireplace, looking up at Ariel's picture above the mantel, his back turned to me. But though I couldn't see his face, I knew his pain by the drooping of his shoulders as he studied her photograph. After a moment he picked up the twin to the slipper I held and stared at it—as though he too tried to hold something of her essence in his hand. My heart seemed to break into tiny bits, and I knew a worse hurt than I had ever felt before. It was one thing to imagine that he loved her, but far worse for me to see how intense his loving had been.

Finally he dropped onto the sofa before the fire and sat

there, holding her slipper. It was shameful to watch him suffer, and it was torture for me—yet it would be worse if he found me here. More humiliating for us both. Thunder crashed, and a flash of lightning flicked through the room as rain slashed against the glass. Oddly, I thought of young Kiov driving down the Hudson toward the bridge that would take him to the highway on the eastern side. Another one who had loved Ariel in his own way. And suffered guilt for her death.

Brendon hadn't moved, his head still bent, the slipper between his hands. If only I could assuage his pain. If only I could go to him and give him the comfort of my love. But that was no longer what he wanted. The illusion that had nurtured our marriage had been shattered, and the pieces could never be put together again. What was I to do? What could I possibly do?

All unwittingly, and out of my anxiety, I must have made some sound. Brendon startled me by jumping to his feet and looking around more carefully. Now he saw me, sitting in my dim corner, prim and quiet in a velvet chair, with the mate to the slipper he held in my hands. Across the gloom of the room that Ariel had brightened with so much red, he stared at me, and his face seemed utterly white, as though all life had drained from it. There was nothing I could do or say that would help, but I had to try.

"I—I'm sorry," I faltered. "I thought I'd be alone here, and—"

He stood very still, staring at me. "You might have let me know when I walked in."

"I was afraid." The words were only a whisper.

"Why did you come here?"

"To find her," I managed. "To *try* to find her. The way she used to be. When we were young and she was my marvelous older sister. The sister I could never be like."

"If only she could have been a woman first—and a dancer second," he mused.

How strange it seemed that we should be talking about her quietly like this. We two whom she had damaged. If he had stormed out of the room in a fury, it wouldn't have surprised me, but to have him stand there leaning against the mantelpiece, each of us with one of Ariel's slippers in our hands as we spoke of her—it seemed strange and unreal.

"I'd never met a witch before," he said.

I almost smiled at the word, because I knew exactly what he meant.

"She was a witch," I agreed, ". . . bewitching others. You had only to see her dance—"

"No!" The sound was explosive, repudiating. "I hated her dancing. I wanted her to be something apart from it. A woman."

"Then you didn't accept her as she was—since she always had to be a dancer first."

"Until she came here. Here with me she was a woman. Yet she always had to go back."

"Of course," I said in surprise. "If you couldn't understand that, you didn't know her. Not really."

"But I began to know her. In the end I began to know her. That's why I sent her away."

I stared at him. "*You*—sent *her* away?"

His look seemed uneasy, dropping after a moment. "You never gave me the opportunity to tell you that. She had decided to marry me—after all my asking. She had decided to take the chance. I think she loved me a little— you'll have to grant me that. But I had to be wise enough for both of us. I had to 'accept the fact that it would never work."

"It was *you* who broke it off?" Something that had died in me a little began to come to life again.

"Come here, Jenny," he said. "Come here to me."

I moved slowly because I was afraid. Hurt was something I'd suffered long enough and I didn't want anything to start it up again. Yet I moved toward him while rain slashed the windows, and thunder rumbled farther away.

"I've missed you, Jenny," he said, and his arms opened for me.

I stopped before I reached him, still afraid, and saw the tenderness in his eyes.

"We were both angry the other night," he went on.

"And you wouldn't have listened if I'd tried to tell you. What could I say to you then? That I walked into a theater and saw the Ariel I had wanted to love? And that I knew at once you were everything she was not—everything I really wanted. There was no deception—I fell in love with *you* from the beginning."

I don't know why I hesitated. He was saying all the things I wanted to hear, wanted to believe, yet I was still afraid, distrusting. Something in the very sound of the words made me uneasy.

"I watched you come into this room just now," I told him. "You stood before her picture, you took that slipper from the mantel, and you sat on that sofa, mourning her."

"No, Jenny. Mourning you because I thought I'd lost you. Only blaming her and trying to see a way out."

I stayed where I was, unable to move into his arms, where I wanted to be. He tried again.

"What I at first thought I loved in her never existed. I had to make her understand that in the end. She doesn't exist for me now. She was never anything but a mirage."

With a sudden quick gesture he turned, and before I could cry out he flung the pink slipper into the fire. I could only stare in hypnotized shock as flames caught pink ribbons first, blazing up for an instant, and then began to char satin and leather, burning slowly, not consuming all at once. For me it was as though he had thrown some living part of Ariel into the fire.

He came to me then and pulled me into his arms, put his cheek against mine, holding me fiercely, tightly. And I *knew*. Gently I released myself and stepped back to look into his face—to see the agony there. He had tried to rid himself of Ariel by sending her away. He had tried just now to fling the very memory of her into the fire. And he had failed. When he reached for me again—reached for the anodyne, the opiate—I held him away.

"Wait," I said. "Please wait." Very carefully I placed Ariel's other slipper on the mantel, where Naomi would find it. Then I turned back to him. "Did you know she was going to have a child?"

He stared at me blindly, out of a pain that I could understand all too well.

"You didn't know, did you?" I went on. "I didn't think you could have. When Naomi told me, I phoned Mother, and she said that Ariel had had an abortion. There was a baby coming."

He closed his eyes and put a hand against the mantel. "It wasn't mine. She wasn't pregnant at the time when I told her we couldn't see each other anymore."

"Why did you give her up? Why did you let her go?"

This time he looked at me directly—in surprise at my lack of understanding. "She wanted me to leave Laurel. She would never have stayed here. She could never have made it her life, as it was mine."

So now I understood—everything. He had never stopped loving Ariel, but he had thought that in me he could have Ariel and Laurel too. But at this very moment when he had made his desperate gesture of casting her away, she was more alive to him than I had ever been.

I had to be gentle with him, I had to be kind, even when my own heart was hurting, but I had also to tell him the truth.

"Ariel won't go up in flames for you, any more than she will for me. Loving a mirage can be very real." I knew. I too had been in love with a mirage. "Look!" I said, pointing.

In the fire the pink slipper had turned black, with only sparks of red glowing here and there. He looked—and again I saw his face. For a moment longer he stood before the fireplace and his gaze wandered to the portrait above. When he turned and walked out of the room, I knew he would never come back to me.

A little time has passed and my heart is no longer thumping wildly, painfully. It seems a heavy, inert thing that hardly beats at all. I sit here with tears drying on my cheeks because I can't even cry for long. In the fire, resting upon a flaming log, the slipper is only a black shape, not yet fallen into ashes. I pick up the iron poker and thrust it into the form of the slipper so that it falls to nothing, leaving only a few red sparks that quickly die.

How long I remained before the fire in Naomi's sitting room I don't know. After a time I walked out of the room, still unable to think clearly, moving only by instinct. When I went to the front door and looked outside, I saw it was still raining hard. An old slicker hung on a rack near the door and I caught it up and pulled it around me.

As I ran down the steps, and started along the road that led past the hotel, rain beat upon me, wetting my unprotected hair, gathering in streams across my face. I ducked my head and ran again. The Mountain House loomed huge above me in the murk, scores of its windows lighted against the gray day. None of the guests was out on the balconies and their glass doors were closed upon the chill. I had no desire now to go inside. Even though I was cold, it didn't seem important. For some reason I must hurry, hurry—because there was only one place that might hold answers for me now. Answers about my sister Ariel.

As I walked around the end of the lake, its surface shone with dancing steel needles of rain. A memory of icy death threatening returned to me for an instant, but I cast it away. At that moment I would have walked heedlessly into any danger that might threaten without counting the cost.

The forest paths were wet, the bushes moisture-heavy as they slapped against me. All this was another face of Laurel—that Laurel to which Brendon must always give his first devotion. I came upon an open place high above the lake where I found leaves and small branches scattered across a small space of ground as though some great fist of wind had thrust through the area, ripping away leaves and branches and flinging them across the path. I stepped over the debris and went on.

My way took me up through the glen and I found the bull standing in the center of his ring, black and wet as

I had imagined him. Magnus' work remained on its stand, covered against the rain, waiting for my return, but I had no time for it now. I hurried on to the second clearing, where the house stood, and saw with relief that blue smoke rose from the chimney, blowing first this way, then that. No truck stood beside the cabin, so Magnus was alone. I ran up the steps and banged on the door, suddenly aware that I was wet and cold and felt a little sick.

Magnus pulled the door open and wasted no time in astonishment. He jerked me into the room without gentleness, had me out of the oversized slicker in seconds and plumped me down on cushions before the fire. When he had brought a towel and begun to dry my wet hair roughly, I started to talk.

"I'm sorry—I mean sorry to burst in on you like this. But he threw her slipper into the fire—and—and I understood everything. I couldn't bear it!"

"Just shut up and get warm," he said. "Talking comes later. Do you like mulled cider? Never mind. That's what you're having because that's what there is."

He brought me a brown mug and it warmed my hands, and sipping the tart brew with its hint of cinnamon seemed to thaw a little of the ice that had coated me inside. Magnus sat down on a worn hassock nearby, a second mug in his own hands, his eyes very green and his red hair and beard ashine in the firelight. But this was no small, tame fire in a Victorian grate. Magnus' hearth was wide, and huge logs burned in its heart, throwing out a fierce heat that was beginning to warm even my icy reaches.

"That's better," Magnus said with authority. "You're looking more human now. So if you want to talk I'll listen."

"Did you know Ariel was going to have a baby?" I asked.

His great head moved in assent. "Yes. She told me before she left. It would have been mine. Perhaps another son, or even a daughter. I'd have liked that. Floris wouldn't have another baby after our son died, so I'd given up hope of children. I watched the papers for any word of her pregnancy, but there was nothing."

For the first time I thought of Magnus, who must have suffered too in silence, holding back his pain. Always wondering, with no one to ask. Now I had to tell him.

"There was nothing in the papers because my mother helped her to get rid of the baby. Perhaps it was more my mother's fault than Ariel's."

"Ariel wasn't intended to have children. She was meant to be a dancer. Only a dancer."

"Yes. Brendon doesn't understand that. Naomi told me that she left him because she didn't want marriage and he did. Naomi told me about the baby and said it was his."

"Naomi builds her own fantasies. It was the other way around. Perhaps it was the fact that he never recognized her as a dancer that drew her to him. He saw something in her apart from her dancing, and that pleased her. Perhaps it made her real to herself for the first time."

"Then he saw something that wasn't there," I said dully.

"Perhaps it was what she wanted to be." Magnus' tone was gentle.

I drank the last of the cider and set the mug aside. "I've just begun to face the truth about Brendon. He will never get over loving Ariel. He will never love anyone else."

"I doubt that's true," Magnus said. "Perhaps, when he's had enough time to heal a little, he'll do the only wise thing. He'll look for someone who doesn't remind him of her in any possible way. Someone who will also marry Laurel."

I knew why I had come to Magnus. If Brendon was part of a mirage, Magnus was reality. He might live in a world of marble and granite, but it was a real world where he could accept human beings for what they were—not merely for what he wanted them to be.

"One of the things that hurts me now," I said, "is the reason why Ariel died. I think she really cared about Brendon. She must have felt torn because she couldn't any longer be a dancer happily without him, and yet she knew she couldn't give up her dancing as he would have wanted. She must have understood that Laurel would always come first with him."

"You've worked it out pretty well," Magnus said.

"But then—why did she come here to you? How could she come to another man if she loved Brendon?"

"She came because she thought she could win him over. I don't think she'd ever been rejected before. I was only an instrument. A willing one. She mattered to me the way she was. And she trusted me. I didn't make any bargains with her. There were no terms between us. She needed to be comforted and I could give her that little at least. I'm sorry it wasn't enough."

He had turned his great red head away to stare into the fire, and I watched him with a lump in my throat. How tangled everything was, yet I would see Magnus standing like a rock through it all—a little like his own stone bull out there in the rain. I liked him a lot, and I was glad that he had given Ariel the comfort of his love. But there was no way I could tell him how I felt just then, how grateful I too was for his rough kindness.

After a moment he turned his head and looked at me, and that wide grin appeared in the red beard.

"No matter how he feels, Brendon wouldn't be pleased to find you here." He sounded a little pleased himself—almost triumphant.

I smiled back at him. "You don't disguise your motives, do you, Magnus?"

"Never. When they're small, they're petty, and I enjoy them."

Somehow we were laughing together and I felt enormously better. But when he would have brought me a second mug of cider, I shook my head.

"No more. I'm warm now. In a little while I'll go back to the hotel."

"Why did you come?"

The point-blank question left me a little shocked by my own actions, now that I'd stopped to consider them. Without thought, without any real purpose, I'd gone rushing off into the rain, somehow sure that I would find answers to all my pain and confusion here with Magnus. Answers that went back to Ariel. And perhaps I had— though without ever asking the questions I thought I'd come to ask.

"I suppose I came to find—me," I said. "I'm not sure how you've done it, but I think I can pull myself together now and start figuring out what to do next. Thank you, Magnus."

"What you do next is to go back to New York," he said. "There's nothing more for you to do here."

"Of course there is. You must finish your sculpture, for one thing. My one chance at immortality! And there's still the matter of Floris' death and the suspicions about Ariel. Now that I know how it was with her, I feel all the more strongly about that, and I don't trust Loring."

He shook his head, scowling at me, but he didn't frighten me anymore, and he didn't try further to persuade me.

"How are you going to get back to the hotel?" he asked.

"Walk, I suppose. That's the way I came up."

"And freeze in the rain all over again. To say nothing of running around alone in the woods, as you've been forbidden to do. No—I'll arrange something. Just sit tight and I'll give Dad a call. If he's around he can pick you up."

I couldn't argue with that and I waited while Magnus called the hotel and left a message to be sent out on the intercom to the truck, wherever it was.

"It may be a little while," he said as he put down the phone. "Come back to the fire, Jenny."

He drew me to the cushions I'd left, his hands unaccustomedly gentle, as though I were a child who must not be frightened. With the rosy warmth on my face and hands, I looked up at all the breadth and height of him where he leaned against the chimney. When I spoke, it was like that child he allowed me, in my need, to be.

"It all hurts so much," I said. "Everything hurts terribly."

"A common state of man. But hurting can also stop.

Eventually. There's always the antidote of time, if we give it a chance. The old cliché holds because it's true."

"If only I'd never walked into that theater lobby! If only I'd never come to Brendon's notice!"

"Then you would have missed something, wouldn't you? Just as I would have missed something if Ariel hadn't come here."

"What about Floris?" I asked. "What about the thing you and Ariel did to her?"

His tone hardened. "That was done by Floris to herself long ago. Though I'm not without blame. It was done when my son died because of her indifference."

"Indifference?" I repeated, startled.

He shook his head. "It doesn't matter now. Let it go. I even tried to forgive her and she stayed on, though she hated me for her own blame. I owed her nothing."

In the long silence I sighed heavily. He heard the sound and pulled his hassock closer to me, taking my hands in his.

"Very few humans love only one person and hold that love forever, Jenny. Most people grow, and change, and if two people don't move in the same direction and change together, love between them gets lost. But it's always unique while it lasts and you've had something that might otherwise have been missed. I'm not talking about casual affairs. There's more to life than only one loving. It will come again—with someone else."

"I don't want it with anyone else!" I cried.

"Sometimes you are such an innocent. Ariel never was a child. She knew what she wanted—sometimes mistakenly, but with her eyes open."

"She loved him," I said, choking on the words. "And he did let her down. He threw her away because he loved Laurel best!"

"No. He made a choice for both of them. Brendon isn't an innocent either."

"She killed herself because of him."

He shook his head at me gently, contradicting. "She was losing confidence in herself as a dancer. She was afraid of having a baby because it might destroy her career. For the first time she couldn't keep a man she reached for until she was ready to discard him. She was afraid of growing old. More than anything else she wanted the comfort of an absolute adulation, and that isn't to be had in life. Except perhaps on a stage. And then only for a few moments at a time while the applause rings in your ears. She had it there and it gave her an insatiable appetite for something that doesn't otherwise exist."

"But she took those pills."

"If you want to know what I think, she only intended to cause concern and fright in those who loved her. Perhaps she wanted to punish Brendon. She wanted you all to come flocking around her so she could believe that she was alive and real and much loved. I don't for one minute believe that in spite of her torments she ever meant to kill herself. If you and her mother and Brendon—perhaps even I—had all run to her and groveled at her pretty feet, she would have drawn sustenance from us, and come back very soon to triumph again. I don't think she died by her own choice, but it was certainly by her own blame, and no one else's."

Magnus was a man to be believed and I drew from his strength and managed to smile at him tremulously.

"Thank you," I said, as I had said to him before.

He leaned forward and tilted my head with one big finger. Then he bent and kissed me lightly on the lips. I felt the brush of his beard and I didn't move.

"You're every bit as special as Ariel, but in a different way. A way all your own. Just don't forget that. Only now you must become the woman you haven't really tried to be before."

Tears started in my eyes and when they spilled he nodded his approval. "Go ahead and cry. Tears can wash everything away. Do you know what I did when I learned of Ariel's death? I went out in the woods and sat on the grass beside my stone bull, and I think we both wept. For something magical that would never touch our lives again."

Strangely, I didn't mind his words because for the first time in my life I had stopped trying to compare myself with Ariel, and I too had known that magic he meant. He had given me back my sister in a new way.

Outside in the storm we heard the sound of a truck coming up the trail and I brushed my tears away hurriedly. Magnus brought my borrowed slicker and helped me into it.

"Take care," he said. It was like a caress—and a warning.

The door banged open with no advance knock, and Naomi McClain burst into the room. A bright yellow scarf was tied under her chin, a yellow oilcloth slicker engulfed her small body and there were boots on her feet. She was only a little wet in her rush from the truck.

"I've come for you," she told me abruptly. "I was at the desk when you called, but Keir is miles away, so I said I'd borrow the ranger's truck and come after you. Everyone's mad today anyway—completely insane!—so I suppose your rushing off up here in the storm is more of the same."

Magnus smiled at me over her head, and I found myself smiling back; smiling warmly, as I hadn't been able to do in a long time. Naomi was in a hurry and shrugged aside the offer of mulled cider, pulled me out the door, her arm linked in mine as we hurried down the steps to the idling truck. I saw again the emblem of the panther— wild and beautiful—and knew how well it stood for Laurel. When I'd climbed into the cab and she'd put the truck into gear, I looked back at Magnus, standing in the open door against the fire glow of his cabin, watching as we drove away. Something had happened to me, though I didn't know quite what it was. Something healing had begun. Magnus was good medicine.

Naomi chattered all the way back to the hotel, her state one of aggravated excitement.

"Brendon's stalking around as though he was cracking up. What on earth did you do to him? No—never mind— I don't want to know. It's Irene and Loring who have really gone crazy. The mouse is roaring. They're having a bang-up fight and I want to get back there before it's over."

"What are they fighting about?" I asked in surprise.

"Everything! Laurel Mountain and Loring's plans. Floris and how she died. I think Loring's threatening them if they won't go his way. It's all pretty wild."

"Threatening them—how?"

"Oh, with his theories about the rock that fell. Those pictures. It could be pretty ugly if he went to the police now with all that."

"But he doesn't want a scandal for Laurel any more than anyone else. Surely he wouldn't—"

"You're right," Naomi said flatly. "He won't."

She sounded thoroughly keyed up, and I stole a look at her sharp, tense profile, with the bony thrust of her nose poked toward the windshield where the wipers zipped back and forth.

In the hotel driveway, she parked the truck out of the way, shoved me from the cab and jumped down. In a moment she had me by the arm and was rushing me inside.

"Come along!" she cried. "We must see this."

We didn't bother with an elevator, but took the stairs to the second floor with furious speed. Bcause of the rainy weekend, what guests there were were all about, occupying the little Victorian sitting rooms, one of them picking out tunes at the piano, others in the game room, engaged in bridge. Naomi rushed past them all, dragging me behind her. The door to the McClains' private parlor was closed, but she thrust it open with as little ceremony as she'd used at Magnus' cabin.

The fight was over, however. Irene sat alone upon a plush sofa, staring at nothing, and a small welt was rising visibly on her cheek. She looked at us without surprise.

"He slapped me," she said dully. "Loring slapped me. Bruce would never have done a thing like that."

"Loring's an oaf, and it's time you found it out," Naomi snapped. "He's heading for trouble—that one. Does Brendon know about this?"

For the first time life showed in Irene's eyes. "No! You mustn't tell him. He left before it happened. He'd be horribly angry. He wouldn't stand for this."

I leaned awkwardly against the closed door, wishing myself away, but unable to leave gracefully. Naomi was hopping around the room, chirping like an indignant sparrow. Loring's downfall was apparently something she would relish.

"What are you going to do?" she demanded after a third journey around the room.

Irene looked strangely calm and controlled—emotionless. "I shall leave him, of course. I shall divorce him," she said quietly.

"Hah!" Naomi cried. "He'll never stand by for that. He didn't marry *you*—he married Laurel Mountain and everything it stands for."

"Don't," I whispered to Naomi. "Don't hurt her."

Irene heard and answered quietly. "I'm through being hurt. I've been trying so hard to make things work, trying not to displease him, afraid of having him angry with me. But when he struck me everything stopped. I don't need him anymore."

Just as everything had stopped for me, I thought, when Brendon threw Ariel's slipper into the fire, and I faced the truth for the first time.

I left my post at the door and went to bend over Irene. "Is there something I can do? Would you like to go back to the house? Naomi has a truck outside, so she could drive us there. Would you like me to stay with you for a little while?"

She looked at me as though for a moment she didn't remember who I was. Then she smiled and nodded wordlessly, took my hand and let me pull her to her feet. Naomi hopped along behind us down the hall to the elevators, and Irene managed to bow with her usual friendliness to guests who greeted her. I suppose our curious little parade didn't really look curious to the casual eye.

This time we took the elevator down one floor, and Irene began to lean on my arm more heavily as we walked past the desk and outside. Keir Devin was coming up the steps, and he stared at Irene. But her hand was up to her cheek, concealing, and she gave him a quick, tremulous smile.

He blocked our way to speak to me. "I thought you needed a lift down the mountain, Jenny?"

"I'm sorry if they called you back," I apologized. "Someone should have told you it was all right. Naomi came up to get me."

He nodded curtly and went past us to the desk. He hadn't seen the welt on Irene's cheek, and she didn't take her hand away until we were in the front seat of the truck. As we left the driveway, one nasty moment came when we saw Loring walking bareheaded ahead of us in the rain.

"Shall I run him down?" Naomi asked gleefully, and Irene, sitting between us, gave her arm a slap.

"Don't talk like that. And stay away from him. He doesn't play games. He's dangerous."

With deliberate intent, Naomi drove through a puddle, throwing water out from the wheels, and I saw Loring jump to the side of the road. When I looked back I knew he was cursing us. Brendon had to know about this unhappy development, and as soon as possible. Yet even as the thought crossed my mind, I realized that I would have no angry feelings about seeing Brendon again. Something had really ended, and I was beginning to accept it. Perhaps in the long reaches of the night I would remember my love. Perhaps it would strike through to me at odd moments during the day when some reminder stabbed me, but recognition that it was over helped to some degree.

At the house we spilled out of the truck again. No chambermaid was about and we went into the living room to sit down, as though a certain formality was necessary.

It was the first time I had been in this room and I looked about in appreciation. The room was, I suspected, Irene's achievement. The walls were white, and a wheat-colored sofa stood in the bay window, with the dark green of Norway pines beyond. Two jewel-toned Moroccan rugs covered the polished floorboards—rugs of dark garnet and deep ruby, with touches of topaz, warm and glowing. Tall bookcases painted eggshell had been built into the walls, and again the fireplace was white marble, with tall brass candlesticks branching at either end. A painting of lake and mountain hung above the mantel, High Tower dominating the scene.

Naomi, taking charge again, had pushed Irene into a chocolate-hued armchair and pulled up an ottoman for her feet. Irene allowed herself to be arranged in the chair, and she nodded when Naomi offered to fix her a cup of tea. When she had gone off toward the kitchen, Irene turned her new, quiet look that seemed all too unemotional upon me.

"It was Loring who fixed that rock to fall," she said as calmly as though she commented on the rain. "It was Loring who coaxed Floris into the Lair and waited for Ariel to go at her usual time to that rock over the lake."

I sat down heavily in a white chair, unable to speak.

"I've suspected this for a long time," she went on. "Floris and he never got on and she was threatening to cause a scandal by using Ariel's name. She would have dragged us all into it. Loring was afraid of what she might do. I couldn't feel sorry when she died. But I think that recent anonymous call to the police was something Loring did himself—in order to threaten Brendon and make him do what Loring wants."

"Does he know you believe all this?"

"Of course. That's why he struck me. He told me to keep my mouth shut about such lying nonsense. I suppose I really was pretty aggravating."

Under her calm there seemed a hint of satisfaction—as though his striking her had released her from some bondage. As though provocation had been deliberate.

"Why are you so sure?" I asked.

But at that moment Naomi came back with her tray of cups and teapot, and we all sat down to a cozy afternoon tea party—like the Mad Hatter's—so that I began to wonder if I were Alice, and Naomi the Red Queen. Increasingly, I had the feeling that we were all marking time, waiting for something dreadful to happen.

15

It did happen—and very soon.

Now it is days later. Only an accident, of course. What else? Yet we are all badly shaken, and I have been questioned endlessly, both by the police and by the family. Undoubtedly I am whispered about throughout the hotel. Because I was there. I saw what happened—but no one quite believes me, and I am looked at askance.

It's true that the family, including Brendon, has stood by me, that I've been as protected from unpleasant intrusion as any McClain could be, but underneath the surface banding-together lie all the unanswered questions —which may never be answered. We wait anxiously.

Now, more than ever, I am urged to leave, and they have all pointed out that there is no reason for my staying. Since Brendon and I have parted for good, there is nothing to hold me here. Yet I must search. I am not satisfied about anything.

That Mad Hatter's tea seems a long time ago now, though only a week or so has passed. It is October, and the woods are gloriously aflame. I have never seen such riotous beauty. I walk the trail to Panther Rock and look across a chasm of color to High Tower on the mountain. The falcons are gone now. Every hillside is an artist's palette of colors, yet I have no heart for painting. I have not even retrieved my sketching kit from Magnus' cabin. Futile little drawings I put on paper don't seem to matter anymore.

There are guests here for the fall beauty, and I am not afraid to walk anywhere alone. Someone is always around, and there have been visiting groups besides, to help fill the rooms.

But on that rainy Saturday night of the day when Irene and Loring quarreled, there were fewer visitors than usual over the weekend. Most of the elderly ladies, or couples who come every year to spend the summer, were gone, and there was a slight lull before full autumn splendor brought those who came to relish the painted forests for the first time.

That night a movie was to be shown in the big room that served as meeting room, music room and ballroom, and guests gathered there after dinner. I had spent a restless afternoon and didn't feel like settling down to watch imaginary figures on a screen. I didn't know or care what movie was being shown.

Dinner had been another uncomfortable meal, with Irene absent, though the others were all there. Loring gave no indication of the quarrel with his wife, except that now and then I caught his eyes on me speculatively. Naomi treated him rudely, but didn't explain why, though I think her behavior surprised Brendon, who still didn't know that Loring had struck Irene.

After dinner, I wandered idly about the hotel, and when the time came for the film showing, I looked into the big lighted room that occupied an annex, protruding from the second-floor corridor over the lake, with its own peaked roof and wide, encircling veranda.

The rain had turned to no more than a drizzle, and even that was lessening by the time I stepped out on the veranda, with the lighted room behind me and a sheltering roof over my head. The rail was wet, the night chill, but I wore a jacket, and as I walked damp boards, the lake seemed a dark steel mirror reflecting the lightening sky. All around the edge shaggy trees left their reflections in black lace trimming, and up on High Tower the beacon shone serenely. The woods were quiet, except for the endless dripping that went on after a rain.

Tonight a wind was blowing, rolling away the storm clouds, leaving a hint of full moon to be seen now and then. The room behind me buzzed with voices, and someone was playing a piano—"Let It Rain." My footsteps echoed on the wide boards as I walked, trying once more to find order in my thoughts.

What of Brendon now? I knew only that something had died. Something wild and exciting and beautiful that I had thought to treasure forever was gone. Was it always like this—that one loved a mirage? I, no less than Brendon in his love for Ariel. We imagined the being we thought we loved, but when the veil was snatched away, we saw only a stranger.

What of Magnus? I didn't know. I knew only that when I was near him I felt safe and warm and reasonably unafraid. But this feeling had nothing in it of the exciting, headlong emotion of falling in love that I had felt toward Brendon. I remembered what Magnus had said about more than one kind of love, yet I felt empty and lost, no more than a shell, now that I knew the Brendon I'd imagined didn't exist.

Other thoughts troubled me as well. The things Irene had spoken of without emotion—her flat statements about Loring and the preparation he had made for Floris' death. How much of that was true? How much was spite on Irene's part because Loring had slapped her? Why had he really slapped her? He was usually self-controlled and above emotion, yet she had managed to break down that careful reserve.

The voices and laughter from the room behind me were dying down as the lights dimmed. When I looked through long glass doors I saw only the flickering from the screen reflected upon upturned faces, and heard the sound track as the movie began.

I strolled to a far corner of the veranda protruding from the face of the hotel. Here I could look up at the outline of turrets, black against a lighter sky. From across the lake a floodlight played upon the face of the structure, but its illumination didn't reach to where the towers of Camelot were silhouetted, somehow faintly sinister and overpowering. What was it like up there where one could command a view of the entire countryside?

A whimsy seized me in my restlessness. Now that the night was clearing, the moon full and sailing free of clouds, now that Camelot towers beckoned, I remembered that Brendon had told me that part of the roof was accessible and that stairs near our room led up to it. What a tremendous view there would be up there—of Laurel Mountain by moonlight, of the valleys that lay beyond the hotel, stretching clear to Catskill peaks on the far horizon. I'd seen all the other views—why not this? And why not tonight while the opportunity offered? Who knew how soon I might leave this place forever and the chance might not come again? The thought of this small adventure was exhilarating, drawing me from apathy.

Inside, the corridors were empty as I hurried along, though in the sitting rooms here and there guests who were not moviegoers lingered. I flitted past without looking in, and took the elevator to the fourth floor. Here there seemed no one about and I followed long hallways past the rooms where I had been so happy, without glancing at their closed doors. In the alcove beyond, narrow stairs rose into shadow.

When I reached the bottom step, I hesitated, with one hand on the rail, remembering that I did not walk without danger in this place, and the roofs would be dark and lonely. But no—there was bright moonlight, and anyway no one knew I had come up here. Perhaps this was one place where Ariel had never gone.

Resolutely, I climbed the stairs and found a door at the top. It was unlocked, but heavy to move, and it creaked on unoiled hinges as I struggled to open it. Once I'd pushed it ajar, I could step out upon the surface of the flat roof.

As I had known, no one roof covered the Mountain House. With all its additional construction over the years, a variety of rooftops abounded. But only this one flat section was intended for observers to visit. There were protecting parapets all around, chimneys of light-colored stone rose here and there and a raised pavilion stood on the far side, with a tiled roof that shone dark in the moonlight and would be red by day. A sharp wind made me shiver in this high, exposed place, yet it was glorious, and I was glad that I had come. I moved behind the parapets looking down upon conglomerate lower roofs, including the one over the room where the movie was being shown. Some roofs were brown-shingled; one just below where I stood was steeply peaked and seemed gray now, though I knew its color was green. Farther away was the long section of steep red roofs above rooms currently in use.

Now and then an intensified gust of wind howled around the chimneys, and overhead ragged clouds raced the sky. I turned up my jacket collar and thrust my hands into pockets as I faced into the wind, looking west over the great valley with its sprinkling of lights spreading clear to scalloped Catskill peaks in the distance. Then I crossed the wide space of roof to look out toward High Tower and its light, riding the cliff above the dark lake. The grounds below seemed far away, but there were lights down there and I could make out paths and great slanting lawns shimmering in the moonlight.

Perhaps it was fortunate for me that the door to the roof was heavy and did not open easily. Because of the events that followed, I still don't know what was truly intended. I only know that as I stood enjoying the view, I heard someone struggling with the door as I had done, heard creaking hinges as it opened, and I acted instinctively. If someone had followed me up here, I had better not be seen, and I stepped quickly behind a massive stone chimney that hid me from view.

Footsteps crossed the roof, and as he went past my hiding place, I saw Loring Grant. He stepped through the arched doorway of the pavilion and at once I sidled around the chimney, keeping out of sight, frightened by his presence. If the things Irene had said were true, Loring was not someone I wanted to face on this lonely rooftop. But hiding places were limited unless I ventured onto a neighboring roof.

Stepping carefully, silently, while he was out of sight in the pavilion, I moved to the edge of a parapet where the flat portion ended and an unguarded, slanting roof spread ahead of me, dropping to either side from a central ridge. Here were more chimneys, and the curves of adjoining roofs to offer hiding, if I could reach them. I could see that a board catwalk followed the ridge, and without daring to hesitate I went over the parapet and onto it. The slant of roof on either side was not as steep here as in some parts of the hotel roofs, and I could probably walk it without difficulty. I tested it first, since it was still wet with rain. Then I stepped swiftly toward the shelter of a chimney, where I could once more crouch and feel well hidden.

Loring was still on the other section of the roof and I couldn't see him from behind my shelter, nor had I any intention of peering out. It was bad enough to hear him moving about, making no attempt to conceal his presence. The sounds came nearer, and I knew that he must have come close to the parapet between him and the catwalk.

"Jenny?" He called my name above the rushing sound of the wind, and I held my breath and clung to the stones of the chimney. He knew I was here. He must have seen me go by downstairs, and he had followed me. He must have known that he had me trapped on the roof.

"Jenny, you shouldn't be up here alone," he called. "This is a dangerous place, and you've been here long enough. It's time to go downstairs, Jenny."

It was indeed time to go—but not with him. When I heard Loring climb onto the wall to let himself down to the catwalk, my fright increased. There would be no Magnus to rescue me this time, and my danger was very real. Yet Loring blocked the way to escape, and my only hope was to be still and pray that he wouldn't find the place where I was hiding. A wild chase over the rooftops didn't appeal to me.

Momentarily, the moon went behind flying clouds, and I peered cautiously from behind my chimney. Loring stood on the parapet, silhouetted against the sky, while well below him I was in dark shadow. As I watched I heard a second screeching of hinges as the roof door swung open again, and someone I could hear but not see ran out upon the roof.

Whoever it was must have glimpsed Loring poised on the high parapet, his back to the intruder. There was a rush of steps across the roof and I saw Loring turn and recoil. A moment later a long pole like a broom handle came into view, thrusting at Loring like a lance. I think it never touched him, but he leaped to my side of the roof, slipped on the catwalk and went sliding down the shingles. I held my breath in shock as he reached the edge. There was a moment when he struggled to catch himself. Then I heard him scream as he went over. Somewhere below there was a dreadful crash, followed by an equally dreadful silence. I shall hear that scream echoing in my nightmares for the rest of my life. For moments longer I cowered behind the chimney with hands over my ears as though I could wipe out the memory of that terrible sound.

But I knew I must listen for something else. Was the person with the broomstick still there on the other roof? When I took down my hands, I heard running steps, the sound of the door again, followed by silence. There was a long, dreadful hush before an outcry of voices sounded far below. Loring's scream and his fall had been heard, and there were shouts of alarm, men running about.

I left my chimney cautiously and went back to the flat section of roof on legs that felt weak and unsupportive. The roof stood empty now, and the door was closed. I looked down from the parapet and saw a cluster of figures in the lighted area below. Some of them were looking upward.

The moon sailed the sky again and now I could make out Loring's body lodged on one of the lower roofs, unmoving as an empty sack. I shouted down to those on the ground.

"He's caught on that roof down there! Come and get him quickly before he slides off!"

Those below scurried like ants, and I turned away, too sick and shaken to watch.

Somehow I managed to cross the empty expanse and open the heavy door to look down the stairs. Would someone be waiting for me around the turn into the corridor? But the very hush of the hallway seemed deserted. I went down a few steps and sat upon the stairs, leaning my head against the wall, waiting for my trembling and my fright to subside.

It was Brendon who found me there. I must have looked at him in a dazed, half-witted way, because he shook me, trying to jar some sense into me. Others were around us now, staring at me. Vaguely I recognized members of the hotel staff.

"It's all right, Jenny," Brendon said. "They've brought him in through a window, and an ambulance is coming."

I looked up at him, still shivering. "Is he . . . ?"

"He's alive. We don't know how badly he's been injured."

I tried to stand up, and then did something I've never done in my life before—I fainted.

When I came to, choking because Naomi was waving an old-fashioned bottle of smelling salts under my nose, I found that I was lying on a plush sofa in the McClains' parlor near the dining room. There were others in the room, staring at me from a distance, but Brendon was gone. Only Naomi knelt on the floor close beside me waving her little green bottle.

"Take it away!" I gasped.

She replaced the glass stopper and I breathed pure air thankfully. But she wouldn't let me alone. With quick little taps she patted my face, as though she expected me to go out again.

"You've got to come to," she said. "You've got to tell us what happened."

"Loring," I murmured. "He—he fell."

"Yes—we know. He's still alive, but unconscious. The ambulance has taken him away. How did it happen, Jenny? Why were you up there?"

I closed my eyes and took long deep breaths, grateful

when Irene came quietly into the room and began to shoo everyone away, including Naomi. Apparently she could be as strong a person in a crisis as I had once thought she might be, because whatever emotion she felt now was being held sternly in check. At the moment she appeared to have only one concern—me.

When they were all out and she had closed the door, she pulled up a chair and sat beside my sofa.

"Now then, Jenny, tell me exactly what happened. Brendon says you were on the roof. Collect yourself and talk to me. We only want to help you."

"Help *me?*" I opened my eyes fully and stared at her. She had used careful make-up over the welt on her cheek. "Why aren't *you* on the way to the hospital with your husband?"

Her expression softened momentarily into more familiar lines. "They took him away before I knew he was hurt. Brendon will drive me in soon. But Jenny—I lost my *husband* years ago. Bruce was my real husband. I couldn't ever put Loring in his place. Right now Brendon wants me to find out what happened up there on the roof. Why did you go up there?"

My voice cracked as I tried to explain. "I—I only wanted to see the view. Loring must have followed me and—"

"Yes. I asked him to. You were behaving strangely, running about aimlessly. When I saw you running down the hall toward the stairs I asked him to go after you."

Someone spoke behind her and I tilted my head to see that Brendon had joined his mother.

"You went up on the roof in the rain and the dark?" he asked.

"The rain had stopped." I felt a sudden eagerness to explain to him, to make him understand. "It wasn't dark. There's a full moon tonight. But I was—afraid when Loring came. I hid from him. I didn't know why he'd followed me up there."

Gently Brendon removed his mother from my side and took her place. "Did Loring speak to you at all?"

"Yes. He called my name. He said it was dangerous

for me to be up there alone and I should come downstairs with him."

"And then?"

"I didn't trust him. I didn't answer and I stayed hidden."

"Where?" Brendon asked.

"I climbed over the parapet onto the next roof where there's a catwalk."

"And no protection!"

"It's not very steep, and I had no choice. I clung to one of those chimneys that could hide me."

"How did he come to fall? Answer me carefully, Jenny. Loring was muttering some sort of accusation when they carried him to the ambulance. But it made no sense."

I closed my eyes again, seeing that terrible moment when he had gone over the wall, slipping and flailing his arms, until he slid over the edge.

"Maybe he was pushed," I said.

Beyond Brendon, Irene cried out, and Brendon bent toward me. "Easy now, Jenny. Be careful how you answer. Who pushed him?"

"I don't know," I said wearily. "I didn't see. I heard someone else come out on the roof and I saw a long pole like a broomstick being shoved at Loring. He tried to escape onto the other roof, but he slipped and fell."

Irene moved in beside her son. "The girl is out of her mind. She's making it all up—or imagining it."

"I know what those door hinges sound like," I said stubbornly. "And I heard steps that weren't Loring's. He wasn't walking about by that time. And I saw the stick that was thrust at him."

"Listen to me." Brendon's tone was low and firm. "The police have to be called in when there's an accident of this sort, and they will be here soon. If you tell them you think he was pushed, they may believe you pushed him. There's no need to let yourself in for that. It could be very uncomfortable for you—though of course we know it isn't true."

I closed my eyes again. Somehow, somewhere, we had stopped loving each other, and it no longer mattered to me what he thought. I didn't care what anyone thought. My life had been smashed as surely as Ariel's had, even though I could live and breathe.

"Perhaps someone was trying to punish Loring for Floris' death," I said, hearing my own strange, rather conversational tones.

Both Irene and Brendon stared at me, then looked at each other. I knew Irene must by now have said to Brendon the things she had said earlier to Naomi and me—the accusations she had made against Loring. Again I wondered if they had been true at all.

Once more, Brendon bent over me. "How are you feeling? Can you sit up, Jenny? Perhaps your mind will clear a bit if you start moving around."

"I'm not out of my head," I assured him, but I allowed him to pull me to a sitting position. There was nothing wrong with me except an enervating despair. "Could it be," I went on, "that Loring had nothing to do with Floris' death, but that he knew something that pointed to whoever caused that boulder to roll?"

Brendon's patience with me ended. He shook me again —hard, so that my head fell back, and I jerked away from him.

"Don't do that!" I cried. "Don't ever do that again!"

"Then listen to me. None of these wild ideas of yours are to be told to the police. I would hope they'd consider your state of confusion and make allowances, but I don't want to see the past resurrected at this late date to make trouble for us."

It was Laurel again. All he cared about was Laurel. He had even sacrificed Ariel to Laurel.

I rose and began to walk about the room with Brendon watching me darkly, and Irene's attention cool upon me.

"Don't you think Irene had better start looking like a grieving wife?" I asked, facing them abruptly.

Before either could answer, there was a tap on the door and one of the clerks from the desk looked in.

"Lieutenant Blair is here from Kings Landing," he said.

The officer came into the room, greeting Brendon and Irene, whom he knew, looking questioningly at me.

"Is this the young lady who was on the roof?" he asked.

I answered before anyone else could answer for me, and my words came out in a rush. "Yes, I was there. Loring Grant came after me because he thought it might be dangerous for me to be up there alone. Then someone else came up to the roof—someone I didn't see. Someone who tried to push Loring off."

Now that the whole uproar has quieted and the worst of it is over, I can look back and almost laugh at the expressions I saw around that room. Brendon's anger because I had disobeyed him, Irene's distress. But they had to accept what I had done, and the whole kettle of fish was opened up for the police. My one concession was to let the matter of Floris and Ariel alone. The present affair was complicated enough.

It was late by the time all the questioning was over and the police had gone. There was no evidence to back up the story I had told—not even a broomstick to be found on the roof—and I don't think they put much stock in my words.

By the time I was free for the night, I felt horribly tired and shaken, but my nerves were on edge, and I couldn't bear the thought of turning in right away. I left the hotel and walked around the end of the lake toward one of the gazebos, where I had gone before after dark. It was public enough, safe enough in this lighted area near the hotel, and nothing more was likely to happen tonight. Whoever had been on the roof with Loring would probably lie low for a while.

Not until I set foot on the rocks leading up to the little summerhouse did I realize that someone was there ahead of me. My heart leaped and I would have turned to run back—trusting no one—when Magnus' voice spoke to me out of the dark shelter.

"Come and talk to me, Jenny. Come and tell me what has happened. My father has been in on some of it, but I'm not particularly welcome around the Mountain House."

I took Magnus' hand and let him pull me up on the

rocks to sit beside him on the rustic bench. In a few moments I had told him everything that had happened, beginning with that Mad Hatter's tea in the afternoon. He heard me out with his usual air of attentive listening. When I told him about Brendon and Irene trying to keep me quiet, and of my rush of words to the police, he put an arm about me.

"That's my girl," he said. "Listen to your own drummer always."

He was so big and warm and comforting that I clung to him and cried a little in relief. He asked nothing of me —he just gave. Of himself—his strength and his belief in me and in what I said. It had been hours since anyone had believed in any words I'd spoken. But when at length I began to shiver, he stood me on my feet.

"Let me walk you back to the house now, Jenny. You're tired and you're cold. Ask Irene for a sleeping pill and let yourself conk out. You can't have your mind going in circles all night."

"But now whoever was up there knows I was there too, Magnus. So I'm afraid—"

"You've also made it very clear that you saw no one. Just stay off roofs for a while, will you, honey, and out of lonely woods."

"What will happen now?" I asked him as we followed the path around the end of the lake.

"There's no telling. Maybe they'll ask more questions. Maybe they'll dig up the fact that I tried to give Loring a beating the other day, and I'll be next on the mat."

"Oh, no!" I cried.

His arm about me tightened. "It doesn't matter. I can answer whatever they ask. Unfortunately, I don't think they have a thing to pin solidly on anyone. Unless you can recall something more definite, they'll probably drop the whole thing."

That was exactly what happened. My own vague impressions were apparently unconvincing, and no one was found who might have wanted to injure Loring. Magnus was questioned, but his father vouched for the fact that he had been in his open-air studio back of the cabin working on a piece of granite by the lights he'd rigged up there.

Through it all, Loring said nothing. Even when he recovered consciousness, his memory of what had happened remained hazy and he had less to tell than I had. His injuries were serious and he would be slow in mending. Much of the time his drugged mind wandered.

In the end, the idea that it was an accident seemed to let everyone off the hook, just as it had done in Floris' case, and it was decided that I wasn't too clear about what had happened anyway. I was the only one who was convinced that a murderer was still at large, and that it was my responsibility now to unmask whoever it was. A responsibility I didn't relish. This time, at last, I had sense enough to do no more talking.

16

This has been a strange day and not without event—for me, at least. A little more than a week has passed since Loring's terrible fall, and there is a continuing uneasiness in the air. It seems strange not to see him around the hotel, and rather sad that, like Floris, he is being missed so little. Guests, of course, come and go, and some are not even aware of what has happened.

Strangely, only Irene seems to miss him. There has been an unexpected change in her. Seeing Loring broken and helpless, their roles reversed, appears to have roused some new, protective instinct in her, and she has been behaving like a loving and conscientious wife. Not a day passes that she is not at Loring's bedside, and she is already making elaborate plans for his convalescence at home. He will not walk easily for some time, and he will need her help and compassion. He is still unable to remember what happened on the roof.

Toward me, Irene has been friendly enough, yet more than a little inquisitive—as though she may believe that I am holding something back concerning that terrible night. I no longer trust her, and I try to avoid her as much as possible.

Until this morning, I hadn't seen Magnus since the night of the accident, though I know the fault was mine.

I had only to climb the mountain to his cabin, yet I couldn't bring myself to do that until today. Perhaps some uncertainty about myself and my own feelings toward him has held me back. If I went to him, he would welcome me, I knew. But if I chose to leave Laurel without seeing him again, he would let me go without any effort to hold me here.

I like that—and I don't like it. It suits my own sense of independence as a woman to be left with a choice that is mine. Yet at the same time, when I recall Brendon's stormy and overwhelming wooing, something of Eve in me enjoys a slight frisson at the memory.

I have told myself that I would never be overpowered in that way again—yet perhaps I was not above a secret fantasy in which Magnus descended from his mountain like his own bull, to bear the not-too-reluctant maiden away. Was that really what I wanted? To have my mind made up for me again? Because if that was the case, I didn't like myself very well. I didn't want to follow in Brendon's footsteps. I mustn't try to make the pain of loss stop by filling in with any substitute that offered.

This morning Naomi surprised me by appearing at the door of my room with an unfamiliar look of entreaty about her.

"Come for a ride with me, Jenny. I've planted bulbs until I'm dizzy. And you haven't ridden a horse since you've come here."

I hadn't, but I could hardly think of a less welcome riding companion. She was persistent, however, so I put on my warmest slacks and a turtleneck sweater under my jacket. Naomi wore her usual jeans and sweater and red bandanna. She often seemed impervious to the cooling weather.

We walked down to the stables, where horses were waiting for us, saddled and ready, since she had phoned ahead of time. Her own mount was an ungainly animal with a slightly sway back and the name of Dulcinea. I gathered that she was one of Naomi's rescued lame ducks. A properly quiet mare called Juniper had been chosen for me and I found myself in the saddle with an unexpected sense of pleasure.

I had been living too much with myself, and it was good to do something physical that would distract me from my own thoughts. Besides, there is something reassuring to the ego about mounting a horse and achieving that sense of command that belongs to a human on horseback.

"Let's not go far," I said to Naomi. "It's been a long time since I've ridden, and I don't want to get miserably stiff."

She nodded and headed off toward the gardens. It became quickly evident that our ride was not without purpose. Naomi took the lead, following a trail above the formal plantings—one that had become familiar to me. I knew where we were going, but by that time I was curious to learn why she was taking me there. On the way, I savored autumn sunshine and woods that were bright with color. There was no talk between Naomi and me, and it was a pleasure to have a horse moving strongly beneath me, carrying me without effort.

When we reached the gate to the cemetery, she dismounted and tied her reins about a gate post, motioning me to do the same. We walked through together and she led the way to Floris' grave. I found myself thinking of Loring, who might so easily have been resting here. And of me.

For once, someone had placed a small bouquet of wild flowers upon Floris' grave. They were already wilting—but at least someone had remembered.

"Magnus," Naomi said. "He's the only one of us big enough to do that, even though he was the one Floris injured most."

"Why have we come here?" I asked.

She gave me a twisted grin. "You know what they say—never speak ill of the dead. Only it's necessary to speak ill of her, so I wanted to do it openly—right here at her grave. If she's anywhere listening—then let her listen. Let her strike me down!"

I had a feeling that she half meant her own words, but I waited, saying nothing.

Naomi sat on a patch of grass and poked with a grass stem at a crawling ant. After a moment, I dropped down beside her, still waiting.

"From the time she first came here," Naomi began, "all Floris wanted was to get away. Wherever she was, that would have been the place to dissatisfy her. Somehow she was always programmed for unhappiness. But since Magnus made this his home, and the place where he wanted to work, she hated it and only wanted to be off to a city. She'd have liked Loring to come in with his bulldozers and drive Magnus and Keir from the cabin. Of course if he was driven away from Laurel, he'd simply move to his land in Pennsylvania, but Floris never accepted that."

"Didn't their child help to hold her here?"

"Chris? He was a lovely little boy. I'm not mad about children, but I was fond of him. Magnus doted on him— so Floris was jealous. Of her own son! She was the sort of person who never understood her own motives—never looked at herself. And she acted against Chris to punish Magnus."

"How do you mean?"

"A small boy shouldn't be around a lake unwatched. But Floris never watched him. Magnus was to blame too because he was busy with his work and he left Chris in Floris' hands. It was Brendon who found the little boy's body when he drowned. He would have been eleven years old by now. Magnus nearly went mad. Floris came through all right, but she wouldn't have any more children."

I was silent for a little while, feeling the pain of so great a tragedy.

"It's a funny thing," Naomi went on, "but there was a time when Floris and I were friends. Neither of us drew people around us the way Irene does, so I suppose we turned to each other in a sort of prickly loneliness. I don't think she really liked me, or I her. She used to drive Magnus right up the wall with her deliberate tormenting. Keir could ignore her, but Magnus had to live as her husband. Maybe he'd have strangled her, or done something desperate, except that he had his own way to get rid of his rage. Every once in a while he would carve some dreadfully ugly creature out of rock from the quarry. I've seen one of them—something out of a nightmare world— huge and threatening and wicked."

"Like his stone bull?"

Naomi looked shocked. "Oh, no. The bull is beautiful. He's pure and primitive and natural. This creature wasn't natural."

"I remember seeing a strange, frighteningly tortured head in Magnus' outdoor studio," I said.

"I know the one you mean, but that was only a small horror. The one I saw was huge."

"What did he do with it? Was there a buyer?"

"Perhaps. I don't really know, and it's not something one would dare to ask him. I think he was a little ashamed of those outbursts and he never talked about them. Floris said the big one just disappeared one time when she was away for a couple of days, and he's never done anything like that since. Perhaps Ariel exorcised his demons for him. She could have, you know—she was an angel."

I had been seeing Naomi in a new role—a more understanding role than I'd ever seen her in before. But now she was back with her own blindness in her adulation of Ariel Vaughn.

"I'm sure we didn't ride up here so you could tell me all this."

"Didn't we? How do you know? You're following in your sister's footsteps, aren't you?"

I thrust back my quickly rising annoyance. "What makes you say that?"

"You and Magnus. It's obvious, isn't it? Though he can't put you in her place, any more than Brendon could."

Annoyance won out and I sprang to my feet. "Let's go back. There's nothing you have to say that I want to hear."

"Isn't there?" Naomi clasped her hands about her knees and rocked back and forth beside Floris' grave.

In spite of myself, I waited. The engraving Magnus had done so carefully on Floris' headstone stood out clearly in the sunlight—stark, somehow, and without delicacy. He had made this stone out of duty, not love. Yet he had met his duty.

All around us in the woods leaves were falling, dry and crisp on the autumn air. They made a little clatter as they fell, rattling the dry bones of coming winter.

"There's so much you don't know," Naomi went on. "So much you would like to know. Don't you think you'd better listen?"

I stayed where I was, looking down at her. "Go on, then."

"Floris hated it when Magnus said Ariel could stay with them."

"Why wouldn't she? I know what my sister was like."

"Do you? Do you know how desperate she was? Magnus had been kind to her when she had come here before to be with Brendon. She went to him because there was no one else to turn to. Even I couldn't help her. He was afraid she might kill herself—as she did, eventually. He had to try to rescue her if he could. And what difference could it make to Floris? She hadn't been a wife to Magnus for years. She only wanted to be a leech and punish him for all the things that were her own fault."

I looked down upon Naomi's head with its red scarf, feeling more kindly toward her—quite unexpectedly. "You seem to have thought a lot about all this, and perhaps you've figured things out rather well. Magnus and Ariel, that is."

"Of course I have! But Ariel's gone—and now there's only you to take her place."

I must have made some sound of exasperation, for she looked up at me forlornly.

"You can't really, of course. You're not a very good substitute. But you're all I've got. So you ought to understand about Magnus and not blame him for anything that happened."

"I've never blamed him," I said. "I think he's the only truly good person I've ever known."

Her small features twisted into a grimace. "You have to have an ideal to worship, don't you? You want a man you can look up to every minute."

"Me?" I cried in astonishment. "I've always been independent. I've always—"

"Until you let Brendon sweep you away. Magnus won't do that. He's a man, and sometimes he's not a very good man. He's suffered the nightmares that used to drive him into carving those weird creatures. Just look at him as he is, Jenny. I don't really like him, but I can see him without blinders."

Once more I was wordless. This was a Naomi I'd never seen before. Wry, as always, yet speaking out of a natural wisdom that she usually kept hidden. The intentness of my look must have spoken for me, because she went on.

"Do you think I don't know what Ariel was like away from her dancing? She could be an angel. But she could also be selfish and inconsiderate and cruel. I saw all of that. Yet she had her own perfection when she danced. And perhaps in her case it justified everything else. The difference between her and Floris was that Ariel really had something to give to life. Floris was an evil person, and she never gave anything. Maybe evil is a melodramatic word, but that's what she was. She knew Ariel was pregnant and she knew Magnus was the father. Oh, I know I lied to you—because I wanted to hurt you then. I don't think I do anymore. Anyway, Floris wanted to punish them both. Not because she cared, but because she liked to hurt people. I talked to her the day before she died and she told me what she meant to do. She was going to expose everything to the nearest reporter who would listen. With anyone else it wouldn't have meant anything. But Ariel couldn't sneeze without hitting the headlines. Someone had to stop Floris. There'd have been bulldozers, all right. Irene would have seen Floris ruin everything Bruce and his father and grandfather had built. Brendon would have seen the things he cares about most destroyed. But it didn't happen. She was stopped in time."

Naomi dropped her voice and looked straight into my eyes. "I think Loring knew who it was."

"Do you know?"

She was watching me quizzically, as though she wondered how far she could trust me. "Perhaps. But I'm not going to do anything about it. At least not very much. Just one small thing, perhaps."

She began to laugh softly to herself, rocking back and forth there on the ground, and the sound was eerie. The clear light of sanity she had displayed until now was gone, and this was the Naomi I knew better—a troublemaker who liked to cut and wound and stir things up, so that sometimes I wondered if she was any better than the Floris she decried.

"Such a joke!" She was choking on her own laughter. "Such a surprise I have for all of you! When I get ready to spring it. Perhaps I'll do it tonight. Yes, tonight after dinner would be a very good time. I'll even invite Magnus and his father down from the mountain. And of course you and Irene and Brendon. To the Red Barn. That's where it must be done."

I reached out and clasped a hand about her wrist. "Stop it, Naomi. You're beginning to sound hysterical. What do you know that no one else knows?"

She jumped to her feet, making an effort to suppress that bubbling, eldritch laughter. "Oh, I do know something! Something lovely. Tonight I'll show you all. You'll come, won't you—because you want terribly to know who killed Floris and pushed Loring off the roof, and substituted that boat, hoping you would drown. Because you can't be safe until the truth is out, can you?"

Before I could press her with more questions, she ran away from me across the cemetery, mounted her sway-backed nag and rode off through the woods. I was left to sit in the sun staring at the headstone on Floris' grave, while my own mare cropped vegetation a little way off. In a few moments I would mount her and ride back to the hotel. I remembered Magnus' words, "Don't stay alone in the woods." But I felt no danger here and no one had molested me since the incident with the boat.

"Good morning, Jenny," a voice said from the cemetery gate.

I looked around to see Keir Devin standing there, regarding me with just the hint of a smile.

"Hello," I said. "I rode up here with Naomi, but she's gone back without me."

"That's like her." He came through the gate. "You'll never find Naomi going for more than ten minutes in one direction. Then she's off on a different course."

"Just the same, she was talking some very good sense just now," I said.

Naomi's good sense did not appear to interest him. He patted Juniper and stroked her nose, talking to me over his shoulder.

"I suppose you'll be going back to New York soon?"

"Soon," I told him.

"It's really over then between you and Brendon? For good?"

I nodded. "I'm afraid so. We both got off on a wrong course."

He seemed to think about that for a while as he stroked the mare. The antagonism I had sensed in him when Brendon and I had first parted seemed to have lessened.

"What about Magnus?" he asked abruptly.

The words surprised me and I started toward him across the enclosure. "What do you mean?"

"He's still working on that marble of the bull. Europa, he says. I think he needs you there. Why don't you go up and see him now?"

"When did you change your mind? You've always warned me away from Magnus."

"And you've never listened. First Ariel and then you. Brendon has been more like a son to me than Magnus, but I didn't want to see it happen all over again."

"Yet now you're urging me to see Magnus. Why?"

"He's suffered enough."

"Has that anything to do with me?"

"You're the only one who can answer that. Don't be too much like your sister."

I changed my course. "It was Brendon who sent Ariel away."

I had surprised him, and he looked at me long and steadily.

"You didn't know that? But Brendon will always love Laurel first and best."

He said nothing as he helped me into the saddle, and I sat looking down at his strong, weathered face. After a moment he spoke.

"Anyhow, it doesn't matter now, one way or the other. You and Brendon have settled that. There's only Magnus left."

"You promised to help me find out the truth about Floris' death."

The dark look he gave me was not a happy one. "You'd better forget about that.".

"Because you've found out something you don't want to tell me?"

"Go and see Magnus," he said, and strode away down the mountain.

I slapped the reins, spoke to Juniper and rode off up the trail toward the cabin. The way steepened shortly, but the mare carried me without objection. When we reached the circle surrounding the bull, I found Magnus standing before his block of marble, busy with mallet and chisel. As I drew near, I saw that he had worked down to perhaps half an inch of the figure he was freeing from the stone. The work he was engaged in now was delicate.

"Would you like me to pose for you again?" I asked, feeling suddenly unsure of myself.

He had been deeply absorbed and hadn't heard me when I dismounted. Now his red head came up quickly, so that I saw once more the green gleam in his eyes.

"So you've come," he said. "It took you long enough."

This was not the welcome I wanted. "If you needed me you had only to phone the hotel."

He stared at me with a look that seemed to cut away all pretense—just as he had cut away the superfluous stone from what lay hidden in the block. I felt uncomfortably exposed and without defense.

"I knew you would come if I waited," he said calmly. "If you hadn't—then I'd have been given a different answer."

Because he confused me, because I hadn't grown up in an atmosphere devoid of subterfuge, I moved from him toward the bull.

"Would you like me to pose today?" I asked again.

He shook his massive red head and began putting tools away, covering the marble block, and I sensed a change in him, his usual exuberance subdued.

"Come up to the cabin, Jenny. I think we need to talk a bit."

Strangely, I was reluctant to go. In me there seemed a warring of impulses. One an impulse to flight—as must have seized Europa in the face of Zeus's blandishments, the other a desire, equally instinctive, to follow wherever this man led. When Magnus left the clearing without looking back, I took the path after him to the cabin, leaving Juniper tethered behind.

Inside, he busied himself lighting the fire, and it was I who tackled the big graniteware coffee pot this time, pouring steaming mugs for us to drink beside the fire. Perhaps I felt it was safer if I had something in my hands. When I chose the worn sofa, he took the hassock near the hearth again, not too close, not too far away.

"Are you satisfied with the decision that Loring's fall was an accident?" I asked when the silence grew too long.

He recognized the side road away from what might become too personal, and accepted it soberly.

"I think the trouble is over," he said.

I couldn't agree with that. "There have been three attempts at murder. One was successful. How can anything be over? There's someone on the mountain with a twisted, dangerous purpose. We can't ignore that."

"Floris and Loring were the real sources of trouble," Magnus pointed out quietly. "Perhaps what happened to you was only a mistake. Unless you go stirring things up again, I don't believe anything more is likely to happen. You don't know enough to be a threat to anyone."

I listened with a sense of outrage. "Do you mean that

you would allow all this to go unresolved, and a murderer left unpunished?"

"How can any of us do anything else at the moment?" he asked. "If there *is* a murderer, I don't know his identity. Do you?"

"You're all protecting someone!" I cried. "I've felt it with every one of you. Brendon, Naomi, your father—now you."

"You haven't mentioned Irene," he said wryly.

"Yes—there's Irene too. Each of you has behaved strangely about all this."

"That names us all, doesn't it, Jenny? So which of us is protecting not one of the others but himself?"

My outrage grew. "I didn't think *you* would be dishonest."

He gave me his blazing white smile. "I'm glad you used to approve of me. But of course you shouldn't. I could be dangerous too. I've known what it's like to have murder in my heart. Perhaps I can even sympathize."

"To the point of protecting someone who has taken a life?"

"No." The smile was gone. "Forgive me for baiting you, Jenny. You have a habit of leading with your chin that brings out the worst in me. If I was convinced that there had been deliberate killing and I knew for certain who had done it, I would go to the police. I just don't happen to know."

"And don't want to know!"

"In any case, I have no facts to go to the police with. But since this isn't something that needs to be settled now, must we talk about it this morning? When perhaps there isn't too much time left to us for talking about other things?"

"What do you mean by that?"

"You'll leave here before long, won't you? Isn't that your plan?"

I took a long sip from the hot mug in my hands. "Yes. I suppose it is. So what do you want to talk about?"

Magnus surprised me. "Let's talk about your painting,

for a start," he said, and left his hassock to pick up my sketchbook from a table.

I'd forgotten that I'd left it there, and I watched a little defensively as he brought it back to the fire and opened it to one of the finished water colors I had done.

"Is this really what you mean to give your life to?" he asked.

I wriggled self-consciously. "Oh, I know they're not very good. But they might be suitable for a textbook. To be used in schools, I mean. Or by beginning botanists."

"That would be useful. And quite possible. It could make a handsome book—though expensive."

"I don't know much about that. I'd just like it to be useful."

"Admirable, but sometimes impractical. One thing though—you're much too good not to be better. Here—look at what you've done."

He handed me the open book and I stared at my water color of a clump of Queen Anne's lace I'd come upon by the roadside. It had been a painting I was rather proud of, and I looked back at him, puzzled.

"I don't know what you mean."

"You haven't learned to use your eyes yet."

This affronted me. "I don't know anyone who is more careful and accurate in copying nature than I try to be. Everyone says my drawings couldn't be more meticulous and exact."

"Meticulous is a good word. All these exquisite little paintings you do—with every petal perfect, every stamen and pistil in place—all terribly exact and flawless and without life. As though you were drawing for a seed catalogue."

I could feel the flush of angry blood surge into my face, but before I could speak he plucked me off the sofa with one great hand and marched me to a window.

"Look out there and tell me what you see."

My voice shook with indignation as I answered. "What do you mean—what do I see? Your workshop is out there, with the woods behind."

"No—look closer to the cabin."

Now I saw the shaggy growth of Queen Anne's lace at the side of the yard.

"Come along," he said, taking the coffee mug from me, setting it on a table and pulling me out the back door after him with almost a single gesture. When we'd reached the white stand of wild flowers, he stopped. "Now look again. Look as though you'd never seen such flowers before. They've been beaten by rain, and chewed on by insects and animals, and touched by frost. They're beautiful and wild—and also imperfect. Just the way a good many things in nature are imperfect, including men and women."

"But that's not what I want to show!" I protested.

"No! You want to fix everything up so it will look like —like Ariel on a stage. But real beauty isn't like that. There are always imperfections. When you begin to accept the imperfections, you'll begin to be a very good artist. There's a lot of promise in your work. When you stop being so prissily exact, you'll be a lot better. You're afraid of imperfections, aren't you? In yourself or anyone else."

If I'd had my jacket with me, I'd have gone back to where Juniper was tethered and ridden straight down to the hotel. But I had to return to the cabin and he came with me and took the jacket out of my hands when I picked it up.

"Sit down for a little while longer, Jenny. What you do with your talent, what you do with your life from now on matters a lot. You grew up with everyone looking at your sister's perfection from the time you were small, didn't you? Your mother probably held Ariel up constantly as someone to emulate, to live up to."

I couldn't look at him, too busy trying to resist his words.

"So everything in your life has to be perfect—the work you do, the man you love. Imperfection scares you because you think it means failure. In your way you've probably been just as demanding as Ariel. Asking too much. Because life happens to be like that clump of weeds out there—full of frayed petals and bent stems. Maybe we all have to learn not to ask for something that never exists in nature. Can't you learn to accept that and become a real painter?"

I sat before the fire with my hands clasped about my knees, feeling young and defenseless and ignorant. I, who'd thought I knew so much!

"*You* know about perfection," I said in a small voice. "In your marvelous work—"

"Never! The dream is always bigger than the reality. That's what keeps us going—coming back every time to try to match the dream."

He had been standing near the fire, and now he came to sit beside me on the sofa, turned me toward him gently. There was only kindness in those strange green eyes, and I no longer thought his mass of red hair and beard fierce-looking.

"Don't ever forget, Jenny, that you have a greater potential for living than Ariel had. She was a genius in her art—but lost and clumsy when it came to living. Your own talent and its development can be a source of satisfaction to you all your life. So can your talent for loving and giving. Don't let either be stunted because of one mistake you've made. Or because of your ambivalence toward your sister. Or because of anything that has happened here. There comes a time for growing, Jenny."

My eyes were aswim with tears because his gentleness destroyed my defense. He was very close and in a moment, if I chose, I could be in his arms and he would hold me tenderly, kindly. Yet that wasn't all I wanted, and I made no move.

The telephone shrilled across the room, making me jump, and Magnus went to answer it. While he talked, I picked up a book that lay open face-down on the sofa and let my eyes wander idly down the spine. Oliver Goldsmith, of all things. I hadn't known anyone read Goldsmith anymore. I turned the book over and found a verse on the open page:

> *The only art her guilt to cover,*
> *To hide her shame from every eye,*

*To give repentance to her lover,
And wring his bosom, is—to die.*

I closed the book quickly and put it aside and Magnus came back to me.

"That was Naomi. She wants me to come down to the Red Barn at eight tonight, but she wouldn't say why. Some sort of showing she's planned. Do you know what it's all about?"

"Only that she has a scheme afoot that she's being mischievous about."

The moment when he would have held me out of kindness was gone, and I made no effort to bring it back, but stood up and held out my hand.

"Thank you, Magnus."

His smile flashed. "For what?"

"For being more patient than I've deserved. For being wiser than I am. I won't try to stay on here. I'll leave in a day or two."

"You've made the right choice," he said and took my hand in his big one.

"I'm sorry not to finish posing for you."

"I've those sketches of you I can use. And I've already got the thing strongly in my eye."

"You'll finish it then?"

"Of course. Perhaps I'll show it in New York sometime—and then you'll come to see it?"

"Oh, I will!" I told him, and felt that I might easily cry again unless I went away quickly.

"I'll walk back to Juniper with you," he said.

I was fumbling into my jacket before he could help me with those big hands that could create such astonishing beauty.

"No, don't bother. I'll see you tonight—at Naomi's affair, whatever it is." I picked up my sketching kit and put it under my arm.

He didn't insist, but stayed in the doorway watching me go. Neither of us said good-bye, though I had a feeling that it was really that. When I looked back and waved, he was still there.

In the glen Juniper neighed at the sight of me, bored with her grazing and glad to see a little activity. I went first, however, to stand one more time beside the magnificent bull. I put my hand on the curve of a lowered horn, and for just an instant I wanted to climb up there again and view the world from that massive back. I knew this was a childish impulse and I refrained.

"Good-bye, Zeus," I said, and went over to Juniper.

When I'd pulled myself into the saddle and we had started down the mountain, tears came, though just for a second or two. I wasn't altogether sure what I was crying about. Perhaps because I knew I would never be alone with Magnus again, and that I would miss him more than I could have believed possible. No good-byes had been said between us and I would see him for a little while tonight, but I knew there had been an unspoken farewell, and something—I didn't know quite what—had come to an end.

17

Naomi's "showing" is over, and I am back in my room at the house. It is after midnight and everyone else is surely asleep. I sit here in the dark beside the window and stare out into the deeper darkness of the pines. I am bundled warm in my coat, but I still feel chilled and frightened. I'm not altogether sure of what happened tonight, not sure of its implications—yet I am frightened. Tomorrow I will be leaving as soon as possible. There is no reason for anyone to want me to stay.

I am uneasy about this last thing Brendon wants of me, but surely it will be a small matter and quickly done. I think it has nothing to do with last night.

We were a thoroughly reluctant crew this evening when we showed up at the Red Barn. Naomi had gone ahead to make her preparations, whatever they were, so I walked over with Irene, who seemed a little keyed up. Loring had had a relapse and she was worried about him. When we reached the hotel Brendon joined us, as stiff with me as he always was these days, yet gentle and considerate with his mother.

Brendon and Irene knew where we were going; I went with them up to the barn's second floor and into a small room where camp chairs were set in rows, and a screen hung against the far wall. Irene whispered that old films taken around Laurel Mountain were sometimes shown here. There was a projector at the back, where Naomi waited, her eyes bright with an anticipation I didn't like. I had come to know that, more than anything else, Naomi enjoyed malicious mischief, and I had a feeling that this was what she was about tonight.

Keir and Magnus arrived shortly after we did, and Naomi waved us all into seats. Magnus' look rested on me briefly, kind, but somehow remote, and I looked quickly away. Keir was apparently feeling disgruntled by having a quiet evening at the cabin disturbed, and was probably here only because Magnus had insisted that he come. Naomi was not one to thwart, and in a sense she was still crown princess of Laurel Mountain.

The rest of the barn was dark and empty tonight, without other visitors, and with no one on duty. From an inner window I had looked down upon the long rectangle that had once been the old stables, and had almost fancied I could hear the restless movement of hoofs, the jingle of long-silenced harness.

When I sat down next to Irene, Naomi's voice took up a short introduction from her place at the projector.

"This won't keep you long," she told us. "It's something neither the police nor anyone else know about. Not even Loring knows. I've had my reasons for keeping quiet about it. Mainly because I don't think it proves anything. Nevertheless, I think you all ought to see it. Perhaps it will lead to questions that ought to be asked. Though I've never wanted to ask them."

The machine started whirring behind us, and Brendon went to turn off the lights. Naomi's voice seemed to float above us in the darkened room, with only the light from the screen upon our faces.

"First," she said, "I want to show you something else. Something to help us all keep a memory green."

Dread made a heaviness inside me, as I sensed what might be coming. I wasn't sure I could endure this without jumping up and running from the room. When Irene whispered to Brendon, Naomi's voice cut through.

"Be quiet," she said. "Just watch," and we were all very quiet indeed.

The filming had been done in the little meeting room where I had found Naomi playing the piano on that day that now seemed so long ago. The film was black and white, and for an instant the room remained bare. Then that incredibly graceful figure in leotard and tights went across the floor in *grands jetés* and pirouetted to face the camera. Someone gasped softly. Perhaps it was I.

It seemed strange and eerie that she could be up there on the screen dancing—as I had seen her dance so many times in life. Ariel Vaughn—of the long legs and lovely slender feet, the great dark eyes and dark hair, the beautiful neck and proudly held head—moving now before us as she had moved so many times before the audiences of the world.

Pain cut through me, penetrating all defenses, and I became aware that I was biting hard on the knuckles of one hand. I put my hand down and watched, scarcely breathing.

There was no sound accompaniment, but I recognized the steps. She was dancing the solo variation from *Giselle*. Those *dégagé* turns, the series of *chaînés,* the pose in fourth position—I recognized them all. The performance lasted for only moments of time, and it seemed that no one in the room moved while she danced. Then it was over and Ariel came laughing toward the camera before the strip of film ended, and Naomi turned off the machine.

Brendon, his voice harsh with pain, said, "Why are you doing this?"

"I wanted you all to remember her," Naomi said softly. "Sometimes I think you are beginning to forget. But this isn't why I've brought you here. Wait while I change the film, and you'll see."

We waited and now someone in the room was breathing heavily. I wanted to close my eyes, to jump up and run out of the barn so I would have to see no more. But I knew I must stay. All my sense of loss, of long-ago love for my sister had swept back in a wave that shook me with emotion. I could not hate her now.

Naomi spoke to us again. "I used to take shots of Ariel around the grounds sometimes when she didn't know I was filming her. I'd just set up the camera and keep out of sight. Perhaps I'll show them all to you someday. She used to go out to those great rocks above the Lair at nearly the same time every afternoon, so I knew I could catch her there with my camera."

The machine began to whirr again, and this time we saw the great boulder above the Lair, and I knew it must be the one that had fallen. For seconds the screen was empty of movement, and I think no one in the room exhaled a breath. Then, as we watched, a figure stepped out upon the rock. A tall, slim figure in a sweater and dark slacks. It was not Ariel but Irene. Again there was a soft gasp somewhere in the room.

She stood in the center of the rock looking out toward the hotel and the lake, lifting her face to the sun. Her presence in that spot meant nothing, of course. Dozens of people must have stood on that rock every day, and this strip of film could have been taken at any time.

Then the woman on the screen seemed to test the rock with an outstretched foot—as though she felt movement under her. At once she backed toward the hillside, and the camera watched her without moving until she disappeared among the rocks on the far side of the boulder.

Still the camera remained motionless, and for a moment or two longer the scene stayed empty. Then a second figure appeared on the trail at the edge of the woods beyond the rocks, moving into the eye of the lens. I stiffened as I recognized Ariel descending the path. She was wearing jeans, an oversized sweater and dark glasses, and she walked slowly, her shoulders drooping as she never allowed them to droop when she knew someone was watching. There was no confidence in her carriage, no authority. This was not the presence one saw on a stage, but a woman deeply troubled.

As we watched, she turned from the trail and stepped out onto that sea of rocks, found her way to the big boulder and stood poised and graceful upon it, in full focus now before that steady, relentless camera that must be resting on a tripod. For a moment or two she appeared to be staring out over the lake toward the opposite cliff of Panther Rock. Then she edged forward, and looked down into the chasm below. I think we all gasped as the boulder under her feet began to teeter. She took a great sideways leap, landing on another rock, with no loss of balance. Before our eyes the boulder where she had stood seemed to dissolve into the air as it tumbled out of our sight. Dust rose in the pictured scene and in the silence of the room I could almost hear the terrible echoes of that crash, the sound of Floris' scream. The lack of sound from the screen made these frozen moments of time past seem all the more eerie. I was aware of some sound in the room, but I couldn't remove my attention from the screen to look about and identify it.

Naomi stopped the film and the screen went blank.

"I'll get the lights," Magnus said, his voice hushed.

In a moment a switch clicked and we were blinking against the brightness overhead. For a little while no one spoke, no one moved, and then Naomi broke the silence by laughing softly, maliciously.

"I thought you might be interested," she said.

I looked about for Irene, but she was gone. The movement I had heard must have been her chair being pushed back, her feet moving softly, carrying her from the room.

"Why haven't you shown us this before?" Brendon asked sharply.

"I didn't want to upset your mother. She never knew I had this film. And I'm sure her presence in it is innocent enough. I just didn't want to stir things up."

"You might have warned me before you showed this," Brendon said. "I'll have to find her, talk to her."

"Yes, you will now, won't you?" Naomi said slyly and began putting her equipment away.

Magnus and Keir had not spoken, but both looked solemn as they moved toward the door, and neither had a kindly word for Naomi.

I went to Brendon's side. "There's something that keeps bothering me. Something I keep trying to remember. It might be important."

They all stopped to stare at me, waiting. But after a moment I shook my head.

"I'm sorry. I can't recall the words. When my sister telephoned me that last time, she said something—something I could make no sense of. But I think it might have meaning now, if only I can remember what it was."

The silence was intense—as though they all waited breathlessly for me to remember what Ariel had said on the telephone. To one of them her words might mean—betrayal—and suddenly I didn't want to remember.

Brendon spoke first. "Stop it, Jenny. Let it go. Don't try to recall what she said."

The words were like a warning. I looked into his face that I had once been so sure I had loved, and I felt nothing at all. Yet at the moment I knew what he meant and knew he was right. It would be a good deal safer for me not to announce in public any remembering I might do.

"It's no use," I said. "I've lost the gist of her words."

Brendon moved on beside Naomi, and Magnus' hand came beneath my elbow as he spoke to his father.

"Go along, Dad. I'll see you out in the truck in a few moments."

Keir nodded and went ahead, while Magnus led me outside.

"I meant to let you go without saying good-bye," he told me. "But now I find I don't want it that way."

Faint moonlight lay in a patina over the landscape as we followed a walk toward the hotel.

Irrelevantly, I thought of the words by Goldsmith that I had read in Magnus' cabin that morning, and I mentioned them to him.

"I don't think she died just to punish Brendon," I said.

"No, of course not. A good many things were troubling her. In any case, I still don't think she meant to die. It was only a cry for help."

I must have sighed, for he put an arm about me. "I know what you're feeling. I feel the same way. To see her again up there on that screen—so alive, so gifted and beautiful—and to know that it's all gone, finished forever."

I touched his hand where it rested on my arm. "I'm

sorry," I said, remembering that he'd loved her. "I understand."

"Do you? Do you really understand what I feel, young Jenny?"

"Don't call me that!" I cried. "I won't ever be 'young Jenny' again."

"I apologize," he said readily. "And, sadly enough, I think you may be right. Though I expect I will always carry a picture of you in my mind—standing on Zeus's back, the way I first saw you. You were very young that day."

"Because I believed in love. Because I believed in forever. Oh, I believed in so many things that don't exist—perhaps never existed."

"Love exists," he said gently. "It will come again. We all make mistakes, lose our heads, behave like fools. You felt free of her that day you met Brendon, and you were ready to fall in love. But we grow a little and we go on."

Perhaps, I thought. I didn't know whether this strange numbness I sometimes felt was growth or not.

"What about Irene?" I said.

"I don't know. I suppose Brendon will find out what happened."

"Magnus—" I turned toward him within the curve of his arm.

My sentence was never finished, however, because a dark figure stepped into our path as we neared the lights of the hotel. Silhouetted against them, I recognized Brendon.

He spoke coldly to Magnus. "I'll take my wife back to the house. You needn't come any farther."

Magnus released me at once, and turned without a word to walk back toward the truck. We still hadn't said good-bye.

"That wasn't necessary," I said to Brendon, moving stiffly beside him because I had no other choice.

"It was necessary," he said coldly. "I've seen what's happening. First Ariel, and now you. Rebounds are dangerous, Jenny—if that's what you think you're doing—and I won't have you turn in that direction."

"The only direction I'm turning in is toward home!" I told him angrily. "I've had enough. I want to leave tomorrow, Brendon. There's no point in my staying any longer. I don't think the tide will be stemmed this time, no matter who might like to stop it. Everything will have to come out now. And I don't think I even want to know what happened. We have the proof that it wasn't Ariel's fault."

Behind us I heard Keir's truck start up and a moment later it passed us on the road up the mountain, its headlights sweeping briefly over us and then away. I didn't look after it.

"I thought you were going to find your mother," I said.

"I know where she is. She's sitting up there in the gazebo above the garden. I'll go up there to talk to her in a little while. First I'll take you back to the house."

I dared not speculate aloud and I knew Brendon wouldn't either. For the moment any further mention of Irene was taboo.

"At least we know where Naomi was," I said.

"Do we?"

The two words were laconic and I thought about them uneasily as we walked on. How fortuitous that Naomi had been there at all. And her camera hadn't moved. It had simply run in a set position, and Naomi had turned off the projector tonight on an empty scene still being recorded. But this wasn't a speculation I could put into words now.

"Are you going to see Magnus again?" Brendon asked abruptly.

"Magnus? How can I? I never expect to come here again."

"In any case," Brendon went on, "there's something I want to show you tomorrow before you leave. I want to make sure you will never try to see Magnus again."

"Don't bother," I told him. "I've had enough of men who fell in love with Ariel first."

"I'll drive you to New York tomorrow myself," he said, as though I hadn't spoken, and I knew his sense of duty was operating. He still felt responsible for me. "But first," he went on, "there's something I mean to show you in the morning."

There was no point in arguing with him. Tomorrow I would try to make some other arrangements for my return. I couldn't bear a long drive to the city with Brendon, when all the way I would be remembering the foolish happiness I had experienced on the trip here. Where had it gone? Why had I ever thought it existed, or that it would last?

He walked with me to the steps of the house, told me shortly that he would pick me up at nine in the morning and went off in the direction of the gardens, with that dark gazebo waiting above. I stood for a moment on the veranda, watching him go. He could still walk with the old arrogance in the very way he held his head—an arrogance that had once fascinated me. But now I felt only a haunting sadness. We both knew it was over. What a maze of hurt Ariel had left behind, wherever she went. Brendon, Naomi, me. Magnus too, but he had learned the secret of using pain and going on. He knew how to live with bitter unhappiness, and yet he could bring out of it the genius behind those marvelous sculptures. Would I ever be as wise as that? At least, thanks to Magnus, I would look with a new eye when I painted my next flower or tree. I would stop trying for a patterned perfection that never really existed in nature or in men.

No one was about when I went upstairs and I was glad to be left alone. For a time I tried to read, but too many thoughts were crowding my mind, and a vision of Ariel seemed to dance between the print and my eyes— that lithe and supple figure in the leotard that I had seen again tonight.

What were those tumbling words Ariel had poured out to me that day on the telephone? I hadn't understood and so I'd remembered only that she was threatening to take her life—the old threat that I had heard before. But she had said something else—was it something about a son? That word seemed to return to my mind, but it meant nothing to me now, any more than it had then.

What might she have seen that day? Which of them

would she have protected—if that was what she was doing? As everything had begun to come clear in retrospect, there seemed only one man she had loved. Brendon. But if he had been there that day, his presence would surely have been innocent. I thought I knew that much about him at least. My mind kept returning to Naomi and her camera—what did *she* know that she might not be telling? What had Ariel really said to her? And what about Irene? Somehow I didn't want to think of Irene.

So the hours have worn away with all my confused pondering, and midnight has come and gone. Yet I still sit by the window, unable to sleep, thinking at last about Magnus. I feel an emotion toward him—I am strongly drawn. But I'm not sure that this feeling is love. I don't think I will ever be so positive of love again as I was with Brendon. How can one ever know, ever be sure?

I think of the elderly couples I have watched walking together around the hotel, their arms linked, their attention rapt upon each other. They are the ones who know because they have something that has lasted, and I envy them. Perhaps love is only a *learning*—something that takes years to grow.

My flash of useless insight dies. It is useless because I am young and I can't wait until I am old to find the answers. At last I return to my bed and pull the covers over me. But still I do not sleep. Still there are questions that will not leave me alone. What is it that Brendon wants to show me tomorrow? What is it that may destroy my trust and admiration for Magnus?

Surely nothing can do that. The thought of Magnus is with me constantly. What a strange thing he said to me today when we were talking about murder. He had said that perhaps I was a "mistake." A puzzling word. I remembered his strong arms pulling me from the lake and carrying me to the truck. How fortunate for me that he had been there at the right moment that afternoon.

No, nothing is going to shake my trust in Magnus. There is a tenuous thread stretched between us, and perhaps it is already stronger than Brendon can dream. Only

Magnus and I can break it. I do trust Magnus, and I don't trust Brendon—and that's the end of it.

Nevertheless, the next morning I was ready when the man who was still my husband came for me. I hadn't gone over to the hotel for breakfast, but had eaten something with Irene and Naomi.

Naomi looked pale as we sat in the little breakfast room with its green and white wallpaper, and the sun coming in the windows. Perhaps she had put a good deal of emotion into her effort last night, and it had left her drained. Irene, on the other hand, had a strangely keyed-up glitter about her—as though she waited for something she knew was going to happen. She seemed to approve of my leaving today for New York, but her thoughts were really on other matters, and there was no more pretense that I was a loved daughter who had come here to live. She wanted only to be rid of me now. Even Naomi came out of her pale preoccupation to comment on Irene's electric state of being.

"What's the matter with you?" she asked. "You're acting like a spark ready to set off the dynamite. And you still haven't told us about being up there in front of my camera that day."

Irene put her coffee cup down with a thump that spilled liquid over the brim. "Everything's going to be all right," she said brightly. "I have a feeling that everything will be all right now."

"You mean when Jenny leaves?"

"Perhaps that's part of it," she said, and subsided to eat her breakfast more quietly, perhaps deliberately quenching that spark.

I had a worry too. My real concern—one that had crystallized this morning—was how to see Magnus again. When I was through with Brendon and whatever he had to show me, I must go to the cabin in the woods for one last time. New York would have to be postponed until Magnus and I had at least spoken to each other again. It was quite possible that he would be glad to see me go, but if that was the case, then I had to know it from his own lips.

When Brendon came over from the hotel, driving a truck, I was waiting for him on the veranda in an old-fashioned rocking chair. We greeted each other as politely as strangers, spoke about nothing for a minute or two and then I got into the front seat beside him.

"I won't make you climb the mountain today," he said. "I've borrowed Keir's truck."

"Where are we going?" I asked as he put the truck into gear.

"Up to High Tower," he told me, and after that I asked no questions.

I felt uneasy, and ready to resist anything he might say against Magnus, but I had to go with him. I had to *know*.

When we had followed the road for a while on its gradual climb, Brendon braked near the top and looked out at the hillside rising beyond the road.

"That's funny," he said. "It seems as though that door has been opened. Wait, and I'll have a look."

He got down from the front seat and climbed up the bank to the metal door set in the mountain. I knew what it was because he had shown it to me on our very first climb together up here. Deep in the hillside an underground tunnel led to the tower, carrying cables for the electricity that was needed for the beacon, as well as pipes for water. The water had never been needed because the underground room Bruce McClain had planned had not been finished, but the tunnel was still in use and this was its upper door.

After a moment or two of investigation, Brendon returned to the seat beside me. "The door is unlocked. I don't have a key with me, though they're available at the hotel, but I've closed the door. I'll have to speak to someone about this. We can't have one of our guests going into that tunnel, where he might be trapped."

As we drove on, I asked a question. "Did you see Irene last night?"

He nodded and was silent.

"Is it going to end soon?"

"Yes," he said, and the ring of that one word had a grim sound.

"You don't want to tell me?"

"I don't want to tell anyone! I wish it could lie buried under all those rocks. But I won't open it up until you've gone, Jenny."

I knew he would tell me nothing more.

When we reached the top, we parked in the empty space below the tower. The morning was bright and cool, and as it was a weekday, fewer guests had come to the hotel. As yet no one besides ourselves had ventured up the mountain.

My uneasiness was increasing. I hated to walk unprepared into an unknown situation. Something unpleasant was in store for me up here, I felt sure, but I had no inkling as to what it might be.

Inside the entrance room, Brendon went to a door near the foot of the stairs that zigzagged to the top of the tower. For this door he had brought a key, and he slipped it into the lock, turning it.

"I hope it's not bolted on the other side," he said.

Under his hand the door swung open easily upon empty darkness beyond. When I pulled back, he moved down the first steps ahead of me.

"The stairs are steep, so be careful. This wasn't intended as the main entry to the room. I'll go first. I have a flashlight."

I still held back. "Why should we go down there at all?"

He smiled at me, teasing. "Surely you can't leave Laurel Mountain without seeing our famous underground room?"

"I'm quite happy not to see it." I was aware that my heart had begun a steady thumping because of a rising dread of this underground place. He hadn't brought me here to show me a *room*.

When I turned back toward the exit from the tower, however, Brendon came to swing me around in no uncertain manner.

"I *want* you to see this room," he said. "I want you to

see what's down there. I have a light and you won't fall on the stairs. Electricity was put in when the room was built, and when we get down I'll light it up."

I knew his determination from the past, and there was nothing to do but follow the moving beam of the flash down a flight of stairs that were as steep as the companionway of a ship. Stale air rushed up to meet us, with a smell of dampness and rot, and cold seeped into my bones.

"Now then," he said when I reached the bottom step, just behind him, "come here where you can see."

He touched a switch on the wall and, with a suddenness that made me blink, overhead lights flashed on part way down the ceiling of the great room. Not all of it had been finished, but the walls at this end were paneled in wood that was showing neglect. A portion of the floor was wood-finished, though this intent too had apparently gone uncompleted when plans had been abandoned. The floor that stretched away to the other end of the room was rough concrete, as were the distant walls.

The entire space was empty except for one huge object that stood in the center of the floor at the far end. Brendon started toward it, drawing me after him.

The overhead lighting stopped before we reached the figure that stood upon its high pedestal, but the mingling of light and shadow at this end made the thing all the more frightening. Once more a larger than life-size creature had been carved from granite—a monstrous panther with two heads—one alert and watchful, the other snarling in ugly rage, somehow grotesque and utterly evil.

"Do you see how hideous it is?" Brendon said at my elbow. "It's a mockery, dreamed out of a twisted imagination. Can you look at that thing and not see what Magnus is truly like?"

I had been frightened when I came down to this cold room, dreading the unknown, afraid of what I might find. But I was frightened no longer. I looked up at Magnus' terrible panther and smiled.

"It reminds me of Laurel Mountain."

"What are you talking about?"

"The two faces of Laurel. One beautiful and wild and natural. The other hideous and snarling."

"But don't you see—" Brendon began.

I put a hand on his arm, silencing him. "You don't understand Magnus at all, do you? Sometimes one can get rid of inner torment by externalizing it. By creating something as ugly as one's own inner thoughts. That's what he's done here. Afterward he could go on to create both the beautiful panther that stands at Panther Rock and his superb bull."

"But this is evil!" Brendon protested.

"Of course. That's why he wanted to transfer his feelings into stone and be rid of them."

Dazedly, Brendon shook his head. "Jenny, it's you I don't understand anymore. I felt sure that when you saw this—"

I stopped him again. "I'm glad I saw it, Brendon. Don't look like that. Please don't regret—anything. We had something marvelous for a little while, and I think we'll always remember it. But next time you'll turn to someone who will never remind you of Ariel—if you're wise. And perhaps in the same way I'll find someone who will never remind me of you."

There was a sorrowing in his eyes, even while he smiled at me with an uncertainty that was uncharacteristic.

"You've changed since you came here, Jenny."

"I'm trying to grow up," I said. "I'm trying to grow into *me*—not Ariel."

He bent and kissed my cheek, and I knew it was both salute and farewell.

Before we could start back toward the stairs, however, there was a sound at that end of the room. Brendon called out, "Who's there?" and waited.

There was no answer—only the clatter of his voice echoing down the long room.

"Wait here," Brendon said. "I'd better investigate. I don't want any guests wandering down into this place. Magnus' nightmare isn't for the public eye."

He hurried off toward the stairs, his feet rousing more

echoes on the concrete. I saw him run up out of sight—and then two things happened. All the lights went out, and at the head of the stairs I heard the slamming of a door.

18

In that vast cavern where a monster panther reigned, I
stood lost and frightened. With a voice that caught in
my throat I called out Brendon's name, but the further
crashing of echoes only alarmed me. Had this been deliberate? Had he locked me in down here? No, I knew
him better than that.

Then I heard the footsteps coming from the direction
of the stairs—not running openly, but moving with stealth
along the concrete toward me. It was not Brendon this
time. I knew he must be shut beyond that slammed door,
and when he rattled it violently, I knew the heavy door
must have been bolted against him on this side. As he
struggled to open it, those secret steps came closer.

I managed to move behind the granite panther, hoping
it would hide me.

"Jenny?" The voice was a whisper, unidentifiable.
"Jenny, have you remembered what your sister told you
on the phone that day?"

As I crouched behind the great stone block, my breath
held as long as possible, lest by an exhalation I betray
my presence, a strange, clear memory flashed through my
mind. In that instant I remembered very well what Ariel
had said, and I knew with deepening horror who it was
that stalked me in this ghastly place.

As the sudden beam of a flashlight cut the darkness, another memory flashed back. There had been all too much that I had never questioned: that truck, for instance, parked so conveniently and coincidentally when Magnus had fished me out of the lake. That boat set out for me to take so easily had been a "mistake," as Magnus had suggested. He had meant that the threat against me was pointless, unnecessary because at that time I was really harmless. Why hadn't I questioned the truck's being there? Or the old boat?

The whisper came again. "Jenny? Where are you? You needn't be afraid. It will be very quick. As quick as it was for Floris. Though I'm sorry it's you. I liked you, Jenny. I could have grown very fond of you."

In the distance Brendon was pounding on the bolted door, shouting to me. But I dared not answer and reveal myself to the hunter. Softly, I moved, circling the panther, hiding from the darting flash that tried to catch me like a spotlight on a stage. My heart was thumping wildly in my ears.

There was a savoring now in the whispers. "How easy it was to prepare that boulder so it would fall. How simple to phone Loring with a lie that would bring Floris into the Lair. But I meant to send that rock crashing myself. It was ready to fall, and I was down there working at it with a crowbar, but I never meant for your sister to do it for me. When Ariel went out on the rock there was nothing I could do except get away as fast as I could. Your sister saw me. She knew that I was up to something. But she left the next day without speaking. And when she died, I thought I was safe. Until you came."

The voice paused, and I heard the quick, light breathing. Then it went on.

"I didn't know that Irene had been there earlier. I don't know what she saw or guessed. But I think she didn't want to betray me. We were friends when we were young. Once I even thought she might have married me —if it hadn't been for Bruce. She should have married me instead of Loring. Then all Laurel would have been safe in our hands."

He still didn't see me where I crouched, but the flashlight might move faster than I at any moment. Yet I dared not try to flee into the open. He would be upon me at once and I would be helpless in those strong hands.

His voice went on again, relentlessly. "I didn't have anything against you, Jenny, until that day when I met Irene coming from the cemetery and she told me what you planned to do. I threw those stones down on you, hoping you'd be scared away. But you weren't, so I put that old boat where you'd find it. That was needless, I thought afterwards, and I wrote you off because there was nothing you knew and I thought you harmless. I grew quite fond of you, Jenny. That was another mistake, wasn't it?"

I felt sick over what he was saying. Because I had grown fond of him too—and trusting. But what lay behind the mask was something as monstrous as the horrid stone panther above me.

The banging at the top of the stairs had stopped, and I felt more alone than ever. If Brendon went down the hill to the tunnel entrance, it would take a long while, and it would all be over before he could reach me. While Brendon knew something was wrong, he couldn't guess my danger or the need for haste.

"Floris was an ugly person. You already know that." He had dropped the whispering to speak in his normal voice and the very ordinariness of his tone made my flesh crawl. "She would have destroyed Laurel and everything it stood for. She would have played into Loring's hands and brought in the bulldozers. Of course I felt Loring had to go—though I`had bad luck that time on the roof. And if I'd known you were there—ah, that would have been bad for you, Jenny."

I clutched at cold stone, with terror striking through me. Now I would never see Magnus again. I would never tell him how I felt.

"When we talked yesterday," Keir went on, "I thought everything would be fine and you would go away. I needn't worry about you anymore. And then last night when Naomi showed her film you began to remember.

You do remember, don't you, Jenny? Whatever it was that Ariel told you?"

I dared not answer, dared not make a sound.

"When Brendon borrowed my truck this morning to bring you up the mountain, I took the shortcut through the tunnel. He'd talked to me before about showing you what was down here, so I knew where he was coming. But that's enough of talking, Jenny. Come out from behind the panther or I'll come and get you."

The flashlight beam moved again as Keir moved, and in a moment it would impale me. Then I heard a great crashing of sound from the tunnel opening at this end of the room. There was a roar of fury as the door burst open, and at the same instant I screamed.

"Magnus—I'm here! Help me, help me, Magnus!"

A second flashlight illumined our end of the room, and before Keir could move around the panther, his son was upon him, hurling him away from me. He crashed into a concrete wall, then righted himself, staring at us in the beam Magnus turned upon him. Somehow the terrible look on his face reminded me of the panther Magnus had hidden in this room.

Before his son could move, Keir ran for the tunnel door and disappeared into the passage. Magnus made no move to follow, playing the light over me.

"Jenny, are you all right?"

Without question or hesitation I went into the arms he held out for me.

This time it is really over. Keir is dead and the full truth will never need to be known outside of the family circle.

When he ran from the tunnel this morning he went straight up the mountain to where the cliff drops steeply down to the talus below. He threw himself out where the falcon had soared, and they found his body later. There were those on the tower who saw it happen, and there is no question that it was anything but suicide.

Brendon had begun to guess, and Irene had told him more last night, but he had wanted me away and uninvolved before he took action. Then it was too late. Magnus, too, loving his father, had closed his eyes to much that he might have seen, had he been willing to look and believe. That day when he had rescued me from the water, he'd walked along the lake road looking for his father, knowing he had driven in that direction. But even when he found the truck from which Keir had been watching me row, and which he had abandoned when he saw Magnus coming—not even then did Magnus accept what was happening. He had rescued me and been thankful for the accident of the truck being there, so he could take me to the hotel quickly. But he hadn't put it all together until recently, when he had begun to suspect that "mistake" about the boat. Even then, he'd felt that his father wouldn't touch me again. He had no proof of anything, and was still stunned by his own suspicions, still pondering what to do.

His putting it together had come almost too late, as it had for me, when Ariel's words on the phone had flashed into my mind. What Ariel had said was, "I can't injure the father when his son has been so good to me."

This morning Magnus saw Brendon driving me up the mountain in Keir's truck. Earlier, since he had been watching, he had seen his father go into the underground tunnel, so he posted himself near its entrance to wait. But when time passed and Keir didn't come out, he grew anxious and started into the tunnel himself to find out what was happening. When he heard Keir's voice, he stopped to listen—and then burst through the door.

So now, in the late afternoon of this dreadful day, I sit in Magnus' cabin. And I know at last that this is where I want to be. The log fire blazes before us, warming away the long chill, and I am safe within the circle of Magnus' arm. We have talked a great deal. I understand his pain over his father's death, and even more for Keir's guilt. But that guilt has been paid for, and perhaps it is better this way.

There was one question Magnus asked—and that was

why Brendon had taken me to the underground room this morning.

"He wanted to shock me," I told him. "He wanted to turn me away from you. But the panther he thought was so horrible didn't frighten me."

Magnus laughed. "He belonged to my gothic period. I got rid of some things in me that were not very pretty when I did that two-headed beast. Perhaps I got rid of an extra head of my own."

I leaned into his arm. "There'll be time to finish your marble bull now. All the time in the world."

He nodded, his beard scratching my cheek. "Yes. After I've moved away, and you've come back to me."

"Come back? But I'm not going anywhere!"

"Of course you are. Tonight you're going down to the house to stay with Irene, who probably needs your company now. Tomorrow you're going home to New York. For a while. So you can think about everything that's happened and begin to digest it. When you're sure of what you want to do, we'll see. No more reckless falling into a love that won't last. I want you to be happy, Jenny. And I want something for myself. I'm going to build a cabin on that land out in Pennsylvania and try to forget about Laurel."

I began to shake my head and his arm tightened about me as he bent to kiss me—hard.

"Shut up, my darling Jenny. It's time to stop and think. This time it's got to be for real."

The common-sense part of me knew how right he was and thrust the emotional part back. For Brendon's sake I must go away at once, of course, and stay away until matters were settled between us. Brendon was coming through his own storms, and he still had his first love—Laurel—to keep him company. But I mustn't stay where my presence would distress him—as Ariel's had done.

Magnus moved abruptly, taking me by surprise, even though I was by now used to being plucked into the air and set down in another place. I didn't even struggle.

"Come along," he said. "Get into your jacket. We have a rendezvous. With a bull."

I asked no questions, but followed him meekly enough along the path to the glen, where Zeus awaited us.

"Take a good look," Magnus said. "He's not like that panther up there under the tower. But he's a lot like me. Are you going to be able to live with all that?"

The stepping stone was familiar to my foot, and I was up between the horns and onto that great stone back in a moment. There I sat on cold stone and stroked the hump of muscle behind the horns.

"He's like you," I said, "and he's not like you. You'll say it better in marble—with the maiden on his back. But how can you bear to leave him behind when you go?"

"I shan't. He'll go with me."

"Then I'll see him again," I said.

He flashed me that smile I had come to know. "I'll walk you down to the house now. You can telephone me from New York. And I'll let you know when I move."

I sighed. "Poor Europa—with a bull who won't even run off with her."

"Not because he doesn't want to, my darling," he said, and pulled me down into his arms.

I will always remember Laurel Mountain. But now there will be another hillside in another place that I will come to love and learn from. And Magnus and the stone bull will be there—waiting for me.